The rain was still trailing down their faces.

Antonia's breath was still hitching like a frightened child's. But when her lashes dropped half shut, and her face tilted ever so slightly, he did it. Gareth kissed her. And in that surreal moment with the rain pounding down all around them, and thunder rumbling ominously in the distance, it seemed as if that was what she begged him for.

He had meant it as a gentle kiss. A kiss of comfort and of reassurance—or so he told himself. But when she opened her mouth beneath him, inviting him to deepen the kiss to something more, he accepted, sliding his tongue deep into the warmth of her mouth as if he, too, were desperate. Perhaps he was. Gareth had not kissed a woman with this sort of irrational hunger in . . . well, perhaps never.

He had forgotten the rain which still drenched them. He had forgotten that anyone, as he had done, might look out from one of the second floor windows. His breath was coming roughly now. His head was swimming with the need to keep her close; to draw her into him somehow. To bind her to him.

Praise for national bestselling author Liz Carlyle and her sizzling romantic novels

"Hot and sexy, just how I like them! Romance fans will want to remember Liz Carlyle's name."

—Linda Howard,
New York Times bestselling author

THREE LITTLE SECRETS

"In her usual brilliant fashion, Carlyle brings her Sins, Lies, and Secrets trilogy to a splendid conclusion with a dark, deliciously sensual, richly emotional story. . . . Exquisitely complex characters and luscious writing . . . simply superb."

—*Booklist* (starred review)

TWO LITTLE LIES

"With effective, emotional writing and a complex heroine, Carlyle's story stands out in a crowded field of Regency-era romances."

—*Publishers Weekly*

ONE LITTLE SIN

"All of Carlyle's signature elements—deliciously clever dialogue, superbly nuanced characters, gracefully witty writing, and sizzling sexual tension—are neatly placed."

—*Booklist* (starred review)

THE DEVIL TO PAY

"Intriguing . . . engaging . . . an illicit delight."

—Stephanie Laurens,
New York Times bestselling author

"Sensual and suspenseful . . . [a] lively and absorbing romance."

—*Publishers Weekly*

A DEAL WITH THE DEVIL

"Sinfully sensual, superbly written . . . nothing short of brilliant."

—*Booklist*

THE DEVIL YOU KNOW

"Sweep-you-off-your-feet romance, the sort of book that leaves you saying, 'More, please!' "

—Connie Brockway,
award-wining author of *Bridal Season*

"Rich and sensual, an unforgettable story in the grand romantic tradition."

—Christina Dodd,
New York Times bestselling author

NO TRUE GENTLEMAN

"One of the year's best historical romances."

—*Publishers Weekly* (starred review)

"Carlyle neatly balances passion and danger in this sizzling, sensual historical that should tempt fans of Amanda Quick and Mary Balogh."

—*Booklist*

A WOMAN OF VIRTUE

"A beautifully written book. . . . I was mesmerized from the first page to the last."

—*The Old Book Barn Gazette*

Never
Deceive
a Duke

LIZ CARLYLE

POCKET BOOKS
New York London Toronto Sydney

Pocket Books
A Division of Simon & Schuster, Inc.
1230 Avenue of the Americas, New York, NY 10020

This book is a work of fiction. Names, characters, places, and incidents either are products of the author's imagination or are used fictitiously. Any resemblance to actual events or locales or persons, living or dead, is entirely coincidental.

First Pocket Books paperback edition August 2007

POCKET and colophon are registered trademarks of Simon & Schuster, Inc.

For information about special discounts for bulk purchases, please contact Simon & Schuster Special Sales at 1-800-456-6798 or business@simonandschuster.com.

Cover illustration by Alan Ayers; lettering by Ron Zinn

Manufactured in the United States of America

10 9 8 7 6 5 4 3 2 1

ISBN-13: 978–1–4165–2715–2
ISBN-10:   1–4165–2715–X

Prologue

The strange saga of the Ventnor family began with the tale of a traitor, then rambled on aimlessly for better than a century before coming to a near end. They were an arrogant, noble people of mostly Norman blood, and so thoroughly taken with themselves that they rarely married elsewhere. Mathilde Ventnor was no exception, and at the advanced age of fifteen, she dutifully married her second cousin, the third Duke of Warneham, then began to bear him children at a rate so prodigious that even the Ventnors were impressed.

All was well until a cold November's day in 1688, when the duke, long known as a hardened loyalist, made a calculated decision to betray his king—and, depending upon whom one asked—his country. With bloody rebellion looming, the king was on the verge of being crushed by the Protestants, who had been breathing down his neck since his contentious coronation. The Ventnors were not Catholic. They were devout opportunists, who worshiped in the Church of the Impertinent Presumption. And seeing the way of things, the duke turned tail somewhere just north of Salisbury—as had many both higher and lower than himself—and bolted to the other side. The *winning* side.

Warneham had much to live for. His ducal holdings were amongst the grandest in England, though they were not secure, for despite her remarkable fertility, Mathilde had thus far had the ill luck to bear naught but daughters—six of them, all very pretty in their own way. And all perfectly useless. Warneham needed a son, and he needed a victory.

Morally confident in his decision, Warneham rode out ahead of the pack of turncoats, crested a leaf-strewn knoll, and beheld with relief the Protestant banner of William of Orange snapping smartly in the breeze. Beneath it stood William's noble supporters, shouting out Warneham's name and waving for him to come down. So gratified was the duke by this welcome that he did not see the burrow which some industrious fox had dug near the foot of the grassy slope. Spurred to dramatic action, his horse caught the hole full on, stumbled, and pitched Warneham headlong into the encampment. The duke landed on his skull, snapped his neck, and promptly breathed his last in the service of his new king.

England's Glorious Revolution ended almost as summarily as Warneham. William of Orange was easily victorious, James fled to France, and nine months later to the day, Mathilde gave birth to twins—strong, lusty boys, the both of them. No one dared point out, however, that the babes looked not remotely alike—with the elder his mother's miniature, a pink, plump cherub, and the second-born a knobby, long-legged creature with a shock of golden hair—and neither looked remotely like their dead father. No, it was a miracle. A godsend.

King William and Queen Mary decreed the babes be brought to court, and the king himself pronounced them both the very spit and image of the dead duke. No one dared gainsay him because—well, because this is a tale of romance. And what is romance without a touch of drama and a dash of deceit?

To Warneham's firstborn son, of course, William reaffirmed the ducal coronet. But to the youngest, he promised command of a regiment—for him, and for his heirs ever after, in acknowledgement of his father's bravery. And thus, according to family legend, was the family's fate forevermore divided.

The boy who now stood in the center of Warneham's vast library was all too aware of this legend. Indeed, after more than two hundred years, it was no longer a division which separated the family but an unbreachable black chasm. And now he was going to puke. Right on the duchess's shoes.

"Stand up straight, boy." The duchess circled him, her tiny heels clicking neatly on the marble floor as if she assessed a piece of statuary.

The boy swallowed hard, the bile burning in his throat. As if this morning's miserable five-mile journey in a lurching farm cart had not been torment enough, the duchess now bent forward and gave him a sharp poke in the belly. His eyes widened, but the boy stood as straight as he was able and forced his gaze to drop subserviently toward the floor.

"Well, he looks sturdy enough," mused the duchess,

cutting a glance at her husband. "He does not appear to be wormy. He seems appropriately humble. And at least he is not *swarthy*."

"No," admitted the duke churlishly. "He is Major Ventnor made over, thank God—those gangling legs and that gold-colored hair included."

The duchess turned her back on the old woman who had brought the boy. "Really, Warneham, what choice have we here?" she murmured. "We must ask ourselves, I think, what is the *Christian* thing to do? Your pardon, of course, Mrs. Gottfried." This last was tossed carelessly over her shoulder.

But the old woman was watching the duke assessingly from her corner. His handsome face was contorted with doubt and distaste. "The Christian thing!" he repeated. "Why is it always the Christian thing which wants doing when one is faced with an unpleasantness?"

The duchess folded her hands primly before her. "You are quite right, of course, Warneham," she agreed. "But the child is of your blood—a *tiny little bit,* at least."

The duke seemed to take umbrage at this suggestion. "Barely at all!" he said brusquely. "And he cannot very well stay here, Livie. We cannot have his sort sharing the schoolroom with Cyril. What would people say?"

The duchess hastened to her husband's side. "No, no, of course not, my dear," she soothed. "That would not do at all."

Mrs. Gottfried rose on arthritic knees and curtsied again. "Your Grace, have mercy," she begged. "The lad's father died a hero's death at Roliça fighting for England. Gabriel has no one else to whom he can turn."

"No one?" said the duchess sharply as she cut another

condescending look over her shoulder. "Really! Have you no family in England, Mrs. Gottfried?"

The old woman bobbed humbly. "No blood kin, Your Grace," she murmured, preparing to lay down her only trump. "But my people will take Gabriel, of course, and raise him as one of their own—if that is indeed your wish?"

"No, by God, it is not!" Warneham jerked abruptly from his chair and began to pace the floor. He was an elegant man, still young and vigorous, and he strode about like one born to the purple. "Damn Ventnor for putting us in such an untenable position, Livie!" he continued. "If a man is going to make an unsuitable marriage, then by God he has no right to go off and get himself shot in foreign parts, king or no king. That's what I say."

"Quite so, my dear," cooed the duchess. "But it is too late for remonstrance. The man is dead, and the child must now be dealt with."

"Well, he cannot live here at Selsdon Court," the duke said again. "We have Cyril to think about. And what would people say?"

"That you are a decent Christian man?" his wife gently suggested. Then she paused and clapped her hands together almost girlishly. "Warneham, I have it! He shall live in the dower house. Mrs. Gottfried can attend to him. We can have that odd little curate—oh, dear, what is his name?"

"Needles," huffed the duke.

"Yes, yes, Needles," said the duchess. "He can come round and tutor the child." She urged her husband gently back into his chair. "It will not be so bad as all that, my dear. And it will be only for a time. Why, in another ten years or so, the boy can be bought a commission. He may go into the army, as his father and grandfather did."

"The dower house, eh?" The duke seemed to be considering it. "The roof leaks and the floors are rotting. Still, we could repair it, I daresay."

In the center of the room, the boy stood as quietly and as rigidly as he could. He tried very hard to look like a soldier. Like his *father*. And this meeting, he knew, was his only hope. Had he not known it, his grandmother's tears and prayers before leaving their shabby wayside inn this morning would have told him so. He swallowed his nine-year-old pride and his roiling bile and pushed back his shoulders.

"May I speak, sir?" he piped.

The duke's head jerked in his direction, and a deathly silence settled over the room. For the first time, the duke actually eyed the boy up and down. "Yes," he finally said, his voice impatient. "Speak up, boy."

"I . . . I should like to be a soldier, Your Grace," he offered. "I should like to go to the Peninsula, sir, and fight against Napoleon, like Papa. Until then—well, I shan't be any trouble to you, sir. I promise."

The duke eyed him almost nastily. "No trouble, eh?" he said. "No trouble! Now why do I somehow doubt that?"

"No trouble, sir," the boy echoed. "I promise it."

He could not know—indeed, they could none of them have known—what a dreadful lie that was to be.

Chapter One

*T*he sun beamed down, warming the fragrant grass of Finsbury Circus. Gabriel played with his wooden animals, queuing them up across his blanket. Papa bent down, his thin, brown hand plucking one from the queue. "Gabe, what is this one called?"

Gabriel moved his tiger into the empty space. "Frederick," he said simply.

His father laughed. "No, what kind of animal is it?"

Gabriel though it a silly question. "Frederick is an elephant. You sent him to me from India."

"Yes, that's right," said Papa.

His mother laughed lightly. "Gabriel had memorized the entire animal kingdom, I think, by the time he was three, Charles. I rather doubt there is much you can teach him now."

With a sigh, Papa leaned back on the bench. "I have missed so much, Ruth," he said, taking her hand in his. "Too much—and I am to miss a great deal more, I fear."

Mamma's face fell. "Oh, Charles, I did not mean—"

Abruptly, she drew a handkerchief from her pocket and delicately coughed into it. "Oh! I beg your pardon. I sound frightful, do I not?"

Papa frowned. "You must see to that cough as soon as I am gone, my love," he chided. "Gabriel, can you help Mamma to remember? She is to see Dr. Cohen tomorrow—and not a moment later."

"Yes, sir." Gabriel plucked one of the monkeys from his queue and handed it to his father.

Papa balanced the monkey in his palm. "This is for me?"

"It's Henry," said Gabriel. "He will go back to India with you. For company."

Papa tucked the monkey into his regimental jacket, then ruffled Gabriel's hair. "Thank you, Gabe," he said. "I shall miss you terribly. Are you all right here, you and Mamma, with Zayde and Bubbe?"

Gabriel nodded. His mother set her hand on Papa's knee. "It is better we continue on this way, Charles, until things settle down for us," she said softly. "Truly, it is. Do you mind terribly?"

Papa laid his hand over hers. "The only thing I would mind, my love, would be your unhappiness."

The offices of Neville Shipping along Wapping Wall were a beehive of activity, with clerks rushing up and down the stairs carrying last-minute contracts, bills of lading, insurance policies, and the occasional cup of tea. London's muggy August heat did little to calm the fervor, though every window had been thrown open to the morning breeze, which was just strong enough to carry in the stench of the Thames, and very little else.

Standing over her desk, Miss Xanthia Neville scarcely

noticed the smell of putrid mud and fermenting sewage. Nor did she hear the rattle of the cooperage's carts, or the lightermen bellowing at one another along the water below. After less than a year in Wapping, she was inured to it all. But this blasted accounting—ah, that was another matter! Exasperated, Miss Neville threw down her pencil, and raked the hair back off her face.

"Gareth?" She glanced up at a passing clerk. "Siddons, where is Gareth Lloyd? I need him at once."

Siddons nodded sharply and dashed back down the stairs. In seconds, Gareth appeared, his broad shoulders filling the doorway to the cavernous office which they shared. For a moment, he let his eyes roam her face.

"Haste makes waste, old girl," he said laconically, setting one shoulder to the door frame. "Can you not get those numbers to add up?"

"I haven't even got that far," she admitted. "I cannot find Eastley's voyage reconciliation sheets to carry over the amounts."

Slowly, he crossed the room to her desk and slid the reconciliation report from beneath the accounting papers. Xanthia's shoulders fell and her eyes rolled heavenward.

Gareth studied her quietly for a moment. "Nervous?" he finally asked. "It is understandable, Zee. By this time tomorrow, you will be a married woman."

Xanthia closed her eyes and set a protective hand over her belly; a telling, intimately feminine gesture. "I'm scared to death," she admitted. "Not of marriage—I *want* that. I want Stefan desperately. It's . . . it's just the ceremony. The people. His brother knows *everyone*. And he has invited all of them. Yet I dare not put it off . . ."

Gareth braced a hand on the back of her chair. He did not touch her. He would never touch her again; he had sworn it—and this time, he meant it. "You had to know, Zee, that it would come to this," he said quietly. "And this is not the worst of it. When you are Lady Nash and people discover that you have the audacity to actually work for a living, they will say—"

"I do not *work* for a living!" she interjected. "I own a shipping company—or rather, you and my family own it. All of us. Together. I just help . . . *oversee* it."

"That's an awfully thin hair to split, my dear," he said. "But I wish you success in attempting it."

She looked up at him then, her face crumpling a little. "Oh, Gareth," she said quietly. "Tell me it will be all right."

She spoke not of the marriage, he knew, but of the business, which was almost like a child to her. Indeed, it was far more important to her than he had ever been. "It will be all right, Zee," he promised. "You are not leaving on your wedding trip for another week or so. We will get all this caught up. We will hire someone if need be. I will be here every day until you come home."

She smiled faintly. "Thank you," she answered. "Oh, Gareth. Thank you. We shan't be gone long, I promise."

Then he broke his pledge not to touch her and slid one finger beneath her chin. "Please don't worry, Zee," he murmured. "Swear to me you won't. Think of the new and happy life which awaits you."

For an instant, her face brightened in a way which was attributable to only one man. "You will be there tomorrow morning, will you not?" she asked almost breathlessly. "At the church?"

He cut his gaze away. "I do not know."

"Gareth." Her voice was suddenly raw. "I *need* you to be there. You are my . . . my best friend. Please?"

But Gareth did not get the chance to answer. A faint knock sounded. Gareth turned to see an elderly, silver-haired man standing in the doorway, and their chief accounting clerk, Mr. Bakely, hovering in the shadows behind, looking gravely ill at ease.

"May we help you?" Xanthia's voice was a little impatient. It was Bakely's job to keep visitors in the counting house below, not in the management offices above.

The man stepped fully inside, allowing the sunlight to fall across his simple but well-cut suit. He wore a pair of gold spectacles and carried a burnished leather satchel. A banker from the City, Gareth guessed—or worse, a solicitor. Whatever he was, he did not look as if he brought glad tidings.

"Miss Neville, is it?" said the man, bowing stiffly. "I am Howard Cavendish of Wilton, Cavendish and Smith in Gracechurch Street. I am looking for one of your employees. A Mr. Gareth Lloyd."

Inexplicably, the tension in the room leapt. Gareth stepped forward. "I'm Lloyd," he answered. "But you'll have to take up your legal business with our solicitors in—"

The man lifted a staying hand. "I fear my errand is of a more personal nature," he said. "I urgently require a moment of your time."

"Mr. Lloyd is not an employee, sir, he is an owner." Xanthia's voice was haughty as she swished from behind her desk. "One generally makes an appointment in order to see him."

Surprise sketched across the solicitor's face but was quickly hidden. "Yes, I see. My apologies. Mr. Lloyd?"

Resigned to what seemed inevitable, Gareth returned to his glossy mahogany desk and motioned for the solicitor to take the leather chair opposite. The man made him deeply uneasy, and Gareth was inexplicably glad that Xanthia had just spent a small fortune refurbishing their once-shabby office, which now looked as elegant as any solicitor's might.

Mr. Cavendish flicked an uncertain gaze at Xanthia.

"It's quite all right," said Gareth. "Miss Neville and I have no secrets."

The man's dark brows flew up. "Indeed?" he murmured, snapping his leather case open. "I trust you are quite sure of that."

"Dear me!" said Xanthia sotto voce. "This sounds exciting." Curiosity etched on her face, she took the armchair to the left of Gareth's desk.

The solicitor was withdrawing a sheaf of papers from the satchel. "I must say, Mr. Lloyd, that you have proven an admirable quarry."

"I was unaware of being hunted."

"So I gather." The man's lips had an unpleasant curl, as if he found his duty distasteful. "My firm has been searching for you for some months now."

Despite his cool tone, Gareth's unease deepened. He cut a glance at Xanthia, suddenly certain he should have sent her away. Sharply, he cleared his throat. "Precisely where were you looking, Mr. Cavendish?" he asked. "Neville Shipping was headquartered in the West Indies until a few months past."

"Yes, yes, I managed to discover that," Cavendish said

impatiently. "Though it took me long enough. There are not many people left in London who remember you, Mr. Lloyd. But I finally managed to locate an elderly woman in Houndsditch—a local goldsmith's widow—and she remembered your grandmother."

"Houndsditch?" said Xanthia incredulously. "What has this to do with you, Gareth?"

"My grandmother lived the last months of her life there," he murmured. "She had many friends, but I imagine most of them are dead now."

"Quite so." Mr. Cavendish was sorting through his papers. "The only one left was senile. She told us you had written your grandmother once—from Bermuda, she claimed. And when that turned up nothing, she decided it was the Bahamas. Alas, no. So she decided to try another letter of the alphabet, and sent us haring off to Jamaica."

"It was Barbados," murmured Gareth.

Cavendish smiled faintly. "Yes, my clerk has practically managed to see the world whilst attempting to find you," he said. "And it has cost rather a fortune, I fear."

"How regrettable for you," said Gareth.

"Oh, I am not paying for it," said the solicitor. "You are."

"I beg your pardon?"

"Or rather, your estate is," the solicitor corrected. "I work for you."

Gareth laughed. "I'm afraid there must be some mistake."

But the solicitor had apparently found the paper he wanted, and he slid it across the desk. "Your cousin the Duke of Warneham is dead," he said flatly. "Poisoned, some say—but dead nonetheless, most conveniently for you, Mr. Lloyd."

Xanthia was gaping at the solicitor. "The Duke of *who?*—"

"Warneham," repeated the solicitor. "That is the coroner's report. *Death by misadventure* was the verdict, though scarcely anyone will believe it. And this is the research from the College of Arms designating you as the heir to the dukedom."

"The . . . *what?*" Gareth felt numb. Sick. There must be some mistake.

Xanthia leaned toward him. "Gareth—?"

But Cavendish was still speaking. "I also have several items which urgently require your signature," he continued. "Things are in rather a mess, as you might imagine. The Duke died in October of last year, and the rumors surrounding his death have only grown more speculative."

"I am sorry," said Xanthia, sharply this time. "What duke? Gareth, what is he talking about?"

Gareth pushed the papers away as if they had burst into flame. "I don't know." He felt suddenly unsteady. Angry. He had not thought of Warneham in a dozen years—at least he had tried not to do so. And now, his death caused Gareth not the pleasure and satisfaction which he had long expected but instead just a strange, unpleasant numbness. Warneham *poisoned?* And now he was to inherit the dukedom? No. It was impossible.

"I think you had best be on your way, sir," he said to Cavendish. "There has been some mistake. This is a busy counting house. We have real work here to do."

The solicitor's head jerked up from his papers. "I beg

your pardon," he said. "You were born Gabriel Gareth Lloyd Ventnor, were you not? Son of Major Charles Ventnor, who died in Portugal?"

"I have never denied who my father was," said Gareth. "He was a hero, and I was proud to be his son. But the rest of the Ventnor family can burn in hell so far as I am concerned."

Mr. Cavendish glowered over his gold eyeglasses. "That is the very point, Mr. Lloyd," he said impatiently. "There really *is* no Ventnor family. You are it. You are the eighth Duke of Warneham. Now if you would kindly turn your attention to these documents—"

"No," Gareth firmly interjected. He glanced at Xanthia, whose eyes were wide as saucers. "No, I want nothing to do with that bastard. *Nothing.* Good God, how can such a thing have happened?"

"I think you know how it happened, Mr. Lloyd," said Cavendish sharply. "But we must put the past behind us, and move on, mustn't we? And by the way, the law does not permit you to refuse the dukedom. It is done. Now you may attend to your estate and your duties, or you may let it all go to rack and ruin if that is your wi—"

"But Warneham lived a long and vigorous life," Gareth interjected, jerking to his feet. "Surely . . . surely there were other children, for God's sake?"

Mr. Cavendish shook his head. "No, Your Grace," he said solemnly. "Fate was not kind to the late duke."

Gareth well knew what the unkindness of fate was like—and he had Warneham to thank for it. Was it possible the son of a bitch had got what he deserved? Gareth began to pace the floor, one hand set at the back of his neck. "Good God, this cannot be happening," he muttered. "We were barely related—third cousins at best. Surely the law cannot permit such a thing?"

"The two of you were both great-great-grandsons of the third Duke of Warneham, who fell heroically in battle fighting for William of Orange," said the solicitor. "The third duke had twin sons—posthumous sons—born but minutes apart. Warneham is dead, his son Cyril predeceased him, and you are the only living blood heir of the second-born twin. Ergo, the College of Arms has determined that—"

"I don't give two shites what the College of Arms determines," said Gareth. "I want—"

"Gareth, your language!" Xanthia gently chided. "Now do sit down and explain all this to me. Is your last name really Ventnor? Did someone really murder your uncle?"

Just then, another dark-haired gentleman came breezing into the room, this one dressed with an almost dandyish elegance. He carried something enormous and shiny before him. "Good morning, my dears!" he sang.

His patience already tried, Gareth wheeled around. "What the devil's good about it?"

Xanthia ignored him. "Heavens, Mr. Kemble," she said, rising. "What have you there?"

"Another of his overpriced trifles, no doubt." Gareth loomed over him.

Mr. Kemble drew the object protectively away. "It's a Tang Dynasty amphora," he snipped. "Don't touch it, you philistine!"

"What is it for?" Xanthia looked disoriented.

"It is the accent piece for the marble window pedestal." Mr. Kemble waltzed across the room and delicately positioned it. "There! Perfect. I now pronounce you Fully Decorated." He spun around. "Now, pardon my intrusion. Where were we? Mr. Lloyd has offed his uncle, has he? I am not surprised."

"I misspoke," said Xanthia. "It was a cousin, perhaps?" Swiftly, she introduced Kemble to the solicitor.

"And I haven't 'offed' anyone," snapped Gareth.

"Actually, we looked into that," said the solicitor dryly. "Mr. Lloyd has the perfect alibi. He was in the middle of the Atlantic Ocean at the time."

Xanthia seemed oblivious to the sarcasm. "And the most shocking thing, Mr. Kemble!" She laid a hand on his coat sleeve. "Gareth is going to be a duke!"

"Oh, good God, Zee!" Gareth felt his blood begin to boil. "Just hush, *please*."

"I am perfectly serious," she said, still addressing Kemble. "Gareth has a secret duke in his family."

"Yes, well, don't we all." Mr. Kemble smiled tightly. "Which one is yours?"

"Warnley," said Xanthia swiftly.

"Warne*ham*," corrected the solicitor.

"Neither of them," said Gareth grimly. "Cavendish here is going to have to shake this family tree until another monkey falls out."

Mr. Kemble lifted his hands. "Well, I cannot help you with this one, old fellow," he said to Gareth. "*C'est la vie, non?* Now, my dears, I really must run. I wouldn't have barged in at all—but the mention of a murder was too delicious to ignore. I'll get the gory bits later."

"Thank you again for the lovely decorating, Mr. Kemble," said Xanthia.

The dapper gentleman paused to snatch Xanthia's

hand, and bowed over it. "I shall wait to kiss this until tomorrow on the portico of St. George's, my dear," he said, "when I may properly call you the Marchioness of Nash."

At that, the solicitor seemed to sit a little straighter in his chair. "I beg your pardon," he said as Mr. Kemble vanished. "Do I gather that congratulations are in order?"

Xanthia blushed. "I am to be married in the morning."

Just then, another shadow appeared at the door. Gareth looked up in frustration. "I do beg your pardon, sir," said Mr. Bakely. "We've just had a rider up from Woolwich. The *Margaret Jane* has been spotted coming up the Blackwall Reach."

Xanthia pressed her hand to her chest. "Oh, thank God!"

"About bloody time," said Gareth, shoving back his chair with a sharp scrape.

"Do you wish her to put into the West India Docks, sir?" Bakely pressed. "Or shall she come upriver?"

"She's to put in," said Gareth urgently. "And send round for my gig. You and I will go down and see how bad things are."

Xanthia, too, had risen. "I apologize, Mr. Cavendish," she said. "As intriguing as your story is—and I confess, I am indeed agog—we must see to the *Margaret Jane* at once. She's been three months at port in Bridgetown, and lost a third of her crew to typhus. We are gravely concerned, as I am sure you can understand?"

"You are not going down there, Zee." Gareth's voice was stern. He was already drawing on his driving coat, oblivious to anything but the duty before him.

Xanthia's hand returned instinctively to her belly. "No, I suppose I oughtn't." She smiled at Mr. Cavendish, and with grave reluctance, he, too, rose.

"But what am I to do with the ducal papers?" he asked.

Intent on collecting his things, Gareth said nothing.

"Just leave them on Mr. Lloyd's desk," Xanthia suggested. "I am sure he will review them later."

Mr. Cavendish looked irritated. "But we have a number of pressing issues," he protested. "His Grace's attention is direly needed."

Xanthia smiled gently. "Do not despair, sir," she murmured. "Gareth will do his duty. He always has. And I have every confidence he shall handle whatever problems you set before him with his usual cool competence."

The solicitor paid her scant heed. "Sir," he said to the back of Gareth's head, "this really cannot be put off."

Gareth snatched a ledger from the bookshelf. "I'll be back in an hour or two," he said to Xanthia. "I shall give Captain Barrett your regards."

"Wait, Your Grace!" said the solicitor a little plaintively now. "You are expected at Selsdon Court immediately. Really, sir! The duchess awaits."

"The *duchess*?" said Xanthia.

Cavendish ignored her. "Everything has been left hanging, sir," the solicitor insisted. "It really cannot wait any longer."

"It will bloody well have to," said Gareth, without looking at them. "Indeed, it can hang 'til Kingdom Come, so far as I care."

"Really, sir! This is unconscionable!"

"Blood does not make a man, Cavendish," Gareth

snapped. "Indeed, it is more often his undoing." He thundered down the stairs behind Bakely without another word.

Xanthia ushered the solicitor to the door. He looked down at her, his brows drawn sharply together. "I really cannot comprehend this," he murmured. "He is the duke. Surely he realizes his good fortune? He is now a peer of the realm—one of England's wealthiest, in fact."

"Gareth possesses a self-confidence which can sometimes seem abrasive, Mr. Cavendish," she answered. "He is a self-made man—and yet money means very little to him."

Both concepts were clearly beyond Cavendish's grasp. After a few more murmured platitudes, Xanthia at last got the solicitor out the door. At the top of the steps, however, a question struck her. "Mr. Cavendish," she said, "might I ask, who is believed to have wished the duke dead? Are there . . . suspects? Any hope of an arrest?"

The solicitor shook his head. "As with most powerful men, the Duke had enemies," he admitted. "As to suspects, the rumormongers have regrettably targeted his widow."

Xanthia felt her eyes widen. "Good Lord! Poor woman—if, indeed, she is innocent?"

"I believe that she is," said the solicitor. "And the coroner believed it. Moreover, the duchess is from a powerful family. No one dares accuse her too loudly—not without evidence."

"Still, in English society, the mere whisper of scandal . . ." Xanthia felt suddenly chilled, and shook her head. "The duchess must be ruined."

"Very near it, I daresay," said Cavendish sadly.

The solicitor went down the steps, his fine leather satchel in hand, looking a good deal wearier than he had upon his arrival. Xanthia's head seemed to be spinning. Quietly, she closed the office door and set her forehead to the cool, well-polished wood.

What on earth had just happened? What had Gareth Lloyd been hiding all these years? Something a little more serious than a miserable childhood, apparently. But Gareth a *duke*?

Then she jerked her head up. Her brother Kieran might know the truth. Abruptly, she crossed the room, rang the bell, and began to haphazardly stuff the contents of her desktop into her bulging leather satchel.

"Send for my carriage," she said to the young clerk who cracked open the door. "I am going to take luncheon with Lord Rothewell."

Chapter Two

*G*abriel held tight to his grandfather's hand, terrified by the spinning carriage wheels and flashing hooves. Everyone was rushing. Shouting. Dashing into traffic— meshuggenehs, *his grandmother would have called them.*

"Zayde, I . . . I want to go home."

His grandfather looked down, smiling. "What, you don't like this place, Gabriel? You should."

"Why? It is too busy."

"It is busy," agreed his grandfather, "because this is the City. This is where the money gets made. Someday you, too, will work here. Perhaps you shall be a merchant banker, eh? Or a broker? Would you like that, Gabriel?"

Gabriel was confused. "I . . . I think I'm to be an English gentleman, Zayde."

"Oy vey!" His grandfather swept Gabriel up into his arms. "What nonsense those women have taught you. Blood does not make a man. A man is nothing if he does not work."

And then they were dashing across the street together, a part of the madding, teeming throng.

* * *

The Duchess of Warneham had slipped away to Selsdon's rose garden for an hour of solitude when Mr. Cavendish arrived the following afternoon. She carried a basket on her arm, but after an hour of aimless wandering had cut but one stem, which she still carried in her hand.

She was thinking again. Thinking of the children, though she had been told time and again she must not. That it did no good to dwell on the past. But here, beyond the constraining walls of the house, her mother's heart could bleed in peace. She had surrendered much. She would not surrender this, her grief.

The late summer sun was hot, with the threat of a shower heavy in the air, but the duchess was scarcely aware. Indeed, she did not hear her husband's solicitor approach until he was halfway along the garden path. She looked up to see him waiting a respectable distance away, wilted rose petals skirling about his feet in the breeze.

"Good afternoon, Cavendish," she said quietly. "Your return to London was brief."

"Your Grace." The solicitor hastened forward and sketched an elegant bow. "I've just this instant arrived."

"Welcome back to Selsdon," she said mechanically. "Have you dined?"

"Yes, Your Grace, in Croydon," he said. "Have you?"

"I beg your pardon?"

"Have you dined, ma'am?" he pressed. "Remember that Dr. Osborne says you must eat."

"Yes, of course," she murmured. "I . . . I shall take a little something shortly, perhaps. Pray tell me what you found in London."

Cavendish looked vaguely uncomfortable. "As I promised, ma'am, I went straight to Neville Shipping," he said. "But I am not sure what I achieved."

"You found him?" she asked. "This man who works for the shipping company?"

Cavendish nodded. "Yes. I found him."

"And?—"

Cavendish exhaled sharply. "It was Gabriel Ventnor, I am quite sure," he admitted. "The man is the very image of his late father. The height. The golden eyes and hair. I am certain we have the right man."

The duchess remained impassive. "So it is done, then. When shall we expect him?"

Cavendish hesitated. "I am not at all sure, ma'am," he confessed. "He seemed . . . disinterested in our news."

"Disinterested," the duchess echoed hollowly.

The solicitor gave an embarrassed cough. "I fear he is not just some sort of dockhand or shipping clerk after all," he explained. "He is an owner. He looked . . . well, rather prosperous, actually. And intractable."

Her smile was wan. "Hardly the impoverished orphan you expected."

"No." Cavendish's voice was sour. "And I am not perfectly sure he comprehends his good fortune in inheriting the title. I am not even certain if or when he will deign to return to Selsdon Court, ma'am. He would make me no answer."

Nor did the duchess. Instead, she looked down at the rose, which she still clutched. The petals were bloodred against her skin. Bloodred. Deathly white. Like flesh when all the life was leached out—and yet she still lived. For a long moment, she studied it, wondering at fate's twisted path. Thinking of death, and all that it wrought. All that it so indelibly altered.

What did it matter if the man came or not? What would change? What could his power and his pride possibly do to her that would make her life more unbearable than it already was? The days ticked by in silent oblivion, as they had these past four years. Or perhaps it was five. She was not sure. She no longer counted.

Gabriel Ventnor. He held her fate, or so they all believed, in his hands. But he did not. He was nothing. He could neither wound her nor torment her, for she no longer flinched at earthly pain.

"Your Grace?"

She looked up to see Cavendish peering at her intently. She realized she had lost her train of thought. "I—I beg your pardon, Cavendish. What were you saying?"

The solicitor frowned, stepped hesitantly nearer, and forced her fingers from the stem. "Your Grace, you have cut yourself again," he chided. He plucked two thorns from her palm, one of them quite deep, and blood beaded from her flesh. "Ball your fist tight about this," he ordered, pressing a handkerchief to the wound.

"It is just blood, Cavendish," she murmured.

He laid the rose in her empty basket. "Come, Your Grace, we must go back into the house now," he said, taking her gently by the arm.

"My roses," she protested. "I should like to finish."

Cavendish did not relent. "Ma'am, it has begun to rain," he said, leading her toward the terrace. "Actually, it has been raining for some moments now."

The duchess looked up to see that spatter was indeed bouncing off the garden wall. The sleeves of her gown were already damp, another earthly discomfort beneath her notice.

"Do you wish to make yourself ill again, ma'am?" Cavendish pressed. "What good would that serve?"

"None, I suppose." The words came out throaty and tremulous.

"Indeed, it will but make Nellie's life more difficult," said Cavendish, "for she will have the inconvenience of nursing you."

The duchess halted abruptly on the garden path. "Yes, Cavendish, you are quite right," she said, looking at him directly now. "And as I have always said, I should hate— above all things—to be an inconvenience. To anyone."

In Berkeley Square the following afternoon, Baron Rothewell toed off his fine leather slippers and poured himself enough brandy to put a lesser man under the table. Damned if he didn't need a drink. The day had thus far been a misery—though his sister, thank God, had not noticed it.

Zee's wedding day. He had often thought never to see it. Other times, he had thought perhaps she might make a marriage of convenience, and of friendship, to Gareth Lloyd. But the day had come, and it had not been enough that Rothewell had had to watch his sister drive away from Berkeley Square with a man who was all but a perfect stranger to him—and a damned dangerous-looking stranger at that. No, Gareth had had to watch it, too.

Xanthia's bridegroom, the Marquess of Nash, had taken the news of Gareth Lloyd's societal elevation with his usual cool grace and had introduced him to all their wedding guests as "a dear family friend, the Duke of

Warneham." He had not meant ill by it, but Rothewell felt for Gareth, poor devil. Nash's plain speaking would surely set society's tongues a'wagging.

Just then his study door opened, and Gareth came in. "There you are, old fellow," said Rothewell. "I was just wondering what went with you."

"I've been belowstairs, helping Trammel carry the extra chairs."

"A duke helping the butler move furniture," mused Rothewell. "Why am I not surprised?"

"A man is nothing if he does not work," Gareth remarked.

"Ugh!" grunted Rothewell. "Perish the thought. Will you join me in a brandy?"

Gareth flung himself into one of Rothewell's wide leather armchairs. "No, it's too early in the day for me," he answered, then hesitated. "But not, perhaps, for the Duke of Warneham?"

Laughter rumbled deep in Rothewell's chest. "You are one and the same now, old friend."

"Then yes, damn you, give me a tot," Gareth grumbled. "I think we both deserve one for having survived this day."

"Well, now you outrank him," said Rothewell, returning to the sideboard. "The Marquess of Nash, I mean. You take precedence, Gareth, over your competition. I find that rich."

"Oh, I quit competing years ago." Gareth's tone was suddenly grim. "And we celebrated a marriage this morning, you will recall."

"Yes, only too well." Pensively, Rothewell swirled the brandy in the glass, then handed it to his guest. "You have lost the object of your youthful infatuation, Gareth, but I . . . well, I do not deceive myself. I have lost a sister. You think it not at all the same, I do not doubt. But when you have been left alone as the three of us were—Luke, Zee, and I—with no one else to depend upon, you forge a bond which is not easily explained."

Gareth was quiet for a moment. "Luke is gone, but you have never been without Xanthia, have you?"

Rothewell shook his head. "Indeed, I remember the very day she was born." His voice caught a little on the last word. "Ah, but enough maudlin sentiment for one day. What is it to be for you, Gareth? Must I set about dragging you off to do your duty?"

"You refer to the dukedom, I collect." Gareth's voice was emotionless. "No, I promised Zee I would be at Neville Shipping every day until her return. I won't leave you in the lurch."

"I never imagined you would," murmured Rothewell. "Since the day my brother hired you as his errand boy, you have been the one we all depended upon. It was for that reason—and to keep the competition from stealing you, of course—that we entered into this joint ownership venture."

Gareth's smile was muted. "Shackled me with golden chains, eh?"

"Bloody well right." The baron swallowed another sip of brandy, his muscular throat working up and down like a well-oiled machine. "And now you mean to uphold your end of the bargain. I respect that. However, whilst your share of Neville Shipping has left you quite wealthy, it can hardly compare to the wealth you have apparently inherited."

"What is your point?" Gareth's words came out more sharply than he'd intended.

"Perhaps you are watching the wrong pot boil." Rothewell had begun to roam restlessly about the room with his glass in hand. "Far be it from me to lecture a man on duty and responsibility, but I strongly suggest you go down to—to—what was it called again?"

"Selsdon Court."

"Ah, yes, Selsdon Court," Rothewell echoed. "How very grand it sounds."

"It is. Obscenely so."

"Well, obscene or not, it is yours now. Perhaps you ought to go attend to it. It is not far, is it?"

Gareth lifted one shoulder. "Half a day's drive, perhaps," he said. "Or one can take the Croydon Canal down from Deptford."

"Half a day?" said Rothewell incredulously. "That is nothing. Go attend to the matters which are pressing, and pay your condolences to the black widow—those are Zee's words, by the way, not mine."

Gareth grunted. "The duchess is a coldhearted bitch, all right," he said. "But a murderess? I rather doubt it. She would not risk being ruined in the eyes of society."

Rothewell looked at him strangely. "What is she like?"

Gareth cut his gaze away. "Supremely haughty," he murmured. "But not overtly cruel. She had her husband for that."

"I wonder if she has been left a wealthy widow?"

"There is no doubt," said Gareth. "Warneham was disgustingly rich. Her family would have seen to generous settlements."

"And yet she awaits you?" murmured Rothewell.

"Perhaps you are expected to make some decision with regard to her future?"

That thought had not occurred to Gareth. For an instant, he let himself wallow in the fantasy of throwing her out into the cold to starve—or worse. But he could take no pleasure in it—indeed, he could scarce imagine it. And surely the choice would not be his?

"You are considering it?" asked Rothewell.

Gareth did not answer. He hardly knew. In all the dreadful days which had followed his exile from Selsdon Court, he had never once wished to return. Oh, at first he had wished for many things which were not to have been. Things children, in their naïveté, longed for. A kind touch. A warm hearth. A *home*. But he had found instead the very opposite. He had been pitched headlong into the bowels of hell. His childhood longing had boiled down to a man's pure, unadulterated hatred. And now that he might go back to Selsdon Court—now that he might be master of them all—he wished to return even less. What a trick fate had played him this time.

Rothewell cleared his throat, returning Gareth to the present. "Luke never said much about your past," he admitted. "Simply that you were an orphan from a good family who had fallen on hard times."

Hard times. Luke Neville had always been a master of understatement. "It was pure luck which brought me to Barbados," Gareth admitted. "And by God's grace, I met your brother."

Rothewell actually smiled. "I recall he caught you bolting from the dockyard with a gang of scurvy sailors on your heels."

Gareth glanced away. "He snatched me up by the

coat collar, thinking me some sort of pickpocket," he answered. "Luke was a brave man."

Rothewell hesitated. "Yes. Very brave indeed."

"And I . . . good Lord, I must have looked like a drowned rat."

"You were skin and bone when he brought you home," Rothewell agreed. "It was hard to believe you were what—thirteen years old?"

"Barely that," said Gareth. "I owed Luke my life for saving me from those bastards."

Again, Rothewell smiled, but it was tight and humorless. "Well, their loss was our gain," he said. "But when Luke said 'of good family' he rather understated the matter."

"I never precisely told him," Gareth admitted. "About Warneham, I mean. I said only that my father was a gentleman—an army major who fell at Roliça—and that my mother was dead."

Rothewell sat down on the corner of his massive desk and pensively regarded Gareth. "Luke knew what it was to be orphaned young," he said simply. "We have been pleased to account you as—well, as almost a member of our family, Gareth. But now a higher duty calls."

"Oh, I doubt it," Gareth sneered, then tossed off the last of his brandy.

"Go down for a fortnight," Rothewell suggested. "Just to make sure there is a competent estate agent in place. Have a good look at the account books to ensure you are not being cheated. Put the fear of God into the staff—and make sure they know for whom they work now. Then you can return to London, and quit that shabby little house of yours in Stepney."

Gareth looked at him incredulously. "And do what?"

Rothewell made a circle in the air with his glass. "One of these grand Mayfair mansions hereabout must belong to the Duke of Warneham," he suggested. "If not, buy one. You need not rusticate the rest of your days—and you certainly do not need to continue slaving in the service of Neville's."

"Impossible," said Gareth. "It cannot be let go, even for a fortnight."

"Zee is not leaving for a few days yet," Rothewell said. "And if worse comes to worst, I daresay old Bakely and I can hobble along well enough to hire—"

"You?" Gareth interjected. "Rothewell, do you even know how to find Neville's offices?"

"No, but my coachman has gone there almost every day for the last nine months," he answered. "Look, Gareth, who is Neville's nearest competitor?"

Gareth hesitated. "Carwell's over in Greenwich, I suppose. They are a little larger, but we have been giving them a run for their money."

Rothewell set his glass on the sideboard. "Then I shall simply hire away their business agent," he replied. "Every man has his price."

"Hire him to replace *me*?"

Rothewell plucked the empty glass from Gareth's hand and returned with it to the sideboard. "My friend, you are just kidding yourself if you think that your old life is not over," he said, drawing the stopper from the brandy decanter. "I know what it is to be saddled with a duty one does not want. But you have no choice. You are an English gentleman. A state of denial will get you nowhere."

"You are a grand one to give advice about denial," said Gareth churlishly, "when you are drinking too damned much, and letting your life and your skills rot away."

"Et tu Brute?" snapped Rothewell over his shoulder. "Perhaps I ought to dress you up in a muslin gown and call you 'sister.' I daresay I'd not miss Xanthia in the least."

Gareth fell silent. Rothewell refilled both glasses, then gave the bellpull a sharp jerk. Trammel appeared almost instantly. "Tell the staff to prepare my traveling coach," he ordered. "Mr. Lloyd shall have need of it at daybreak. They are to meet him at his home in Stepney."

"Really, Rothewell, this is unnecessary," said Gareth, springing to his feet.

But Trammel had vanished. "You cannot very well go to Selsdon Court in a gig," said Rothewell. "Nor in a canal boat."

"Well, I won't go in a borrowed carriage, by God."

Rothewell crossed the room and pressed the drink into Gareth's hand. "The coach, if I am not much mistaken, is technically a company asset belonging to Neville's."

"By whom I am no longer employed," snapped Gareth.

"But of which you are still part owner," Rothewell answered. "I am sure any number of fine carriages await you at Selsdon Court, old friend. Send mine back once you are settled."

"You will let me see no peace, will you?"

"I have seen none. Why should you?" Then, with mock solemnity, the baron raised his glass. "To His Grace, the Duke of Warneham. Long may he reign."

Chapter Three

*T*he house was still as death, the scent of fresh bread and cabbage hanging thickly in the air. The ropes of the bed groaned as his mother pulled herself up, inch by agonizing inch. "Gabriel, tatellah, come to me."

He crawled up the mattress on hands and knees, then curled against her like a puppy. His mother's fingers were cold as they threaded through his hair. "Gabriel, an English gentleman always does his duty," she said, her voice weak. "Promise . . . promise me you will be a good boy—an English gentleman. Like your father. Yes?"

He nodded, his hair scrubbing against the coverlet. "Mamma, are you going to die?"

"No, tatellah, only my human form," she whispered. "A mother's love never dies. It reaches out, Gabriel, across time and across the grave. A mother's love can never be broken. Tell me you understand this?"

He did not, but he nodded anyway. "I will always do my duty, Mamma," he vowed. "I will be a gentleman. I promise."

His mother sighed, and relaxed again into the blessed oblivion of sleep.

"All I am saying, my lady, is that it does not seem quite fair." Nellie drew the brush down the length of her mistress's heavy blond hair. "A woman ought not be put out of her own home—not even a widow."

"This is not my home, Nellie," said the duchess firmly. "Women do not own homes. Men decide where they will live."

Nellie grunted disdainfully. "My aunt Margie owns a home," she said. "And a tavern, too. No man will be putting her out of 'em anytime soon, depend upon it."

The duchess looked up into the mirror and smiled faintly. "I rather envy your aunt Margie," she said. "She has a freedom that women . . . well, women like me are brought up never to expect."

"Noblewomen, you mean," said Nellie knowingly. "No, my lady, I've seen how some folk live. And I'd rather earn my crust with my own sweat any day."

"You are very wise, Nellie."

The duchess's gaze dropped to her hands clasped tightly in her lap. They had been together, she and Nellie, for ten years now. Nellie's competent hands had begun to show her age, and her brow was permanently furrowed. And when they were alone—which was often—the maid frequently regressed to her mistress's former names or titles, sometimes even a combination thereof. The duchess did not bother to correct her. She had no fondness for the lofty position fate had bestowed upon her. Before this marriage, she had hoped only to live out her years in quiet widowhood. Now, perhaps, she might at long last get her wish.

"Has there been nothing, then, from Lord Swinburne?" Nellie laid aside the brush, to pick through a porcelain dish filled with hairpins.

"A letter from Paris." The duchess tried to brighten her expression. "Papa is to be a father again—and quite soon. His wedding trip has apparently been all one might wish for."

"But what about you, my lady?" Nellie's eyes met hers in the mirror. "Can't you go back home? Greenfields is such a big house—not quite as vast as this, I know, but surely 'tis enough for the three of you?"

The duchess hesitated. "Penelope is very young, and newly wed," she said. "Papa says that perhaps—perhaps after the child is born . . ." She let her words drift away.

Nellie pursed her lips, and twisted up the first section of her mistress's hair. "I think I see the way of things," she muttered, wrestling with a pin. "One house, one mistress?"

"Penelope is very young," the duchess said again. "And why should I wish to return home? I would feel out of place, I daresay. Papa is right—in this, at least."

"Lord Albridge, then?" Nellie suggested.

"Heavens, Nellie! My brother is a gazetted womanizer. A sister underfoot is the last thing a rakehell would wish for." She stilled the maid's hand by covering it with her own. "Do not worry, Nellie. I am not poor. Once we know the new duke's wishes, why, perhaps I can lease a small house?"

"Something, ma'am," said the maid. "Anything.

There's been a cloud hanging over this place since the old duke's death. And people do talk."

"It is gossip, and nothing more," the duchess answered. "But we shall find something—in Bath, I think. Or Brighton? Would you like that?"

Nellie wrinkled her nose. "Ooh, I don't think so, ma'am," she said. "I'm a country girl. And it's not myself I'm worried for. I can go to work for my aunt Margie."

The duchess smiled wanly. "Has she room enough for the two of us?" she asked. "I think perhaps I should make a tolerable chambermaid."

"Poo!" Nellie snatched up her fingers. "With these hands? I doubt it, my lady. Besides, I'll go where you go. You know that."

"Yes, Nellie. I know that."

Just then, the room dimmed, as if a lamp had been turned down. Nellie glanced over her shoulder at the wide bank of windows. "Here it comes again, ma'am," she warned. "That dratted rain."

"Perhaps it will pass us by," the duchess murmured mechanically.

"Aye, well, you can wish," said the maid. "But I feel it, ma'am. I truly do."

"Feel what, precisely?"

The maid lifted one shoulder. "There's something queer in the air," she said. "Something . . . I don't know. Just a storm, I reckon. It's this miserable August heat. We're all wilting."

"It has been unpleasant," the duchess acknowledged.

But Nellie just shrugged again, twisted another hank of hair aloft, and studied it. "I think I'm going to do this up high," she said. "Something very . . . duchessly—is that a word?"

"It is now," said the duchess. "But the hair—really, Nellie. Do not waste your time. Just throw it up."

"Come now, ma'am," the maid cajoled. "He won't be like all those other fellows who've been trotting down from London in droves. He's the wicked prodigal cousin. You ought to get all togged out and properly impress him."

It really did matter to Nellie, the duchess realized, so she forced anther smile. She had worried very little about her appearance of late. Still, as Nellie pointed out, it had not stopped the suitors who sometimes vied for her hand. Oh, they called, ostensibly, to express sympathy, and to see how she "got on." But the duchess knew vultures when she saw them—polite, well-bred vultures, of course, but in search of carrion, just the same. Apparently, every scoundrel in London was fishing for a fortune. The more respectable men kept their distance.

"Of course you are right," she finally said. "Yes, by all means, Nellie. Let us be duchessly."

The maid's deft hands made short work of the duchess's tresses, drawing them up into an elegant pile of gold, which spilled into curls at the nape of her neck. "Will you wear the aubergine silk, ma'am?" asked Nellie as she wound the last strands into place. "I'll thread some black ribbons through here to match."

"Yes, and my black shawl, I suppose."

Nellie unfurled a length of black ribbon, which was looking a little worn. "I reckon this ought to be replaced," she muttered. "But just a few more weeks, my lady, and you can put off this black for good."

"Yes, Nellie. That will be lovely."

But she would not put off her mourning. Not really. She would, the duchess imagined, wear it all the days of her life—inwardly, if not otherwise.

Suddenly, a commotion sounded in the cobblestone courtyard below. The clamor of horses' hooves along with the grind of carriage wheels, and, above it all, the butler barking anxiously at the servants. Inside, footsteps began to thunder up and down the servants' stairs. The house was on edge today—and not without reason.

"Sounds like a carriage coming through the gateposts," said Nellie grimly, going to the window. "Ooh, and it's a fine one, too, ma'am. A glossy black landau with red wheels. And black-and-red livery, too. Must be a regular nabob, that one."

"Yes, our poor little orphaned cousin!" murmured the duchess.

"Oh, I'd say the new master hasn't lived hand-to-mouth in a mighty long while, ma'am," said Nellie, peering round the drapery. "And now he's about to get the royal treatment. Coggins is queuing the staff down the steps, somber as a row of gravestones."

The duchess cut her gaze toward the windows. "Isn't it raining, Nellie?" she asked. "Mrs. Musbury still has that dreadful cough."

"Aye, it's peppering down all right." The maid's nose was almost pressed to the glass now. "But Coggins has the evil eye on 'em, ma'am, and no one's so much as twitching. And he—wait! The carriage has stopped. One of his footmen is getting down to open the door. And he's getting out. And he's . . . oh, holy gawd . . ."

The duchess turned around on her stool. "Nellie, *what* on earth?"

"Oh, that's the very thing, ma'am," said Nellie in a voice of quiet awe. "He doesn't look earthly. More like an angel, I'd say—but one of the grim, bad-tempered kind. Like the ones on the ballroom ceiling slinging down those lightning bolts and looking all angry?"

"Nellie, please don't be fanciful."

"Oh, I'm not being fanciful, ma'am." Her voice was oddly flat. "And he's awfully young, ma'am. Not what I expected a'tall."

For a long moment, they listened to the murmur of the introductions below as Nellie kept up a commentary about his hair, the breadth of his shoulders, the cut of his coat, and precisely which step he now stood on. The new duke was taking his time, it would seem. The audacity of him to keep loyal servants standing in the rain!

Slowly, the duchess felt an almost foreign emotion begin to stir. It was *anger*. It surprised her to feel it. She dearly hoped Mrs. Musbury would not worsen. She half-hoped the new duke took consumption. And she really wished Nellie would not continue to rattle on about lightning bolts. A bad-tempered angel indeed!

Just then, thunder rolled ominously in the distance, and the sound of the rain on the roofs ratcheted up into a cacophonous roar. Downstairs, doors began to slam. Shouts rang out. Harnesses jingled and the carriage began to rattle away. For an instant, everything was chaos.

"See, ma'am?" said Nellie, turning from the window. "It's about to happen."

The duchess frowned. "What, pray, is about to happen?"

"The lightning. The *storm*." Brow oddly furrowed, Nellie smoothed her hands down the front of her smock. "It's about to break, ma'am. I—I feel it."

The great entrance hall of Selsdon Court was almost grandiose in its emptiness. Only the very rich could afford an empty room containing little more than marble, gilding, and fine art. Gareth stood in the midst of it and slowly turned in a circle. It was the very same. Vast, polished perfection.

Even the collection of old masters, Gareth noted, hung in precisely the same arrangement. The Poussin above the Leyster. The van Eyck to the left of de Hooch. The three Rembrandts in a massive, magnificent grouping between the drawing room doors. There were a dozen more, each of them well-remembered. For an instant, Gareth closed his eyes as the servants swarmed around him; the footmen attending to the luggage, the maids and kitchen staff returning to their tasks. It sounded the same. It even smelled the same.

And yet it was not. He opened his eyes and looked around. Some of the under servants, he had noticed, looked perhaps vaguely familiar. But other than that, he recognized no one. Perhaps that was because few dared lift their eyes to him. What had he expected? They had doubtless heard the rumors.

Gone was Peters, Selsdon Court's condescending butler. Mr. Nowell, his uncle's favorite flunky, must have gone on to his great reward as well. Even Mrs. Harte, the grumpy old housekeeper, was nowhere to be seen, and in her place was a thin, mouse-haired lady with kind eyes and a frightfully bad cough. Mrs. Musgrove?

No. That was not quite right.

"Coggins," said Gareth, leaning nearer the butler. "I want a roster of all the staff by name and position, to include their ages and their years of service."

The servant's eyes flared with alarm, but it was quickly veiled. "Yes, Your Grace."

"And this estate agent, Mr. Watson," Gareth added. "Where the devil is he?"

Again, the faint look of alarm. That instant of hesitation. It made Gareth wonder what these people had been told of him. That he ground servants' bones to make his bread?

"I did not have an opportunity to inform Mr. Watson of your arrival, Your Grace," the butler murmured. They all *murmured*—as if the house were some sort of mausoleum. "I fear he has gone to Portsmouth."

"Portsmouth?" said Gareth.

"Yes, sir." The butler gave a strange, stiff bow. "He is to collect a piece of equipment—a threshing machine—which is coming down from Glasgow."

"They make such contraptions nowadays?"

The butler nodded. "It was ordered by the late duke prior to his death, but"—here he paused and let his eyes dart about the room—"they are not popular in certain circles. There have been, shall we say, *difficulties* further south."

"Ah." Gareth clasped his hands behind his back. "Put men out of work, do they?"

"So some would believe, Your Grace." A passing footman caught Coggins's eyes, and nodded. The butler swept his hand toward one of the magnificent staircases which rose in splendid, symmetrical curves from the great hall. "Your chambers are ready now, sir, if you would care to follow me?"

"What I wish to do is to see the duchess," Gareth returned. His tone was sharp, he knew, but he was anxious to get it over with.

To his credit, Coggins did not falter. "But of course, Your Grace," he said. "Will you wish to freshen your wardrobe first?"

Freshen his wardrobe? Gareth had forgotten that the denizens of Selsdon Court changed their clothes about as often as regular folk drew breath. No doubt the duchess would be appalled to receive a man still attired in clothes which he'd had on for . . . oh, all of seven hours. Gareth would be considered unforgivably travel-stained. *Quelle horreur!* as Mr. Kemble was fond of saying.

"Have you no valet, sir?" asked Coggins as they started up the stairs.

"No, he was insolent, so I chopped off his head."

Coggins stopped abruptly on the stairs. He began to quiver almost imperceptibly, but whether from fear, outrage, or barely suppressed laughter, Gareth could not say.

Outrage, no doubt. These folks took clothing seriously. "Good God, Coggins, get on with it," Gareth said. "It was a jest. No, I haven't a valet at present. I shall send for one eventually, I suppose."

Suddenly, he had a mental flash of Xanthia, who never gave a fig what anyone wore. Indeed, she had herself been known to wear the same gown three days running—not because she had so little but simply because such things were beneath her notice. She thought only of the business which needed doing on any given day.

He was going to miss her, he suddenly and acutely realized. Their lives had diverged now and would likely never join again in any meaningful way. His old life—the life he had fought so hard to build out of the rubble which had been his childhood—was gone. It felt as if he was back where he started. This dukedom was not a boon to him. It was a curse. A bloody damned curse.

Just then, they arrived at a set of double doors, which looked to be carved of solid mahogany. With another sweeping gesture, Coggins pushed them both wide, then stepped aside so that Gareth might take in the glory.

"The ducal bedchamber, Your Grace," he said, motioning about the vast room. "To your right is your dressing room, and to the left, your sitting room."

Gareth followed the butler and tried not to gape. These were rooms which he had never before seen—and they were, he conceded, truly magnificent. The bedroom was hung with ice-blue silk, and a darker shade of blue decorated the massive canopied bed. The blue-and-silver rug was Persian, and looked big enough to cover half the hold of some of Neville's smaller ships.

They crossed into the sitting room, which was similarly decorated but fitted with furniture that looked rather dainty by comparison. On the opposite wall was another door. Gareth drew it open. "What is this?" he asked as the soft scent of gardenia assailed his nostrils.

"This is the duchess's bedchamber," said the butler, "when, of course, there is a duchess in residence."

Gareth drew in the scent again, deeper this time. There was something exotic and alluring about it. An underlying hint of lotus blossom, perhaps? "There *is* a duchess in residence, Coggins," he finally said. "What's become of her?"

The butler inclined his head again. "The dowager duchess has moved to another suite of rooms," he explained. "She believed it was what you would wish."

Gareth set one hand on his hip. "Well, I do not wish it," he said, abruptly shutting the door. "Put her back again. Where is the second-best suite? I shall have that."

On this point, however, Coggins was not cowed. "It would be best, perhaps, Your Grace, if you had this discussion with the duchess herself?"

"Very well," he said. "I shall."

Two footmen had brought in hot water and were filling a hip bath which had been drawn into the center of the dressing room. Gareth's hands went to the knot of his neckcloth. "You will tell the duchess to expect me in twenty minutes," he said, stripping it off. "I shall see her in the study."

Coggins hesitated. "Perhaps, Your Grace, I might suggest the morning parlor?"

Gareth's hands paused at the buttons of his waistcoat. "The morning parlor? Why?"

Again, there was an instant of uncertainty. "The duchess greatly dislikes the study," the butler finally answered. "She . . . does not care for dark rooms. The study. The library. The north parlors. Indeed, save for dinner, she rarely leaves the south wing."

Gareth frowned. This did not sound like the indomitable woman he had known. "Since when has she adopted such odd notions?"

The butler's lips thinned. "I wish I knew what further to tell you, sir," he answered. "The duchess is . . . unusual."

"Unusual?"

"Er—*delicate,* Your Grace," he answered.

"Ah!" said Gareth, shrugging out of his coat. "You mean she has been indulged. Very well, then. It isn't my job to disabuse her. The morning parlor—in *eighteen* minutes."

"Eighteen?" the butler echoed.

"Yes, Coggins." Gareth hurled the waistcoat onto the bed. "Because time is money—and it is time everyone here learnt it."

Chapter Four

Gabriel pressed his ear to the keyhole, frightened. Zayde was sobbing. But men were not supposed to cry. Zayde himself said so—at least once a week.

"Gone, Rachel!" he cried. "Everything. Gone. Oy, a shkandal! A thousand curses on them!"

"B-But they are English gentlemen," whispered his grandmother. "They must pay it. They must."

"What, from France?" His grandfather's voice was bitter. "Accept it, Rachel. They are gone. Ruined. We've lost it—all of it—even the house, I fear."

"No!" His grandmother gasped. "Oh, not my home. Malachi, please!"

"Insolvents cannot live in Finsbury Circus, Rachel. We'll do well to lease a filthy hekdish in Houndsditch again."

"But what of Major Ventnor?" said his grandmother. "Perhaps he can help us?"

"Help! Help! Rachel, there is no help!"

"But here—I will write to him, yes?" Gabriel heard her

footsteps crossing to her little chestnut writing desk. "He will send us money."

"What, on an officer's pay?" Zayde's voice was a low groan now. "No, Rachel. No. This is God's will. It is over."

Gareth stood outside the door of Selsdon Court's morning parlor and dragged a hand through his still-damp hair. In the other hand, he clasped the documents Cavendish had supplied him, most of which he'd not yet read. He did not welcome this meeting. Scarcely two days had passed since his untimely visit from the solicitor, and already Gareth was tired of pretending to be something he was not. But he would have done with this miserable business straightaway—for until he did so, he could not move forward. Forward into what, he scarcely knew.

He rapped harshly on the door and went in.

The room was bathed in muted afternoon light which emphasized its pale gold and cream furnishings. A woman—not the duchess—stood by the bank of French windows, staring out into the gardens. She wore an elegant gown in a shade of purple so dark it appeared almost black, and thin black ribbons which twined delicately through hair which shone with gold light. A gossamer black shawl had slithered off her shoulders and now hung from her elbows. She gave the vague impression of being quite beautiful, but how could one tell? The woman did not deign to turn around or to acknowledge his presence in any way whatsoever.

A regal snub, then. He might have expected as much. "Good afternoon," he said, loudly and brusquely.

The woman whirled around, her eyes widening. Perhaps she had not heard him enter after all? No, that was unlikely.

"I am Warneham," he said coolly. "Who the devil are you?"

The woman curtsied so deeply and so gracefully that she might have touched her forehead to the floor. "I am Antonia," she said, smoothly rising. "Allow me to welcome you, Your Grace, to Selsdon Court."

"Antonia?—"

She cocked her head to one side. "Antonia, the Duchess of Warneham."

Understanding, swift and a little embarrassing, surged through Gareth. *The duchess.* Good Lord, he was an idiot. "You . . . you were Warneham's second wife?"

The woman smiled faintly, a slight curving of the lips which was at once knowing and a little bitter. "His fourth, I believe," she murmured. "The late duke was nothing if not determined."

"Good God," he said. "Determined to do what, kill himself?"

She averted her gaze, and again understanding struck. Upon Cyril's death, Warneham would have grasped the rules of succession all too well. He would have been desperate—desperate for an heir to displace the boy he had come to hate with his every fiber, rather than to merely loathe. And, just to make doubly sure Gareth could not inherit, Warneham had got rid of him with every hope he would not survive to see England again. But survive he had.

And this woman . . . good God. She was more beautiful, even, than first impression suggested. She was also young—well shy of thirty, he thought, which was certainly young enough to give an embittered old man a child. But if she had any children by Warneham, they were daughters, else Gareth would not be standing here, and she would not be gazing politely at the gardens, as if to spare him his embarrassment. Well, to hell with her mercy. He did not need it.

"Allow me to extend my condolences on your bereavement," he said briskly. "As you are doubtless aware, my cousin and I did not communicate, so I do not know if—"

"And I know nothing of my husband's personal affairs," she interjected tightly. "Certainly you need not explain them to me now."

"I beg your pardon?"

She looked at him in obvious impatience. "Ours was a brief marriage, Your Grace," she returned. "And it was arranged—arranged for just one purpose. He was not interested in my personal affairs, nor I in his."

She could not have cut off the conversation more cleanly had she sliced it through with a corsair's blade. He stared at her almost blankly for a moment. She seemed an enigma; fragile as fine china to look at, but cool and spiteful in her heart. A porcelain princess, haughty and regal.

"Tell me, ma'am," he finally said. "Is there anyone in this house who does not resent me? Anyone at all who does not wish me to the very devil?"

Her finely etched eyebrows rose. "I'm sure I haven't the faintest notion," she said. "But I do not wish you ill, Your Grace. I wish merely to move on with my life, such as it is. I wish . . . for my *freedom*. That is all."

"Your freedom?" he echoed. "Yes, I see. I have kept you waiting."

"Fate has kept me waiting," the duchess corrected. "And speaking of waiting, Your Grace, might I ask that you kindly not demean the servants by keeping them waiting in the rain again? Mrs. Musbury has a weak chest."

"Believe me, I have no interest in pomp or ceremony," he said, scowling. "It must have been Coggins's idea to line everyone up."

Her chin went up a fraction. "And yet you detained them?"

"As opposed to what?" he snapped. "Walking past them as if I didn't give a damn? *That* would have been demeaning, ma'am. That would have suggested that their employment was of no consequence to me—and had you ever *been* employed, ma'am, you would know that that can be the cruelest cut of all."

What little color she possessed drained away, and a look of instant guilt sketched across her face. "I beg your pardon," she said quietly. "I have spoken out of turn."

"No, you have spoken *wrongly*," he snapped. "We are not taking turns. You may speak when and where you please. And whilst we are arguing, ma'am, let me give another unequivocal order: you are to return to your chambers in the south wing at once."

She blanched. "I hardly think that would be appropriate, Your Grace."

"Appropriate?" he echoed, fleetingly confused. "Oh, for pity's sake, woman! I am moving to another suite."

Her discomfort shifted to bewilderment. "Well, I am not sure that is appropriate, either."

"An opinion which I shall instantly disregard," he said. "That, you see, is why I used the word *unequivocal.*"

"Dear me," said the duchess quietly. "You *are* Warneham's cousin after all, aren't you?"

"Yes, and a pity he hadn't another," Gareth returned.

She looked at him with curiosity, but no anger. "What is that supposed to mean?"

"Never mind," he answered. "Forgive me." Gareth cleared his throat a little sharply, then realized with yet another flash of discomfort that he had not invited her to sit. This was, after all, his house, not hers. She realized it, too.

With a motion of his arm, he gestured toward a pair of chairs by the window. "I see you have a fondness for that particular view of Selsdon's garden," he said somewhat drolly. "And we have got off to a rather awkward start. Will you have a seat, ma'am?"

The duchess recognized his command, tempered though it was. She returned to the bank of windows, her spine rigid beneath the dark purple silk. She sat down almost regally and adjusted her skirts.

Gareth forced his eyes from her and glanced out at the magnificent view beyond; at the verdant sweep of perfectly manicured boxwoods, at the pea-gravel paths which were doubtless still raked with a comb every morning, and at the ostentatious fountain which spewed streams of water some ten feet into the air. The "fish fountain" they had called it, he and Cyril, since the water spouted from the mouths of the mythological creatures which surrounded a sculpture of Triton. They had loved to play in it on warm summer days.

It reminded him yet again that all of this should have been Cyril's. He had been born to it. Prepared for it. *Expected* it. Gareth had not. No, not in his wildest dreams. But he settled himself into the chair opposite the duchess and forced himself to look at her again. This time, their eyes met, causing his breath to oddly catch. But what nonsense. He did not know her. And she clearly had no wish to know him.

"What plans have you made for your future, ma'am?" he stiffly enquired. "And how may I expedite them?"

"I have made no plans as yet," she answered. "Mr. Cavendish said I might not, until your permission was sought."

"My permission?" Impatiently, Gareth tapped the edge of the file against his thigh. "Not my advice? Or my guidance, perhaps? You have a dower right, have you not?"

"I have been granted one-twentieth of the income from the ducal holdings," she replied. "I will not starve."

"One-*twentieth*?" Gareth looked at her incredulously. "Good God, what possessed you to agree to such a thing?"

Again, the gently arched eyebrows rose. "You must have been abroad a great many years indeed, Your Grace," she murmured. "England is still a patriarchal society."

She was right, of course. Gareth had become too accustomed to Xanthia's independence. Most women had not the privilege of living her sort of life.

"My father handled the marriage settlements," the duchess continued. "I knew nothing of them until the solicitors came down after the funeral. Cavendish has likely provided you a copy. But one-twentieth of the income of Selsdon alone could keep a frugal family of ten in comfort. As I said, Your Grace, I shan't starve."

"Your father was either a fool, or in one hell of a hurry to marry you off," he muttered, sorting through the papers in the file. "English common law would have given you a third, wouldn't it?"

When she did not answer, he lifted his head to look at her. A stricken look was upon her face, and much of her color had gone. Gareth felt instantly ashamed.

"I beg your pardon," he said stiffly. "My remark was inappropriate, given your grief."

But she did not look precisely grief stricken. She looked . . . well, just stricken. But her color was swiftly returning. She squared her shoulders and said, "It was a carefully negotiated marriage, Your Grace. My father felt I should be grateful for Warneham's offer, as my prospects were few."

What utter nonsense she spoke. The duchess was the sort of woman who could reasonably expect men to fall at her feet. "Few prospects, eh?" he muttered.

"Oh, do not feel sorry for me, Your Grace," she said coolly. "I was everything the late duke wished for in a bride."

Gareth cleared his throat and pressed on. "As the dowager duchess, ma'am, you should have the right to remain in your home," he said. "No one expects you to leave it. My visits here will be as infrequent as possible, so we shall hardly be under one another's feet."

Something like relief seemed to pass over her, and Gareth saw her shoulders relax just a fraction. "Thank you," she said throatily. "I . . . I do thank you, Your Grace. But I am not perfectly sure—"

"That you wish to remain here?" he supplied. "Yes, the place is a dreadful old mausoleum, despite its grandeur. What of your family? Your father, perhaps?"

"No," she said swiftly. "He . . . he is traveling at present."

Something in her words warned him not to press that point. "Have you any children, ma'am?" he asked instead. "A daughter, perhaps?"

Her gaze shot toward him, and for an instant he saw something raw and poignant in her eyes. "No, Your Grace," she said quietly. "I have no children."

Good God, was there no safe topic with this woman? "What does Cavendish think you should do?"

She clasped her hands in her lap. "He feels I should retire to Knollwood Manor—that is the dower house—and live a quiet life away from the prying eyes of society. He believes that would be . . . best for me, under the circumstances."

The dower house? Inwardly, Gareth cringed. But outwardly, he remained expressionless. "You are far too young, I think, to live such a quiet life unless you wish it," he said. "Pardon my ignorance, but haven't we a house in town?"

She nodded. "In Bruton Street, but it has been let."

"Then I shall un-let it," he answered.

"You are very kind," she said again. "But no, I cannot return to London. And I am not sure that sort of life would suit me. I am just . . . not sure."

But he was sure. She was young and breathtakingly beautiful. She had the whole of her life before her. Though she had not been left a great deal of income, surely she could marry well on her looks alone, once the rumors about Warneham's death died down? Unless there was something she was not telling him.

Perhaps she had a scandalous past? He looked at her and considered it. No. More likely she was damaged goods—damaged in some way which was not readily apparent. And would those rumors ever really die down? Warneham had been dead nearly a year. Perhaps they would not. Society was quick to talk and slow to forgive. Ah, well. They all had their crosses to bear, hadn't they? Her past was none of his concern. And his was none of hers.

Swiftly, he shuffled through the papers to see if there was any information about the lease on the house in Bruton Street, but there was nothing. He looked up at her. "Well, we need not decide in haste, ma'am," he said. "You are welcome to remain at Selsdon Court as long as you wish. But if indeed you prefer Knollwood . . . well, I suppose we may consider it."

She dropped her gaze to the carpet. "It is in a dreadful state, I'm told," she replied. "Cavendish says it will take a vast deal of money to set it to rights. It was abandoned, I collect, some years past."

He felt his jaw harden. "Indeed it was," he said. "I lived there, you see, as a boy. And even then, it was a run-down, rotting mess."

Her head jerked up. "I . . . I did not know," she stammered. "It was said, of course, you once lived here—"

"I never lived here," he interjected. "I have never lived in this house."

"Oh." She looked away. "I have never been inside. Knollwood, I mean."

"There is nothing to see," he said sharply. "Indeed, it must be perfectly uninhabitable now. Twenty years ago, the roof leaked and the floors were rotting. There is no plumbing whatsoever, and the cellar is so damp the downstairs reeked of mildew."

At that, the duchess wrinkled her nose and made a face. It made her look perfectly girlish—and it made him want, inexplicably, to laugh. Not at her, but with her. For an instant, he forgot about the cold and miserable nights he had spent in that grim old house—and the nights which had come after.

"It actually looks quite lovely from the outside," she said apologetically. "Like a little fairy castle, I sometimes think."

"It's the turrets, I suppose." He forced himself to smile. "They appear rather romantic from the exterior. And if you really wish to live there—and never mind what Cavendish wants—then the necessary repairs can be made. Assets must be maintained, and I've no doubt the estate can afford it."

"Indeed, you are one of England's wealthiest men now, Your Grace." Suddenly, she paled. "Not to suggest, of course, that you weren't before. I cannot presume to know your circumstances—"

She had succumbed to blushes. "Just what did that old prune Cavendish think he was getting when he ran me down?" Gareth muttered. "Some back-alley blackleg? A cutpurse? A grave robber, perhaps?"

The blush deepened. "A stevedore, I believe he said," she answered. "Or a dockhand? Are they the same?"

"More or less." Gareth smiled. "I'm almost sorry

now that I wasn't one. I'd have had a devilish good time watching him mince about the docks with a handkerchief clamped to his nose."

For an instant, she looked as if she might laugh. He found himself waiting for the sound with an inexplicable eagerness, but she kept silent.

He laid the file aside and set his hands on his thighs as if to rise. "Well, we can do no more at present, I think," he said musingly. "What time is dinner served these days?"

"Half past six." Suddenly, her eyes widened. "And it is Monday, Your Grace."

"Monday?"

"Sir Percy and Lady Ingham usually dine at Selsdon on Monday, along with Dr. Osborne," she answered. "And usually the rector and his wife. But they are on holiday in Brighton. Do you mind terribly?"

"I mind it a great deal indeed," he returned. "I should much prefer to be on holiday in Brighton myself."

The duchess gave another serene smile. "I meant Dr. Osborne," she clarified. "He is our village doctor in Lower Addington. And Sir Percy and his wife are quite nice people. They have all—well, stood by me, I suppose, during this terrible time."

"Then I shall look forward to meeting them," he said, rising. And it would have the added benefit, he inwardly considered, of helping him avoid another hour alone in her company. With a deliberately distant smile, Gareth offered his hand and helped the duchess rise from her chair.

At the door, however, she hesitated and turned to face him. Her expression was once again bleak.

"Your Grace?"

"Yes?"

"I realize this is your first afternoon at Selsdon." Her eyes were focused somewhere beyond his shoulder. "It is but a matter of time, however, before you . . . well, before you hear the rumors."

"Rumors?" He smiled a little bitterly. "I should think Selsdon is rife with those. To which do you refer?"

She returned her gaze to his, her eyes bleak. "There are some who believe my husband's death was not an accident," said the duchess quietly. "It has been whispered that perhaps—well, that perhaps I was unhappy in my marriage."

The words, spoken so emotionlessly from her own lips, sent a chill down his spine which Xanthia's rumor had not. "Are you saying that you have been openly accused?"

She gave a muted half smile. "Accused? No. That would be too complicated. It is far easier to simply blight my reputation with whispers and innuendo."

Gareth held her gaze steadily. "And did you kill him?"

"No, Your Grace," she said softly. "I did not. But the damage is done."

"I learnt long ago what an ugly, destructive force rumors can be," he answered coolly. "In this case, I suggest we pay them all the heed they are worth—which is nothing."

But as he left her standing by the door, he was not at all sure his suggestion was a good one. There was something strange and a little otherworldly about the Duchess. Something haunting in her eyes. But a murderess?

He was utterly certain she was not, though why he felt such confidence, he could not have said.

Unfortunately, in her world—the world of the *ton*—that sort of rumor could be worse than ruinous. Perhaps he was beginning to comprehend why she might prefer to shut herself away in a lonely, ramshackle place like Knollwood rather than return to that world and try to build a life for herself.

But none of this was really his problem, was it? He had come here merely to look over the estate, and make certain it was being profitably run. He was not here to save the world—not even the duchess's elite little corner of it.

Upon her return, Nellie greeted Antonia at her bedchamber door. "You've come back!" she said, as if she'd expected her mistress to have been eaten alive. "What was he like, ma'am, the new duke?"

Antonia gave a grim smile. "Arrogant," she said, tossing her black shawl onto the bed. "Now pack up my things, Nellie. We're going—"

"Oh, ma'am!" the maid wailed. "He must be heartless! Truly!"

"—back to the ducal suite," Antonia finished.

Nellie's mouth dropped shut. "Well, bless me!" she said after a moment had passed. "Back to your old rooms, then? That's right and proper of him, if I do say so myself."

Antonia had crossed the room to the window. It was clear Nellie wished to hear more about the meeting, but Antonia drew away the sheer drapery and stared down at the graveled forecourt. She was inexplicably reluctant to allow the maid to gauge her mood just now. She was not perfectly sure she understood it herself.

What had just happened to her in the morning room? Something . . . strange. She felt oddly aware—but aware of what? It was as if she was shaking—or perhaps the word was aquiver? As if something inside her had been stirred up.

She had expected, really, to dislike the new Duke of Warneham, not that she had cared much one way or the other. At her very first glance, the man had appeared high-handed and arrogant—which he was. He had looked every inch the haughty aristocrat, with his form fitting coat and snug breeches. His golden gaze had seemed to pierce her. His jaw had been too hard, his nose too aquiline. His leonine mane entirely too luxurious. And inexplicably, she had found herself almost spoiling for a fight. That was not like her. It truly was not. There was no longer anything worth quarreling over in life. *Was* there?

And that spate of temper! Where had it come from? She had not raised her voice to anyone since . . well, in a very long while. But something about the duke had provoked her. The man had seemed so cocksure. So . . . apparently *comfortable* in wielding his new power. And in the end, to her shock, he had been almost kind. He had believed her, she thought.

She had expected, she supposed, that he would be rough-edged and ill-mannered; a rustic who would have gazed about his easily-got gains in gaping stupefaction. She had not expected him to look so young, and she had assumed that his years drifting about in the navy and the colonial islands would have rubbed off any bit of bronze which had been left from his brief life at Selsdon. But he was not like that at all. He was something far more dangerous.

"Yes, Nellie, the new duke said everything which was proper," Antonia finally responded. "I do not believe him a warmhearted man by any estimate, but I have hope that he is just."

Nellie touched her lightly on the arm. "But he was arrogant, you said?"

"Yes . . ." Antonia was not sure how to describe it. "Perhaps it really is bred in the blood, Nellie? I think this man would have been imperious had he been raised in a cow byre."

"Well, we don't really know where he was raised, do we, ma'am?" said Nellie suspiciously. "We only know what's said belowstairs: that he killed his little cousin, and broke the old duke's heart—not that I ever saw as he had one."

"Nellie, that will do," Antonia gently admonished. "By the way, he tells me he actually lived at Knollwood. Had you ever heard that?"

"No, ma'am." The maid had returned to her task of folding stockings. "Just that he was brought up here."

"But it's not quite the same, is it?" Antonia mused. "Tell me, Nellie, what are they saying belowstairs?"

"Most everyone is kind of quiet-like," the maid admitted. "There are some as say the new duke was very kind to take the time to meet everyone, seeing as how it was beginning to pour the rain. And some remarked favorably on his way of plain speaking. But one or two are saying how they don't fancy working for a jumped-up piece of—well, never mind that."

Antonia shot her a sidelong glance. "Yes, never mind that indeed."

Nellie shrugged. "Metcaff says there's been whispers

that the new master had something to do with the old duke's death, ma'am."

"The only whispers are Metcaff's," said Antonia. "An idle tongue is Satan's tool, Nellie. And you'll recall that it was I who had done the dastardly deed until this new opportunity turned up."

"No one really believes that, ma'am," said Nellie, but Antonia knew she was just being kind. "Anyway, Metcaff says he's thinking of giving notice."

"Does he?" said Antonia incredulously. "To do what, pray?"

"I couldn't say, ma'am," answered the maid. "But he's egging on some of the others to go with him."

"Then they shall all starve together," Antonia retorted. "People are already without food in London, and this damp is like to ruin the harvest. They had better be grateful for employment."

Nellie was quiet for a moment. "Begging your pardon, ma'am, but are you perfectly all right?"

"Yes, Nellie, perfectly." Antonia turned from the window. "Why do you ask?"

This time Nellie lifted just one shoulder. "You seem in an odd frame of mind, ma'am," she answered. "And your color . . . but never mind that, either. If you are well enough, then—"

"I am fine."

"Then, as you say, I ought to pack."

"Yes, thank you." Antonia had returned her gaze to the window. "But be so good as to lay out my dinner dress first."

Nellie opened the dressing room. "Which would you have, ma'am?"

"You choose," Antonia said, gazing not at the fore-court but at her own watery reflection in the glass. Nellie was right. She did not look quite herself. Her color was a little high, and her expression not one she easily recognized.

"Nellie," she abruptly added, "choose something with just a little color. Perhaps the dark blue jacquard satin? Is it too soon, do you think?"

"Of course not, ma'am." Nellie extracted the gown and gave it a healthy shake. "The new duke has come. It is your duty to welcome him."

"Yes, Nellie, I suppose you are right." Absently, Antonia lifted her hand and lightly touched the stranger in the glass. "It is my duty, isn't it?"

That evening, Gareth greeted his guests with both a measure of dread and at least a modicum of relief. After his meeting with the Duchess of Warneham, he was not perfectly sure he wished to be alone with her again. He was not certain why he felt that way. Visually, the woman was an indulgence—but like a too-rich dessert, better cut with something bland, perhaps, like tepid coffee.

He got his wish in Sir Percy Ingham. If the duchess was a chocolate gâteau with crème anglaise, Sir Percy was weak tea. He was also a relative newcomer to the village of Lower Addington, which Gareth found a relief. He was a little tired of the whispers which already went on behind his back. Not that Sir Percy seemed above it—certainly his wife was not—but at least Gareth did not know them from his childhood. He found the same favorable trait in the doctor, a man named

Martin Osborne, who was well spoken and obviously well educated. Osborne looked to be a bit less than forty, and he possessed all the polish of a gentleman.

Gareth was also relieved to discover that Selsdon was gifted with a chef of outstanding skill. He looked down the dinner table in some satisfaction as the third course was removed and a selection of fruit tarts and ices was brought in.

"Let me say again, Your Grace, how pleased we are to dine with you on this, your very first night at Selsdon," said Dr. Osborne solemnly. "You are most gracious to carry on our little tradition."

"Very gracious indeed," said Sir Percy, picking judiciously over the platter of tarts. "On the whole, Your Grace, how have you found your first day in your new home?"

Gareth nodded at the footman, who was offering more wine. "What was it, Sir Percy, that the Reverend Richard Hooker once said?" Gareth mused as the servant leaned over to pour. " 'Change is not made without inconvenience, even from worse to better?' "

"Quite so! Quite so!" Sir Percy looked surprised. "Have you by chance read Hooker's masterpiece *Of the Lawes of Ecclesiastical Politie*? It is one of the rector's favorites."

"I have read it," said Gareth a little tightly, wondering if any insult—or worse, some probing question—hid behind the baronet's words. Reverend Needles had crammed Hooker into his head *ad nauseam*—not that it was any of their damned business. But the remark had passed without notice. Gareth relaxed.

"What, pray, do you find inconvenient about this

change, Your Grace?" twittered Lady Ingham. "I vow, I can find nothing about Selsdon Court to dislike."

"You misunderstand his point, my dear," said her husband.

"It is not a matter of dislike, ma'am," Gareth calmly lied. "I am inconvenienced in having to leave my business unattended in London."

Lady Ingham smiled benightedly. "But surely you must have clerks?"

Gareth felt suddenly and inordinately weary. These people were kind enough, but they knew little of the real world. "We've a dozen clerks, ma'am, but it would be a bit much for them to take on," he answered. "And my business associate is newly wed, so she—"

"*She?*" Lady Ingham pounced on the morsel of gossip. "Why, what sort of business associate do you have?"

Gareth was tempted to say he'd gone in halves on Mrs. Berkley's latest flagellation house, since that was the sort of salacious reply she obviously hoped for. He restrained himself. "The Marchioness of Nash is my associate," he answered. "We are part owners in a company called Neville Shipping."

The duchess said nothing, but Gareth saw her eyes widen in obvious surprise.

"Neville Shipping," mused the doctor. "Have you an office in Wapping High Street? I think I've seen it."

"On one of your trips up to town, I daresay?" said the duchess, breaking her silence.

"Yes, I remember seeing the sign thereabouts," Osborne confessed. "I use a chemist near Wapping Wall. What a small place the world has become."

"Not too small, I hope," said Gareth. "If it is shrinking, Neville's shall soon be out of business altogether."

"But surely, Your Grace, you do not mean to continue on with it?" Mrs. Ingham's tone was faintly chiding.

At that, Gareth finally felt his temper slip. "Why would I not?" he asked pointedly. "Hard work never did a man much ill—and often a vast deal of good."

"Quite so! Quite so!" said Sir Percy again.

The doctor leaned forward as if to emphasize his words. "There are vocations, Lady Ingham, and then there are passions. Perhaps this business is a passion for the duke?"

Gareth glanced down the length of snowy linen to see that the duchess was watching him attentively, as if wondering what his answer would be. "It was a necessity which has become a passion," he said. "Shall we leave it at that?"

Moments later, the desserts were cleared and port was brought in. The gentlemen did not linger long. When they rejoined the ladies in the withdrawing room, it was to see Lady Ingham already being helped into her cloak.

"I heard a little thunder," she said almost sheepishly. "I think, Percy, we must go at once."

Sir Percy winked at Gareth. "The wife does not care for thunderstorms."

"Nor does Her Grace," Osborne gently added.

The duchess, who had been neatening Lady Ingham's cloak collar, froze. She looked at no one, not even the doctor. Osborne must have realized his faux pas, and he began prattling in more general terms about the weather.

"May we set you down in the village, Osborne?" Sir Percy interjected. "I fear my wife is right about the rain."

"Thank you, no," said Osborne. "I brought an umbrella."

Gareth accompanied the Inghams to the front door, but the duchess held back almost deferentially. When Gareth returned to the withdrawing room moments later, however, he wondered if deference had anything to do with it. Osborne stood just inside the door, the duchess's hands clasped lightly in his own. He was holding her gaze intently.

"And the sleeping draught?" he murmured. "Promise me, Antonia, that you will not forget it?"

She caught the plump swell of her lower lip between her teeth, and something in Gareth's stomach did a flip-flop. "I dislike it immensely," she finally said. "It makes me feel very queer afterward."

"Antonia, you must promise me," he said more firmly, lifting her hands as if he might kiss them. "You need it—otherwise you know you will not do well with this storm coming in."

She dropped her gaze in a sweep of dark eyelashes. "Very well. I shall consider it."

Gareth cleared his throat sharply and stepped inside the room.

The pair sprang apart almost conspiratorially. The duchess lowered her eyes again and drifted toward the cold hearth, rubbing her arms as if she felt chilled. Dr. Osborne began to express his thanks for the dinner.

When Gareth returned from escorting the doctor out, he was somewhat relieved to discover that the duchess had vanished.

Chapter Five

Gabriel stood at a distance as the older boys played, kicking their ball along the swath of green. He had seen them in Finsbury Circus before. And he had seen the ball, too; an amazingly round and bouncing sphere which skittered across the grass at lightning speed, and made a satisfying "thunk!" when kicked.

The smallest boy caught Gabriel's eye and crooked a finger. With a glance back at his dozing grandfather, Gabriel dashed onto the grass.

The boy held out the ball. "We need a sixth," he said. "Can you kick?"

Gabriel nodded. "I can kick."

The biggest boy elbowed past him. "Give it, Will," he said, snatching the ball from between them. "We ain't playin' with Jews."

Gabriel let his arms drop.

The bigger boy danced backward across the grass, sneering. "What?" he said. "You want the ball? You want it? Here—

catch!" He dropped the ball and punted hard, his long leg swinging wide.

The ball caught Gabriel in the gut. The breath burst from his lungs. He fell to the grass in a heap, the pounding of blood in his ears almost—almost—shutting out the peals of laughter. At first just the laughter of one. And then another and another, until all the boys were laughing.

His humiliation was complete when Zayde snatched him from the grass. "A broch tsu dir!" he said, shaking his fist at the boys. "Go back to Shoreditch, you little pigs!"

Still giggling, the boys dashed away. Zayde began to dust Gabriel off. "Oy vey, Gabriel! What were you thinking?"

"I—I liked their ball."

"Eingeshpahrt!" His grandfather sighed. "But I can buy you a ball, yes?"

"And I want someone to play with."

"Then keep to your own kind!" Zayde seized his hand and set off across the grass towards their house. "They don't want us, Gabriel. When will you learn, eh?"

That night, the heat broke and a rainstorm hammered across Surrey with a vengeance. Gareth went to bed to the sound of howling wind and the incessant rattle of overflowing drainpipes. Inordinately weary from the day's travel—and the thoughts of the duty which lay before him—he fell at once into a deep but uneasy sleep. He awoke sometime after midnight in a cold sweat, caught in a tangle of sheets, unable to catch his breath. He jerked upright, terrified and disoriented.

Selsdon Court. He was at Selsdon. A burning sconce in the passageway beyond limned the outline of his door. A very wide and very solid door. His cousin was finally dead, thank God. There was no ship, no chains. But the dream clung like damp, moldering sailcloth. He could smell it thick in his nostrils, along with the stench of tarred rope and the press of rancid, unwashed bodies. The *Saint-Nazaire*? Good God. He had not dreamt of that rotted old hulk in months.

He did not realize until that moment just how badly he was shaking. Dragging a hand through his tousled hair, Gareth tried to steady himself. Lord, what did it mean that he should dream of his lost youth tonight, of all nights?

Nothing. It meant noting. He was not a child any more. He could defend himself now. But at the moment, he needed a drink. Yes, a generous tot of brandy— Rothewell's infamous cure for all ills. He extracted himself from the sheets, sat up on the edge of the bed, and wiped the sweat from his brow. Beyond the windows, lightning flashed; once, then again. Seconds later, thunder rumbled, but far in the distance.

The brandy sat on a side table between the windows. Gareth lit a lamp, pulled on his dressing gown, then poured a glass. And then a second. He was well into his third, and growing impatient with himself for brooding, when the restlessness struck. He looked at the mantel clock. *Half past two.* Why did it seem another lifetime?

It was this place. Returning conjured up too many memories. He thought, strangely, of his grandmother, and of Cyril. His life here, by and large, had been one of childhood misery. But he had not realized how relatively pleasant misery could be until he'd ended up in hell—on the *Saint-Nazaire*.

Abruptly, he tossed back the last of the brandy, savoring the burn as it slid down his throat. Good Lord, Rothewell would laugh to see him now, cowering in the gloom like some timorous boy, and slightly sotted from a mere fraction of what the baron himself might put away before breakfast.

Gareth, however, had never been much of a drinker. He'd always believed it a habit for blue bloods, men who need not rise at dawn to work for a living—a category which, he abruptly realized, now included *him*.

On that thought, Gareth jerked from his chair and began to roam restlessly through the room. His grandfather had been right; he had never been meant for this sort of life. So how had it happened? For a time, he was lost in a whirl of thoughts and half-wrought memories; he could not later have said what, for at last he found something which could thoroughly distract him. He drew open the heavy draperies and looked out across the courtyard below.

Selsdon Court had begun as a Norman keep, which had become a fully crenellated castle in the reign of William II. Eventually the castle had become an elegant mansion, which had retained many of its original features, amongst them the south and east bastions, which were connected by a towering curtain wall, the oldest part of the house. Gareth could see it looming across the inner courtyard, its rough stone walls yellow-brown in the flickering light cast upward by the gate lamps. From his vantage point just above, he could make out the crenellations, but the interior rampart was steeped in shadow.

He peered higher, toward the sky. The rain was coming in sheets now, but with less ferocity, perhaps. Another bolt of lightning lit the sky, illuminating the house. Gareth's gaze swept the curtain wall again. He had glimpsed something on the rampart. Motion? Light? Both, he thought. Another flash, this one more distant.

This time, he saw her clearly. A woman in white. She was pacing like some ghostly specter, her white-draped arms lifted heavenward. Good God, was she begging to die? Again the sky lit, bathing her in pale, otherworldly light. She seemed oblivious to the nearing storm. Gareth had both slippers on before he knew what he meant to do.

Later, of course, he realized that he should have summoned a servant. It would have saved him a pair of wet slippers and a vast amount of angst. But in the press of the moment, he rushed headlong down the twisting passageways, and up and down the stairs which led from one section of the house to another, and all the while praying he remembered how to find his way onto the wall. Surely he did? He and Cyril had played in the towers as children, battling one another up and down the spiral staircases.

Suddenly, he saw it. An arched wooden doorway banded with iron and set at an odd angle in the wall. He pushed through into the bastion's circular room. The stairs were just beyond. He went up half a flight and saw the next door, a narrow, planked affair. It gave onto the curtain wall. But the damned door was stuck.

With a mighty blow, Gareth shouldered his way through. The door swung into the gloom on squalling hinges. On the rampart beyond, the woman was still pacing, her back turned to him. Again the horizon lit, throwing the east bastion ahead into stark relief. But he had no need to see her face. He knew at once who she was; he had known it, perhaps, from the first.

"Your Grace!" His words barely carried over the roar of the rain. "Antonia! *Stop!*"

She did not hear him. Gingerly, he approached, heedless of the puddles. Tension seemed to radiate from her body. Her pale blond hair hung below her waist, sodden from the rain. She looked shockingly thin and small.

"Antonia?" he said softly.

When he touched her shoulder, she turned without alarm and looked—well, not *at* him, but *through* him. It was utterly unnerving, especially when he realized she wore nothing but a sheer muslin nightgown which was now plastered to a pair of exquisite breasts.

He forced his gaze to her face. "Antonia," he said quietly, "what are you doing out here?"

She pulled away, dragging a hand through her wet hair. "Beatrice," she murmured, not looking at him. "The carriage—do you hear it?"

Gareth grasped her forearm in a gentle but uncompromising grip. "Who is Beatrice?" he asked over the racket of the rain.

"It's late," she rasped. "Surely . . . surely that must be them?"

"Antonia, get inside! No one is coming tonight."

Obviously agitated, she shook her head. "The children, the children," she muttered. "I must wait."

She was sleepwalking. Or a little mad, perhaps? Certainly she did not know where she was. Damn it, he had to get her off this bloody wall. A bolt of lightning was apt to strike them both dead. "Come inside, Antonia," he said, tugging on her arm. "I insist."

"No!" Her voice was panicked. "No, I cannot leave!" She jerked away, forcing him to lunge for her.

She fought at him like a little hellcat then, striking out with both hands, clawing and struggling to throw off his grasp. Again, she escaped, and this time, he captured her against him, banding her to him with one arm, trying not to hurt her as she flailed. But Antonia's body was lithe and surprisingly strong—and surprisingly lush, too, God help him. For what seemed an eternity he fought her as she twisted, writhed, and struck at him, high on the rampart, with the storm drawing ever nearer, and nothing but the low crenellations to keep them both from tumbling over, and onto the cliffs below.

Finally he managed to pin her against the bastion with the weight of his body. "Antonia, stop!" She was breathing hard now. He clung to her, the rain running in rivulets down his face. "For God's sake, hold still!"

She had begun to cry—more of a gut-wrenching wail, really—and something inside him felt as if it was being wrenched from his chest with the sound. It was horrific. Heartbreaking. Her knees began to give, her entire body sliding weakly down the wall. Gareth drew her up, pulled her head to his shoulder, and let her sob. He had the other arm tightly around her at last, and the fight, he could sense, was going out of her. He drew her fully against him and felt the life or the consciousness or whatever it was slowly return to her body.

"Antonia," he whispered into her damp hair. "Oh, Christ Jesus, you scared the life out of me!"

"I—I'm sorry!" she whimpered, still sobbing. "I'm sorry! Oh, God!"

"Come, we must go," he said. "The storm is nearing again."

But instead, she threw her arms around his neck as if she were drowning. "No, don't leave me!" she whimpered. "Just . . . I cannot . . ." She began to sob in earnest, a sound like a wounded animal, and something inside his heart tore. "No one is coming," she rasped through the tears. "I am sorry. I—I got mixed up."

"It's all right, my dear." He tightened his grip around her waist and shoulders and felt her lush, womanly curves press enticingly along his body. She felt wonderfully warm despite the rain and the chilling remnants of what had been blind terror. Good God, what a pig he was! But her head was on his shoulder again, and she was still sobbing as if her heart might break.

"I won't leave you," he promised. "Come, Antonia, let's go inside."

At long last, she lifted her head, her arms still entwined behind his neck. Their gazes locked. Her eyes brimmed with emotion; fear and anguish, and yes, something more. Something haunting and painfully inescapable. Her lower lip trembled. And against him, her body began to tremble, too, as if from desperation, and from that raw emotion which one often feels when danger has brushed too near. An emotion which could oftentimes take the form of a desperate hunger; a wish to be fully, reassuringly alive.

Good God, this was ludicrous. And he was a cad. The rain was still trailing down their faces. Her breath was still hitching like a frightened child's. But when her lashes dropped half shut, and her face tilted ever so slightly, he did it. He kissed her. And in that surreal moment, with the rain pounding down all around them, and thunder rumbling ominously in the distance, it seemed as if that was what she begged him for.

He had meant it as a gentle kiss. A kiss of comfort and of reassurance—or so he told himself. But when she opened her mouth beneath him, inviting him to deepen the kiss to something more, he accepted, sliding his tongue deep into the warmth of her mouth as if he, too, was desperate. Perhaps he was. Gareth had not kissed a woman with this sort of irrational hunger in . . . well, perhaps never.

He knew, of course, that it was wrong; that he was taking advantage of an emotionally vulnerable woman. And yet he was unable to stop himself. How could he? Antonia was kissing him back with a heated urgency, coming onto her toes, and allowing her breasts to press flat against him. She smelled of soap and rain, and of gardenia. The sodden nightgown clung to her every curve, lush and tempting, leaving nothing to the imagination.

At that, he closed his eyes, and set one hand over the swell of her hip, telling himself it was what she desired. When he touched her, she made a sound deep in her throat and pressed her hips into his. *Yes, she did want this.* And it was madness. A madness he strangely understood.

He had forgotten the rain which still drenched them. He had forgotten that anyone, as he had done, might look out from one of the second-floor windows. That the two of them might be struck dead at any moment. His breath was coming roughly now. His head was swimming with the need to keep her close; to draw her into him somehow. To bind her to him.

Yes, it was madness. Vaguely, he knew it would pass. But when she hitched one knee high, and let it stroke the outside of his thigh, he did it. He slid his hand fully beneath the lush weight of her buttock and gently lifted, parting her so that his fingertips might stroke deeper despite the wet muslin of her gown.

Her mouth still open beneath his, she gasped, and then hitched her leg higher, wrapping it almost desperately around him. Good God, what was she asking for?

He tore his mouth from hers. "Antonia," he rasped. "What do you want?"

She lifted her face to the rain. "Make me forget," she whispered. "Like this. I want to feel . . . something else."

"Come inside with me."

"No." Her eyes flared with alarm. "No. Now."

He let his mouth slide down her cheek, then skim hotly along her jaw. "Antonia, I don't think . . ."

"No!" she said sharply. "We . . . we *cannot think*. I want only to *feel*."

She kissed him again, hot and openmouthed, with a feverish desperation. She was an enchantress. A secret siren, calling to him. Oh, yes. Antonia had learnt the art of seduction well—and in that moment, he willed himself not to think of *where* she had learnt it.

In the heat and the madness, he had somehow lifted her against the bastion wall. Her leg was all but around his waist now, her warm hands and honeyed mouth more than a little reckless. He could not think about the storm. The lightning. The utter incredulity of what he was about to do. She was desire incarnate. Blood thundered in his head and throbbed in his cock, readily apparent beneath his scant nightclothes.

Antonia slid her delicately warm tongue into his mouth, thrusting and parrying with his own in a dance of rash desire. Spurred to urgency, Gareth fisted her wet nightgown in one hand and dragged it up. She did not resist but instead began to paw urgently at his dressing gown. He knew what she wanted. He pushed away his clothes and felt their warm flesh meet beneath the tangle of muslin and linen. He could not wait.

"Your other leg," he choked. "Put it—put it around— yes, my waist."

He set her back to the tower wall and, lifting her delicately in his hands, spread her wide. "Antonia, is this what you want?" he demanded.

"Yes." Her voice was feverish. "I want you. Desperately. Don't stop."

He kissed her again, then let his cock slide into the welcoming folds of warm, creamy flesh. Balancing her weight against his body, he lifted her up, and thrust.

"Ah!" In the gloom, he could sense her shock.

"Antonia." Gareth closed his eyes and prayed for control. "Oh, God. I—can't—I don't—"

"No," she said swiftly. "Don't think. Don't *stop*."

He thrust again, pulling her pelvis to his. It was all he could do to control his motions, to keep himself in check rather than ravish her like an animal. Antonia exhaled in a long, breathless sigh. A sound of yearning. Rain spattered all about them. Thunder rolled far in the distance. Again, he lifted her, thrusting deep. Then somehow, he found a shred of sense and managed to free one hand and slide it delicately between them. Her cry of shock had told him more than her bold actions had. He found her clitoris, sweetly firm beneath his fingertips, and lightly rubbed. In response, Antonia gasped again and let her head fall back against the stone tower.

He pumped himself into her, watching the rain run down the swanlike length of her throat. Watched her swallow hard, then begin to moan. He sensed he ought not speak; ought do nothing to spoil the impulsiveness and the near-anonymity of what they did. The passion between them was palpable. Never had he felt so unrestrained; so desperate to possess a woman, body and soul. Deep inside her, his cock throbbed with heat and blood. His body cried out with the urgency of his need as he thrust.

Antonia's breath was coming sharp and fast. Lightning lit the horizon again, revealing her face, which was lifted to the sky in an expression of nearing ecstasy. He worked her more furiously, touching and thrusting, their bodies rain-slick and sweating. Antonia's fingers dug deep into the flesh of his shoulders. Her entire body shuddered. She cried out like a wild thing, her gaze locking with his. And then she was lost to it.

Gareth drew out and thrust deep again. Over and over he pounded his flesh into her throbbing sheath, his head thrown back in release when at last his seed flooded forth, spurting inside her in waves of guilty pleasure. Spent, they clung to one another in the rain, her legs and arms still about him, their bodies still throbbing. For a time, Gareth shut out all thought and simply felt. Felt the heat of her slender body through their wet clothes. Felt her warm sheath relax about his cock. The softness of her breath on his ear. And then he felt vaguely ashamed of what he'd just done.

Antonia's spine still rested against the tower wall. "The stone," he finally managed. "It must hurt."

She said nothing. As if by mutual agreement, they unwrapped one another, Antonia sliding down his length until her feet touched the wet flagstone of the rampart. His wet robe slithered damply down his legs. Antonia dropped her head, and tenderly, he restored her clothing to order.

The rain was slacking off now. The storm had passed.

Gently, he slid a finger beneath her chin and lifted her gaze to his. The blank look was returning to her eyes. Dear Lord, what had they done? Everything about this troubled him. Even the seductive anonymity no longer felt right.

"Antonia," he rasped. "Antonia, I want you to say my name."

In the gloom, he sensed uncertainty sketch across her face. He set both hands on her shoulders as if he might shake her. "Antonia, *who am I?*"

Suddenly, a faint light trembled inside the tower beyond. Shuffling footsteps echoed far below in the stairwell. Antonia moved as if to go, and he caught her arm.

"My name," he repeated. "I just want to hear it once from your lips."

"Gabriel," she whispered, looking back at him. "You are . . . the angel Gabriel."

He let her go.

Gabriel. It was not his name. Not any longer.

"My lady?" A servant's voice called gently up the stairwell. "Your Grace, are you up there?"

She slipped through the bastion's opening, then vanished down the dark and twisting stairs. She was safe. She was gone.

So what was he waiting for? Gareth turned and walked swiftly back along the rampart to the opposite end. The drizzle was cold on his face now, his slippers and clothing were sopping. He was chilled, he realized. But all the anguish and all the physical discomfort could not shut out that one awful question—what in God's name had he just done?

Chapter Six

Gabriel's grandfather led him by the hand through the labyrinthine alleys of Moorgate. Dusk was fast turning to night, and shopkeepers were drawing their shades.

"Are we far from home, Zayde?"

"Almost there, Gabriel," he said. "Did you enjoy your visit to the bank? Impressive, eh?"

"I guess so," he answered. "It was big." Just then, a door further up the alley flew open, flooding the cobbled passageway with light. A rowdy gang of men burst out. The one in front was cursing and struggling to break free, but his arms were pinned.

"Sha shtil!" whispered Zayde, yanking Gabriel into the shadows.

Pressed against a cold brick wall by his grandfather's body, Gabriel could see nothing. But the shouts and the sound of a man's boots being dragged past he could too easily hear.

"Let me go, damn you!" the man shouted. "Help! For God's sake, help!"

"*Bugger it, Nate!*" *grunted one of the men.* "*Thought you said 'e was too sotted ter fight!*"

"*Tie his feet then, damn you!*"

"*No! No! I'm a sailmaker!*" *the man bellowed. Gabriel could hear him struggling to throw off his captors.* "*I have a letter! I have protection! You cannot take me!*"

"*Oy gevalt!*" *murmured his grandfather.* "*Poor devil.*"

Soon the commotion was gone. Zayde grabbed Gabriel's hand, and hastened away. The gang had vanished into the gloom. "*What did that man do, Zayde?*"

"*Drank too deep with men he did not know,*" *he said.* "*The English need sailors, and to the press gang, almost anyone is fair game.*"

"*But . . . but they cannot do that,*" *said Gabriel.* "*They cannot just take you away—c-can they?*"

"*Oy vey, Gabriel!*" *said his grandfather.* "*This is why I tell you,* stay away. *Keep to yourself,* tatellah, *and to your own kind. But do you ever listen? Do you?*"

He waited for her at breakfast; waited until the flames beneath the chafing dishes had sputtered their last and the coffee had gone cold. Waited until the footmen began to shift their weight uneasily, as if duty called them elsewhere. Still Antonia did not come.

Yes, Her Grace normally took breakfast in the parlor, one of the footmen confirmed. Yes, agreed another, Her Grace was a punctual and early riser. And so Gareth kept picking at his food and sipping at his coffee, waiting. He waited, in fact, until one of the passing housemaids actually poked her head inside the door of the breakfast parlor to scowl at the still-laden sideboard.

Coggins followed on her heels. "Mr. Watson has returned, Your Grace," he said with a stiff bow. "He has sent the threshing machine down to the granary and awaits you at your convenience."

There was no putting off the day and the work which lay before him. She wasn't coming anyway. And what did he care? They could have no meaningful conversation with the damned footmen hovering over them like languid bumblebees. He supposed he had just wished to see her. To reassure himself that she was well.

But that was nonsense. The woman had a maid and an army of servants to fret over her. Gareth pushed back his chair with a scrape and tossed down his napkin. But as he strode through the house and out onto the long, rose-covered pergola which connected the main house to the estate offices and shops, he seethed with frustration.

He was being avoided. He sensed it.

Perhaps, he thought, as he hastened down the last flight of steps, she was just embarrassed? That he could understand. He felt fairly shamefaced himself. The mere thought of how desperately they had touched one another—the hunger, the raw, driving passion—could still make his hands shake. What they had done together in the rain last night could not now be undone. They would have to live with the memory of it, both of them, throughout the whole of their lives together.

Fleetingly, he considered refusing her permission to renovate Knollwood Manor. Then, surely, she would leave Selsdon and take up residence in Town? Perhaps they would need never see one another again.

But what if she did not leave? He had told her she might remain at Selsdon as long as she wished. And even if she went to Town, he might well have to see her.

Both he and Xanthia would now be required to move in circles they might otherwise have managed to avoid. On the other hand, forcing Antonia to Town might be sending her into the gnashing teeth of the *ton*—where it was entirely possible she would be shunned, or worse.

Damn it. He jerked to a halt and felt his jaw begin to twitch. This was a fine mess he'd landed himself in. It was untenable, in fact. They would have to discuss this, the two of them, and come to some sort of resolution. He would call upon her as soon as this estate business was done. So resolved, Gareth jerked open the door to the estate office.

A rangy, rough-faced man in a wool surtout stepped forward, his hand extended. "Your Grace," he said promptly. "I'm Benjamin Watson, your agent."

Antonia was on her knees in the family chapel when Nellie found her there near midmorning. The chapel was in an unheated part of the old castle, and musty with the scents of melted wax, moldering velvet, and dank stone. There was little light save that which came through the narrow mullioned windows flanking the chancel and from the three candles which Antonia had lit near the altar.

"Your Grace?" Nellie peeked into the gloom. "Ma'am, are you in there?"

Slowly, Antonia rose, the heavy folds of her cloak unfurling from the cold stone floor. "Yes, Nellie. I'm here."

"Lud, I wondered where you'd got to!" Nellie made her way through the chancel. "How long have you been on your knees like that, ma'am?"

"I am not perfect sure," Antonia hedged.

"Ooh, this is a damp, gloomy place." Nellie rubbed her arms and looked about. "You'll get the rheumatism if you stay in here, my lady. And you have missed your breakfast."

Antonia smiled a little weakly. "I had no appetite," she murmured. "I wished to spend some time alone. I should have told you."

Nellie looked down at the flickering candles. "Three candles today, ma'am?"

"Yes, one for Eric," she quietly acknowledged. "I suppose . . . I suppose I was feeling charitable this morning." *Or guilty,* she silently added.

Nellie shifted her weight uneasily. "I wanted to say something, ma'am," she said. "About last night."

Antonia turned and started down the aisle. "Must we speak of it, Nellie?"

Nellie followed her. "I'm sorry, ma'am," she said, touching her lightly on the arm. "But it was dangerous for you to be up there alone. And in the rain, too. You might yet take ill from it. And you scared the life out of me."

Antonia stopped by the chapel door. "Forgive me, Nellie," she answered. "I did not mean to be so thoughtless."

"You did not take your sleeping draught, did you?" the maid pressed.

Antonia shook her head. "I . . . I thought I would not need it," she answered. "So I poured it out."

"You scared me, ma'am," Nellie said again more firmly. "I have not seen you quite like that in an age."

"You needn't worry." Antonia pushed open the door and went out into the fresher air of the passageway. She paused and drew the air deep into her lungs. "I just think the apprehension yesterday ran deeper than I grasped, Nellie. I will be more careful in the future."

"You mean the new master's arrival?" asked the maid. "Aye, everyone was on tenterhooks. But you have more at stake than any of us."

Antonia said nothing and drew the folds of her cloak tighter.

"Pardon me, ma'am," said Nellie. "But was there something else you wished to tell me?"

"Such as?"

"Something about . . . about last night, perhaps?"

Swiftly, Antonia shook her head. "No, nothing," she answered. "Nothing at all."

"Very well then," said Nellie as they started up the stairs. "Shall you walk this morning, Your Grace? I didn't know which things to lay out."

It would be good, Antonia realized, to get out of the house. She needed to get away, and Nellie was right. She could not stay on her knees in the damp chapel all day.

"I'm going down to the village," Nellie suggested. "I'm going to replace all your black ribbons and pick up that gray velvet bonnet."

"No, not the village," murmured Antonia. "But thank you, Nellie."

Antonia wished for solitude. A walk in the woods, perhaps? Or perhaps she would make the long trek up to the dower house and have a look around. It mightn't be in such bad shape after all. Besides, she could scarcely afford to be choosy now. Perhaps she could make do with something which was a little shabby and get out of Selsdon even sooner than was planned? Perhaps God was already answering her prayers.

"Not the village," she said again. "No, I think, Nellie, that I shall walk up to Knollwood. Or perhaps down to the deer park, and have a poke about the pavilion."

Coggins was in his narrow office by the great hall sorting through the morning's post when Gareth returned from his meeting with Mr. Watson. The butler seemed surprised when Gareth appeared at his elbow.

"Has the duchess come down this morning?" Gareth cut a glance down at the tidy piles of letters the butler had laid out across the green baize of his secretary.

"No, Your Grace," said Coggins. "Not as I've seen. But her maid went out perhaps a quarter hour past."

Gareth tapped his finger thoughtfully atop one of the letters. It was from London, and addressed to Antonia. "Does the duchess have a great many acquaintances in Town, Coggins?" he asked musingly.

"I believe she once did, Your Grace."

"People whom she met through my late cousin?"

Coggins hesitated. "His Grace's companions were mostly country gentlemen," said the butler. "He and the duchess had few friends in common."

"Ah," said Gareth.

The butler took pity on him. "I believe the duchess's brother resides in Town, Your Grace," he explained. "He is a very sporting sort of fellow, I collect, and popular in certain circles."

"Gaming and horse racing, eh?" said Gareth a little cynically.

Coggins smiled faintly. "I believe he has a fondness for both, yes," he answered. "And the duchess knew many of his friends prior to her marriage to the late duke. Some of those gentlemen, I believe, have taken it upon themselves to console Her Grace in her widowhood."

And sniff around for a fortune in the process, too, Gareth did not doubt. "How altruistic they sound."

Coggins lifted his brows a telling fraction. "I couldn't say, sir."

But Gareth could see that Coggins shared his own opinion. With the black cloud of Warneham's death hanging over her good name, scoundrels were likely the only suitors she would attract.

On impulse, Gareth snatched Antonia's pile of letters. "I was just on my way up to speak with the duchess," he said. "I'll drop these by, shall I?"

Coggins had little choice. "Thank you, Your Grace."

Gareth made his way back upstairs to the sitting room which connected the ducal bedchambers. If her maid was indeed out, Antonia would not be able to avoid him. She would have to answer the door.

He knocked and was relieved when Antonia appeared. But her face drained instantly of all color. "Your Grace," she murmured. "Good morning."

He did not ask if he might come in, for he had the distinct impression she might refuse him. Instead he strode into the room and laid Coggins's tidy stack of letters on the rosewood secretary just inside the door. "I've brought the morning's post."

"Thank you." She still stood by the open door, her hand upon the knob. "Was . . . was there something else, Your Grace?"

He clasped his hands behind his back as if restraining himself from something he did not understand. Damn it, he wished she'd not been so beautiful. So fine-boned and fragile. A porcelain princess, truly. He paced to the bank of windows opposite, then back to the door again.

"It's like this, Antonia," he finally said. "There's no sense avoiding it. I think that we must talk about what happened last night."

She did not move from the door. "About . . . last night?"

Since she seemed incapable of doing so, Gareth pushed the door shut. Her hand fell to her side. "Antonia, are you all right?" he demanded. "I have been worried sick. When you did not come down to breakfast, I feared you might be ill."

"But as you see, I am fine," she answered, stepping back from him.

Gareth was not perfectly sure he agreed, given her lack of color. And he did not like the distance which lay between them this morning; distance which the duchess was taking pains to maintain, both literally and figuratively. She had circled behind a giltwood settee now, as if doing so might somehow protect her.

"Antonia," he finally went on, "we made a dreadful mistake last night. It was . . . imprudent. And I will admit, I am mostly to blame. You were not yourself. You were obviously distraught and—"

Something like horror flashed across her face. She whirled about and went at once to the bank of windows. He followed on her heels, lightly touching her shoulder. "Antonia?"

He felt her tremble beneath his touch.

"Antonia, I am sorry. I think we must put this behind us, my dear."

She leaned forward and set her fingertips to the glass,

as if longing to meld into it and vanish. "I do not know what you are referring to," she rasped. "Will you kindly go now?"

"I beg your pardon?" His grip tightened.

Another deep shudder ran through her. "I thank you, Your Grace, for your concern," she said. "I . . . I did not sleep well. I often do not. Whatever—that is to say, if something happened—then I cannot—"

At that, he forced her around. "*If* something happened?" he demanded. "*If?* By God, woman, you know as well as I what we did last night."

She shook her head, her eyes wild. "No," she whispered. "I can't—I don't—really remember. Please, let us just forget it."

"Antonia." He set both hands firmly on her shoulders now. "Antonia, why are you lying?"

Her eyes shied away. He gave her a gentle shake. "Antonia, there was something between us last night." His voice was oddly hoarse; not his own. "How can you say this? How can you just pretend it didn't happen?"

She shook her head and said nothing.

"Antonia, we made love," he went on. "It was wild and it was passionate—and yes, it was madness, too— but it was not remotely forgettable. Don't lie to me about this. It is too important."

"I'm sorry." The words came out throaty and a little tremulous. "I cannot talk about this."

Without realizing it, he had backed her up against the wall by the window. "Why? Does it scare you that much? Well, by God it scared me. No one can deny that sort of passion."

"You just said it was a dreadful mistake," she choked.

"How . . . How can it be if I do not remember? How can it be? Please, Your Grace, just *leave me alone*. I don't want passion. Can't you understand?"

"No, by God, I cannot." And then, somehow, he was kissing her, his hands still braced on her shoulders. He took her mouth roughly, only half-aware of what he meant to do. Antonia set her hands flat against his chest and pushed, but he ignored her, deepening the kiss. She made a strange sound; a sob or a sigh of surrender, then opened her mouth to his. On a rush of triumph, he let himself surge into her mouth, ravenous and desperate. Like molten silk, their tongues entwined in a heated dance of passion. Her hands curled into the soft wool of his coat at last, her face lifted to his in submission.

"There, Antonia," he rasped when their lips finally parted. "That is what runs so hot and fierce between us. Passion. Madness. You don't for one moment deceive me."

Still trying to catch her breath, she tore her gaze from his and set her hands flat against the wall behind her. He sensed her drawing back inside herself, shutting him out. It was as if she'd ripped his heart from his chest again.

"Is it me, Antonia?" he demanded. "Is that it? You want me—but I'm not good enough? Then by God, just say it!"

"You won't believe anything I say," she answered, refusing to look at him. "Why should I say anything? You have had your way with me, Your Grace. You have made me . . . respond to your caresses. May we not end this charade?"

Her words were like a thinly veiled slap. She desired him. But she would not stoop to have him. "Yes, I suppose we may," he retorted. "And I hope you enjoyed it—because it will be a cold day in hell before I warm your bed again."

It was only as he strode toward the door that he recalled that there had been no bed involved, and precious little warmth. No, he had backed Antonia up against a cold, damp wall and taken her like some Covent Garden tart. And now she did not want to remember. Rather than ponder the meaning of that, however, it was easier to just throw open the door and storm out. To his chagrin, a pair of housemaids went skittering off into the shadows, and he caught the tail end of what looked like a footman vanishing round one corner.

Perfect. Now the servants would have something to gossip about besides his mongrel bloodlines and whether or not their mistress was a murderess. Gareth held up his head despite his anger, and set off in the direction of his study. He needed a place of solitude in which to lick his wounds.

But his solitude was not long-lived. After wearing a tread into the carpet, he had just decided on a tentative course of action when an ill wind burst into the room in the form of the duchess's ruddy-faced maid. He pushed away the paper he'd been scratching on, then stood, though why the devil he should have done that was beyond him.

"Now you see here, sir," said the maid, marching up to the desk. "I want to know what you've done to her ladyship, and I want to know now."

"I beg your pardon?" said Gareth. "*You* wish *what?*"

The maid had two beefy hands set high on her hips. "You got no cause wheresoever to go about bullying and sharp-talking her ladyship, sir," she went on. "You're neither her husband—"

"Thank God for that small mercy."

"—nor her father, and you have no right, do you hear?"

"Madam, what, pray, is your name?"

That caught her up short for an instant. "Nellie Waters."

"Miss Waters, do you value your employment?" he snapped. "I will have you dismissed for your insolence."

"It's *Mrs*. Waters, Your Grace, and I do not work for you," said the woman. "I work for Her Grace, as I did for her mother before her, and her aunt before that—and I will thank you to leave that poor, sad woman alone. Hasn't she suffered enough but what you must come in here talking ugly to her and making her cry?"

"She hadn't shed so much as a tear when last I saw her," he snarled across his desk.

"Why, she's beside herself!" charged the maid, who had begun to wring her hands most affectedly. "Can't get a straight word out o' her—"

"Nor could I," he said.

"—and her just lying there across the bed sobbing like her heart be broken all over again. And for what? So you can let off a little temper? I hope it was worth it to you, sir, I truly do."

"You know nothing of it," he snapped. "Furthermore, it is none of your business. Your mistress seems a stranger to the truth, *Mrs*. Waters."

"The *truth*?" demanded the maid. "What's that to do with anything? Do you think this is easy for her, sir? To have people whispering that she's mad, per'aps even a murderess? To have to live here in what was once her home, under your thumb—a man she does not even know?"

And does not wish to know, Gareth mentally added.

"She's buried two husbands, Your Grace, and it goes hard on a woman, I'll tell you it does. A man just picks up and marries him another, and what's the difference? Not much. But a woman—it's not like that."

But Gareth was so enraged that he was barely listening. "You don't know a damned thing about it," he retorted. "Ask your mistress what the trouble is when her tantrum is done. And don't be so quick to paint every man with your broad brush. She's enough to drive a good man mad."

The woman's face fell like soft dough. "But she's never had a good man, Your Grace." Her voice had gone quiet now. "Wouldn't know one from a dead trout, I daresay. Me, I had a good husband. The kind a woman don't have but once—and I'll never have another. But she can't make that choice. She can't make any choice, she's so locked up with fear inside."

Gareth did not wish to feel one iota of sympathy for Antonia—and he very much suspected he knew the cause of her tears. It was shame, and something a good deal worse—outright bigotry. He thrust his finger at the door. "Get out, madam," he said quietly. "Perhaps I cannot fire you, but I can bloody well have you thrown out of my house."

"Aye, that you can do," she agreed. "But if I go, she'll go, for she don't know what else to do, sir. And I think you don't want that—do you? No, don't answer me. Time will tell it, one way or t'other."

Gareth balled his fists at his sides. Damn her. *Damn her.* He'd never had an employee he couldn't dismiss on the spot—and he'd cheerfully let a few go, too. But he really didn't know if the insolent hag was paid out of the duchess's funds or his. Worse, she was right on the second point, too, damn her to hell.

"Get out." His voice was quiet with fury. "Just get out, Waters, and never let me lay eyes on you again."

With one last cutting glance, the woman left.

Antonia dragged herself up off the bed and dashed a hand beneath her eyes. For once Nellie had surprised her by doing as she'd asked and left her alone with her misery. At last Antonia had cried herself out. Her sobs had stilled, and now she was merely sniveling. That, apparently, was how she measured progress nowadays.

Dear God, what had she been thinking to lie to the duke? And she had lied; both of them had known it. But after years of being told what she *should* think and how she *should* feel, and how so much of what she believed and felt was just the result of her overwrought imagination, it had seemed so easy to simply . . . well, to imagine nothing had happened. To pretend that she had not made a moon-calf fool of herself, throwing herself at a man she did not know. A man who, in no small part, held her future in his hands.

In truth, there was much she did not remember, though it happened far less often than it once had. Certainly she did not remember getting out of bed, or going up onto the rampart in the rain. Indeed, she was not sure how she'd managed to get the heavy wooden door open, much less end up in the duke's arms. Dr. Osborne called it sleepwalking, but most doctors had been less charitable.

The physician whose services her father had retained had termed it acute female hysteria. Antonia had been kept under lock and key in his isolated country house in the months after her first husband, Eric, had had his accident; a house so deep in the vales that no one heard her screams. The doctor's treatment had consisted of a regimen of ice baths, physical restraints, purges, and drug-induced stupors, most of which had been administered by a brutal staff. One soon learned not to cry or to show distress of any sort. One learned to be numb.

Antonia's reward for her good behavior had been the Duke of Warneham, who had needed another pretty young wife—this time one who'd been *proven* to be fertile. But Antonia had possessed yet another desirable trait: she'd come unencumbered by another man's children. A history of madness, Warneham had apparently decided, had been no great obstacle. His new duchess had needed to do only one thing with competence. Otherwise, she could have locked herself in the chapel to pray and to mourn until hell froze over.

Antonia set her palms against her feverish cheeks. What had she been thinking? To jeopardize *this,* the only sanctuary she had ever known? Warneham had been a selfish, soulless man; a man obsessed by the notion of revenge, but he had given her this. A place of peace. A home where, though the servants might whisper behind her back, they at least showed a modicum of respect to her face. And while she had not wanted his children, she would have borne them had God willed it.

But God had not willed it. Now the thing which her husband had most dreaded had happened. Warneham had spent much of his life wishing Gabriel Ventnor to the devil. Perhaps he had done a good deal more than wish. But it had all been for naught. The new duke was here, and Antonia had made the most humiliating mistake imaginable, all for a few moments of comfort. No, of *pleasure*. Exquisite, tormenting pleasure. There had been, just as he had said, an undeniable passion between them—a passion which was now all the more unbearable to recall.

Why, oh why could he not have played along and simply pretended that it had never happened? She had offered them both a way out—she was mad; surely he knew?—but the duke had refused it. Now she looked worse than mad. She looked like a liar. A lonely, desperate liar. And he had looked angry beyond words, like an avenging angel indeed. He would almost certainly send her away now. He might even begin to wonder if she *had* killed Warneham. That was a terrifying thought. Antonia set a hand beneath her breasts and dragged in a ragged, unsteady breath.

No. She would not cry again. She had got herself into this mess, so now she must either get herself out of it again or bear the duke's punishment with all the grace she could muster.

Just then, Nellie burst back into the room. "Well, lovie, I've done it," she declared, going to the tall mahogany wardrobe and throwing it open. "I hope we don't have to pack up tonight."

"What?" Antonia rose from the edge of the bed. "Lud, Nellie. What have you done?"

"Gave that man the razor's edge of my tongue," she declared, eyeing Antonia's heaviest cloak, as if sizing it up for the trunks. "He tried to sack me, o'course. But I told him he couldn't."

"Oh, Nellie." Antonia sank back down onto the mattress. "Oh, this is very bad indeed."

Nellie must have heard the odd edge in Antonia's voice, for she came at once to the bed. "There, now, my lady," she said, taking Antonia's hand. "We were to leave anyways, weren't we?"

Antonia found herself biting back tears again. What a watering-pot she was! "Oh, Nellie, I don't think you understand."

"Understand what, ma'am?"

"I did something awful, Nellie," she whispered. "I am so ashamed."

"Ashamed, my lady?" Nellie gently patted her hand. "You've never done a thing in your life to be ashamed of."

"This is different."

Nellie settled herself on the edge of the bed. Lips pursed, she let her gaze drift over Antonia's face. "Dearie me," she finally said. "I thought something was amiss last night."

Antonia hung her head.

"Aye, there was a look about you, lovie, that worried me," she said softly. "So t'was something to do with him, then? Well, he's handsome enough, Lord knows. And you have been alone an awful long time. Did he try to seduce you?"

"No, I—I just made a mistake," Antonia confessed. "I used very poor judgment."

"Aye, and so did I, perhaps," acknowledged Nellie. "So, what's the worst he can do now? Put us up at the White Lion?"

"I think you underestimate him, Nellie," said Antonia warily. "He is a hard man, I fear. I'm not sure he will bother with the niceties."

Nellie bit her lip a moment. "Aye, you're right,"

she finally admitted. "You're a lady born and bred, but what will that mean to him? They do say Jews are hard-hearted folk—and clutch-fisted, too."

"Nellie!"

"What?"

"How many Jews are you acquainted with?"

Nellie considered this. "Well, none as I know of."

"That's like saying all Irish are lazy, and all Scots are cheap!"

Nellie lifted one shoulder. "Well, Scots *are* cheap," she countered. "If you don't believe it, just ask one. Brag about it, they do."

"Perhaps some are proud of being thrifty," Antonia conceded. "But don't say any of it ever again in my hearing, do you understand? Perhaps the new duke is a Jew—I cannot say—but we are still living under his roof."

"Yes, ma'am."

Antonia let her shoulders sag. "Oh, Nellie!" she said quietly. "What am I to do?"

The maid patted her on the knee. "Just hold your head up, ma'am, like the lady you are," she said. "Let him do his worst. You are the daughter of an earl, and the widow of a baron and a duke. You are ten times better bred than he can ever hope to be."

"Oh, Nellie, it's just not that simple," whispered Antonia. "Nothing is simple anymore—and I am afraid it never will be, ever again."

Nellie squeezed her hand again. But she said no more. The truth was painfully apparent, and there really was nothing more to be said.

Chapter Seven

Gabriel watched as his grandmother's careful fingers smoothed the wrinkles from the freshly embroidered pillow slips. "Pretty, Bubbe," he said. "Who are they for?"

"Malka Weiss." His grandmother stood back to admire her handiwork. "Tomorrow, Gabriel, on the way to synagogue, I take them to her. It is Malka's bat mitzvah."

Gabriel's brow furrowed. "What is that, Bubbe?"

"It means she is a woman now," said his grandmother. "Malka may give testimony, and even marry if she—"

"Marry!" said Gabriel. "Old buck-toothed Malka?"

"Shush, tatellah," his grandmother chided. "Tomorrow is a special day. Her mother will bake poppy-seed cakes and we will kiss Malka, and give her little gifts."

Gabriel scrubbed one scuffed shoe against the other. "Bubbe," he said hesitantly, "can I go to synagogue, too?"

His grandmother smiled a little sadly. "No, Gabriel."

"But why?"

His grandmother hesitated. "You cannot," she finally said.

"It is because I am not one of you!" he said petulantly.

"Why don't you just say it, Bubbe? I am not a real Jew."

"Gabriel, shush!" His grandmother came down on one knee and gave his shoulders a little shake. "You are a real Jew!" she whispered. "Do you hear me? Being a Jew is more than a synagogue! You are as much a Jew as I am, tatellah—but you will someday live in a world where one must never speak of it carelessly. Do you understand me? Do you?"

Halfway along the road which led down to the village of Lower Addington, Gareth reined his mount around to a halt. Shifting his hat, he looked up at the edifice of Selsdon, its impressive stone façade aglow with a pure, almost sumptuous afternoon light. From this angle he could still see the south bastion hanging dramatically out above the cliffs, and to the north, the impressive stable block and estate shops, which together were larger than the village itself. The part of Selsdon beyond his view was just as grand, and stretched further still. He still could not fathom how all this had come to be his. But it *was* his—and he wondered vaguely if ever he would see a moment's peace within its walls.

A man makes his own peace, his grandfather had been fond of saying. And there was a certain amount of truth in that. Gareth had spent the last three days trying to come to terms with what had happened between him and Antonia, and trying to accept that he might never understand it. Since their argument, they had not seen one another save at dinner, which they suffered through in stoic restraint, treating one another like—well, like the perfect strangers they were.

Abruptly, Gareth slapped his hat back on his head

and spun the fine, long-legged bay around again. He very much hoped the doctor was in when he reached the village. Seeing Osborne would be just one small step, perhaps, toward making his own peace. Gareth was determined to discover if there was any medical explanation for Antonia's alleged—and very selective—spate of amnesia, though precisely how he meant to glean this was not yet clear to him.

The doctor's house lay at the end of the road, about a quarter-mile beyond the village proper. It was a lovely half-timbered manor with a wide, welcoming door topped by a rambling vine, which was beginning to show perhaps a hint of burnished red. Gareth tethered his mount to the gatepost, then went up the stairs to ring the bell. A housemaid dressed in starched black and white bobbed, awestruck, and showed him at once into a sunny front parlor. Five minutes later, Dr. Osborne entered, his forehead creased with worry.

"Your Grace." He bowed perfunctorily. "What is wrong?"

Gareth stood. "Wrong?" he said. "Nothing, I trust. Why?"

Osborne waved him back into his chair. "Lord, I don't know," he said wearily. "I suppose I've come to expect bad news when anyone from Selsdon turns up unexpectedly."

He was speaking of Warneham's death, no doubt. Gareth tried to smile. "No, we are fresh out of tragedies today," he said. "I wished merely to ask you a few questions about the people at Selsdon."

"The people?" Osborne looked at him coolly as he seated himself opposite Gareth. "The staff, do you mean?"

"Yes, the staff," Gareth agreed. "Everyone, actually. You are the only doctor hereabouts, are you not?"

"I am," Osborne agreed. "Was there anyone you were particularly concerned about?"

Gareth propped his elbows on the chair arms and leaned forward. "I am concerned for all of them," he said. "They are a responsibility I have inherited, whether I like it or not. But yes, some concern me more than others. Mrs. Musbury, for example."

"Ah, yes." The doctor steepled his fingers thoughtfully. "A hardworking woman, Mrs. Musbury. But she always has a chronic cough this time of year."

"The duchess tells me Mrs. Musbury has a weak chest."

The doctor gave an amiable shrug. "Oh, I doubt it," he responded. "This is an annual ritual. The cough comes on in August and vanishes after our first hard frost. By Advent, she's fit as a fiddle."

"So the duchess has overstated the matter?"

The doctor rolled his shoulders, as if his coat were too tight. "The duchess has a kind heart," he finally said. "And she has not known Mrs. Musbury nearly so long as I have."

Gareth held his gaze assessingly for a moment. "The duchess seems unwell herself at times," he remarked. "I could not help but notice your concern for her last Monday evening."

Osborne looked suddenly distant. "It is true that the duchess is not entirely well," he answered. "She is a fragile, rather restless soul. And sometimes, she is . . . well, out of touch with her surroundings."

"She daydreams? She is fanciful?"

Again, the doctor shook his head. "It is more than that," he reluctantly admitted. "She sleepwalks, too. Nellie, her maid, must be constantly on guard. On occasion, the duchess must be sedated. Her case is most complex—a form of hysteria, to be honest."

Again, Gareth leaned forward in his chair. He did not like to probe in this direction, and yet he seemed unable to stop himself. "Dr. Osborne, I must ask you something in the strictest confidence," he said quietly. "Something which might sound strange."

The doctor smiled a little grimly. "Few questions shock a doctor, Your Grace," he said. "But let's ring for tea first, shall we? A little fortification might be in order."

He got up at once and did so. They made small talk about the weather until the black-garbed housemaid returned with a broad, ornate tea tray as fine as any at Selsdon. She followed with a plate of thin sandwiches. Gareth's stomach growled at the sight, and it was only then that he realized that he had once again forgotten to eat luncheon—the third time in as many days.

The doctor poured, then offered the plate of sandwiches. "Well, I can put it off no longer, can I?" he said. "You wished to ask me something about the duchess, I collect."

Gareth paused to carefully consider his words. "Yes, something of a personal nature, I'm afraid."

Osborne looked resigned. "I thought as much," he said. "Go on."

"What I wish to know is"—Gareth considered how to pose the question—"Well, whether the duchess might do something and . . . and not be aware of what she was doing? Could she later simply not remember it?"

Dr. Osborne blanched. "Oh, dear," he murmured. "Back to that, are we?"

"I beg your pardon?"

Osborne shifted uncomfortably in his chair. "I do wish those rumors would die down," he admitted. "As her friend and her physician, I have never believed them."

Rumors? Clearly, they were speaking at cross-purposes, but Gareth was curious. "Precisely why did you not believe them, Doctor?" he probed.

Osborne's gaze grew distant. "In my opinion," the doctor finally said, "the duchess does not possess the ruthlessness necessary for such a violent act—not even when she is in one of her disturbed states."

"A violent act?" The doctor was referring to Warneham's death, then. "I think you'd best tell me everything you know, Dr. Osborne."

"About Warneham and . . . and all the gossip?" A look of sadness passed over the doctor's face.

Gareth hesitated. It seemed Antonia had been right about the rumors. This was his chance to learn more, perhaps. "I have a right to know, have I not?"

"It might be best, Your Grace, if you spoke to John Laudrey, the local justice of the peace."

"No, I wish to hear from you," Gareth pressed. "You were often in the house, were you not?"

Osborne lifted one shoulder. "I was the duke's personal physician for some years," he admitted. "We often played chess together. I dined at Selsdon at least once a week. Yes, I was there frequently."

"So, tell me what happened," Gareth pressed.

"In my opinion, Warneham died of potassium nitrate poisoning," said the doctor.

"At whose hand?" Gareth demanded.

Osborne opened both hands expansively. "Well . . . mine, perhaps."

"Yours?"

"I was prescribing it." Fleetingly, the doctor looked grief-stricken. "For Warneham's asthma. The night of his death, Warneham had some guests down from London, which was unusual. The gentlemen played billiards late into the night—and they smoked, of course. I had persuaded Warneham to give up the habit, but his friends—"

"I see," said Gareth. "Did he complain of breathing difficulties?"

"I was not present," the doctor admitted. "But Warneham had become deeply preoccupied, shall we say, with his health."

"Who usually prepared the drug for him each night? The duchess?"

"Rarely, but she knew how," said the doctor. "His Grace usually prepared the medication himself. I think it possible that when he went to bed that night, he simply took too much of it, perhaps fearing that the smoke had affected him."

"No one else could have done this?"

"Given him the potassium nitrate?" asked the doctor. "Yes, anyone, I daresay. But why would they?"

"You would suggest there are some who believe the duchess did so."

Osborne shook his head. "I cannot believe it of her," he said. "I never have, and so I told Laudrey. Moreover, the bottle was labeled merely as his asthma medication. No one ever asked me what was in it."

"Did anyone else handle the medication?"

"What do you mean?" Osborne looked a little insulted. "I use an excellent chemist in London. I bring the drugs here—Lower Addington has no apothecary—and I hand-deliver them to my patients."

"Always?"

The doctor hesitated. "My mother used to help occasionally," he said. "Especially if it was something . . . well, of a female nature. It saved embarrassment."

"I understand."

"But Mother died almost three years ago," he went on. "There are servants in the house, of course. But they have been here for years and are totally trustworthy."

"I believe you," said Gareth. "Tell me, Doctor, were the duke and duchess unhappy in their marriage?"

The doctor hesitated. "I cannot say."

Gareth watched him warily for a moment. "I think you can," he finally said. "I'd rather hear it from you than have the bloody servants whispering behind my back. It's bad enough they think I deliberately killed his son. Now to suspect that his wife may have done him in? It won't do."

Dr. Osborne was silent for a long moment. Gareth realized he had said too much; revealed too much of himself. What did he care if Antonia had poisoned her husband? Warneham had deserved worse—and but a few weeks past, Gareth would have cheerfully danced on the bastard's grave.

But he did care. Murder was wrong, of course, but that was hardly his reason for caring. Gareth felt vaguely troubled by that realization. Good God, this was not what he had come to learn.

Finally, Osborne spoke. "I should preface anything I say further, Your Grace, by telling you that I accounted the late duke a friend and benefactor," he answered.

"Yes, there is no doubt that everyone has been on edge at Selsdon this last year. Yes, there have been whispers. As to the marriage, it was arranged against the duchess's wishes. That much I knew. But I think she came to be at peace at Selsdon."

"They had no children," Gareth remarked.

Osborne shook his head. "The marriage was a brief one," he explained. "Little more than a year."

"Just a year?" Gareth was surprised.

"Eighteen months, I believe," Osborne went on. "And Warneham was no longer young. It can take time to conceive a child." Again, he twisted in his chair uncomfortably, and Gareth sensed he would say no more on the subject.

"Thank you, Dr. Osborne," he said, his voice flat now. "Will you now answer my first question? Could the duchess do something and later not remember it?"

Reluctance was etched on Osborne's face. "Yes," he finally said. "It is entirely possible."

"How?" Gareth pressed. "Is she . . . mad?"

The reluctance deepened. "The duchess suffered an emotional trauma a year or so before she wed Warneham," he admitted. "One which, in my opinion, she never fully recovered from. Certainly she had not recovered at the time of her remarriage."

"Her *remarriage*?"

"Yes." The doctor's eyebrows lifted. "She was a widow, Lady Lambeth. Did you not know?"

Something stirred in the back of Gareth's mind. What was it Mrs. Waters had been screeching about all those days ago? Something about burying two husbands, but Gareth had been too angry to absorb it. "I did not even know of the woman's existence, Osborne, until I arrived here," he answered sharply. "So far as I knew—and for all that I cared—Warneham was still married to his first wife."

"Oh, no, she has been dead many years," said the doctor. "Lady Lambeth was his fourth wife."

"Yes, it seems Warneham was cursed with bad luck," said Gareth dryly. "What happened to the other two?"

"The first died tragically," said the doctor.

"Is there any other way?" asked Gareth.

A rueful smile curved the doctor's mouth. "I suppose not," he admitted. "But this was doubly tragic. The girl was carrying a child—the duke's son—and she fell from her horse during the village's autumn hunt and was badly injured. In the end, neither she nor the child survived."

Gareth looked at the doctor incredulously. "She was fox hunting whilst with child?"

Osborne hesitated. "From what I am told, the second duchess was very young, and a little impulsive," he confessed. "She was wed at eighteen to a man much older than herself, and perhaps none too pleased to be settled down. The marriage might have been strained."

"I daresay it was," said Gareth.

The doctor shrugged. "I was still at university, myself," he said. "At Oxford. I know nothing firsthand."

"And the third wife?" said Gareth. "Was she an impulsive debutante, too?"

"A debutante, yes," said Osborne. "But an older, rather solemn girl. I quite liked her, really. Though she was not a beauty, everyone thought it an ideal marriage."

"But it was not?"

The doctor looked sad. "She was barren," he answered. "It was a terrible disappointment to His Grace."

"Yes," said Gareth grimly, "and I daresay he never let her forget it."

Osborne did not deny Gareth's allegation. "Her failure to conceive left her deeply unhappy, too," he said. "She felt she had failed the duke, and she became melancholy to the point of illness. She began to depend upon laudanum to sleep."

Gareth saw what was coming. "Did herself in, did she?"

The doctor smiled wearily. "For regular users, Your Grace, there can be a fine line between sedation and death when ingesting opiates. I believe it was an accident."

"And then the duke was free to marry again," Gareth suggested.

"It was an *accident,* Your Grace," said Osborne. "She would never have taken her life out of sheer melancholia, and no one meant her any harm."

Gareth felt instantly ashamed. "No, I am sure they did not," he said swiftly. "As you say, a tragedy."

"The Ventnor family has suffered more than their share," the doctor agreed.

Gareth wondered how much Osborne knew about his history at Selsdon. But did it really matter? He set both hands on his thighs and abruptly rose. "Thank you, Doctor, for your candor," he said. "I shall leave you to your work."

Gareth rode back through the village with his mind in turmoil. He had gone to Dr. Osborne with some very firm suspicions. So why did he now feel so unsettled by having those suspicions confirmed?

Perhaps Antonia really did not recall making love to him. Gareth considered it, then shook his head. The truth, he suspected, lay somewhere in the middle. She had been incoherent when he'd found her, yes. But at some point, Antonia had returned to herself. The woman with whom he had shared unbridled passion had been, at least fleetingly, whole and quite thoroughly in her right mind. She *did* remember. The morning of their quarrel, he had seen the truth and the shame in her eyes. Oh, she was clearly an emotional creature, even a little erratic, perhaps. But was she mad? No, not precisely.

There had been a man aboard the *Saint-Nazaire*—an old salt by the name of Huggins—who had been abandoned by the Royal Navy as unfit for duty. Huggins had fought aboard HMS *Java* with General Hislop off the coast of Brazil, not far from where the *Saint-Nazaire* had taken him on. It had been a long and brutal battle, and in the end, the Americans had been merciless. *Java* had struck her colors and was burnt. The survivors had been few and broken.

Huggins, too, had had that look—the wild, haunted look he had seen in Antonia's eyes in the rain that night. It was as if they looked through you even as their eyes became a portal to a terror almost unimaginable. On the ship, Huggins had proven delusional and useless. The captain had set him ashore again in Caracas, where he had likely died.

Good God. How could he think of Antonia and that pathetic creature in the same breath? They were nothing alike. But the eyes . . . dear Lord, the eyes.

Gareth shook off the memories and spurred his mount to a quicker pace. He needed a few moments of peace and quiet in which to consider all that Osborne had said. Actually, what he needed was advice. He was too blinded by lust and anger to think clearly. He had an estate to learn to run, and a staff to manage—one which was far larger than Neville's. He needed to meet his tenants, introduce himself to the local gentry, and hire a decent valet. He needed to learn about crop rotation and irrigation, for pity's sake. And yet his mind kept turning to the past, and to Antonia. Did people really imagine her a murderess? And why did he wish to prove she was not?

He did not know her. Indeed, he knew nothing of anyone at Selsdon. Almost anyone in the house could have wished his cousin dead. He himself had often done so.

And what was the truth about Antonia? What was it that had left her so tormented? Suddenly it dawned on Gareth that what he needed was Xanthia. Xanthia would know how best to get at the truth of things. She could advise him. Help him find clarity. Suddenly, he laughed aloud at the incongruity of the notion. *He wished his old lover to give him advice on his new lover?*

No. No, Antonia was a duty. An obligation. But she was not his lover. He could not go on thinking in those terms. Moreover, Xanthia was on her way to the Aegean on Nash's private yacht. She would be away for weeks—and she was another man's wife. Which left only Rothewell.

Gareth slid his hand pensively along his jaw and considered it. Just how desperate was he?

Damned desperate—but for what, he hardly knew. A friend, he supposed. A sounding board. He spurred up his mount yet again, and this time, he kept a steady pace until home was well within his sights. Once there, he went straight into his study and withdrew a sheet of Warneham's fine, heavy foolscap from the desk.

* * *

By Saturday, Antonia was beginning to relax just a fraction. Nothing had been said about her and Nellie leaving, and life at Selsdon with the new duke had assumed a pattern of sorts these last few days. As was customary at Selsdon, they were to dine that evening in the small dining room, a chamber which seated eight, as opposed to the grand state dining room, which could accommodate forty in utter opulence. Antonia glanced at it as she passed by on her way to dinner. The state dining room had never been used during her short tenure as duchess. She wondered a little absently if the new duke meant ever to entertain. Perhaps not. He seemed a solitary sort of man.

At the door to the small dining room, she paused to gather her nerve and adjust her shawl, which felt a little twisted. Then, forcing her chin up and her shoulders back, Antonia entered. In the last few days, she had almost grown accustomed to this; the sense of her breath catching and her stomach bottoming out when she entered a room to find him there.

Tonight the duke was dressed simply but elegantly in black and white. He did not seem to own a great many formal clothes, Antonia had noticed, but those he owned were of excellent fit and quality. As often was the case, his hair was still damp, which dulled its warm, golden sheen to a honeyed brown. His lean, well-tanned face appeared freshly shaved, emphasizing the strong angle of his jaw.

"Good evening, Your Grace," she said stiffly.

He had risen at once. "Good evening, ma'am."

It was the way they had greeted one another for the past three evenings; so rigidly that their lack of emotion was almost an emotion in itself. Antonia dropped her gaze and swiftly took her seat at the end of the table—in the duchess's chair, as he had insisted from the very first.

The duke gave a nod to the attending footman—tonight it was Metcaff, and there was an almost disdainful curl to his lip. She hoped that the duke did not know him well enough to notice it. As the first course was brought in, Antonia observed Metcaff as he served. There was a decidedly sullen inattention to his motions. Perhaps it was time to dismiss the man? But that was not her business.

She shut Metcaff from her mind and got on with the trouble of dinner. However, after they had made their way through the second course, sole in herb butter, and the third, veal cutlets, Antonia found they were swiftly running out of bland topics like the weather, the harvest, and the king's health. The duke, too, had noticed it. He motioned for Metcaff to pour the next wine. "Thank you," he said then. "You may leave us."

Metcaff hesitated. "I beg your pardon?"

"We do not require your attention just now," said the duke. "We shall ring for you later."

Metcaff bowed stiffly and withdrew.

Uneasy, Antonia laid aside her fork, accidentally striking it on her plate rim.

The duke took up his wineglass, drew in the scent, then drank from it approvingly. "Coggins keeps an excellent cellar, does he not?" he remarked.

"Yes, he is quite knowledgeable." Antonia's voice was thready.

The duke studied her over the rim of her glass.

"Madam, I do not bite," he said quietly. "At least, I have not yet done so."

Antonia cut her gaze away. Warmth flooded her cheeks.

He set his glass down with a thud. She could feel the steady heat of his eyes upon her. "We need not continue with this charade, Antonia," he finally said. "I take no joy in it. Clearly, you do not."

"Wh-what charade, Your Grace?"

He made an expansive gesture about the room with his glass. "This charade of dinner," he said. "It is supposed to be a time of relaxation when the household comes together, isn't it? But we are neither of us relaxed. We do not enjoy this. And there is really no need for you to be uncomfortable when you might as easily have a tray in your room. Or I can dine in my study. Would that better please you?"

Strangely, the notion did not please her. In fact, his offer inexplicably stung. She cleared her throat and lifted her eyes to his. "No, Your Grace," she said in a surprisingly strong voice. "Dinner is an important tradition here at Selsdon."

The duke began to swirl his wine around in a lazy circle. "And are you a woman who enjoys traditional things?" he asked quietly.

"I was brought up to greatly respect tradition," she answered. "It is the backbone of all we stand for, is it not?"

Surprisingly, the duke shrugged. "I've never given a tinker's damn for it, myself," he said, without a hint of disdain. "Tradition has never done a thing for me. But I am willing, I daresay, to give it another chance if you think it proper."

There was something in his voice—a strain, perhaps—and a hint of fatigue about his eyes. And suddenly it occurred to Antonia how hard this must be for him. Perhaps it had never occurred to this man that one day the mantle of duty—and yes, of *tradition*—would fall upon his shoulders.

She made a vague, fluttery gesture with her hand, then jerked it back into her lap. Damn it, she was *not* a witless schoolgirl. Why was it that in the duke's presence, she became so painfully aware of her own shortcomings? So fully conscious of the fact that she was no longer the vivacious, confident woman she had once been? What was it about him that made her . . . *feel*?

"I am so sorry," she said quietly. "I have handled this badly, Your Grace. You have been unexpectedly saddled with me, I know. And I . . . I have been a poor hostess. I have been of no help to you whatsoever."

"I do not require your help, Antonia," he said calmly. "Merely your happiness, as much as it is within my power."

He meant it. She could hear the sincerity in his voice. And when she looked at him, with his solemn, dark gold eyes and his too-handsome face, something inside her seemed to give way. It was a rush of appreciation and admiration—and other emotions best left unnamed. "I should have helped you to settle in," she said, as much to herself as to him. "I should have been . . . more gracious. Instead, I have—well, I should rather not remember how I have behaved."

The duke was quiet for a long moment. "Grief does strange things to us all," he finally said. "Just know, Antonia, that I am sorry for all that has happened to you. My personal feelings for my cousin aside, he was your husband. I know you miss him. I know, too, that a certain amount of security has been stripped from your life with his passing—and it is not my intention to compound that loss."

Antonia felt an unexpected pressure well in her eyes. "You . . . You are very kind, Your Grace."

The duke shoved his glass a little away. "Look, Antonia, I can only imagine what has been said of me around here." His voice was sharper now. "I know Warneham loathed me. He never wanted me here to begin with—and God knows I never wanted to come back. But tell me, Antonia—what choice do I have? Any? If you can think of one, for God's sake, let's have it."

"None," she quietly acknowledged. "You have no choice whatsoever. Everyone here at Selsdon depends upon you, and upon your ability to make wise decisions. The dukedom is a large and momentous responsibility."

"But I could simply walk away," he suggested. "Even though Cavendish tells me the law does not provide for it. If I did walk away, however, what would happen to the workers and tenants?"

She shook her head. "I do not know."

The duke was staring into the depths of the room now. "Eventually, I suppose, this whole bloody mess will be the Crown's," he said pensively. "But I can stand here with my finger in the proverbial dyke for a few years, I daresay—and eventually, perhaps some long-lost Ventnor will turn up after all."

Antonia gave a sharp laugh. "Oh, I do not think so, Your Grace," she said, taking a healthy sip of her wine. "If there had been one, trust me, my husband would have found him long before now."

The duke smiled a little bitterly. "So the Crown's it shall be, then, when I turn up my toes," he said. "I'll bet old Prinny is already salivating at the thought."

Antonia looked at him blankly for a moment. "You . . . you do not mean to begat an heir, Your Grace?"

He shook his head. "I doubt it. Not unless . . . unless we—" His voice fell to a whisper. "Oh, Christ, Antonia. What the devil would we do if—"

She heard the glass snap before she felt the pain. She looked down to see a drop of blood, bright red on the tablecloth. She must have cried out, for the duke was out of his chair and bending over her before Metcaff could burst into the room.

"Good God, let me see your hand," said the duke, raking away the broken glass with the back of his fist.

"Your Grace," said Metcaff sharply. "Are you all right?"

The duke was blotting away the blood with his napkin. "I snapped my wine stem," she said. "It is nothing. I—I forget, sometimes, what I am holding."

"Shall I fetch Waters, Your Grace?" he asked. "Or a bandage?"

"No, leave us," barked the duke, glancing up.

Something which looked like outrage flashed across the footman's face. He turned abruptly, then he slammed the door behind. Antonia was glad to see him go.

The duke was still dabbing gently at the cut, which had almost stopped bleeding. "I wonder if that man could possibly make his dislike of me more apparent," he murmured.

"Metcaff can be insolent."

"So I noticed." He withdrew a freshly starched handkerchief from his pocket and applied it tenderly to the wound. "Here, just press this on the cut. Does it hurt?"

She shook her head. "No, really, it is just a scratch," she said. "I apologize for Metcaff's manners."

The duke straightened up, and with him went his reassuring warmth and scent. Antonia felt suddenly cold. "Yes, I begin to believe it is time to give Mr. Metcaff good cause for his bad mood," he said grimly. "I hate to, the economy being what it is just now. Does the man have a family?"

Again, Antonia shook her head. "I believe he has been spreading tales, Your Grace." She felt her face heat. "Not about anything we have been—I mean, there are rumors about—well, you. Your background. But that is none of my business. Certainly it is none of Metcaff's."

"Well, at least you acknowledge that there might be something to gossip about." The tenderness had left his face now, and the fatigue had returned. "But that footman's expression had little to do with gossip. I saw unmitigated hatred on his face just now—and not for the first time."

Antonia pressed the linen handkerchief to her hand and looked away. "I think"—She paused to swallow—"I think that it is because he does not wish to work for you."

"A burden from which I can swiftly relieve him," said the duke. "But what the devil have I done to him?"

"It is not you, Your Grace," she whispered. "Metcaff is just . . . ignorant."

He set his hands flat on the tabletop and looked her straight in the eyes. "Ignorant?" he said, eyeing her appraisingly. "No, it's more than that, isn't it? Tell me, Antonia. What is it?"

Her eyes shied a little wildly toward him. "It is because they say . . . they say you are a Jew."

The duke looked neither surprised nor angry, but merely disgusted. "Ah, both a murderer and Jew now, am I?" He straightened up and sat abruptly in the chair to her right.

"No one has said that, Your Grace." *Not since my husband died,* Antonia silently added. Inexplicably, she wanted to know the truth. "*Are* you a Jew?"

The duke looked at her unflinchingly. "Absolutely," he answered. "In my heart, at the very least. Certainly, my mother was. But my upbringing was unusual."

"I see," said Antonia hesitantly. "Was . . . was your mother frightfully rich?"

Gareth gave a bitter bark of laughter. "Yes, that's the only reason a blue-blooded English gentleman would stoop to marry a Jewish girl, isn't it?" he said rhetorically. "A fat marriage portion."

Almost violently, Antonia shook her head. "No, no, that's not what I meant," she said. "I just meant . . . that you seem . . . perfectly ordinary."

His gaze hardened. "Ordinary?" he repeated. "Is that meant to be a compliment?"

Antonia had been bred to handle any sort of social discomfort with ease. How had she bungled this one so badly? "I mean ordinary, like any Englishman," she continued, her voice stronger. "You seem like . . . well, like everyone else I know."

"Only one head, do you mean?" He flashed a grim smile. "And no talons or fangs?"

"You are making a jest of me," she said quietly. "I meant wealthy, well-bred, and frightfully English. I knew

Major Ventnor was a soldier. But I thought perhaps your mother had money? Or are you truly a self-made man?"

The duke gave a muted, inward smile. "No man is self-made, my dear, much as he might like to think it," he said. "I have had the help of many. My grandparents. The Nevilles. And yes, the Jewish community in which I spent my early years. They were honest, diligent people who influenced me greatly. But if I had come from money, trust me, I would never have come to Selsdon. As a child, I was here because I had no choice."

"I must apologize for my own ignorance," she answered. "I have only met a few Jews, you see—like the writer, Mr. Disraeli? I met him and one of his brothers at a literary salon once. They seemed lovely gentlemen. But they are very dark. Spanish, I believe?"

"Italian," said Gareth.

"Yes, perhaps you are right," she went on. "But then, they are not Jews, really, are they?"

"The Disraelis are about as Jewish as I am, I suppose," he answered quietly. "They were born of a Jewess— which some say is the definition. But like me, Disraeli was baptized in an Anglican church, and has likely never seen the inside of a synagogue."

"Have you?"

"No," he said softly. "My mother forbade it."

Antonia was deeply curious. "Why would she forbid such a thing?"

"I am not perfectly sure," he answered. "My parents were unusual. Theirs was a love match—a very passionate one, by all accounts. And my mother vowed that I would be raised as my father was raised—as a privileged English gentleman."

"Your father asked this of her?"

Antonia realized she had begun to chatter like a magpie, but she found giving voice to her thoughts strangely liberating. And the duke was amazingly easy to talk to. She felt as if a floodgate had been opened; not just the floodgate to her curiosity, but to something deeper. She wanted desperately to know more about this enigmatic man.

His gaze was focused not on her now but upon the broken wineglass. "I do not know if my father insisted," he admitted. "I know only that it was what they agreed upon when they married. Perhaps she thought it was her duty, because she was so utterly devoted to him. Or perhaps she simply wished me to have an easier life, free from prejudice. She knew that as a Jew, I could not go to university, or sit in Parliament, or do a hundred other things regular Englishmen do with ease."

"You never asked her why?"

"I never got the chance," he answered softly. "I was quite young when she died. She made my grandmother promise to raise me as she and my father had agreed. It was hard for my grandmother. It went against all that she believed in, and my grandfather thought it utter balderdash. But she did it."

"And your father?"

"He was on the Peninsula with Wellington," said the duke. "He died there a few years later."

"And your grandparents continued to care for you?"

"No, my grandfather was gone by then." His voice was flat. "His business had suffered a setback from which neither fully recovered. Whilst my father was alive, he provided for my grandmother and me as best he could.

But when both of them were gone, my grandmother brought me here. She did not know what else to do."

"I see," she said quietly. "How . . . how old were you?"

The duke's mood had oddly shifted. He sat slightly slumped in his chair now, his shoulders rolled forward as if he was totally at ease in her presence, but a little weary, too. She saw him, suddenly, as vulnerable; as a vigorous, breathtakingly handsome man who should have been enjoying life and all the temptations beautiful men usually enjoyed. Instead he looked weighed down by it all. He was like no man she had ever known; neither a faithless liar, as Eric had been, nor a charming rake, like her brother. And strangely, he seemed neither bitter nor vindictive—and she was beginning to wonder if of all of them, her second husband included, he did not have just cause to be both.

"I don't recall how old," he finally murmured. "Eight? No, nine, perhaps."

Antonia was taken aback. "Eight or *nine?*"

He looked at her strangely. "Yes, why?"

Antonia's late husband had painted his young cousin as the very embodiment of evil. Antonia had imagined him as some sort of miscreant, wreaking havoc across the countryside. But nine? Nine was just a child.

"How old were you when you decided to leave Selsdon?" she asked.

Gareth looked at her in surprise. "When I *decided?*" he echoed. "I was twelve when I left Selsdon. Is that what you meant?"

"Yes, I suppose." But she didn't see. Not precisely. "Might I ask, Your Grace—how old you are now?"

"I shall be thirty in a few weeks' time," he said, quietly studying her.

"Heavens," she said.

The corners of his eyes crinkled softly. "Looking a little worn, am I?"

She allowed herself the pleasure of taking in his face again. "No, frankly I expected someone much older," she finally said. "But you are only thirty? You seem older in some way which I cannot quite put my finger on—and yet—no, you do not look it."

Again, he shrugged, as if it did not matter to him whether he looked thirty or sixty. "And how old are you?" he said instead. "Turnabout, madam, is fair play."

Antonia felt her cheeks warm again. "I am six-and-twenty . . . I think. I stopped keeping count, to be honest."

He gave a muted, inward smile, but if one looked deeper, one could see that a warm, masculine appreciation had begun to kindle in his eyes; a lazy, sensual heat which seemed to strengthen as his gaze drifted over her. "You are very beautiful for twenty-six," he said quietly. "And you have not even reached the prime of womanhood. You have many wonderful years ahead of you, Antonia. I hope for your sake you will not waste them."

Antonia felt her breath catch again, and a startling memory—his hands on her breasts in the rain, her drenched nightgown, the roughened sound of his breath against her ear, all of it—cut into her consciousness. She felt her skin heat and her toes curl. The memory was both sensuous and shocking. She caught his heated gaze, and for an instant, a question seemed to linger between them. A desire unspoken. She waited on the razor's edge of expectation, wondering if he would ask. And what she would say in return.

To her dismay, he simply cleared his throat and stood. "Well, I am sure you must wish to have that cut attended to," he said, offering his hand. "I think dinner was over anyway."

With a surprising sense of disappointment, Antonia laid her hand in his larger, warmer one and rose. She had misunderstood. Misinterpreted. What did she know, really, about men and their desires?

They stood but inches apart now, and again she drew in his remarkable warmth and scent. He felt rock-solid and steady, and fleetingly she wondered what it would be like to be held close against him when one was thoroughly and completely in one's right mind.

The duke's mind, however, seemed elsewhere. "I shall be riding up to Knollwood sometime next week," he said, his voice oddly emotionless. "After I have done so, I will be able to give you some idea of when the house can be ready for you."

Antonia stepped away. "Thank you."

The duke crossed the room and held open the door for her. "Goodnight, then, Antonia," he said. "I shall see you tomorrow."

Chapter Eight

Gabriel watched his grandmother's gnarled hands close the heavy lid of the trunk, then smooth almost lovingly across the top. "Bubbe, that looks old," he said as she stood.

"Old, yes." She smiled down at it almost wistfully. "When your grandfather came here as a young man, this trunk held everything he owned. And when they carried it up to the attic a dozen years ago, I thought never to see it again. But life surprises us sometimes, does it not, tatellah?"

Two servants came in and, at his grandmother's nod, lashed the trunk shut, then hefted it up between them. Gabriel watched them carry it down the stairs. "Will we like living in Houndsditch, Bubbe?" he asked. "Is it far away?"

His grandmother ruffled his hair with her hand. "Not far, Gabriel," she answered. "And we shall like it about as well as we choose to, I think."

"What does that mean?" he asked. "I like it here, Bubbe. I like Finsbury Circus."

The wistful smile returned. "Grandfather says we have

*put it off as long as we can," she said. "A new family is com-
ing to this house, tatellah. It is God's will."*

*Gabriel flung his arms across his narrow chest. "I am
tired of God's will," he said. "Someday, Bubbe, I shall have a
home of my own. And God shan't will it to be anyone else's.
Never, ever again."*

Little more than a week after his meeting with Dr. Osborne, Gareth was in the estate office when Terrence, the
second groom, burst in. "Your Grace!" he said excitedly.
"Mr. Watson! A carriage!"

Gareth and Watson were bent over one of the estate
ledgers. "What carriage, Terry?" said the estate agent
absently.

"A great, high-perch phaeton, sir!" he said. "Painted
solid black. It just went ripping through the village—right
through Mrs. Corey's guinea hens! Feathers everywhere,
sir. You can still hear her screeching from the stables."

The estate agent straightened up from the table, eyebrows knitted together. "Anyone you recognized?"

The groom shrugged. "Whoever he is, he just turned
up the hill on two wheels, and clipped the edge of the
gatepost," he said. "He'll be up here any moment—if he
lives."

Gareth threw down his pencil and hastened off to
greet his guest. Not many men drove with such a callous
disregard for their own safety—let alone that of hapless
guinea fowl.

As it happened, however, man and beasts survived.
Lord Rothewell threw his phaeton up against Selsdon's
front step—a mere inch away—and leapt down with a
grace which implied sobriety. The gentleman on the seat

beside him, however, was not so sanguine. Mr. Kemble removed his exquisite beaver hat and began to fan himself with it. "I say, Rothewell! If I soiled myself in that last turn, *you'll* be doing the bloody laundry."

"My good man, I cannot even spell laundry," came the reply.

Gareth approached the pair with caution, as one might a loaded gun. "Afternoon, Rothewell," he said. "And Mr. Kemble. This is indeed a surprise."

Rothewell's usually grim mouth turned up into a grin. "I believe we've set a record down from London, old boy."

"Not on my account, I hope," said Gareth. "I want no one's blood on my hands."

Rothewell sobered a bit. "Didn't hit a thing, old chap," he said. "As to those hens, I swerved just in time, and—"

"—yes, by God, he swerved!" interjected Kemble. The slender, dapper man was climbing gingerly down from the phaeton's seat. "Then he hit the gatepost. And tomorrow, I'll have the bruises to prove it."

"Have a care, Rothewell," said Gareth solemnly. "Guinea fowl mate for life, you know."

"More fool they, then," muttered Rothewell, surveying the house with his hands on his hips. "Well, this is quite a show, Gareth. I believe they could drop my house in Cheshire into this place twice over."

"How would you know, never having bothered to see it?" asked Gareth good-naturedly.

Mr. Kemble was critically surveying Selsdon's façade, window by window. "How's the chef?" he asked bluntly. "Will he do? Or shall I find you another?"

"How gracious you are, Kemble," said Gareth speciously. "I should rather you turn an eye to my décor first. It cannot possibly be what it ought."

"An excellent notion," said Kemble, oblivious to the sarcasm. He had begun to pace his way along the front of the house, gaze focused on the second floor. "I can tell you right now, Lloyd, that I don't like what I see in those upstairs draperies. Burgundy velvet is so horridly passé. Is this a south-facing façade? No, more southwest, isn't it? So you'll want greens and golds up there, most likely. I shall have a look, and let you know after dinner."

"Shall you indeed? How thoughtful."

Coggins had come to the door and was surveying the scene in mild disapprobation. The surly footman stood behind him. "Shall Metcaff get their things?" asked the butler hesitantly.

"It would appear so." Gareth turned to Rothewell. "What the devil is *he* doing here?"

Halfway down the front of the house, Kemble seemed to be paying them no mind now.

"I have done as you suggested, my friend," said Rothewell, starting up the steps. "I have brought you some help. A secretary, of sorts."

"He doesn't precisely *look* like a secretary," Coggins remarked, craning his head around the door pediment.

Gareth caught Rothewell's arm. "A what?" he asked incredulously. "A *secretary*? I didn't ask you to bring a secretary. I didn't ask you to bring anyone—not even yourself. I merely asked for your advice. And I casually mentioned that I needed a valet."

"Fine," said the baron, "then he's a valet. Let us discuss this later, *hmm*?"

Metcaff's disdain was apparent. "Well, which is he then?" the footman asked querulously. "A valet or a secretary?"

"Both," snapped Kemble, who had silently crept up on them all. "I'm to do both jobs—and yours too, Mr. Metcaff, if you don't wipe that condescending smirk off your face."

The footman faltered. "But I have to know where to put him!" he protested to Coggins. "Up? Or down?"

Gareth was resigned to the inevitable. He had already been through this with Xanthia. Once Kemble got a toe in the door and a notion in his head, there was no getting rid of him. "Up," he grumbled. "He's a secretary. Put him up."

"Oh, heavens, no!" said Kemble. "Put me belowstairs, Metcaff, by all means."

Gareth hesitated. "But if you are to be an upper servant," he explained, "then I think—"

Kemble laid a stilling hand on his arm. "But that is the very beauty of the situation, Your Grace," he said airily. "You no longer need to think. I am here to do that for you. I shall go *down*. And that is the end of it. Now let us waste no more of Mr. Metcaff's incredibly valuable time. I am going to find the study and pour myself something for my overwrought nerves. Cheerio, all."

"I'm damned glad to see you, Rothewell," said Gareth after the gentlemen's portmanteaus had been taken up the stairs and inside. "But to be honest, I'm shocked. What brings you?"

The baron was gazing approvingly about the great hall. "Magnificent!" he said, his eyes lighting on the Poussin to the left of the massive Carrera marble chimneypiece. "Oh—what brings me? Well, boredom, I daresay. Your letter sounded intriguing—after all, you've never before asked for my advice. And this duchess of yours—"

"No, no, she isn't *anyone's* duchess," warned Gareth. "She is my cousin's widow."

"And widows are fair game," said Rothewell, sotto voce. "A delicate beauty, you said?"

Gareth felt his expression harden. "Don't even think about it, Kieran," he warned. "She is not that sort of woman. Go back to Town and take up with Mrs. Ambrose again, if that's what you are looking for."

Rothewell's black eyebrows went up a notch. "Me?—" he said archly. "I have simply come to the country for a little fresh air, and to see what sort of intrigue my old friend has got himself mixed up in. But what I wonder, Gareth, is this—what are *you* looking for?"

"I can't think what you mean."

Rothewell just shook his head. "There was something in your letter," he mused. "Something written just between the lines. Alas, however, I cannot help you there; you must deal with such emotions yourself. But those other little mysteries—now they do bear a closer scrutiny."

"I thank you for taking my concerns so seriously, but I still don't understand why you've brought Kemble," Gareth complained, jerking his head in the direction of the study. "He doesn't even like me."

"And he mortally hates me," said Rothewell. "But I called in a favor, and—"

"What favor?" snapped Gareth. "You've never done anyone a favor in your life."

Rothewell shrugged. "Zee's favor," he admitted. "Kemble and his cohorts at the Home Office owed her hugely for that debacle with the contraband rifles a few weeks back."

"What, those French smugglers?" Gareth was incredulous. "She's lucky Nash didn't kill her."

"Nash turned out to be innocent, you will recall," said Rothewell.

"Yes, but *she* didn't know that."

Rothewell stopped on the landing and set a hand on Gareth's shoulder. "Look, she read your letter, old chap," he said in a resigned voice. "And she told me I was to bring him. By the by, Kem has the strangest notion you've murdered your uncle. You haven't, have you?"

"I don't even have a bloody uncle," he said. "And I thought Zee was in the Adriatic."

Rothewell patted his back paternally. "Just a slight delay," he said. "They will be off shortly. I think you should retain Kemble's services, old chap. Perhaps an unbiased opinion is in order here?"

"My opinion is not biased," said Gareth a little hotly.

"Indeed?" The inky eyebrows went up again. "Are you quite sure of that, old chap? Don't you wish to know the truth about your lovely widow?"

"I know the truth," he snapped. "What I wish to do is clear her name—though that's none of my business either."

Rothewell looked unaffected. "Why not simply use Kemble for what he's worth, then?" he suggested. "To give the devil his due, the old boy's sharp as a tack, and just a tad vicious. You might find him of some use as a servant."

"As a servant?" Gareth looked at him incredulously. "The man is in my study, drinking my brandy. Does he look like a servant to you?"

Kemble was indeed comfortably ensconced in the study, seated in the brown leather wing chair which had already become Gareth's favorite, and sipping rather tentatively at a snifter of what looked like the good cognac. The man certainly had a taste for life's most expensive luxuries—and a nose for sniffing them out.

"An excellent and well-aged *eau-de-vie,* Lloyd," he said, raising his glass as they entered. "So far as cognac goes, of course. My nerves feel much restored."

"Help yourself, Rothewell," said Gareth, motioning toward the decanter. "It is too bloody early for me."

Rothewell, too, declined. He very clearly had something besides drinking and whoring on his mind, a somewhat uncommon occurrence. They took seats around the tea table, and Kemble began to ask questions—pointed, very specific questions about Warneham, his death, and the estate in general. In time, he left his chair and began to pace as they talked. Rothewell, too, was listening. He was taking Gareth's concerns with surprising gravity— and truth be told, Gareth was damned glad to see him.

After an hour spent sequestered thus, Gareth felt oddly encouraged. He relaxed in his chair and watched Kemble stroll back and forth before the wide bank of windows which overlooked the north gardens. Gareth was beginning to see a decided advantage to Rothewell's plan. Kemble could be his tool; his eyes and ears in the house and about the village. Kemble would be able to ask questions and elicit information the servants would never volunteer to their employer. He now understood quite clearly why Kemble had insisted on being placed belowstairs.

At last, Kemble stopped and set his brandy glass down on the corner of Gareth's desk. "Your cousin sounds like a singularly unpleasant fellow," he remarked. "I daresay any number of people should have liked to see him dead."

"Myself amongst them," Gareth admitted.

Rothewell was looking uncharacteristically pensive. "I think you'd best let Kemble take this on, old chap," he said. "I cannot stay—no one here is going to tell me anything anyway—but I have done the next best thing. I have brought you Kemble."

"And I am grateful, Kieran," Gareth replied. "It's damned good of you. But why did Xanthia think this so important?"

Rothewell hesitated. "Your duchess does indeed have a dark cloud hanging over her head," he said at last. "It is not your imagination."

Gareth studied him. "What, precisely, are you saying?"

Rothewell lifted one shoulder. "Zee and I took it upon ourselves to ask a few questions in Town," he murmured. "Our cousin Pamela, Lady Sharpe, is well connected, you will recall."

"And?—" Gareth leaned forward in his chair.

"Pamela says there were some unfortunate rumors after the duchess's first husband died," Rothewell said quietly. "Rumors that she had a sort of mental collapse. Then this second death . . . well, it bodes ill for her, that's all. There have been whispers. People wonder if she mightn't be a little mad."

"I think the notion absurd." Gareth managed to keep his tone calm. "The woman is perfectly sane."

He neglected to mention, however, his conversation with Dr. Osborne. Nor did he report what had happened between them that night on the rampart, and Antonia's strange behavior afterward. He should have done so. Even in that moment, Gareth knew he was withholding what might be important information. And yet he said nothing. It was a very bad sign, and he knew it.

Gareth looked at Kemble assessingly. "I should like you to take this on, Mr. Kemble," he said. "But it will require some time. Can you leave your business unattended?"

Kemble sniffed. "I owe a debt of honor to Lady Nash," he said a little haughtily. "Maurice can keep an eye on the shop from upstairs, I daresay. Besides, Lloyd, you need all the help you can get. If I cannot clear your lovely duchess's good name, I can—at the very least— burn those burgundy draperies."

At that, Gareth laughed, rose from his chair, and offered his guests a tour of the shops and barns. A former plantation owner, Rothewell leapt at the chance to see the new threshing machine. Kemble declared that manure gave him hives and promptly withdrew.

True to his word, Kemble began his new career as valet with an enthusiasm which was as impressive as it was unnecessary. When Gareth returned to his suite to dress for dinner, it was to find half his wardrobe heaped in tidy piles. A few garments were laid over a chair, and the larger part lay upon the bed. Kemble greeted him at the dressing room door, Gareth's favorite riding coat draped across his arm.

After eying it suspiciously, Gareth went at once to his side table and poured them both another brandy. "How long can you be away, Kemble?" he asked, passing one of the glasses.

"For as long as it takes, and not an instant more," said Kemble, who promptly downed the brandy. "I despise the country. And since I haven't valeted for anyone in almost a decade—"

"You mean you actually *were* a valet?"

Kemble looked at him curiously. "What, you think I make this up as I go along?" he said with a disdainful sniff. "Valeting is a science, Lloyd. One does not pick it up in one's spare time."

"I am just shocked to learn that not all of your careers have been shady," said Gareth, grinning.

"One or two, perhaps." Kemble picked up a brown riding coat and gave it a good snap. "Actually, your wardrobe is not entirely hopeless, Lloyd—I beg your pardon *Your Grace*. Funny how I cannot quite come to grips with that new title."

"Nor can I," muttered Gareth.

"This riding jacket, for example," Kemble went on. "The cut is marvelous and the fabric acceptable. The color, however—" He halted, and glanced at Gareth's hair. "Actually, this *might* work. You have that tall, blond Adonis look, and a good suntan still. Maurice says tobacco always lifts one's natural—"

"I'm not much of a smoker," Gareth interjected.

Kemble cut him a withering glance. "Tobacco is a color, Your Grace."

"Ah, and I thought it merely a vice."

Kemble tossed the coat into the pile on the bed. "Speaking of vices, I saw your arrogant footman under the servants' stairwell groping one of the scullery maids."

"*Groping?*" Gareth felt a surge of anger. "By God, she'd best have been willing."

"Desperately unwilling, I think," Kemble speculated. "Either that or she was playing hard to get like a Drury Lane professional. I don't like the look of him."

"Nor do I."

"Shall I get rid of him?"

"What, and deny me the pleasure?" Gareth answered. "I won't have that bastard oppressing someone smaller and weaker than himself. Find out what happened."

Kemble lifted both brows. "My, you sound serious," he murmured. "Just give me a few days to earn the trust of the other servants, and I'll get at the truth of it."

"Yes, you do that." Gareth fell back into his chair and forced his temper to calm. "Kemble, tell me again why you agreed to this scheme of Xanthia's?" he said, changing the subject. "What, precisely, did she say to you?"

"Well, now, let me see!" Kemble laid a finger along his cheek. "Lady Nash's orders said I was firstly *to improve your wardrobe to one worthy of a duke*. And secondly, *to discover who killed your nasty uncle—*"

"—cousin."

"Whatever." Kemble tossed his hand. "And thirdly, *to determine if the duchess is truly worthy of your regard.*"

"If she's *what?*—"

"Worthy of your regard."

"Xanthia has a lot of nerve putting words into my mouth."

"She did not need to," said Kemble. "Did you read that letter you wrote, or did you channel it from the netherworld, then simply toss it in the morning's post?"

"I know what the letter said, damn it," Gareth grumbled. "And it said nothing about my being infatuated with the duchess."

Kemble pressed his fingertips to his chest. "*Infatuated?*" he said, his eyes widening dramatically. "My, this does sound fascinating. But regard is a far simpler emotion, Lloyd, and your concern for her was writ plain upon the paper. Let me see—'a lovely, fragile creature who immediately captures one's eye and one's sympathy.' I believe that's what you said."

"Yes, perhaps." Gareth propped his chin in his hand. "I don't precisely recall."

"And, as it happens, I know a good bit about the object of your—er, your *regard*."

Gareth's chin came up. "Do you? How?"

Kemble smiled and went back into the dressing room. "In my line of work, Your Grace, it pays to know such things," he said, addressing a stack of folded shirts.

"See, there's another question," said Gareth. "Precisely what the devil *is* your line of work, anyway?"

Kemble poked his head out and flashed an amiable smile. "Why, I am just a simple shopkeeper in the Strand," he said. "A purveyor of unusual antiquities, paintings, and *objets d'art*."

Gareth narrowed one eye. "Now, why is it I've never quite believed that?"

"I couldn't say." With a graceful flick of his wrist, Kemble tossed one of the shirts onto the chair. "Certainly the police never do. They have the oddest notion I'm a fence for stolen artwork."

"Lovely," said Gareth. "My first week at Selsdon, and

I've let in a professional receiver and a chronically inebriated madman. But what the hell, right? You said you knew something of the duchess? Let's hear it."

Kemble was sorting stockings now. "Merely the particulars of her background," he answered. "None of the dirt—*yet*."

Gareth opened his mouth to protest, then thought better of it. "Go on."

"Antonia Notting is the second child of the Earl of Swinburne." Kemble kept rolling and unrolling Gareth's stockings as he talked. "The family has pots of money. Her father recently married some whey-faced debutante of no significance. Antonia's elder brother James, Viscount Albridge, is a rake of the worst sort, and a favorite with the bookmakers. He runs with a fast, dangerous crowd, one of whom used to be his sister's husband, Eric, Lord Lambeth—a minor baron with a major conceit. They married in the middle of her first season. She was just seventeen."

"Heavens," said Gareth sardonically. "You are like a Debrett's and a Covent Garden scandal rag all rolled into one."

Kemble smiled smugly. "And yet you hang on my every word!" He crammed his hand down one of Gareth's stockings and held it to the light. "Ah, threadbare in the heel." He tossed it onto the bed.

It was an especially warm, woolly stocking, but Gareth did not argue. He knew when a battle was not worth fighting. "By the way," he said reluctantly, "I am going to need some new clothes, am I not?"

"An entire wardrobe, give or take." Kemble tossed another sock.

"I was wondering," said Gareth, "if you could possibly get your friend Monsieur Giroux to take me on. Giroux & Chenault are the very best, I know, but Xanthia says they aren't taking new clients."

Kemble smiled knowingly. "Maurice will do whatever I ask," he said. "Perhaps I shall discuss it with him when I get home—if you prove yourself worthy of his extraordinary talents."

"Prove myself? In what way?" Gareth demanded. "Look, just forget I asked. What of this Lord Lambeth? Just tell me what sort of fellow he was."

"Breathtaking," said Kemble. "I actually knew him vaguely. But he's been dead at least three years now—so your duchess cannot have been married to Warneham for very long."

No, not long at all. Gareth considered it. Antonia must have wed Warneham almost as soon as her mourning had ended. Not that there was anything wrong with that. "Why did she marry him?" he said abruptly. "Lord Lambeth, I mean?"

Kemble trilled with laughter. "Oh, it was a passionate love-match!" he said. "She loved Lord Lambeth desperately—and he did, too. So they had something in common."

Gareth laughed. "You are a cruel man, Mr. Kemble."

"No," he said with a mystical wave of his hand, "I am Cassandra, Seer of the Truth. Besides, Lambeth left a mistress and two children in Hampstead, and a string of more salacious sex partners over in Soho. Does that sound like love to you?"

Gareth was beginning to wonder if he knew what love was. "I don't know," he said. "How did he die?"

Kemble shrugged. "As he lived," he answered. "Most men do, you know. I heard that he overturned his curricle driving too fast in the rain, but it happened at his country house, so I don't know the gory details—*yet*."

"You keep saying that word in a way which gives me shivers," Gareth said. "I've heard enough, I think."

"Very well," said Kemble. "Then I shan't tell you who killed your uncle."

Gareth's head jerked up. "*Did* someone kill him? Do you know who?"

Kemble smiled. "Most likely, and not yet," he answered. "Nasty people usually meet a nasty end."

Gareth sipped pensively at his brandy. "I want you to find out precisely what happened, Kemble," he finally said. "Find out the truth—and don't spare the horses doing it, either."

Kemble gave a dramatic, swooping bow. "Your wish is my command, Your Grace," he said. "By the by, I feel a dreadful pair of bruises coming on from Lord Rothewell's driving. I think that tomorrow I must consult a physician."

"For *bruises*?" said Gareth.

"Yes, I'm frightfully delicate," said Kemble. "Now, tell me again—what was that village doctor's name?"

The day following their arrival, Selsdon's new houseguests gave every indication of settling in—perhaps until shooting season. Gareth knew that in part Rothewell was simply avoiding his sister's leaving, though he likely did not realize it on any conscious level. That was just how the baron's mind worked. He had stayed drunk for two days following the wedding. George Kemble's motivation was harder to grasp. It was quite likely that Xanthia had simply paid him some exorbitant sum to do her bidding. Gareth should, of course, have been angry at having his life interfered with, but he had other, far greater concerns than Xanthia's meddling. Besides, Rothewell was right. Kemble might prove useful.

After breakfast, Kemble made himself busy in the study with a pile of correspondence, mostly routine letters of congratulations from people whom Gareth did not know, welcoming him to the lofty ranks of landed aristocracy. He doubted any of them sincerely wished him well. Most were secretly appalled, he suspected. After all, he was naught but a cutthroat, working-class Jew whose kinship to the late duke was so distant and convoluted that he himself could not track it. To the aristocracy, such ill-breeding was an abomination.

Rothewell had not yet risen and would not likely do so before noon. Restless and on edge, Gareth dressed for riding and ordered his horse saddled. Since his first meeting with Antonia, he had dreaded the day when he would eventually have to visit Knollwood, but now he was inexplicably impatient to go. He had sat through dinner again last night, unable to take his eyes from her despite his guests. His curiosity about her—one might even call it a mild obsession—was growing. It made him realize that the sooner one of them was out of the house, the easier it would be for both of them. Besides, he was a little tired of catching sight of her unawares, and feeling his heart ratchet up like some besotted schoolboy's.

He would look about for a mistress as soon as he could get back to London, Gareth decided as his mount was brought round. He set off toward the village, turning the matter over in his mind. Perhaps he would visit Madame Trudeau again. A highly sought-after dress-maker, Madame Trudeau was polished and delightful, if not in the first blush of youth, and Gareth had spent one or two delightful evenings in her arms. She appreciated him for what he could give her, and asked no questions. Perhaps now that he was no longer pining for Xanthia, *madame* could be persuaded to something more regular? At that thought, he reined his horse to a stop. *Was he no longer pining for Xanthia?*

No, he supposed he was not. Nowadays when he thought of her, it was with fondness and exasperation. Perhaps her marriage had drawn that fine, bright line he had needed to see. On the other hand, perhaps the change in his attitude was due to something more dire. That did not bear thinking about.

His horse was prancing impatiently. At the foot of the hill, he turned north, away from the village, and sprang the beast. Eager to please, the horse ate up the ground, throwing up dust and stones as he flew. They reached the foot of the carriage drive in short order. As they made their way up the hill Gareth realized that someone—Watson, most likely—had kept the road up to Knollwood in good shape.

It was a pity one could not say the same for the house. Knollwood was a fanciful three-storied house with two stone turrets which served little purpose, an elegant entryway, and what had once been carefully landscaped gardens. The house had been constructed perhaps a century and a half earlier and appeared to have been on the decline ever since. Gareth tethered his mount behind the house in an especially shady spot, then went back around to the stone steps, now surrounded by brambles and covered in moss. The key Watson had given him worked. Gareth turned the lock, pushed open the door, and was struck by a vague sense of dread.

His last days in this sad old house had been the worst of his life. Even the abuse heaped upon him by the sailors of the *Saint-Nazaire* had not compared to this sort of grief. Gareth forced himself to step inside. He looked about the entrance hall as if it were a foreign land, yet realizing in the same breath that almost nothing had changed. Oh, the smell of damp and decay was worse—but the pale yellow walls were the same, just more mold-specked. Even the old oak settle by the door sat unmoved, covered in years of dust.

Upon peering into the drawing room, he realized that someone had simply tossed Holland covers over the furniture and walked away. He could make out the settee, the side chairs, even the lumpy old chaise. The botanical drawings on the wall still hung, mildewing in their frames. The oil landscape over the marble mantelpiece had faded, and one corner hung loose, torn from its stretchers.

Gareth approached his grandmother's favorite reading table and picked up one corner of the dustcover to see that a porcelain *bonbonnière* still sat on the peeling marquetry top, a lumpy black residue lying in the bottom. Calcified chocolate? A dead mouse? It was disgusting, all of it. And yet this place, he suddenly realized, no longer held any power over him. It was as if by stepping inside, he had shattered an evil spell.

He continued to roam the ground floor, his boots echoing hauntingly through the lifeless house. The library with its old wooden panels. The parlor, its great Palladian window cracked. The once-elegant dining room hung with pink silk which had formerly been red. The rotting residue of a life which had long ago died.

From time to time, he could feel the old floor sag suspiciously. He kept to the edges and made his way to the staircase. He realized at once it was rotting, and he went up warily, sidling along the wall. This floor he found much the same, but in better shape, as it was further removed from the damp. The four chambers here had been put to bed with a little more care, their long, heavy draperies wrapped in Holland cloths. The beds still stood in their usual places, dustcovers laid neatly over the mattresses, and beneath, all of their bedding stripped.

In his grandmother's room, however, the curtains had been removed, allowing the midday sun to stream in. It made the room seem almost lived in. Here the smell of damp was no more than a mustiness. His grandmother's writing desk sat uncovered by the windows. He went to her bed and stripped back the Holland cover. This was the bed that, for the first months of his life at Knollwood, he had so often come to in the middle of the night, in order to have his fears assuaged and his demons shoved back into their wardrobes. He felt a sudden wave of wistfulness, and of loss.

In his old room, he looked down at the oak tester bed, and for a few dreadful moments, he was nine again. Gareth shuddered. The wooden canopy had terrified him when he was a child. Heavy and dark, it had seemed to loom ominously overhead, shutting out the light. He had grown accustomed to it, of course. He had had no choice.

Caught in the midst of his brooding, he became vaguely aware of a noise. Mice, he supposed.

The sharp, terrified scream, however, was not a mouse.

Gareth rushed for the stairs to the sound of splintering wood. Antonia was clinging to the banister with both hands, her black riding habit pooled awkwardly on the step above. "Don't move!" he ordered.

Her face was etched with terror. "I cannot," she cried. "Oh, Gabriel! I cannot free my boot!"

Gareth was edging his way back down, his spine to the wall. "Do not move, Antonia," he said again. "Bear your weight on the banister, not your feet. I shall get you free."

She nodded resolutely, eyes wide. "Yes."

He reached her easily. Planting his weight near the wall, he leaned over her and set his right hand on the banister near hers. "How far down has your leg gone?"

"To—to the knee," she said. "Almost."

Quickly, he surveyed the situation. "Keep hold of the banister," he commanded. "I am going to lift up your skirt."

Her leg—a very fetching, well-turned leg—had gone completely through the rotted wood. A splintered chunk of the stair tread had caught the lip of her riding boot, wedging her awkwardly into place. It was so dark beneath that he could not make out the cellar stairs. Perhaps they had already collapsed? *Bloody hell.*

"Is your back foot secure?" he asked, forcing his voice to be calm.

She nodded, biting her lip. There was an ominous groaning sound somewhere beneath them, followed by the crack of wood.

Dear Lord. She was headed for the cellars, and he with her, most likely. "Don't let go of the banister," Gareth said calmly. "I will rip this splintered wood away, then lift you out with my arm round your waist."

She gave a nervous bark of laughter. "Can you?" she said. "I seem to have put on a few pounds."

Gareth smiled reassuringly. "You are the merest feather, my dear," he answered. "The treads and risers have rotted in the center."

"Oh," she said quietly.

Gareth still wore his riding gloves, a lucky bit of happenstance which made ripping away the splintered wood an easy task. When the last one was pulled from her boot, he stripped off the glove and wrapped his left arm about her waist. Antonia did not panic as he'd feared but instead bore her weight on the banister as he lifted her. At the right moment, she let go and threw her arms round his neck. Her riding hat toppled off and went tumbling down the stairs. Gareth swung her across the hole to him, then edged up the stairs as he'd come down, clinging to the wall.

"Oh, thank you!" she managed to say when he set her down upstairs. "This feels like terra firma!"

Chapter Nine

*T*he curtains were drawn in the little flat above the goldsmith's shop. The air was stale, the rooms lifeless. Gabriel could hear the occasional murmurs from the next room and knew without listening what was being said. He felt at once bored and frightened.

Though he knew he ought not, Gabriel went to the window and pushed the curtains wide enough to lean out. Propping his elbows on the sill, he watched the black-garbed jewelers going in and out of Cutler Street below. For a time, he studied them and tried to imagine where they went with their strong, purposeful strides. Just then, he heard a noise, and whirled around.

Rabbi Isaacs! Gabriel sat down on the floor, ashamed.

"Gabriel, my son," said the rabbi, "you do not sit with Rachel?"

He made a face. "I—I was, but I got tired."

"Tired of sitting shiva?" Rabbi Isaacs bent down and rumpled his hair. "Ah, yes. I think I understand." He took the rickety ladder-back chair by the bed and turned it to *face Gabriel, who sat on a rug beneath the window.* "You have covered your mirror. Gabriel. That is right in the eyes of God. And you have put away your shoes. It speaks well of you, my boy."

Gabriel looked down at his worn stockings. "I have tried to do all the right things," *he said.* "But Bubbe keeps crying."

Rabbi Isaacs nodded. "Shiva is the time for tears," *he said quietly.* "But Rachel's tears forge her strength, Gabriel. Never forget this."

Gabriel did not understand. But because it seemed expected of him, he nodded.

"You were a good grandson, Gabriel, to Malachi." *Rabbi Isaacs patted his head, then rose from his chair to go.* "I know he was proud."

Gabriel waited but a moment, then returned to his window, and to his fears. He did not know what else to do.

Across the wide passageway at the top of the stairs, Gareth studied Antonia's pale but otherwise lovely face. She seemed perfectly steady for a woman who had just experienced a near-brush with—well, if not death, then something dank and deeply unpleasant.

"You are all right?" he asked her. "You are not injured in any way?"

She smiled and shook her head. "No, but I must have given you a fright," she said. "For a moment, I feared we were destined to go crashing into the cellar together."

He winced. "That is the last place you should wish to go in this house, trust me. That is the source of all this damp."

"Oh, dear!" Sudden alarm sketched across her face. "How shall we ever get back down?"

"There are stone staircases in the old turrets at either end," he said. "They are dark and nasty, and likely choked with cobwebs, but I will go before you and knock them down."

"Thank you. Oh, you are so kind." Antonia relaxed and began to look about the upstairs. Against the dark gray of her habit, her face was as smooth and pale as porcelain, but there was a dash of color on her cheeks today, and her eyes looked bright and perfectly lucid. "How did you get up here without falling?" she asked.

"A sailor's eye for rotted wood," he said. "It is a hazard in my sort of work."

"In the shipping business?" she said.

"I was at sea for a while, too," he said. "One learns a great many survival skills on a ship."

Antonia had begun to roam tentatively down the passageway. "Yes, you were in the navy, were you not?" she said over her shoulder. "That must have been exciting for a young man."

He followed her, puzzled. "I was never in the navy."

She turned around, the hem of her habit spinning about her ankles. "Oh," she said. "I thought . . . I thought you were trained as an officer?"

"No." He shook his head.

"Then I must be confused." Her smile had faded a little. She turned to peek into the next bedchamber. "What a sad, lovely house this is," she murmured. "Can you feel it?"

"Feel it?"

Her gaze returned to his. "The sense of grief," she said quietly. "It lingers here."

Gareth set his jaw and tried not to grit his teeth. He

had felt the grief and sadness firsthand. He had lived it. But he had no wish to talk about the past, especially not with Antonia. Besides, however he might feel toward his dead cousin, none of it was his widow's fault. "Did you come up to see the house, then?" he managed to say. "I would have invited you, but I feared it mightn't be safe."

That was true, so far as it went. But he had also wished to be alone on his first visit to Knollwood. He had not known, honestly, how it would feel to return here. Now, however, he was strangely glad to see her.

"I had no idea you were up here." Antonia had strolled to the window which overlooked the front lawn. "I just rode up to poke about the place, and when I saw the front door was open—well, I couldn't resist."

He followed her to the window. Their shoulders brushed as they stood looking out. He pointed to a place just above the distant tree line. "Over there is Selsdon's roof," he said. "Can you make it out?"

"Yes, just barely," she answered. "And look, there is the tithe barn! And that break in the trees—is that the old bridle path?"

"Yes, it winds back down to Selsdon's stables. I walked it often as a boy."

"I tried to use it once," she confessed. "But it was overgrown."

"I will have it cleared for you," he assured her. "It will take some time, Antonia, but this place can be a home again. The grief and sadness can be ripped out along with the rotted floors. Do you believe me?"

"I believe you," she answered quietly.

"Antonia?"

"Yes?" She did not look at him.

"Will you be lonely here? I . . . I don't want that for you."

He had set his hands on the frame and leaned nearer the window. She followed suit. "I don't know," she said, still staring through the grimy glass. "Perhaps I shall be. But no one ever died of loneliness."

She was right about that. For a long moment, neither spoke. There was a strange, peaceful stillness which enveloped them. A sense of intimacy which he hesitated to sever. Finally, he cleared his throat. "A few moments ago, on the stairs," he said awkwardly, "you . . . you called me Gabriel."

She turned to face him, her lips almost expectantly parted. "Yes, Your Grace," she answered. "It was inappropriately familiar. I apologize."

He gave a muted smile and shook his head. "You needn't call me 'Your Grace,' " he said. "I meant only that . . . well, that I have not been Gabriel in a very long time." Not since the night they had made love in the rain, and not for many long years before that.

"Oh," she said quietly. "I have rarely heard you spoken of by any other name. You do not care for it? Shall I call you something else?"

He shrugged. "Call me what you wish," he answered. "But that part of me—the Gabriel part—it feels as if it was lost a long time ago, Antonia."

"What do you mean?"

"Within a few months of leaving this place, I knew it would be best if no one ever found me again. And I did not like the weak, frightened person I had become. So I became someone else."

"I see," she murmured. But she did not see. She could not possibly.

Antonia was looking deeply thoughtful. "But if a part of you has been lost," she added, "perhaps it needs to be found again? I know what that is like, you see. I once lost myself—my joy, my faith—everything that made me . . . well, *Antonia*. I have not got it all back, quite honestly. But some days, I see glimmers of hope. Isn't that what we are all working toward? To simply be—oh, I don't know—what we were meant to be?"

Gareth glanced away. "I am happy enough," he said, "with what I have become."

Antonia straightened up from the window. "Then tell me," she said brightly, "which room was yours when you lived here?"

He strolled toward the door, and she followed him in. "This one," he said. "I loved the chest inside the window seat for my toys—what few I possessed. But the bed terrified me."

Antonia looked it at with a theatrical shiver. "Lord, it's positively medieval, isn't it? That horrid wooden canopy. A child would feel quite trapped, I think."

Gareth laughed, but he was strangely relieved that someone understood. He found himself telling her of his childhood notions and nightmares. Of his belief that goblins lived beneath his bed, and ghosts hid in the wardrobe. Of how the utter silence of a country night could frighten a child so accustomed to the hustle and bustle of London.

They strolled through the room as they talked, Antonia picking up the corners of the Holland cloths to see what lay beneath. "You poor thing," she said when he was done. "You had come to live in a strange place. A place nothing at all like the city you were accustomed to. When my husband and I removed to the country, Beatrice was terrified of—"

Gareth turned to look at her. Antonia's face had gone white. Her eyes were round. He caught her gently by the hand and drew her towards him. "Beatrice was terrified of what?" He sensed that he must keep her talking. "Tell me, Antonia. Who was Beatrice? What was it that frightened her?"

Antonia swallowed hard and tore her gaze from his. "Beatrice—she was my daughter," she blurted. "She was frightened of the hedgerows. I—I am not supposed to talk about her."

Gareth did not let go of her hand. "Who told you that?" he gently demanded. "Who said you mustn't speak of her?"

"No one wants to hear it," she said, tripping over the words. "Papa says that another person's grief is very tiring."

"You just listened to a quarter hour of mine," he pointed out. "Do you feel tired?"

"Pray do not make fun of me." She was speaking very rapidly now, and her eyes held that look again—like a colt that had been spooked. "I am trying . . . trying to do my best."

He led her back to the window seat and gently urged her down. "So Beatrice was afraid of the hedgerows?" he prodded. "Because they were so tall?"

Again, she swallowed hard. "Yes, tall," she agreed. "They . . . they shut out the sun sometimes. And trees which hang over the road? They terrified her. And now I think of her—of where she is—and I think how frightened she must be." Her voice caught on a sob, and her trembling fingertips went to her mouth. "I know she must want me. And . . . and I am afraid—oh, Gabriel!— I am so afraid she is in the dark."

Gareth put an arm about her waist. Dear Lord, so much was coming clear to him. He knew what it was to be afraid. To be a child, lost and without hope. But Antonia's child was quite obviously beyond this mortal coil. "Beatrice is not in the dark," he whispered. "She is in the light, Antonia. She is in heaven, and she is happy."

"*Is* she in heaven?" Antonia choked. "Do we know that? Do Jews have a heaven? If they do, how can you know it is really there? How? What if . . . what if everything they taught us was *wrong*? Just lies to—to placate us? To make us hush?"

"Antonia, I think most of us believe in the afterlife," he said, taking one of her hands in his. "I have studied more than one religion, and it is a fairly universal construct."

"Is it?" Her voice was teary.

"Yes, and I believe quite firmly that the wicked burn in hell," he said, "and that all children go to heaven. I am quite sure your Beatrice is at peace. But my knowing it is not the same as your knowing it. There is nothing wrong with fear or doubt, nor anything wrong in talking about it."

Her free hand was really shaking now. "Oh, I just don't know!" she cried. "Sometimes I am just so tired of crying."

Gareth cupped his hand around her cheek and gently turned her face to his. "A wise rabbi I once knew told me, Antonia, that our tears forge our strength," he said quietly. "In my grandparents' faith, mourning is a sacred process which cannot be hurried. We remember our dead at holidays. And on the anniversary of their passing, we honor and commemorate their life."

"How strange that sounds to me." Her limpid blue eyes widened. "I thought everyone believed I ought never to think of it."

"A good Jew would tell you that you *need* to think of it." He massaged her hand as he spoke, forcing her fist to relax. "And to talk about it, too. You should set aside times to do these things, and honor them like the momentous commitments they are. If your father suggested otherwise, then he was wrong."

"It was a long time ago," she said, her voice flat now. "I should get on with my life. People lose children all the time."

"Children are not disposable, Antonia," he said angrily. Good God, it was no wonder the poor woman was half mad with grief—they had forced her to bottle it up. "No one should simply throw a child away. I, more than anyone, know that much. And if God takes a child, you *should* grieve. You must grieve. If anyone has tried to make you believe otherwise, then they should burn in hell."

"That . . . that is what I sometimes thought," she confessed. "But everyone thinks that it is just is a part of life. And that I should forget about Beatrice—and Eric."

"Eric was your husband?" He already knew that, of course. Kemble had told him—but apparently he had not known about the daughter.

"Yes, my—my first husband." Her voice was a whisper.

"And I am sure you loved him very much," said Gareth softly.

"Too much," she interjected harshly. "I loved him too much. Until the end—and by then I did not love him at all."

Gareth did not know what to say. He squeezed her hand again. "Why don't you tell me about Beatrice?" he suggested.

She looked at him through grief-stricken eyes and said nothing.

"How old was she?" he encouraged her. "What did she look like? Was she adventurous? Shy?"

Antonia's face broke into a watery smile. "Adventurous," she whispered, tugging a handkerchief from inside her riding coat. "And she looked like me. We were so very much alike. Everyone said so. But . . . I am not *me* anymore. I am not adventurous. I barely recognize myself. Beatrice was a wonderful child. She . . . she was three years old."

"I am so sorry, Antonia," he said. "I cannot imagine the depth of your loss, but I am deeply sorry."

Gareth meant every word, too. He could not comprehend the horror of what she had been through. He had been twelve when fate had torn him from his grandmother. He had been thrown away like so much refuse, mourned by no one save for her. And Rachel Gottfried—a vigorous, sensible woman—had lived but two years after that. If that sort of grief could strip the will to live from a woman of her strength and faith, then it could bring anyone to their knees.

Antonia had not even been allowed to grieve. Unless he had counted wrongly, Antonia's father had arranged a second marriage for her right on the heels of her first—a marriage which had apparently ended in all manner of tragedy. Gareth almost hoped she did not know what a faithless bastard her first husband had been—but she did. He had already seen it in her eyes.

"Papa thought it best I go on with my life," she said quietly. "He said that the sooner I married again, the sooner I could have another child. He said that I would find it easier to forget what happened to Beatrice, and that Warneham was offering me what no one else would. But I failed, you see. I did not give him a child."

Gareth had no idea how to answer that. Gently, he lifted a stray strand of hair and tucked it behind her ear. "Antonia, when a woman has suffered a crisis, sometimes—well, I cannot be accounted an expert—but does it not make it hard to conceive?"

She looked at the floor, and shook her head. "It was not like that," she whispered. "It was . . . I was . . . just not desirable enough."

"Not desirable enough?" *Was the woman blind?*

"It was my bleary eyes and red nose, Papa said," she quietly confessed. "He said men do not find unhappy women attractive. Eric told me that, too. And so I tried to do what I ought for Warneham. I *tried*. But all I could think of . . . was Beatrice. Then he died—and everyone thought I had wished him dead—or worse. But I did not. I *did not*."

"Antonia." Gareth set his fingertips to his forehead for an instant, carefully choosing his words. "Was it just that Warneham . . . that he was not . . . romantic with you?"

She lifted her narrow shoulders lamely and wadded her handkerchief into a tight ball. "He tried to be," she whispered. "But we could never—*I* could not—fully please him."

He gave her hand another short, hard squeeze. "Antonia, why do you think his—his inability to perform had anything to do with you? Why didn't he discuss it with Dr. Osborne? Wasn't he obsessed with his health?"

"Yes, frightfully, but if he complained to the doctor, I know nothing of it," she said, sniffing. "I do think, though, that Dr. Osborne suspected."

"Did he? Why?"

"Sometimes he would ask questions—delicately, of course," she said. "I supposed he was just worried for me. He knew Warneham married me for only one reason. But I felt like such a failure."

"Antonia, you were not a failure," Gareth said. "Warneham was not exactly a young man."

"Eric was a young man." She twisted the handkerchief around her fingers so tightly that he thought the blood might stop. "He said a husband wants a wife who smiles and is happy. And that if she cannot make him feel worshiped—if she is shrewish and complaining—then he does not want to bed her."

"Ah," said Gareth, reaching across to unwrap the handkerchief. "Was that his excuse?"

She turned her head and looked at him strangely. "What do you mean?"

Gareth did not look at her but instead spread her handkerchief over his knee and began to meticulously refold it. "Your husband was a liar, Antonia," he finally said. "Call me a pig if you will, but I would still want to bed you, even if you were crying, screaming, and trying to stab me all at the same time. And trust me, it really would not matter if your nose was red."

"I . . . I do not understand," she said.

Gareth shrugged. "Why do you think I came up here today, Antonia?" he asked. "I should rather have a tooth drawn than return to Knollwood. This is where my whole life went to hell. But if I keep you within arm's reach . . . if I don't get you out of Selsdon—" He shook his head, cleared his throat, then awkwardly continued. "You *will* find someone again, Antonia," he said. "You will fall in love with someone who will be right for you, and someone your family will approve of. Someone whose blood is blue—and this time, I pray, someone whose heart is as true as yours."

She started to speak, but he turned and set his fingertips to her lips. "Listen to me, Antonia," he said. "You *are* desirable, you are beautiful, and you are just twenty-six years old. You have many years to find the right man and have children again. But you have every right to mourn the daughter you have already lost. You will mourn her, I am sure, for the whole of your life—not every minute, no. But every day—at least for a minute, and oftentimes far more. Until you find a man who accepts that, *don't marry anyone*."

"I don't even want that life anymore," she said, her voice steadier. "I decided that when Warneham died I was going to live an independent life. I know I am not the person I used to be. But I want a home of my own, and a say over my body. I want no man telling me that I must do this thing or that thing, or feel a certain way. And when I wish to cry, I shall do it. If I cannot have those things . . . if I cannot have them . . . I think I will die. I *know* I will—for I very nearly have."

Her determination was surprising. Antonia had clearly given her independence a great deal of thought. Gareth said no more for a time but merely returned her handkerchief, then set his hand atop hers.

"We should go," he said quietly. "Let's get you back to Selsdon. I shall send Watson up to London to hire us a construction crew next week—a big one."

"Yes, I should go back." They rose from the window seat and went out into the passageway. "It is Monday, is it not? We shall have a great many dinner guests."

Damn. He had forgotten that tonight was the night Sir Percy and his coterie came to dine. It was a pleasant enough tradition, but tonight he would be in no mood for it, he feared.

Outside his grandmother's room, Antonia stopped and turned around. "Is my nose red?" she asked. "Do I look a fright?"

Gareth managed to smile. "Your nose is pleasantly pink," he replied. "But you could never look a fright, Antonia."

She held his gaze steadily. "Do you really find me desirable?"

He felt his smile fade. "Many women are desirable, Antonia," he said. "But you are more than that."

She was still looking at him, her eyes wide and luminous. "I wish . . . I wish, Gabriel, that you would show me again."

He narrowed his gaze. "How, Antonia?"

Finally, she glanced away. "You said we had a passion. A madness. That something hot and fierce ran between us. I wish to feel that again, if only for a moment. Kiss me. Kiss me as you did that day in the sitting room."

He took a step back. "It would not be wise, my dear," he said quietly. "What I want when I look at you is—well, never mind that. Your emotions are raw just now. I would be taking advantage."

She set her head to one side, and studied him. "Don't do that," she whispered. "Please just do not . . . patronize me. Don't pretend that I am some fragile, witless thing. I am strong—far stronger than I look, Gabriel. Do not underestimate me."

He stepped toward her and laid a hand on her shoulder. "Antonia, it is not that."

"I think it is." She leaned into him. "You have said that you find me attractive. I . . . I am asking you to show me."

"I am not the man for you, Antonia," he said quietly. "You know that."

"I know that, yes."

"Then don't push . . . *this*. I am not a gentleman, Antonia. I won't say no. And when I am done, you will know precisely how you make me feel. Because I won't stop at a kiss."

But she stepped toward him anyway and set one hand on his chest. "Just show me," she whispered, her mouth barely brushing the edge of his jaw line. "I remember how you made me feel that night. I—I don't know why I lied. I remember it—most of it—and it makes me a little bit ashamed. But I cannot stop thinking of it."

"Antonia, you were alone and frightened," he said. "I gave you what you needed. That's what I'm good at. But beyond it, I have nothing more to give."

"I am asking for no more," she said. "Do you know what it is like, Gabriel, to experience something like that—something so raw and so pure—when everything else you feel is just jumbled, jagged emotion? To be so focused on one's self and one's desire that all else is fleetingly shut out? For me, it is a reprieve. It is like a redemption of—not my soul, but my *self*."

He encircled her with his arm and drew her full against him. He forgot that he hardly knew her; that mere days ago he had thought her haughty and cold—perhaps even a murderess. "Oh, Antonia," he said, burying his face in her hair. "This is going to be a terrible mistake."

Her other hand skated up the back of his coat as she set her cheek to his lapel. "I can hear your heart beat," she said. "It is so strong. So certain. No—this is *not* a mistake. It just is . . . what it is. Two people, Gabriel. Two people alone. It is our secret. Our sin. No one else need ever know what we do here."

She had convinced him. Antonia sensed it. And he did desire her. With this man, perhaps her feminine instincts did not fail her. Gabriel bent his head and kissed her forehead. "Just this once, then," he said, his voice heated. "Just once more, Antonia. And then . . . it must be over."

"Yes," she whispered, for in that moment, she would have sold her soul just to feel Gabriel's touch again. "Gabriel, I swear it."

Antonia felt his mouth settle over hers, firm and demanding. She felt one fleeting instant of doubt, and then was lost, swimming in the sensation of a kiss which weakened her knees and seized her breath.

Gabriel's hands moved over her, urgent and insistent. One warm, heavy palm settled at the small of her back, then restlessly shifted to tug her shirt free. He caressed the skin he had bared, searing her with his touch even as he kept kissing her. She had no specific recollection of how they made their way into the sunlit bedroom, but when Gabriel backed her up against the mattress, she felt the wooden edge of the bed touch her legs.

Dimly, she was aware of tugging at his coat and his cravat. Gabriel unbuttoned her coat and pushed it from her shoulders. She heard it slither into the floor. His breath was already roughening. Her fingers found the buttons of his waistcoat and unfastened them as his mouth moved down her jaw, then lower still. Delicately, he trailed the tip of his tongue down her throat and over her pulse point, making her shiver.

"Oh!" she cried softly.

She wanted this. She wanted him. She needed to lose herself in an emotion which was neither grief nor regret but a celebration of life. And Gabriel was so overwhelmingly *alive*. Impatient now, she pushed his waistcoat away, drew free his shirttails, then ran her fingers beneath the band of his riding breeches. She felt the weight of his manhood press firmly against her belly, and she let her fingers delve lower. But when she brushed the velvety tip of his erection, Gabriel froze.

"Wait," he said, setting her a little away from him. "This . . . this isn't how it should be for you, Antonia."

"How should it be?" she asked.

He turned her about and sat down on the bed, his shirt billowing softly about his waist. "Come here," he said, pulling her between his legs. "Let me undress you slowly, Antonia. I don't want to just toss up your skirts. Let me feast my eyes on your pure English beauty."

Antonia felt suddenly shy. It was all very well to go at one another like mad things. But to slow down. To *think*. Oh, that was harder. "I can't wait," she pleaded as his hands went to the buttons of her shirt.

"You must," he said firmly. "I won't take you again like some—well, like before. We'll go slow, Antonia. This time we do it my way."

She closed her eyes and nodded as his warm, deft fingers began to work their way down her bodice.

"Wait!" she said again, opening her eyes. "You must take your shirt off. Please?"

He looked up at her with a boyish grin. "You may take it all off—all perhaps save these boots, which I am not at all sure will come off without a fight."

Antonia managed to smile back. "Your boots are no impediment to what I require," she said. "They may stay on. The shirt must come off."

"Whatever Her Grace demands," he said, stripping it over his head in one motion.

"Oh!" Antonia let her eyes run over him. "Oh, my."

Gabriel was smooth and lean, his skin a warm shade of honey. His chest was tautly layered with muscle and just a dust of gold hair. His arms were the same. He possessed the body of a vigorous, physical man in the very prime of his life. He reached for her and drew her back into the vee of his legs. "We are going to regret this, you know," he said, lifting her shirt to kiss the tender skin just beneath her rib cage. "But it is too late. We might as well enjoy one another. Here, let's take this off."

To her shock, Antonia's skirt went sliding down her legs. "Oh!" she said, looking at the floor.

"*All of it,*" he growled. "All of it off, Antonia. I want to see you when I make love to you this time." He looked up at her then, his eyes glittering gold in the afternoon sun.

In that moment, beyond the dusty room, nothing else existed. Outside, a faint breeze had kicked up, rustling the branches about the windows. Somewhere in the distance, a cow was lowing. The sun was dropping in the sky. But she saw only him, with his demanding eyes and lean, hard face. She wanted this; had begged for it. And what he wanted was not unreasonable. Without another word, she reached up and began to draw out her hairpins.

All the while he watched her, the simmering ardor growing in his eyes. When the pins were gone, she drew off the rest of her underthings, her hands shaking a little, and dropped them onto the floor. "Good Lord," he choked.

Antonia had never been this naked with a man in broad daylight. She felt awkward, and a little uncertain, but the heat in his eyes was reassuring. "Have you any notion how beautiful you are, my dear?" he whispered, his hands coming up to cup her breasts almost reverently. "Those pink, perfect nipples alone could stir a man from the dead."

"Thank you," she said honestly. "I think these boots and stockings must be the next to go."

A slow, lazy grin curved his mouth. Lightly, he thumbed her nipples, drawing them into taut, tormented peaks. "You may leave your boots on, too, Your Grace, if you wish."

She craned her head to look at them. "I think not," she said. "If you would be so kind as to unfasten the buckles?"

Antonia watched his long, elegant fingers as they made short work of her boots. Then one by one, he rolled her stockings down, as cleverly as any lady's maid might have done. "I see you have some experience at this," she murmured.

"A bit, yes," he said, tossing the last stocking aside. "God knows I'm no innocent, Antonia. But you might as well use me for what I can give you."

It sounded harsh, and oddly self-deprecating. He was more than that to her. Surely he knew? But when she straightened up and opened her mouth to chide him, Gabriel's warm hands settled on her buttocks, urging her toward him. Still a little embarrassed, Antonia closed her eyes but an instant. At that moment, his tongue lightly touched her belly, making her shudder and gasp.

"My dear, you seem easy to please," he murmured.

"Yes, with you, I—I think I might be," she whispered, closing her eyes. "But what I wish to know is . . . how to . . . oh, heavens! What—oh! That is—"

"—delightful?" he supplied, withdrawing his tongue. She grabbed firmly hold of his shoulders and nodded.

He lifted and parted her slightly with his broad, certain hands, and stroked his tongue deep enough to tease. Deep enough to leave her gasping. Several times. Antonia knew a little about desire and—she had thought— her body. But soon she realized she really knew nothing at all.

"Stop!" she heard herself cry after a few tormenting strokes. "Oh, please. *Stop.*"

He did so at once. "Antonia?" The concern in his tone was palpable.

She opened her eyes and looked down at him. "Not

stop," she clarified. She touched the tip of her tongue to her lip. "That was . . . oh! Someday I would like to— what I mean is, for now . . . I just want *you*."

With one hand, he pushed the folds of his breeches and drawers away. Antonia looked down to see his erection spring free of the tangled cloth. It was . . . daunting.

"Climb on me," he rasped.

She looked up at his eyes. "What—?"

He pulled her toward him roughly. "Come here, wench, and stop staring," he commanded.

With a faint, uncertain laugh, Antonia set one knee to the mattress. Gabriel pulled her onto his lap, pushed her knees wide, then urged her down across him, allowing the warm weight of his erection to slide up through her warmth, grazing her most delicate spot.

"Ah," she moaned, shivering in his embrace again. "Don't you . . . wish to . . . undress? Or to lie down?"

"No time, sweet." With a grunt, Gabriel shifted her weight and lifted her ever so slightly. She felt his shaft slide deliciously across her center again. With her hands on his broad shoulders, she rose onto her knees and met his first thrust.

"Good. God." Gabriel's voice was choked. *"Almighty!"*

He pushed deeper, slowly but inexorably, stretching her in a way which seemed impossible.

"Oh, my." Experimentally, Antonia lifted herself up, reveling in the sight of his shaft drawing out of her body. She eased back down, exhaling on a perfect, sweet sigh. This was amazing. On her knees atop him, much of the control was hers. Gabriel set his broad hands at her waist and gently lifted her again.

"This really is . . . quite remarkable," she whispered.

Gabriel laughed. "Put me to work, love," he said, leaning back to watch her.

But instead, Antonia bent her head and kissed him—kissed him with her lips and with her tongue, thrusting inside his mouth as he had kissed her. It was as if something in the room burst into flames. Heat and desire rolled over them, an inferno of raw, emotional lust. Over and over, she rose on her knees, riding him as their tongues thrust and parried. His strong hands never left her waist. His belly drew taut as a washboard as he plunged up and inside her, searing her. Claiming her.

She had never known this—anything quite like this—was possible. Gabriel tore his mouth from hers and found her breast, drawing the nipple between his teeth. He bit—not hard, but enough to hurt. And yet it was not pain. Antonia cried out as his tongue teased and circled the hard little tip, pushing her toward something. It was maddening. Incendiary. Her nails dug into Gabriel's shoulders. She lost herself to the sweet, driving thrusts of his body, matching his strokes, urging herself against him like a hungry wanton, seeking something precious and elusive.

"Come for me, Antonia," he rasped. "Dear God, you're like a wild thing."

"I am." The voice was not her own. "I feel ... different."

"Come for me, love," Gabriel crooned. "Let me see you—let me—oh, God!"

Antonia felt a blinding light explode somewhere inside herself. Felt her body surge to him, surrendering to him, giving him what he had claimed. And then she was lost, and knew nothing more but perfect wholeness. A relief which was at once carnal and sweet and glorious. She came back to herself, unable to catch her breath, and just a little frightened.

She was not stupid. She understood desire. And her body—she had thought. But she was not at all sure what had just happened. It was so much more intense, so much more *everything,* that it was a little disconcerting.

She became slowly aware that they lay almost flat now. Gabriel had at last collapsed beneath her, and was now on his back.

"Oh, my," she said beneath her breath. "Gabriel, this might not be . . . . good."

He tilted his head to look up at her. "It definitely was not my best performance," he said.

Antonia stared at him for a moment. "It . . . wasn't?"

He laughed and let his head fall back onto the bed. "Five minutes is not my norm." Again, she caught the self-deprecating sarcasm. "Thank God you're a little powder keg, love, else you'd be damned disappointed with me right about now."

A powder keg. That was a compliment, she thought. She let herself relax atop him, her breasts flattening against the faint dampness of his chest. His heat and scent surrounded her. Gabriel wore no cologne but smelled instead of plain soap and something wonderful. Something that was uniquely him.

"You are very good," she murmured, her head resting on his shoulder. "You know it, too, do you not?"

He chuckled, the sound rumbling deep in his chest. "I have been told that, yes, from time to time."

She closed her eyes. "But you are more than that, Gabriel," she went on. "You . . . touch me in a way I cannot explain. There is something between us that is almost . . . metaphysical."

He set his lips to her temple. "Antonia, we are good together," he said quietly. "But it is still just sex. Tell me, my dear, that you know that."

Antonia felt sleep overtaking her. She felt suddenly exhausted to her very core. "Yes, I know that," she murmured. "It was just sex. And it was just this once."

But the acknowledgement brought Antonia no peace. Instead, she could think only of her promise. *Just once.* Already she was regretting those words.

Chapter Ten

*T*he church of St. George's-in-the-East was a towering white edifice dwarfing everything which surrounded it. Stark against the Sunday morning sun, the bell tower cast a shadow which ran all the way to Cannon Street, and right over Gabriel's toes.

"Bubbe, I don't like it," he whispered, tugging at her hand.

"What is this, 'I don't like it!'" she chided. "It is a church, tatellah. It is God's house."

"Not your God," he muttered.

His grandmother squeezed his hand. "Gabriel, my child, you must learn to be part of them, these English. In a few years, you will be old enough for your bar mitzvah, yes?"

He narrowed one eye suspiciously. "The English don't have them, Bubbe."

"Oh, yes, but they are called confirmations," she answered. "It was your mother's dearest wish you should have one."

Gabriel scraped his toe across a crack in the pavement and said nothing.

"*Come,* tatellah," she cajoled. "*Go up the stairs, and sit in the back. Just do what the others do.*"

Gabriel looked at the church again. People were pushing past them now, and making their way up the flagstone path. Fine carriages were everywhere. "You won't go with me, Bubbe?"

His grandmother brushed her hand across his cheek. "*I cannot, but you must,* tatellah. *Because I promised your mother—and she promised your father.*"

"But I hardly even remember him!"

His grandmother pinched his cheek. "*It does not matter,*" she said firmly. "*He is still your father. And you must never disappoint him.*"

"*Umm.*" George Kemble smacked his mouth perceptibly. "You do brew a most excellent cup of tea, Mrs. Waters. A North Fujian *wu-long,* is it not?"

Nellie Waters looked at him suspiciously across the housekeeper's table. " 'Tis whatever was left over in Musbury's tea caddy," she said, rising. The servants took tea belowstairs every afternoon at three, but the others had finished and gone. "There, on the sideboard. You may see it for yourself."

Kemble made a fluttery, downward motion with his hand. "Do sit back down, Mrs. Waters," he said. "I have so much to learn about how a ducal household works. I wondered if I might depend upon you to help me?"

Her suspicion did not wane, but slowly she sat. "You'd best ask Musbury," said Nellie. "Or Coggins. They'd be the upper servants."

Kemble smiled and crossed one knee over the other. "Yes, but they cannot know the day-to-day workings of the house," he demurred. "Those intimate details which the personal servants almost innately grasp."

"I don't know what *innately* means," said Nellie Waters. "But I know what you're after is gossip. Don't take me for a fool, Mr. Kemble."

"Oh, no indeed!" said Kemble. "You are *not* a fool. That is precisely why I asked Mrs. Musbury to leave us alone after tea."

"That's all very well, I suppose." The maid's brow unfurrowed a tad. "But I'll not be tittle-tattling about my mistress."

"And who would respect you if you did?" Kemble slipped his hand into his coat and withdrew an engraved silver flask. He tipped it over Nellie's cup. "Frog water?"

"And I'll not be plied with alcohol," said the maid.

"My good woman, this is the finest French armagnac this side of Algiers."

Temptation sketched across her face. "A little tot, then, wouldn't hurt, I suppose."

"Not in the least!" said Kemble, dumping a generous slosh into the empty cups.

Nellie pulled the cup toward her. "I know your type, sir," she said, sniffing at the brandy. "I know you've been snooping round, asking all manner of questions. And I don't doubt for a minute that's just what you were brought here to do."

Kemble made a guilty face. "Dear me, there's no pulling the proverbial wool over your eyes, is there?"

Nellie relaxed and took a healthy sip from her teacup. "Just tell me what you want straight out, sir, and perhaps I'll help," she said. "And perhaps I shan't. But if you try to winkle it out of me, you'll get not a thing for your trouble."

She had convinced him. "Well, it is like this, Mrs. Waters," he explained. "The duke is concerned about certain rumors regarding his late cousin's death."

Her eyebrows snapped together. "What sort of rumors?"

Kemble smiled a little tightly. "Oh, I think you know, Mrs. Waters," he answered. "As you say, you are no fool."

"Aye, rumors he was poisoned, belike," said the maid. "And per'aps he was. But I don't care what the village tabbies say, my lady did not do it. Don't have it in her, poor lovie—and if she was going to poison a husband, t'wouldn't have been this one."

Kemble nodded knowingly. "You are referring, of course, to Lord Lambeth," he said. "From what I hear, he would have deserved it."

Nellie shifted in her seat uncomfortably. "Well, he did himself in, the damned fool," she said. "So that's over and done. What else do you wish to know?"

"Who else might have wished the late duke dead?"

"Lord, make a list!" Nellie rolled her eyes. "The families of those last two chits he wed, per'aps. One or two of the servants. And the Earl of Mitchley—they quarreled over a boundary dispute. 'Twas to have been heard in court last year, so Mr. Cavendish said. And the duke was still hot as a poker at Laudrey, the local justice of the peace, for asking questions about his last wife's dying, as I heard it."

Kemble merely nodded. "The present duke tells me that the village doctor determined it was potassium nitrate poisoning," he said musingly. "That is a drug often used for severe asthma, but usually by inhalation. Was the duke terribly ill?"

Nellie's brow furrowed. "He took a cold in his chest shortly before the wedding," she said. "Coughed for two or three days, and cut up a terrible fuss, wanting flannel and warming pans and running the servants to death. He was peculiar about his health, the duke was."

"*Before* the wedding? You were here?"

Nellie looked wistful. "Lord Swinburne wished my lady to have a few days to settle down," she explained. "And he wanted to acquaint himself with Dr. Osborne—to prepare him, I reckon. The doctor was upstairs, listening to my lady's heart with his ear tube—her sleeping draught was disagreeing—and he said the duke's barking sounded like asthma, so he went down to examine him. Within a se'night, the cough was gone."

"Interesting," murmured Kemble. "Tell me, Mrs. Waters, did you by chance see the duke's body at any time after death?"

"Oh, yes, 'twas I who heard old Nowell screeching at the top of his lungs that morning," said Nellie. "I ran across to the duke's bedchamber to see him all sprawled out on the floor."

"Did you notice anything unusual, Mrs. Waters? About his face, perhaps?"

"That's just what Laudrey asked," said Nellie. "His lips were all strange looking. Brownish."

"Ah, I see. Tell me, was there a chamber pot in the room?"

"Of course," said the maid. "That was the first thing Dr. Osborne wanted to see. About to run over, it was. I allowed Musbury ought to give those chambermaids a good conk on the sconce, but the doctor said it was a . . . a symptom."

"Of nitrate poisoning, yes," Kemble acknowledged. "Your justice of the peace, Mr. Laudrey, did he examine the contents of the duke's medicine chest? And if so, what did he do with it?"

"Yes, I showed him," said Nellie. "Mr. Nowell was fit for nothing by then, and two days after, Coggins pensioned him off somehow. So I showed Mr. Laudrey what was where."

"And what then became of the duke's things?"

"His medicines and such?" asked Nellie. "Why, I boxed them up and took 'em to the stillroom. Waste not, want not, I always say."

Kemble rose at once. "My thoughts exactly, Mrs. Waters," he said with a smile. "Would you be so kind as to show them to me?"

Nellie took him across the corridor, lifted a small ring of keys from her pocket, and led him into a narrow room with stone countertops. "Here, in the cupboard," she said, lifting down a large box which looked stuffed to bursting with brown bottles and tins.

"Good Lord!" said Kemble. "Was he a hypochondriac?"

Nellie considered it. "I never heard of that," she admitted. "But he did have an odd rash back in the spring."

Kemble smiled. "And the duke was deeply anxious about his health, I collect?"

Nellie smiled grimly. "They say Warneham feared he might die before begetting another heir," said the maid, pushing the box to Kemble. "But me, I think per'aps he was just afraid to meet St. Peter. I think he had done something—something he was afraid to be called to account for."

Kemble thought the maid was a woman of uncommon intuition. He began to poke through the box. "Tooth powder, headache powder, bilious liver drops, ointment for sore joints," he muttered. "And—ah ha! *This*."

"That's it," said Nellie. "The asthma draught."

Kemble held the brown bottle to the light. "Christ, that looks like the pure stuff," he muttered. He unscrewed the lid, peered inside, then sniffed it.

"Does it smell wrong?" asked Nellie suspiciously.

"It has no smell at all—as it should."

"So it's just what it ought to be then?" Nellie sounded disappointed.

"Well, it is a dangerous chemical," said Kemble. "Poisonous, even explosive, under the right circumstances." He did not mention its many uses, though the possibilities were tumbling round in his head. He put the bottle back. "I see no dosing instructions," he commented. "How much did he take?"

Nellie shrugged. "The duke dosed himself, most of the time," she said. "You might ask Dr. Osborne."

Kemble did not like the sound of that. "Did the duchess ever prepare his medication?"

Nellie crossed her arms over her chest. "Once or twice, per'aps—but only at first when he was abed with that cough. It was the Christian thing, don't you think?"

"And her wifely duty, of course," Kemble agreed. "Tell me, could any of the servants in the house have entered the duke's room the night of his death?"

"Aye, with the right excuse, I daresay."

"And who else had regular access to the house?"

Nellie considered it. "Well, the squire and Lady Ingham are here at least once a week," she said. "The rector and his wife. The doctor is in and out—his mother used to come, too, but she passed on shortly after my lady and I came here—oh, and that night, the duke had guests. Two gents from Town. One was a barrister—Sir somebody-er-other. The other was his nephew—Lord something—kin through his first wife."

"I am sure Coggins will know their names," said Kemble. "Well! That's that, then. Thank you, Mrs. Waters. Shall we finish our tea?"

Just then, there was a little scream further down the flagstone passage. Nellie scowled and yanked the door wide. "That would be Jane from the scullery," she said darkly. "Poor child. Somebody ought to geld that devil."

She moved as if to march down to the scullery, but Kemble laid a restraining hand on her arm. "Oh, no, Mrs. Waters," he said sweetly. "*Do* permit me."

They were eight to dinner that evening. Gareth tried not to stare down the table at Antonia, who had worn a dark purple gown cut just off her shoulders, which showed her elegant, swanlike throat to great advantage. He failed, of course, and barely attended Reverend Hamm's long-winded discourse on the importance of philanthropy amongst the upper classes.

Mrs. Hamm was a pretty, vibrant brunette who did her best to offset her husband's plodding demeanor with her ability to draw others into the conversation. Nonetheless, her status as a clergyman's wife put her off limits for Rothewell's more aggressive flirtations. The baron therefore fell into a bit of a funk from which no amount of cajoling could stir him.

As the meal was ending, Antonia ordered coffee be prepared for the large withdrawing room while the gentlemen enjoyed their port. As the ladies filed from the room, laughing amongst themselves, Gareth saw Antonia cast one last parting glance in his direction. It was a look which was both sweet and yet remarkably knowing. He felt his knees go a little weak. It was a very bad sign.

I am strong, Gabriel, she had said at Knollwood. *Do not underestimate me.*

He did not. In truth, he was beginning to fear she might have the strength to fell him. But it would be she who came away unsatisfied in the end, he feared. Whatever the truth about Antonia and Warneham, Gareth was beginning to care deeply for her. He had found himself telling her things he had never before shared with anyone—not since Luke Neville had saved his sorry hide and set him on the path toward making something of himself.

But sharing a few sad details of one's life was not intimacy, and Gabriel was not foolish enough to think it was. Perhaps that was what he had liked about Xanthia. She'd never asked him anything about his past. Perhaps Luke had quietly told her all she had needed to know. And perhaps it had been that knowledge which had held her back from a real commitment to him. Or perhaps she simply had not cared about old history. Xanthia was that rare sort of woman—one who did not live and die by her emotions. She was cool-headed and—it had often seemed to him—cool-hearted.

Antonia was neither. Gareth could already sense that

she was the sort of woman who wore her heart on her sleeve. When Antonia fell in love, it would be deeply, heedlessly so, and she would need to share every aspect of life with her lover. He only prayed she did not fall deeply in love with him. She would need the sort of intimacy which was beyond him, for there were too many things he could not bear to share with anyone. And the last thing Antonia needed was to be trapped in another empty marriage.

The door was closed now, and Gareth had lost his taste for port. Rothewell had lit an odiferous cheroot, and Dr. Osborne was chiding him for it. Rothewell's eyes had gone dark, a clear sign he was in one of his bleak moods.

After the wine was brought out, they lingered but briefly, then Rothewell stubbed out his cheroot and they headed toward the withdrawing room. Halfway along the corridor, Gareth stopped and touched Rothewell lightly on the shoulder. "Are you all right, old fellow?"

"Well enough, I daresay." The baron's voice was flat.

"You are bored here in the country," said Gareth. "And missing Xanthia. Admit it."

Rothewell's eyes darkened. "No, I am concerned about her," he averred. "What do we know, really, of this Nash fellow, Gareth? Why must he take her all the way to the Adriatic?"

Gareth smiled. "We know Xanthia chose him," he said. "And that her judgment has always been sound. Perhaps your moods of late have been more about yourself—about the emptiness in your life—rather than the change in hers?"

"You are quite the philosopher these days," said

Rothewell irritably. "I do not need it, damn you. Haven't you troubles enough without poking into mine?"

Gareth grinned. "You have come to help me," he returned. "So I feel obliged to return the favor."

With one last dark look, Rothewell set off toward the drawing room. "There is nothing so thoroughly annoying, Gareth, as a man newly besotted," he grumbled. "Careful it doesn't become something worse."

"I am not besotted," Gareth said quietly. "I am merely—now, what was that word you just used?—yes, *concerned*."

Rothewell gave a loud snort. "And I am queen of the Nile."

"Look, Kieran," said Gareth, relenting. "You were right to bring Kemble down here. And I thank you for coming—it has been damned good to see a friendly face, to be honest—but don't suffer on my account, old fellow. Return to Town whenever it pleases you. You know I will send for you if I need you."

"Yes, perhaps," said Rothewell equivocally.

Together they entered the drawing room mere moments after the other gentlemen. They found the ladies engaged in an animated conversation with Mr. Kemble, who had single-handedly carried in a silver tray large enough to hold a suckling pig.

Gareth motioned for the other gentlemen to be seated. "Where is Metcaff?" he quietly asked when everyone was arranged.

Kemble waved his hand and set the sugar tongs atop the bowl. "Oh, we had a little mishap in the scullery," he answered. "I inadvertently broke one of his fingers—well, two or three, perhaps."

Gareth dropped his voice. "You did *what?*"

"Oh, never mind!" said Kemble. "I shan't bore you with the details just now. Will you have coffee, Your Grace?"

"Don't we have servants to do that?"

Kemble smiled and patted the back of a vacant chair. "And what am I, Your Grace? Eel bait?"

Left with no recourse, Gareth awkwardly introduced him to the guests as his new secretary. Sir Percy and Reverend Hamm seemed a little thrown by being introduced to the person serving their coffee, but Kemble glossed it over. "A pleasure to meet you both, I'm sure," he said, passing the cups around. "Of course, I have already made Dr. Osborne's acquaintance."

Osborne took his cup. "Yes, Mr. Kemble suffered some painful jolts on his trip down from London," the doctor remarked. "I hope the Epsom soak gave some relief?"

"Oh, I feel infinitely better!" Kemble smiled. "Such a small village is fortunate to have so skilled a physician, Dr. Osborne. I wonder you aren't tempted to remove to Harley Street and become fashionable."

"Oh, you do not know our Dr. Osborne!" said Sir Percy. "He will never leave our little village."

"Indeed, he won't," agreed Lady Ingham. "And therein lies a delightful tale."

Rothewell was looking dead bored. "Indeed?" he said dryly. "Let us hear it, by all means."

"Please, Lady Ingham," the doctor protested. "I should think there are a thousand stories more interesting than mine."

But Lady Ingham waved him off. "Mrs. Osborne told me that when her son was a very young man, and quite new to the village, he chanced to meet the duke leading his favorite bay mare," she said. "The duke doted upon this horse—oh, dear, what was her name, Dr. Osborne?"

"Annabelle, perhaps," he said reluctantly.

"Yes, it might have been—in any case, she kept coming up lame." Lady Ingham was nodding vigorously now, causing a purple plume on her turban to bounce vigorously. "He and young Osborne fell into a conversation about why he was leading his mount home, and Osborne suggested a paste made of linseed oil and . . . bless me, I never can recall?—"

"White willow," supplied the doctor almost grudgingly. "And some comfrey, perhaps."

"And it saved the horse!" said Lady Ingham. "She never took lame again, and after considering Osborne's scientific mind, and the fact that the village had no doctor, the duke offered to educate Osborne for just ? career."

"What a charming story," declared L whose cynicism was becoming too ?

The doctor shrugged. "I natural sciences," he ex right place, and th erous to und

Lad

th

"The poor *were* delighted, I am sure," said her ladyship with a sniff.

"He replaced the church roof in just such a way," declared Reverend Hamm. "A general plea for funds was made one June—it was the Feast of St. Alban, you see—and after the services, he came to me and offered to pay for it in its entirety."

"I recall it," said Lady Ingham. "It was your first year at St. Alban's."

Gareth noticed that Mrs. Hamm had begun to shift uncomfortably in her chair. Kemble, who was still puttering about the drawing room, was carefully but discreetly observing her every move.

Throughout this happy interchange, Antonia said nothing. But when the line of conversation regarding her dead husband at last fell away, she promptly suggested whist. Two teams were made up, but for the most part, ewell spent the rest of his evening staring at Mrs. nd drinking Gareth's cognac.

h, however, the ordeal was over and all the ut the door or up the stairs. "Well," ne upstairs to undress him. ed in the Church of St.

here, Your ovely,"

running high, but he was far from sure his relationship with Antonia could be described as good fortune. Tonight, watching her as they'd played cards, it had felt a little as if his heart were being gored out with a dull penknife. She had looked so . . . *pretty.* Almost effervescent. There had been a decided glow to her cheeks, and until the talk of her late husband had come up, she had been fully engaged with everything around her. For the first time in Gareth's experience, Antonia had given every indication of being a happy woman.

"Monday night dinner," he muttered a little wincingly. "Is this what the lord of the manor must do to be seen as interested in the welfare of his neighbors?"

"Oh, is *that* what this is?"

Gareth shrugged. "How the hell should I know? It was my cousin's tradition, not mine."

Kemble took the coat into the dressing room. "I have many clients and friends amongst the aristocracy, Your Grace, and none of them bother to dine with their parish priest once a week," he said. "Let alone the local squire. Osborne, at least, is witty and interesting, but—"

"But what?" Gareth followed him into the dressing room, untying his cravat as he went. "It is a dashed dull business, these dinners, so if you have a scheme to get me out of it, let's hear it by all means."

"No, it is not that," said Kemble pensively. "I was thinking of Osborne."

"Yes? What of him?"

"Tonight over coffee, I thought he looked a little too long and lingeringly at Lady Lovely," he remarked. "And she looked . . . well, almost radiant. Is the game afoot, do you think?"

Gareth felt his blood surge. "Osborne? With Antonia?"

Kemble shrugged. "Don't look at me. I just got here."

But the truth was, Gareth, too, had wondered at it. He remembered the scene in the withdrawing room his first night at Selsdon. The doctor had been holding her hands and—Gareth had thought—gazing into Antonia's eyes. But since then, there had been nothing. "I think you are mistaken," he said. "He is her doctor, and she is—"

"—mad, or so they say downstairs," said Kemble, relieving Gareth of his waistcoat.

Gareth glared at him. "I won't have that said in my hearing," he gritted. "And I shall sack the next person who does so—and that includes *you,* Kemble."

Kemble looked at him for a long moment, then burst into staccato laughter. "What, and force me back to the dreary drudgery of Town?"

Gareth had forgotten Kemble was likely here under duress. "Well, she isn't mad," he snapped. "What? Did Osborne tell you that today? What else did you pry out of the poor devil?"

"Now that you mention it, it was an interesting visit," Kemble said pensively. "I cannot tell if he believes the duchess innocent or if he is protecting her by taking some of the blame upon himself."

"Both, perhaps," Gareth grumbled.

He felt suddenly and inordinately weary. With every passing day, he cared less and less about who had killed Warneham and more about Antonia. Osborne had said she was sometimes out of touch with her surroundings— her "disturbed states" he had termed them.

In the last few days, however, Antonia had seemed

somewhat more focused. When Gareth had chanced to run into her inside the house, she'd been more apt to be actively doing something—writing letters or arranging flowers—rather than simply daydreaming. But on one occasion, when he had been unable to sleep, he had gone down to the library to find Antonia sitting there in her nightclothes and looking rather dazed, with her maid bent solicitously over her. Mrs. Waters had seen him, and lifted a finger to her lips. Gareth had gone back upstairs. Antonia had been sleepwalking again.

"Osborne says the duchess is improving, he believes," Kemble said, cutting into Gareth's musing. "She requires less medication than she once did. Which reminds me—when I went round to see him this morning, I was seated in a pretty little parlor."

"Yes, a blue one, at the front of the house?" Gareth handed him the wrinkled cravat.

Kemble appeared not to notice the outstretched hand. "I saw a portrait there," he went on. "A quite striking young woman with very dark hair and eyes. She looked familiar."

"I recall it vaguely. Who is she?"

"Osborne's mother, he said," Kemble replied. "Mrs. Waters mentioned her, too—but that was later. This morning I thought the portrait looked familiar, but I could not have put a name to it at the time."

"I should have supposed it was Mrs. Osborne," said Gareth.

Kemble did not note the sarcasm. "When I knew her she was Mrs. de la Croix," he said. "Celeste de la Croix. Yes, I really do think I am right."

"Who was Celeste de la Croix?" asked Gareth.

"Lord, you *have* been stuck in the West Indies!" said Kemble. "But then, you are very young, too. Celeste de la Croix was a high-flyer—and the toast of London, very briefly."

"A courtesan?"

"Indeed, and quite sought after," said Kemble. "She must have retired here to live out her last days in rural domesticity."

"How would you know?" asked Gareth suspiciously. "You would have been but a child yourself."

Kemble's introspection faded, and his brisk efficiency returned. "My mother was a courtesan," he said, snatching the neckcloth from Gareth's hand. "Perhaps the most famous of her time."

"Your mother knew this Celeste?"

"Mother had a retinue of scandalous friends," Kemble said, going back into the dressing room. "And yes, for a time, *la belle Celeste* was amongst them. But she was very beautiful, and Mother never suffered that sort of comparison for long."

"So Osborne is not the doctor's real name?" said Gareth, propping his shoulder on the dressing room door.

"Oh, it probably is," said Kemble. "Celeste was about as French as you are."

As he considered it, Gareth went to the side table and poured two brandies. "Anything else I should know?" he asked, handing Kemble a glass.

Kemble tapped one finger on his cheek. "Well, I discovered a bit about Warneham's houseguests the night of his murder," he answered. "Sir Harold Hardell, a barrister and former schoolmate of the duke's, along with his first wife's nephew—a Lord Litting. Does either ring a bell?"

Lord Litting. Gareth remembered him all too well.

"As a boy, Litting often spent his summers at Selsdon," he explained. "The duchess thought him a maturing influence on Cyril. But he was a bit of a bully, really. The barrister I never heard of."

"Oh, well!" said Kemble. "They sounded dull as ditchwater. Now, getting back to the gossip—"

"Good God, what else can you have learnt during your first forty-eight hours?" Gareth sat down by the hearth and tossed off half the brandy.

"Oh, you would be amazed!" Kemble said. "Take that surly footman, Metcaff—he despises you, by the way. Did you know?"

"Yes." Gareth hardened his gaze. "Which reminds me—what did you do to his fingers?"

"Oh, that!" said Kemble, putting his hand into his pocket. "There was a little accident in the scullery. He ran into my hand whist I was wearing this."

Gareth looked down to see a heavy piece of brass with four finger-holes cut into it. He had seen plenty of them around the ports, especially after dark. And he knew at once what had happened. "God damn it!" he exploded, all but slamming down his glass. "Was he pressing his attentions on that poor kitchen maid again? I'll break the rest of his frigging fingers."

"Oh, it didn't get that far this time," Kemble assured him. "Now, do you know what you've done to incur Mr. Metcaff's wrath?"

"Not a damned thing," snapped Gareth. "He despised me before I got here—because I'm a Jew, if you must know."

Kemble shrugged and dropped the brass back into his pocket. "Yes, that's it—in part."

Gareth looked at him strangely. "Well, what is it in whole, then?"

"Jealousy," said Kemble matter-of-factly. "Metcaff is the old duke's by-blow."

Gareth stared at him. "You don't say."

"No, *I* don't say," he replied. "Mrs. Musbury says— but it's taken me two days to winkle it out of her. The duke got one of the upstairs maids with child. Did Mrs. Gottfried never hear *anything* in the way of gossip?"

How the devil had Kemble learned about his grand-mother? Gareth dragged a hand through his hair. "No one here spoke to her," he admitted. "The denizens of Selsdon thought of her as more or less a servant, stuck up at Knollwood to wipe my nose and make me eat my por-ridge so that they would not have to be troubled with it."

"Most unfortunate," said Kemble thoughtfully. "I suppose she did not know about Mrs. Hamm, either. That would be far too recent."

"Mrs. Hamm?"

"The duke once seduced her," said Kemble.

"He *seduced* his rector's wife? Dear God, is nothing sacred?"

"Yes, the duke's memory—according to that syco-phant Lady Ingham!" Kemble laughed. "Mrs. Hamm does not appear to hold him in quite such high regard."

Gareth grunted and sipped at his brandy. "It makes one wonder if she was just seduced or something worse."

"Something worse, I collect," said Kemble a little grimly. "But given the duke's power, there wasn't a damned thing she could do about it."

"No one would have believed her," said Gareth. "Begin-ning with her husband—because he couldn't afford to."

"Yes, and shortly after, the rector got that new roof he was crowing about," Kemble added. "How's that for *quid pro quo*? And the poor woman was stuck dining with the bastard once a week until—well, until one of them died. Funny how that works."

"Good Lord," said Gareth, disgusted. "Is the whole village rotten to its very core?"

"These little villages always are." Kemble held his brandy to the light. "They are a microcosm of society, with all the angst and sin and greed which goes along with it—multiplied times ten, in my experience."

"You are just full of good cheer, aren't you?" Gareth slumped deeper in his chair. "Tell me—was there *anyone* at dinner tonight who didn't have cause to want Warneham dead? Lady Ingham? Sir Percy? Restore just a little of my faith in mankind."

"Very well, Lady Ingham, I suppose," Kemble conceded. "As to her husband, one never knows what skeletons are hidden in *his* closet. Perhaps he and Warneham had something going on?"

"Sir Percy?" said Gareth archly. "He's just a harmless old fool!"

"Yes, but he's as nancy as they come, I'm afraid," said Kemble matter-of-factly.

"If I had to bed that yammering wife of his, I might consider my options, too." Gareth set his elbow on the chair arm and propped his head in it. His temples were starting to pound. "And who told you of this little scandal? Not Mrs. Musbury, I hope?"

"Oh, heavens no!" said Kemble. "Sir Percy grabbed my arse when I bent over with the sugar tongs."

"That's disgusting," said Gareth.

"Easy for you to say," said Kemble. "It wasn't your arse. Trust me, it was worse than disgusting."

"God." Gareth shook his head. "What do you make of all this?"

"That he finds my hindquarters attractive," said Kemble. "And honestly, for my age, it really is quite decent. I mean, it could be a little less—well, *prominent,* perhaps. But with the proper tailoring—"

"Oh, not your arse, for Christ's sake!" Gareth snapped. "*All* of this!"

Just then, the door flew open and Rothewell entered, looking rather rumpled.

"Well, look what the cat dragged in!" said Kemble.

Rothewell didn't blink an eye. "Whose arse are we discussing?" he asked, flopping into the chair on the other side of the hearth. "I rather liked the one on Mrs. Hamm tonight. Is there any hope do you think?"

"No, and we were discussing mine," said Kemble, flipping up his coattails. "What do you think? Too round? Or about right?"

Rothewell squinted one eye. "Turn to your left."

Kemble did so.

"I think it's fine," said the baron. "Now—do you two have any more brandy?"

Gareth just shook his head, then got up to pour another glass. "Tell me, Kieran," he said, pressing it into his hand, "is it thought frightfully bad *ton* for a nobleman to beat the hell out of one of his servants?"

Rothewell sat up a little straighter. "Not if he deserves it, I shouldn't think," he said, his expression brightening. "I'll back you up, old chap. Who are we to pummel?"

"That brutish footman, Metcaff," said Gareth quietly.

"He's been pressing his attentions on one of the house-maids."

Rothewell shrugged. "But that's just the way of things, old chap," he said. "Human nature, if you will."

"Human nature?" Gareth felt his temper spike again. "To force yourself on someone smaller and weaker than yourself? The poor girl wouldn't weigh ninety pounds soaking wet, for God's sake."

The baron looked nonplussed. "Well, did he actually *do* anything to the chit?"

Gareth had stalked toward the fireplace. He set his boot on the fender and stared into the cold hearth. "He has not yet raped her, if that is what you meant," Gareth snarled. "But he won't stop. His sort never does."

"Then you should simply sack him," said Rothewell. "The girl deserves a safe place in which to live and work."

"If I sack him, he will only take his barbarity else-where," Gareth said into the hearth. "He will simply find another victim to prey upon."

"Windmills! Windmills!" sang Kemble from the dressing room. "You are tilting at windmills again, Alonso."

"Kemble is right," said Rothewell quietly. "Sack the surly bastard and let it go, Gareth. You cannot fix all the world's ills."

But Gareth could not escape the feeling that *this* one he ought to be able to fix. Frustrated, he gave the fender a disgusted shove with his boot. It scraped across the marble and slammed into the pilaster below the man-telpiece. Damn it all, he was tempted to go and drag the arrogant devil from his bed this instant.

Rothewell seemed to read his mind. "You are overreacting, old chap," he said quietly. "Just sit down and finish your brandy. Tomorrow will do well enough."

Tomorrow, then, it would be. Reluctantly, Gareth returned to his guests and to his chair. "Come join us, Kem," he ordered. "We have other fish to fry."

Kemble came out of the dressing room and seated himself with languid grace. "Have you a particular fish in mind?" he asked.

"Yes," said Gareth darkly. "I want you to seek out that JP everyone keeps mentioning—what was the name?"

"Mr. Laudrey, I believe."

"Yes, Laudrey." Gareth relaxed in his chair with a dark, inward smile. "Find him, Kem. And then light a fire under his frying pan. I want to find out just what the hell he knows."

Chapter Eleven

*T*he sound of heavy boots echoed up the stairwell, and the knock which followed was sharp and certain. Gabriel opened the door to find a tall man in an officer's uniform looking worriedly down at him. The caller wore the elaborate shako and red sash of the 20th Light Dragoons, and for an instant, Gabriel thought it might be his father.

"I am looking for Rachel Gottfried," said the man, glancing at the letter he carried in his pristine white glove.

Gabriel hesitated. But the caller was, after all, an officer. "My grandmother is at synagogue," he said. "Would you care to come in and wait?"

The man set his shako and letter aside and took the seat Gabriel offered in one of the small parlor chairs. He looked awkward, and a little nervous. He cleared his throat. "You . . . You must be Gabriel," he finally said. "Gabriel Ventnor?"

Solemnly, Gabriel nodded.

The officer almost winced. "Well, Gabriel," he said quietly. "I've come from the War Office in Whitehall. I—well, I am afraid I have brought some bad news."

Gabriel looked down to see that the man was toying with something small and brown. With a sense of inevitability, Gabriel extended his hand. The officer laid the little wooden monkey in his palm, then gently closed Gabriel's fingers around it.

Baron Rothewell remained in Surrey another week before restlessness got a firm grip on him and dragged him back to the stews and hells of London. Gareth was sorry to see him go. Mr. Kemble carried on as valet and secretary, turning up new and sometimes titillating tidbits about Selsdon and the residents of Lower Addington on a daily basis. Thus far, none of them seemed to have had much to do with the old duke's death, nor did they lift any suspicion from the duchess's shoulders, but Gareth felt strangely confident.

Every day or so, Kemble would mail a spurt of letters to Town. Gareth didn't ask why. He was relatively sure he was better off not knowing. Letters returned to him in the same manner. Gareth sacked Metcaff personally with much satisfaction—and without a reference. The footman did not seem surprised and left with a vengeful glint in his eye. Spurred to action by his master's *carte blanche,* Mr. Watson went to Town with a wad of banknotes, and returned with a draughtsman, four carpenters, and a motley crew of stonemasons and ditch-diggers.

A plan was quickly hatched to install French drains around Knollwood's perimeter, to install modern downspouts, and to expose a part of the cellars where an underground spring was suspected. The spring would then be properly encased and piped up to the kitchens, where it could do some good. The carpenters stayed inside, ripping and hammering. Gareth just kept nodding and signing the bank drafts. The entire project was purely a defensive mechanism, designed to save his sanity. He and Antonia were back to dining alone. It was almost more than he could bear. The words *"just this once"* kept haunting him.

The weather was still unusually warm when he caught sight of her one morning in the garden. He had chanced to go into the cream-colored morning room, the room in which he had first encountered Antonia. Today, through the bank of windows which overlooked the fish fountain, he could see her. She sat alone on one of the stone benches, a wicker basket at her feet, her gaze focused into the depths of the boxwoods.

Even from a distance, Gareth could sense that something was not quite right. Her shoulders were bowed a little into the breeze, and she held the ends of her black cashmere shawl, which had slipped from her shoulders, in an awkward knot below her breasts. In her right hand she held a piece of paper, but it was crumpled. The wind had kicked up, and from Gareth's angle, she looked to be almost in the path of the fountain's spray. Something was very wrong.

Forgetting his vow to keep a polite distance between them, he pushed open one of the windows and went out. The flagstones around one end of the bench were wet. "Antonia?"

She jumped at the sound.

Gareth leaned over the bench and took her hand. "Come, Antonia, the wind has shifted," he said gently. "Your hems are getting damp."

She rose like an automaton and followed him across

the little courtyard to a bench which was both in the sun and away from the spray. "Sit down, my dear," he said, drawing her down to join him. "Has something happened to distress you?"

She shook her head but did not look at him. "I am well, thank you," she said, further crumpling the letter. "I am fine."

To his shock, he was flooded with an almost overwhelming tenderness. "Come, Antonia, you need not pretend for me." Gently, he lifted the shawl and drew it back up her shoulders. "I have been watching you awhile through the windows. You look troubled."

At last she turned to look at him, a weak smile turning up one side of her mouth. "I . . . I was lost in thought, I suppose," she confessed, speaking in the small, hesitant voice which, he had learnt, signaled her distress. "I do that sometimes. I . . . I begin thinking of something, and I forget other things. Or I forget precisely where I am."

"Or what you are holding," he murmured, gently extracting the crumpled paper. "You are clenching your fists again, my dear. Your poor fingers have done nothing for which they should be punished—have they?"

Her smile seemed to become more genuine.

"You have had a letter, I see," he continued. "One of your many suitors from Town, perhaps?"

She laughed a little sharply. "No, and for once I wish those rascals had—"

When she stopped, he gave her hand a little squeeze. "What is it that you wish, Antonia?" he asked softly.

Distress sketched across her face. "I wish only to be left in peace," she answered. "The letter—it is from my father."

"Not bad news, I hope?" he asked.

"He and his wife have returned home to London," she replied. "They have been abroad for many months. And now he . . . he wishes me to visit."

"Does he?" Gareth tried to look encouraging. "There certainly is no reason you cannot go. If we have questions about your wishes for Knollwood, I shall write to you."

She made an odd face and shook her head. "No," she whispered. "I . . . I cannot go. Indeed, I should rather not."

He could sense the pain and perhaps even a little fear in her voice. Heedless of who might be watching, he set an arm around her shoulders. "Then you should write him back and give him your regrets," Gareth quietly suggested. "This is your home, Antonia, until Knollwood is ready for you. There is no reason you should leave it unless you wish to."

To his shock, she gave a pitiful little cry and brought her hands to her face. "Oh, Gabriel!" she cried. "I am a bad person. I am so petty, and so spiteful! I wish it were not so."

He turned on the bench to look at her. "Antonia, that simply is not true," he said, drawing her hands from her face. It was then that he saw the marks: two thin, silvery scars on the insides of her wrists, almost savage in their precision. *Good God.* How had he never noticed them before?

For an instant, he could not get his breath. Somehow, he forced his eyes upward. "Look at me, Antonia," he demanded. "You are not bad or spiteful. What has Lord Swinburne said to upset you?"

She looked at him witheringly and seemed almost to

shrink before his very eyes. "She—she—is—to—have . . . a *child*," Antonia said haltingly and through tears. "She is to have a child, and I *hate* her for it. I hate her, Gareth! There, I have said it. She is to have a child, and Papa wants me to come, and to celebrate the birth—and I do not trust myself enough to go."

Gareth was holding both her hands now. "I am sure your father meant well," he said, hoping it was true.

Antonia hung her head. The breeze stirred the soft tendrils of hair at her temples and at the back of her neck. Today she wore dark blue, which emphasized the lighter blue of her eyes and the pale pink undertones of her skin. Such delicate, perfect skin. What in heaven's name had driven her to so mutilate herself? The dead daughter? The unfaithful husband? He felt a well of pity—and yet it was all tangled up with fear and a measure of anger. Anger at her. Anger at fate.

Somehow, Gareth slipped a finger under her chin and lifted it. "What else did your father say?" he asked. "Why do I get the feeling there is something more? I think you should tell me, Antonia."

Antonia's gaze hardened uncharacteristically. "He wishes me to assure him 'that I have kept my figure and my looks,' " she said. "Papa says that hiding myself in the country is the worst possible way to counter all the nasty rumors. He insists I accompany him in society whilst Lydia recovers her health, otherwise people might begin to believe I really am mad. Gareth, he says . . . he says it is time I was married again."

Gareth was quiet for a time. He felt as if someone had just kicked him in the gut. Logically, of course, he was not sure he disagreed with all of Lord Swinburne's argument. When her wounds were less raw, and the speculation about his cousin's death had died away, Antonia should marry again. But to thrust her into society when she so clearly was not ready? And could Swinburne be trusted? Would he give her the time she needed to find the right man? The notion did not sit well with Gareth.

"Antonia," he finally said, "do you wish to remarry now?" His heart leapt into his throat as he waited for her answer.

At last she shook her head. "No, and I have no wish to return to London," she said. "Not for any reason."

Gareth felt both relieved and wounded by her vehemence on the subject. "Antonia, you told me a few days ago that you were strong," he said quietly. "That I should never underestimate your strength. I think your father has done that. He has underestimated your strength. You have only to write to him and tell him that you do not wish to marry. You must be very firm. You must make it plain to him that you are well enough now you will not be bullied."

"It is not so easy, Gabriel, as you make it out." Her voice was soft but stronger. "For the most part, Papa has always tried to help me. He and my brother are all the family I have."

"Antonia, that simply is not true." He knew he was going to regret if not his words, then the fervor in them. "You are a part of this family. You are a Ventnor until you remarry or die. Your father has no power here."

"You are the only Ventnor left," she answered, flashing a faint smile.

"Yes, but one is enough," he assured her. "If you wish to hide behind me, Antonia, you are welcome to. If your father tries to cross me, I'll make damned sure he regrets it. But the truth is, you do not really need me. You are stronger, I think, than even you know."

She looked at him quietly for a long moment. "No, I do not need you," she finally said. "At least—well, I am trying not to. But thank you, Gabriel, for saying that. I won't hide behind you. I am going to have the life I wanted long ago—the life of a widow in control of her own destiny. No one, not even my father, will stand in my way. But I still do not relish the fight."

He understood then what she was saying. And he was beginning to admire her determination. They sat together in silence for a time. There was nothing but the birdsong and the gentle rustling of leaves in the breeze.

At last, she shifted as if to rise. "Thank you," she said again. "I came out, actually, to work in the roses, not to sit and mope. Would you care to join me?"

Gareth rose and extended his hand. "I am afraid I cannot," he lied. "Watson is expecting me."

He watched her quietly as she picked up her basket and walked away. As always, he was unable to take his eyes from her. Their conversation had oddly shaken him. But there was no denying that Antonia was beauty in motion. Her narrow shoulders straightened beneath the dark blue fabric of her gown, and she held her head up like the duchess she was as she stepped from the shadow of the house, and into the brilliant afternoon sun. The light caught her blond hair, warming it to a golden glow.

Although he had known many beautiful women— known some of them in the most intimate of ways—he had never felt drawn to one as he was drawn to Antonia. He was not perfectly sure what he wanted of her.

Sexually, of course, he desired her. But she also stirred his protective instincts in a way no woman ever had, and that was troubling. Certainly Xanthia, the only woman Gareth had ever loved, had not needed him in that way. Actually, she had not needed him in *any* way—save for the physical satisfaction he had given her. That, at least, he knew how to provide.

But their youthful *affaire* had not lasted long. Xanthia had refused his proposals of marriage. They had settled back into their old routine of being, for the most part, good friends and coworkers. Nonetheless, it had hurt and frustrated him. Much of that frustration had been turned inward. Still young and impulsive, he had begun to grasp the fact that while he might be a nice port in a storm—sometimes almost literally—he was not what women needed in the long term. He was just a short-term remedy for an itch that needed scratching.

Was he about to make a fool of himself yet again? Over another woman who did not need him? Gareth shook his head. He did not have time for this. Watson was hitching up the threshing machine. It was time to see if the contraption would do them any good come harvest, which was right around the corner.

The Vicomte de Vendenheim-Sélestat stood at the deep window of his office and looked down at the crush of traffic in Whitehall. In his left hand, he clutched a letter, while his right was braced firmly on the window frame. London was suffering the last of a hot, damp summer, and even the horses looked wilted.

Feeling rather wilted himself, de Vendenheim turned his back to the window and thrust the letter into the light. Again, he read it. "Mr. Howard!" he bellowed to the front office clerk.

Howard came in at once, his spectacles sliding down his nose. "Yes, my lord?"

"When did this bloody letter come?"

"J-Just this morning, my lord."

"Very well," he said. "Is the Home Secretary in?"

"Yes, sir," said Howard. "Do you wish to see him?"

"I am afraid, Howard, that I must."

Five minutes later, he stood before Mr. Peel's desk, two letters in hand. After exchanging perfunctory greetings, de Vendenheim laid the first letter—an *unsigned* letter—down. "I am afraid some old debts are being called in," he said. "George Kemble asks a favor."

"Indeed? Of what sort?" Peel glanced down at the perfect, angular penmanship.

"Kemble is helping with a murder inquiry," said de Vendenheim. "A private case, for the people who own Neville Shipping. He needs someone to hold a little fire to the local justice of the peace."

Peel's eyes were sweeping over the letter. "Ah, I see," he murmured. "And this is to be Kemble's kindling, is it?"

De Vendenheim nodded. "It simply states that Mr. Kemble acts on your behalf in this matter," he said. "And it strongly encourages the justice's full cooperation."

Peel smiled faintly. "Expecting trouble, is he?" But he took up his pen and, in an instant, slashed his signature across the bottom. "Now, what second small favor does Kemble ask? Out with it."

De Vendenheim tried not to exhale aloud. "Do you know Lord Litting?"

Mr. Peel shrugged. "Socially, a bit."

"The dead man is Litting's uncle by marriage."

Some of the confusion fell away from Peel's face. "Yes, the Duke of Warneham's death. There were some nasty whispers, I recall. But it was finally ruled an accident, was it not?"

"Yes, and it probably was," said de Vendenheim. "But the rumors and questions have not died down, and Kemble wishes to pursue it, just to make certain. He wants me to speak with Litting, who was in the house, apparently, on the night of his uncle's death. Sir Harold Hardell accompanied him."

"Hardell." Peel smiled a little grimly. "Is either a suspect?"

"Not so far as I know," said the vicomte. "I'd like to question the nephew. But I may have to send him through the mangle a time or two, in order to press out what little information he may have."

"Yes, well." Peel coughed discreetly and reached for his pen. "I'm sure he will be a better man for it."

De Vendenheim smiled grimly. "Perhaps, but it will likely make him angry," he warned. "Still, we do owe Kem for his work in that smuggling case."

"Pray do not give it a second thought." Peel drew a sheet of letter paper from his drawer and began to scratch out a note. "Give this to Litting if there's any trouble," he said. "If I must choose between angering a nobleman I scarcely know and one of the best operatives we've ever had—well, it may be dashed awkward—but I know whom I shall choose."

Gratefully, de Vendenheim took the note. "I hope you don't regret this, sir," he said.

"Yes." Peel smiled faintly. "So do I."

De Vendenheim was halfway out the door when Peel spoke again. "Wait, Max—what do you mean to do about Sir Harold?" he asked. "I should rather not make an enemy of a preeminent barrister."

De Vendenheim nodded. "I shall leave him out of it, if at all possible," he assured him.

Peel sighed. "Do what you can, then," he added. "But Max?—"

Hand on the doorknob, de Vendenheim stuck his head back in. "Yes, sir?"

Peel looked deeply pensive. "Whatever else you do . . . see justice done."

"I believe, my lady, that you are putting on a little weight," said Nellie on Saturday morning. "This habit is getting just a little snug."

Antonia turned toward the pier glass and stuck her thumb into the waistband of her skirt. "It is a little tighter," she agreed. "Will it do, still?"

"Lord, yes, and you could do with another stone after that one," said Nellie, going into the dressing room to fetch her mistress's boots. "Where does the duke wish to ride today?"

"I don't know," Antonia confessed, following the maid. "He said only that he wished me to meet him at ten, and that it was a surprise."

"Terry says they put in a new staircase up at the manor yesterday," said Nellie. "Likely that'd be it."

Antonia laughed. "I did nearly fall through the old one," she said, pulling on her boots.

"Well, you stay near to the master, my lady," Nellie

advised, shaking her finger. "Don't go wanderin' off in that moldering old heap, do you hear? Next time he mightn't be able to drag you back out again."

"Why, Nellie, you make it sound utterly romantic!" said Antonia. "I do believe you are revising your opinion of our new duke."

"Judgment's still out," Nellie bristled, brushing a speck of lint from Antonia's habit. "But so long as he's kind to you, his doings are none of my concern."

Antonia laughed again and spun around before the mirror. It was a silly, girlish thing to do—but lately, she was feeling a little girlish. When the moment of dizziness subsided, she studied her face in the mirror, paying particular attention to the lines which were beginning to show at the corners of her eyes. She ran her hands down her bodice, smoothing the fabric over her breasts and ribs.

Yes, she still looked well enough, she thought. And she *had* put on weight. The bosom of the jacket was decidedly more snug, and her color was slowly returning. She was resting a little better, too, though she still was not taking her sleeping draught. When Dr. Osborne chided her, she simply changed the subject. She would no longer live her life sedated and uncertain. The choice was hers, and she had made it.

She was inordinately pleased that Gabriel had invited her to go riding today. It was such a simple pleasure, anticipation. It had been a long time since she had had anything to look forward to. But this was just riding, she reminded herself, holding her own gaze in the mirror. *Just riding*. With Gabriel, a man who was not for her. He had said so himself, and Antonia knew that he was right.

No one in their right mind could wish to be saddled with her—not in that way. And for all his kindness, for all the pleasure his touch could engender in her, Gabriel kept a part of himself—a large part of himself—at a distance. She did not know him, and she must accept that she might never do so.

She cut a swift glance at the mantel clock. "Lud, look at the time!" she said, starting toward the shelf which held her hats. "Nellie, which hat do you think—"

The maid was sitting in something of a heap in the chair by the dressing room. Antonia rushed to her. "Nellie!" she said, kneeling. "What is it? Oh, my dear, you look pale as a ghost!"

Nellie dragged a hand across her brow, which was beaded in sweat. "Get up, ma'am, and move away," she ordered. "I think per'aps I've caught something."

Instead Antonia went to the bell and pulled it sharply, then poured a glass of water. "Have you a temperature, Nellie?" she asked anxiously. "Does your throat hurt?"

Reluctantly, the maid nodded. "Aye, since this morning," she admitted. "I ought to have said so sooner. I thought . . . I thought it would come to naught."

One of the upstairs maids came in and took one look at Nellie. "Lord, it's that quinsy that's going round!" declared the girl. "I could just wring the boot boy's neck for carrying it into the house."

Nellie was looking more bleary-eyed by the minute. Antonia felt guilty for not having noticed it sooner. "How many are ill with it now?" she asked.

"Rose and Linnie in the kitchens," said the girl. "Three of the grooms and the stable boy. Then Jane fell ill this morning. Oh, Mrs. Waters, I really think you'd best go upstairs to bed. I shall have Mrs. Musbury make up a mustard plaster. Dr. Osborne's already been sent for, I hope, on account of Jane."

Antonia pointed to the door. "Off you go," she said to Nellie. "You have your orders. And do not come back down under any circumstance until you are well again."

"You will go for your ride?" Nellie demanded.

Antonia hesitated, then nodded. "Yes, if you wish. But I will check in on you as soon as I return."

After a few more moments of protest, Nellie was bundled off in the care of the maid. Antonia grabbed the first riding hat she saw and hastened downstairs.

Chapter Twelve

*G*abriel hunkered behind the gravestone, sitting as motion-less as he possibly could. The sun was hot on his shoulders, the air deathly still. Behind him, a honeybee droned. He could hear Cyril rushing across the grass, his breathing heavy. Gabriel squeezed his eyes shut and tried to shrink.

"Found you! Found you!" Cyril's voice rang out some yards away.

There was a momentary scuffle in the grass. "Cyril, you cheated!" Jeremy's voice trembled with anger. "You were to count a hundred."

"I did!" said Cyril. "I did count a hundred!"

"Cyril? Lord Litting?" A man's voice boomed across the churchyard.

"Oh, bugger it!" Jeremy whispered.

Gabriel peered around the gravestone to see a man in a cleric's frock striding across the stubbled grass. Jeremy looked up at him defiantly and thrust out an arm. "There's another over there," he said, pointing. "It's not just us."

The priest turned around and scowled. Chin down, Gabriel came out to join them.

"I think the three of you know this is not a place for playing," the priest chided. "Lord Litting, you are the eldest. These boys look to you for an example."

"We're sorry, sir." Cyril, at least, looked truly contrite. "It shan't happen again."

"Kindly see that it does not," said the priest. Then he turned to Gabriel and smiled. "You must be Gabriel Ventnor. Welcome to the village. Shall we see you at St. Alban's on Sunday?"

Jeremy's mouth turned down in a sneer. "He cannot come with us," the boy spat. "My mamma says he's just a godless Jew."

"Oh, don't be ridiculous, Jeremy," said Cyril.

The priest set a warm hand on Gabriel's shoulder. "God welcomes everyone into his house, Lord Litting. I hope young Gabriel here will always remember that?"

Gareth waited a little impatiently at the foot of the steps. He held his horse's head, while Statton, one of Selsdon's pensioners, held the reins of the small but beautiful gray gelding which Antonia always favored. Vaguely, Gareth wondered if the wizened old servant remembered him. He did not recall the groom, but that meant very little.

"It looks a good day for a ride," said Gareth conversationally.

Statton spat into the gravel. "Fine, but turning," he said in his raspy voice. "We'll 'ave rain, belike, by supper."

Gareth surveyed the sky. "Yes, I daresay." He turned to face the former groom. "Listen, Statton, I appreciate your coming up from the village. This illness going round is the devil—just be sure you don't take it yourself, all right?"

The old man drew a leather cord from beneath his worn leather jerkin. "Horseradish and cloves," he said, flashing a near-toothless grin. "Wards it off."

"I trust it will work for you," said Gareth doubtfully. The man was taciturn, but Gareth pressed on, having nothing better to do while cooling his heels. The gray, too, seemed impatient, and was wheeling about, kicking up dust and gravel. "That's a prime goer the duchess rides," he commented. "Bred here at Selsdon, was he?"

The old man laughed, but it sounded bitter. "Weren't nought bred here, Your Grace," said Statton just as Kemble came down the stairs, a basket over his arm. "The old duke allowed it cost too much."

"Really?" said Gareth. "I should have thought it more efficient."

Statton shrugged and spat again. "Didn't want the upkeep on the mares," he said matter-of-factly. "Costs a lot to keep 'em in hay through the winter, and 'e allowed they weren't never worth the trouble."

Not worth the trouble! That must have been Warneham's logic for letting Knollwood go to hell, too.

Kemble stopped to admire the gray. "Gorgeous creature," he remarked, turning to Gareth. "Well, I'm off to the village to fetch Dr. Osborne and do a little shopping. May I get you anything?"

"Thank you, no." Gareth was still stroking the gray's nose, but the animal's hindquarters kept shifting restlessly. "What do you need with Osborne?"

"Jane and Mrs. Waters have succumbed to that putrid throat going round."

"Good Lord, this stuff is like the plague," said Gareth. Kemble shrugged and went on his way. Gareth returned his attention to Statton. "Where did they get this gorgeous fellow?"

The old man's squint narrowed. "Off Lord Mitchley back in '21—that was afore the falling out—but 'e was bought for the duchess. Not this one. The one before."

Gareth winced. "Yes, the one who fell."

Statton shook his head. "No," he said. "The lady who went to sleep and never woke."

"Sorry, yes," said Gareth. "I confess, I get them confused."

At that, Statton wheezed with laughter, as if Gareth had just made the world's greatest joke, but Gareth was still thinking of Warneham.

From his long days spent reviewing the estate accounts with Watson, Gareth was beginning to understand that his dead cousin had been a cheap, spiteful bastard. The spat with Lord Mitchley had begun over nothing—a bit of fence not kept in repair—and had escalated to the point of ridiculousness. He had ordered Cavendish and Watson to settle the matter.

Just then, Antonia interrupted his introspection by hastening down the stairs while making profuse apologies to both Gareth and the groom, and explaining Mrs. Waters's illness. "And so we got her upstairs to bed," she finished as Statton helped her mount. "Mr. Kemble has gone for Dr. Osborne."

"Yes, so he said," Gareth remarked. "I trust she will recover quickly."

"I hope so," said Antonia, wheeling the gray neatly around. "Good-bye, Statton!" she said, waving. "Thank you for coming to help out today!"

Antonia glanced across at Gabriel, and despite her worry over Nellie, she felt a wave of feminine admiration. Like anticipation, it was a welcome feeling after what had seemed an emotional drought. Gabriel was dressed for the country today in snug buff breeches and brown tasseled knee-boots which looked as if they had been molded to his calves. He wore the dark brown coat which he favored, and beneath it, a beautiful cream-colored waistcoat and impossibly snowy linen. In fact, his entire appearance was just a touch more elegant, but Antonia could not have put her finger on what it was, specifically. Mr. Kemble, she decided, had a trick or two up his sleeve.

She apologized again for being late. "I fear Nellie has spoilt your surprise," she said as they circled around the carriage drive. "She has told me all about the new staircase at Knollwood."

At that, Gabriel laughed, causing his eyes to crinkle charmingly at the corners. "No, that is hardly a surprise," he said. "Turn here and go up behind the stables."

She did so, but once up the little hill, she saw nothing save the entrance to the old bridle path.

Gabriel motioned towards it. "This is your surprise," he said. "Watson has had it cleared. The shortcut to Knollwood is now yours to use as you please."

Antonia felt her spirits oddly lift. "Shall we take it, then?"

"Yes, I plan to give you the grand tour," he agreed. "As I recall from childhood, it is a pretty path, with a waterfall, and a little folly above the lake."

The trip through the wood was peaceful, with Antonia turning this way and that in her saddle to admire everything around them. The path circled above the estate's small lake, which extended from the pastures well up into the wood, where the pond's source, a little cascade, came splashing down a rocky outcropping, then rushed beneath an arched stone bridge.

As they turned and began the climb toward Knollwood, Antonia spied the folly, a fanciful thing made of rough stone and mortar which matched the bridge. It was primitively built and far from elegant, but it had a magical quality which made it look entirely at home in the forest.

Gareth lifted his hand and pointed at it. "Cyril and I once pinched a pipe and a pouch of tobacco from Selsdon's coachman," he said. "We went up there to smoke it."

Antonia laughed. He seemed so serious-minded now. It was hard to imagine him doing anything wayward. But if her husband's stories were to be believed, he had been very wayward indeed. She found it a sobering thought.

"Antonia?" Gabriel had edged his mount nearer. "Are you perfectly all right?"

"Yes." She lifted her head and smiled. "It is just that you seem so serious-minded now. What happened to you and Cyril? Were you caught and soundly whipped?"

"Oh, our punishment was swift, and entirely self-imposed," he said. "We became deathly ill—you don't wish to know the specifics. Just trust me when I say I spent enough time hanging over that stone balustrade to know that I never wished to smoke again."

"May we walk up there?" she asked impulsively. "Or are we expected at Knollwood?"

Gabriel shook his head. "We needn't even go unless you wish to," he said, dismounting.

He tied his horse to a sapling which had escaped Watson's hand scythes, then turned to help her down. Antonia felt his hands come around her waist, solid and strong, and he lifted her from the saddle with ease. But the path was not wide, and he stood very close as he set her down. Their coats brushed. She felt the heat of his eyes upon her and caught his gaze. Finally, Gabriel let her feet touch the ground. Antonia tried not to feel disappointed.

"I shall tether your horse." Did she imagine it, or had his voice roughened? "There are some stone steps just there, beneath the leaves. No—wait. I shall give you my arm."

The steps up to the folly were indeed slick with damp and leaves. She kicked the first two clear, then Gabriel stepped around her, smiled, and took her hand. It was large and solid, and for an instant, Antonia wished he would never let go. She felt safe, yet oddly in control when Gabriel was near. Perhaps he really was a guardian angel. With a smile playing at her lips, she considered it. No, he was just a little too wicked to be any sort of angel—and far too intriguing.

"It is always damp in this little hollow," he said, sounding perfectly natural again. "There is moss everywhere, and bizarre little toadstools. Cyril used to claim that fairies came out here at night."

"I believe they might still do," she murmured, looking about.

At the top of the stairs, she stepped up into the folly, which was open at one side but was otherwise encircled by a stone balustrade. Deep inside, a wide bench had been built into the shelter. Gabriel stripped off his riding gloves, and she did likewise. Together, they used them to sweep away the dead leaves. When the worst was gone, they sat down together. She could feel the heat and the strength almost radiate from him, though only their arms actually touched.

It was not enough. She wanted more; wanted to know him in every possible way. But it was not what he wanted. Moreover, he was too guarded; too locked up tight within himself. There was a darkness inside him which gave her pause. With a suppressed sigh, Antonia put away such thoughts and looked out across the balcony at the lake's beginning, far below.

"It is beautiful," she finally said. "We are so high up, and the hill is so steep. It is amazing they ever built this here."

"No one uses it," said Gabriel quietly. "No one ever has—save for Cyril and me, so far as I know."

"There is another folly," Antonia remarked. "A pavilion, really. It is a grand, elegant thing made of Portland stone and marble. Someone said they used to have picnics there."

Gabriel did not answer. Antonia felt something inside him shift, and she turned to look at him. His jaw was clenched, his face otherwise devoid of expression. "Yes," he finally said. "It is down that road by the orchard, about half a mile on. There is a deer park, and beautiful gardens—and a lake which is . . . very big."

"Yes, I walk there sometimes," she answered, lightly covering her hand with his. The warmth of his hand and the strong sinewy strength in his fingers when he gripped hers was comforting at first, and then a little disconcerting. "Gabriel? Did I say something wrong?"

He shook his head, but his eyes were focused far into

the distance. "It was there—in the deer park—that Cyril died," he answered. "I wonder no one has asked me about it. I have been waiting—almost wishing, really—that someone would, and just get it over with."

Antonia didn't know what to say. "I had heard . . . yes, that there was an accident."

His head swiveled about, his eyes almost accusing. "No you didn't," he said. "You heard I killed him. And I suppose that I did. But no one here ever once used the word *accident*."

Antonia let her gaze fall. "No, you are right," she admitted. "But then, the only person who ever spoke of it was . . . my late husband."

"Yes, and I'll bet he spoke of little else," said Gareth grimly. "It became, I believe, the focus of his existence."

"He was an angry, bitter man," she whispered, toying with her gloves. "But in his defense, Gabriel, I can only say that I know what it is to lose a child. It . . . it makes you mad with grief, I think."

"With grief, yes," he returned. "But did you look for someone to blame?"

"Oh, I did not have to look, Gabriel," she said hollowly. "I *knew* who was to blame. Me. Me and my awful, shrewish temper."

He shook his head. "No. No, I do not believe that was the cause of a death."

She turned a little on the stone bench and took both his hands in hers. "But I did it, Gabriel," she said. "I caused it, as surely as if I'd killed her myself. I pushed and I pushed, until . . . until the worst happened."

To her shock, he circled his fingers around her wrists and turned her hands over. "Antonia, I think *this* is the worst that could happen to anyone," he rasped. "I want to know . . . I want to know, Antonia, why you did this to yourself. To your beautiful, beautiful body. *This* is a tragedy, too. The burden you bear is a tragedy."

Antonia could not find the words. She stared at the scars, the scars she tried never to look at; thin, white curls like silvery worms drawn over her veins and tendons.

Gabriel cursed beneath his breath. "God, Antonia, I did not bring you here for this," he whispered. "This was to be a pleasant outing. Suddenly I have ruined it, asking things I did not mean to ask. But since I saw those scars, I have been—I don't know. Wounded for you. Cut up a little inside. I just . . . I just can't understand *why*."

"Why?" she echoed. "Why does it matter any more?"

"It matters," he answered, his voice hollow. "I need to understand—these scars, your life—how can you have hated yourself so much? What happened? I find myself frightened for you, Antonia. And frightened for myself."

"It was my husband, Eric," she whispered, drawing her hands away and wrapping her arms around her body. "My husband is what happened. I was . . . so *angry* with him."

"Antonia," he said quietly, "you did not harm yourself because you were angry. You are far too sensible for that."

For an instant, Antonia sat perfectly still. No one had called her *sensible* in—well, years and years. A rush of gratitude choked her for a moment. "No, no, I did not," she finally answered. "He had left us, you see, Beatrice and me, at his country house a few miles from London. I thought we had married to be together. That it was true love. I did not know—no one told me at first—that Eric had a mistress in Town."

Gabriel shut his eyes. "Oh, Antonia."

"He had kept her for many years," she pressed on. "They had *two children,* Gabriel. I never dreamt—I had thought our marriage perfect. He had wooed me and won me, and said that he loved me to distraction. But it all turned out a lie, and me a fool. We fought often over it, and because of that, he moved us to the country. Afterward, Beatrice and I saw him only once a month, perhaps. I became with child again—a desperate gesture, was it not?—but it did not help. Every time, the fights grew worse. I hated him for humiliating me, and I hated him for ignoring his daughter."

"Poor child," Gabriel whispered.

Antonia shook her head, lips pursed. "The thing is, Gabriel, in looking back, I do not think Beatrice really cared or understood," she whispered. "I think it was just me—my jealous pride. I did not mean to, but I used her. And it cost me everything."

"What happened, Antonia?" he asked. "What happened to Beatrice?"

She forced herself to look straight into Gabriel's eyes. "One afternoon Eric started back to London late," she said. "He was oddly desperate to go—to *her,* I suppose. It was overcast and drizzling. I could hear thunder in the distance. And he had his phaeton brought round, of all the idiotic things to drive. We were fighting, as we always did. Fighting about his leaving, fighting about the lateness of the hour. I accused him of leaving us for her."

"It sounds as if he was," said Gabriel quietly.

"Eric called me a shrewish cow," she whispered. "I

accused him of ignoring Beatrice, of never spending any time with her. I don't know why I said it; by then she scarcely knew him. But he looked at me, and it was as if he simply snapped. 'Fine,' he said. 'Put the chit in the damned carriage and I will take her back to London. Perhaps that will put an end to your whinging.'"

"Good Lord," murmured Gabriel.

"I was horrified, of course, and it showed," she said. "But Eric seized upon the notion like a madman. 'No!' he said to me, 'No, damn you, you wish the child to spend time with her father—then by God, let me have her!' Then he snatched her up—no coat, no hat—and drove away hell-for-leather."

"Christ, the child must have been terrified."

"No, no, Beatrice thought it a great joke," said Antonia. "And I shall never forget the look Eric shot me as he whipped up his horses. It was a look of . . . of utter *triumph*. Beatrice was with him, not me. And she was happy—screeching with joy—until they made the turn at the foot of the drive. Later they said . . . they said that the shoulder was soft from the rain. The carriage—it just went over. I saw it all. I knew—oh, God, I *knew*."

"It would have been quick, Antonia," Gabriel rasped. "She would not have suffered."

But Antonia felt almost numb now. "The servants carried the bodies back in a cart," she whispered. "It had begun to pour rain. Someone . . . someone tried to take me away, but I would not go. Blood and mud and water was everywhere. On them, on the floor. And then I looked down . . . and realized it was *my* blood. *My* water. It was like my life's blood—my child's life's blood—flowing out of me. I knew then that my temper had killed

Beatrice—and that it was going to kill the child that was coming."

"Was there . . . no chance?"

A lone tear ran down her cheek, singeing her skin. "I named him Simon," she whispered. "He was so perfect—so beautifully made. They christened him at once. They knew, you see. He lived two days. And then . . . and then I had nothing to live for."

"Oh, Antonia," he whispered. "I am so sorry."

She turned her wrists over and stared at them through a well of tears. "I do not even remember this," she said. "It was the first of many things, Gabriel, that I do not remember. I did not lie to you about that. But Nellie—she found me. In the rose garden. I had a paring knife. Father came, and took me to a place—a country house—where I could rest, he said. And he left me there."

"Dear God. For how long?"

Antonia lifted her shoulders. "Months," she said simply. "And when I came out, Papa took me to Greenfields—that's his estate—and within a few weeks, he told me he had arranged a marriage with the Duke of Warneham. That the duke was willing to have me, and that I was lucky. I did not care enough to fight. I just . . . did not care."

Gabriel set an arm about her shoulders and drew her to him. She let his warmth and comforting scent surround her, and let her eyes drop shut. "I had to know, Antonia," he said quietly. "I am so sorry for making you relive it."

"I relive it every day," she said. "But perhaps a little less? No, that is not right. A little less obsessively. It is as you once said, Gabriel. I will mourn my children every day for the rest of my life, but eventually, perhaps, not with every breath."

"I hope you can reach that point," he said, "for your sake, Antonia."

They sat quietly for a long moment, and Antonia could feel his gaze. He was measuring her. Wondering, perhaps, if he had pushed her too far. But it had been almost a relief to tell him. She was so tired—so desperately tired—of not talking. Not feeling. It was as if she had turned herself off and was only now reawakening—to pain, yes, but perhaps to some of life's joy, too. The warmth of the sun. The sound of the fountains in the garden. The small pleasure of deciding what to wear each day.

And then there was the physical pleasure which Gareth had given her, which was not just reawakening but healing. The comfort of his voice and his touch, and the reassurance of his sheer strength and broad shoulders—things which shouldn't have mattered but strangely did. She was falling; falling fast and hard again. She was waking up, coming back to life, and she could not seem to stop. She was not even sure she *wanted* to stop.

"Have you never been in love, Gabriel?" she asked softly.

He surprised her, answering without hesitation. "Yes, once," he answered. "Passionately so, I thought. But it did not end well."

She laughed a little bitterly. "The passionate ones never do," she said. "I think it is better to fall in love slowly."

He had leaned back into the bench and propped his booted feet upon the stone ledge. "Is that what happened with you and Eric?" he asked, crossing his boots at the ankle. "Was it love at first sight?"

She hesitated. "It is pathetically embarrassing. Must I say?"

"I wish you would," he said quietly.

Antonia drew a deep breath. "He was at Cambridge with James, my brother," she said. "I had known him forever, I think, and had been infatuated with him for just as long. And when I came out, he danced attendance on me. It was like a fairy tale. Then he offered for me—and like the child I was, I really believed I was going to get my happy-ever-after."

"I am sorry you did not, Antonia."

"Don't be," she answered. "I mourn my children, not my husband."

The branches beyond the folly clattered, and a pair of squirrels came racing down the tree. For a long while, she watched them leap and chase one another, all the while wondering if Gabriel was secretly laughing at her girlhood fantasies.

When he said nothing, she turned to him. "What about you, Gabriel? You give the impression of a man whose heart has been broken."

He had tipped his hat down as if he might be drowsing, but he was not. She knew him too well now to be fooled. Finally, he spoke. "I suppose I wanted a fairy tale, too," he said. "But of a different sort. I fell in love with Rothewell's sister."

"Oh," she said sharply. "Your business partner?"

He tipped his hat back up. "You have been paying attention," he said.

Antonia blushed and looked away. "What is her name?"

"Xanthia Neville," he said. "Or Zee, we often call her. Now, of course, she is the Marchioness of Nash."

There was a wistfulness and an affection in Gabriel's voice which was unmistakable. "Zee," she echoed. "It sounds so . . . so light. So pretty and carefree. Is she?"

"Pretty?" said Gabriel. "Yes, she is very beautiful—in an uncommon way. But carefree? No, Xanthia is all business."

"She is married now, you said," she said. "Was that the end of it?"

He scrubbed a hand around his lean jaw, which showed just a hint of shadow. "No, we ended it many years ago," he said pensively. "Zee was not interested in marriage—not to me, at any rate."

"Did you ask her?"

"It was understood," he said a little irritably. "We had . . . things had . . . happened. It was assumed by her brother that we would marry. Yes, I offered for her—often enough to humiliate myself."

"I am sorry," she said. "Were you in love with her for a long time?"

Antonia was surprised when he hesitated. "I have been thinking about that a great deal of late," he confessed. "I have been trying to figure out when and how it started."

"You don't know?"

"Not precisely," he confessed. "You see, her eldest brother hired me into the shipping business—as an errand boy, really. It was a small concern then, just three or four ships, if you can imagine. And it was there I met Zee. We were close to the same age, and I just . . . I just envied her life so much."

"What do you mean?"

"I wanted what she had," he said. "I wanted the security of a family. Zee had two elder brothers at that time, Luke, for whom I worked, and Rothewell, who ran the sugar plantations. They loved her unconditionally and protected her fiercely. I just . . . wanted that. And when I grew older and found myself attracted to her, I believed . . . I *think* what I believed, deep down, was that if we married, then . . . then I would be a part of them. I would be—well, the fourth Neville. They could never turn their backs on me."

"Oh, Gabriel," she murmured. "Did you fear they would?"

"I was just the hired help," he said grimly. "How did I know what they might do? I had learnt to trust no one. I was an orphan they'd taken on charity, without a penny to my name and scarcely a rag to my back. Luke died not too many years after that, so it was just Xanthia, Rothewell, and me. I was afraid of losing them, Antonia."

"I see," she answered. "I think I can understand how you might fear that."

Suddenly, Gabriel laughed and set his fingertips to his temple. "Good God, I cannot believe we are having this discussion," he said. "I asked you one simple question . . . and now I feel like I'm telling you the pathetic story of my life."

"The question you asked me was not simple," said Antonia quietly. "And I should like . . . I should like to hear the pathetic story of your life. Indeed, we have been circling round it for days now."

He looked at her strangely. "I don't know what you mean."

She shook her head. "Do not lie to me, Gabriel," she said. "I know unfailingly when a man is lying to me. It is a skill I learnt in a very hard school."

When he said nothing but merely set his jaw in that hard line which was becoming so familiar to her, Antonia spoke again. "You hold yourself at a distance from me," she said. "From everyone, really. I think . . . I think something very bad happened to you, Gabriel."

He looked away. "It was a bad life," he said. "For a time."

Antonia set her head to one side. "I watch you, you know, with your friend Rothewell. You do the same thing with him—hold yourself at a distance, I mean. And it makes me wonder, Gabriel, if you really have anyone to trust."

The jaw unclenched a fraction as he seemed to ponder it. "I trust myself," he finally said. "And in some ways, yes, I trust Rothewell and Xanthia."

She wished, inexplicably, that he would say he trusted *her*. But he did not. And why should he? She was not precisely stable or clear-thinking. And never—not even when she'd been well and whole—had she been the sort of capable, cool-headed woman this Xanthia Neville sounded. Antonia felt pathetically wanting in comparison. Perhaps she now understood the meaning of Gareth's three little words—*"just this once."* His heart had already been given.

"What was your life like at Knollwood, Gabriel?" she asked, deliberately changing the subject. "Was it a misery? Was Cyril really so terrible to you?"

He looked at her in mute amazement. "Cyril?" he finally said. "Terrible? What a strange thing to say. He was a boy, not much younger than myself. He was too innocent to be thought terrible by anyone."

Antonia was confused again. "You did not envy him? You did not feel less than him?"

Gabriel shook his head. "I liked Cyril a great deal," he said. "He was the only playmate I ever really had."

"Did you play together often?" Antonia was surprised.

Gareth gave a crooked smile. "More than his parents wished, I am sure," he said. "It was never their intent we should be playmates. But Cyril was lonely, too. He was . . . just a boy, like me. Mischievous, sometimes. Even a little petty, as all children are."

"But you were older, were you not?"

"By a few months."

Antonia considered it for a moment. This was very different than the impression her late husband had given. "And you were not . . . you were not in the Royal Navy, either, were you?"

His incredulity was obviously growing. "Antonia, what are you talking about?"

She swallowed hard. "When—after—Cyril died, Warneham did not send you into the navy? That, you see, was what he said. That he had taken you to Portsmouth, because he couldn't bear the sight of you. That you were to become a midshipman."

"No," said Gabriel calmly. "No, Antonia. Warneham hauled me down to Portsmouth and gave me to a press gang. There is a vast deal of difference in the two."

She recoiled in horror. "A press gang? Good God. How old were you?"

"I was twelve," he said. "And barely that. Even the

British Navy won't stoop so low as to impress a twelve-year-old boy. They aren't even supposed to take a grown man if he has no experience at sea."

"So there was no chance of your ever being an officer? . . ."

His face suddenly blazed with anger. "Damn it, Antonia, *listen* to me," he said, carefully enunciating each word. "I don't know what cock-and-bull story Warneham told people about my disappearance, but the truth is this: He threw my grandmother out of Knollwood, snatched me from her, hauled me down to Portsmouth, and made it damn good and clear to the press gang that no one—*no one*—was apt ever to come looking for me. He did not place me in officer's training. He told them to *get rid of me,* and he gave them a fifty-pound bribe to seal the bargain. He wanted me dead—he just didn't have the guts to do it himself."

Antonia pressed her fingertips to her lips. She wanted, suddenly, to cry. "But . . . but that is unconscionable!"

"Antonia, gently bred boys do not just become midshipmen in the Royal Navy," he said. "One's family must petition for an admission. It takes connections. And if you do not have them—if no one of at least *some* importance will vouch for you—it simply won't happen. If Warneham let himself believe I somehow landed in that sort of clover, then he was simply assuaging his own guilt."

"I—I begin to wonder what he did believe," she said. "So . . . what happened to you if the navy would not take you?"

"The press gang traded me for a barrel of port."

"*Traded* you?"

"Yes, to a turncoat merchant ship out of Marseilles—if you could call it that. In truth, they were but one step removed from plain pirates—and traitorous ones, at that."

"My God!" Antonia looked stricken. "Do you think Warneham could have known that would happen?"

Gareth was bloody well sure he had known, but he said nothing. Instead he merely set one boot heel against the stone ledge and bit his tongue.

"What did you do?" asked Antonia. "Were you frightened?"

"Only of the water, at first," he said. "Just walking along the docks made my stomach churn. But the people? No, I just wanted my grandmother. I was too naïve to be frightened. I kept telling the ship's captain who I was, who my father had been, that there had just been a misunderstanding. He found it uproarious. My earnest pleadings kept the crew entertained all the way to Guernsey."

"How . . . how did you survive?"

"I did whatever I had to do to survive," he said grimly. "By the time we'd sailed around the tip of Brittany, I had learnt to keep my mouth shut and do whatever I was told. I was twelve years old, and I was terrified."

"Did . . . did they hold you captive?"

"In the middle of the ocean?" He looked at her oddly. "I was made to work, Antonia. They were traitors. Algerian corsairs. Sicilian pirates. The dregs of Europe, for the most part—and the lot of them traveling under a forged letter of marque from the British government. They would cheerfully slaughter their own brothers, and I was their slave. A cabin boy. Do you have any idea what that means?"

She shook her head. "You had to . . . to do their chores?"

And then some, he wanted to say.

But if he had been gently bred, Antonia had been utterly cocooned. She could not begin to comprehend what his life on the *Saint-Nazaire* had been like—and he did not want her to. Antonia had suffered enough of her own horror. And he could not suffer the utter humiliation of describing his. He could not bear to relive that sickening sense of powerlessness.

Antonia had lost a little of her newly won color. "Gabriel, w-where did they take you?"

"America had just declared war on England," he said grimly. "It was expected to be a bloodbath—and privateers were prowling the Caribbean like sharks in the water. There was business aplenty for anyone with the stomach for it."

"How long were you with these . . . these pirates?" she asked, her voice a little thready. "How did you escape?"

"I sailed with them for well over a year," he said. "I thought about trying to escape every time we made port, but oftentimes, the places were foreign and frightening to me, and I could not understand the language. I had no money. At least on the *Saint-Nazaire* I had food and shelter—if one could call it that." He realized his voice had dropped to a whisper, and he sharply cleared his throat. "When you are held in someone's power like that—well, after a while you . . . you get confused as to precisely who your enemy is. Everyone around you looks rough and dangerous. And sometimes . . . sometimes you just choose the devil you know. Does that make any sense?"

"None of this makes any sense," Antonia whispered.

"None of it. You were twelve years old. I can't think how you survived."

"Ultimately, I made a run for it," he said. "We came into Bridgetown on a brilliant, beautiful day, and I saw that Union Jack snapping in the breeze, and I knew—I just *knew* it was my chance. Likely the only one I would ever get. And by then, my captors had become a little lax. They knew as well as I did that my options were few. I bolted the first clear chance I got. Unfortunately, someone raised the alarm."

"They went after you?" she said. "Could they do that on British soil?"

Gareth laughed bitterly. "They didn't give a damn whose soil it was," he said. "You're bloody well right they chased me—and caught me by the shirt collar twice. Then I had the good fortune to run smack into Luke Neville coming out of a back-alley tavern, and that was the end of it. He believed me. He . . . he saved me. I know it sounds melodramatic, but he literally saved my worthless hide."

"And then you went to work for him?" she asked. "You were twelve years old, and you had to work for your living. What was that like?"

"I was thirteen by then," he said.

"Oh, well, that made it perfectly acceptable," she murmured.

He forced himself to smile. "Antonia, I was glad to work—daylight to dusk, if need be. I learnt everything I know from Luke Neville. Besides, my grandfather had raised me to believe I would go into some sort of profession one day. He never wished me to think of myself as an aristocrat. He felt that the expectation of a gentleman's life too easily instilled a lack of character—and in hindsight, I feel he was right. He was ruined, you see, by a group of so-called gentlemen who borrowed vast sums from him, then chose to flee the country rather than do the honorable thing. There was nothing honorable about them."

"Heavens," Antonia murmured. "That is a little blunt."

He looked at her sympathetically. "I apologize if it sounded harsh," he said. "I'm afraid, Antonia, that the—the quiet comfort of having you near entices me to speak more freely than I ought. I am sure you were brought up quite differently."

Antonia looked still faintly uncomfortable, and pensive, too. Gareth said no more. The conclusions were hers to draw, but from what he had heard so far, both her father and brother sounded spoilt and self-indulgent to him.

Gareth looked up at the easterly sky. Gray-blue clouds were indeed beginning to gather, unthreatening still. But Statton, it appeared, had not been wrong in his predictions. He dropped his boot from the balustrade and picked up his riding gloves. "I daresay we'd best go on up to Knollwood if we are going," he mused. "I think we might get rain later."

She set one small, warm hand on his knee. "We need not go," she said. "Not unless you require my opinion on something. I know how you dislike the place."

His gaze fell to her hand. "Antonia, I—" Gareth stopped and measured his words. "I just want it to be perfect for you. I just want—"

But he could say no more, for he scarcely knew what he wanted. He wanted her—yes. And on some level,

Antonia wanted him. But there had been so much water under the bridge for both of them. So many old hurts and slights. His snide remark about aristocrats, for example, showed his own prejudices in very stark relief. Doubtless her fine old aristocratic family had a few prejudices of their own. They would not welcome the grandson of a Jewish money lender into their blue-blooded dynasty—particularly if they knew what the rest of his life had been like—even if Antonia wanted him.

And was Antonia even capable of making clear-thought choices just now? She had spent the whole of her adult life, since the age of seventeen, in either an unhappy marriage or the moral equivalent of Bedlam. She had been allowed not even the slightest measure of independence, nor any opportunity to make her own decisions. If she was free to live her own life—if this horrid gossip about her dead husband was laid to rest—and she had the wherewithal and the confidence to travel, to socialize, to do whatever she pleased wherever and however she pleased, well, why on earth would she still want him? Other than for the sex, of course. When he was good for nothing else, there was always sex.

Abruptly, he rose and offered down his hand. "They are running the water pipes from the new spring box up to the kitchen," he said. "Perhaps they can pipe some water upstairs as well. We should go and have a look, don't you think?"

Her gaze had grown distant. She put her hand in his. "Yes, thank you," she said mechanically. "Let us go, by all means."

Chapter Thirteen

*T*he Red Indians sat cross-legged inside the folly, sharpening their arrows and awaiting the American onslaught. Tall Feather notched the ends of his sapling branch, bowed it, and looked at it in satisfaction. "That's a good one," he said. "Hey, Cyril, give me the twine."

Cyril scowled up from his whittling. "You're supposed to say Growling Bear," he reminded Gabriel, "or it doesn't count."

"Just give me the twine," said Gabriel a little irritably. "I'm going to string my bow."

Cyril bent forward with the twine, then winced. "Wait," he said, springing up. "I've got to piss."

"Me, too," said Gabriel, following him to the edge of the folly. "But Mr. Needles says you should say 'make water' instead of piss."

"Poo, that's for children!" said Cyril derisively, hitching loose his trousers. "I've got to piss."

"Here, let's aim for that tree," Gabriel suggested. Together, they gave it a royal drenching.

"I won," said Cyril, shaking himself off.

"Did not!" said Gabriel. "If anything, we tied."

"Wait," said Cyril, peering down at Gabriel's trousers. "Take it back out."

Gabriel looked at him strangely. "Take what back out?"

"Your penis, ijit," said Cyril, whipping his from his drawers. "Here, I'll show you mine."

"Well, all right, then." Reluctantly, Gabriel obliged him.

Cyril bent down as if to study it. "It looks just like mine," he said, frowning. "Maybe longer."

"Well, of course it looks like yours," said Gabriel. "Cyril, you're the ijit. All penises are the very same."

"No, they aren't." Cyril straightened up and tucked himself back inside his drawers. "I heard the housemaids talking. Maisie said if you're a Jew, you have to cut it off."

"Eeewww!" said Gabriel. "Cyril, that's horrid!"

Cyril grinned and slapped him in the back of the head. "Well, you're all right—probably 'cause you're a half-breed," he teased. "Hey—I know—maybe we should change your Red Indian name from Tall Feather to Tall Cock!"

Coggins greeted Gareth on Selsdon's top step immediately upon his return from Knollwood. The dark clouds seemed to have intensified, both on the horizon and over the house itself, it seemed, for the butler's face was a little fretful, and his hands were laid neatly over one another, as if he was resisting the urge to wring them.

Curious, Gareth passed his reins over to Statton, who had returned for the horses, then lifted Antonia from the saddle.

"The post came early," said the butler as they ascended the stairs.

Gareth glanced at Antonia. "Not bad news, I hope?"

The butler made an equivocal gesture with his hand. "Well, I *think* not," he said. "But Mr. Kemble seemed to have a great many letters from London. He opened one of them in some haste, then said he must go at once to West Widding."

"West Widding?"

"Yes, Your Grace," said Coggins a little irritably. "And I am afraid . . . well, I am afraid he took your gig, sir."

"Well, it's not as if I have ever used it," said Gareth. "Besides, I instructed him to go. There was some particular business I wished him to take care of, and I daresay there was no other way to get there?"

Coggins looked relieved. "Not easily, sir," he answered. "It's five miles away."

Just then, Dr. Osborne came down one of the staircases. "There you are, Your Grace," he said upon seeing the duchess. "I am so glad you caught me."

Antonia hastened toward him. "Oh, heavens, have you been here all this time, Doctor?" she asked breathlessly.

"No, no, I had to return to the village for more medications," he said. "I've just this instant come back."

"How is she, Dr. Osborne?" asked Antonia anxiously. "How is my poor Nellie?"

Osborne smiled down at the duchess. "She is resting comfortably," he reassured her. "I have given both her and Jane a little something to keep the cough at bay and to help them sleep quite soundly. In a few days, they should both be well on the mend."

"Thank you, Osborne," said Gareth, stepping forward. "How are our patients in the stables?"

The doctor's gaze swiveled toward him, as if he was just now noticing Gareth's presence. "Oh, good afternoon, Your Grace," he replied. "They are much improved, thank God. Now if we can just keep everyone else well?"

After a few more polite exchanges, Antonia excused herself and went up the stairs to sit with her maid. Osborne stood beside Gareth, watching her go.

"She is a lovely creature, is she not?" said the doctor.

"Yes," said Gareth quietly. "A lovely creature indeed."

Nestled between the river and the forest, the village of West Widding was a pretty little gem, save for the eyesore of a massive brick workhouse which sat along the water's edge. The parish boasted an inn, two public houses, a justice of the peace, and a small medieval church whose bell tower had collapsed during the Lord Protector's reign and had never been rebuilt. It was the third of these boasts, however, which most concerned George Kemble.

He drove past the squat, towerless church, turned left at the second public house, and, at the end of the narrow lane, found what he sought. The home of John Laudrey was a wide, hideously modern cottage made of brick, and standing in gardens so new they looked over-pruned and shrunken. A maid in a gray serge dress opened the door and let her eyes sweep down his attire. He easily passed her examination. She showed him into a parlor at the back of the house.

When Laudrey entered, he at once struck Kemble as being overly self-important and moderately intelligent— always a dangerous combination. He was a large, bristle-haired man whose shoulders looked about to burst from his coat seams. The justice opened the letter which de

Vendenheim had sent down from London, a remarkable shade of red burning slowly down his cheeks as he read, until he looked rather like a boil about to rupture.

"Well!" he said. "It is always helpful to have the Home Office step into our business after we've done with it."

Kemble smiled and seated himself without being asked. "I rather suspect Mr. Peel views murder as being very much the Home Office's business," he said tartly. "Particularly when it has gone unresolved for some months."

"Oh, a murder now, is it?" Laudrey thrust the letter at Kemble and sat down. "No one wanted to hear of *that* last year when the deed was done."

"Well, it certainly was a questionable death." Kemble folded his hands neatly over one knee. "And the new duke has ordered me to get to the bottom of it. He hopes a second set of eyes will help." It was not a request, so Kemble barged on. "I'm told you were called to the ducal estate by the local constable on the morning of Warneham's death. You examined the body, found signs consistent with potassium nitrate poisoning, and interviewed the doctor, who ventured an opinion that the duke had used too much of his asthma medication. Do I have that right?"

"If you know all that, why must I be bothered?" asked the justice.

"Right, then, thank you," said Kemble. "Warneham—the new duke—tells me that you and the doctor disagreed as to whether it was a case of murder or an overdose. An inquest was held, and the doctor's opinion prevailed?"

"Yes."

Kemble considered it a moment. "May I ask, Mr.

Laudrey, whether or not you interviewed the two gentlemen who were houseguests at Selsdon that evening—Sir Harold Hardell and Lord Litting?"

"I tried," Laudrey admitted. "But they had left at dawn unaware of the duke's demise—or so they claimed. Afterward, it being a suspicious death, I went up to London to talk to the gentlemen, but I got naught from them except for the fact that there had been a good deal of smoking going on in the billiard room that evening."

"Yes, so I heard," murmured Kemble. "Let me ask, Mr. Laudrey, if there was anything else which made you suspicious about the late duke's death?"

Laudrey shifted uncomfortably. "The London gentlemen were hiding something, I thought," he said quietly. "The upper classes will go to a great deal of trouble, you know, to avoid even the breath of scandal touching them, even if it means a death must go unanswered for."

"Perfectly true!" said Kemble. "And you are thinking, are you not, of the duchess? It's quite all right. The gossip is still going round Lower Addington."

"Everyone knows she was married against her wishes," said the justice. "And while it mighn't be common knowledge up so far as London, it did not take a doctor to see that the lady was not wholly in her right mind."

Kemble imagined that seeing one's husband lying dead on his bedroom floor would unsettle even the hardest of nerves, but he said nothing. Instead, he leaned forward in his chair. "Do you know what caught my attention, Mr. Laudrey?" he asked. "The fact that in ten years, there have been at least three premature deaths in that house. And I am not going back so far as to count the first duchess. What killed her, by the way?"

"A broken heart, they say, over the little boy that died," Laudrey admitted, then his voice flattened. "But the fellow who did the postmortem said it was just an infectious appendix which ruptured and poisoned the poor lady."

"Ah," said Kemble. "Well, that is fairly cut-and-dried, is it not?"

Laudrey reluctantly admitted that it was.

"And the second duchess," Kemble murmured. "Yet another tragedy! Do you recall what happened to her?"

The justice looked at him a little disparagingly. "I daresay you know already. The young lady took a bit of a spill whilst hunting."

"A bit of a spill?" Kemble had never heard it characterized quite so benignly. "Do we know how this spill occurred?"

"Mrs. Osborne said her horse shied at a fence," he said. "The poor lady was beside herself, for she was in the lead. She felt, I think, that she'd led the girl into something which was beyond her skill."

"Yes, the second duchess had a good bit of cheek, I'm told," said Kemble. "Was she not a good rider?"

"She had been raised in Town, as I understand it," answered Laudrey. "Riding to hounds in the countryside is a different kettle of fish."

"Just so," said Kemble. "And it was such a tragedy that the child was lost."

"Well, that part was never clear to me," said Laudrey. "But then, I'm not a doctor. In fact, I was not involved in the matter at all, as it was considered a natural death."

The hair on the back of Kemble's neck suddenly rose. "I beg your pardon?"

Laudrey opened his hands expansively. "The child, as I understand it, was not lost until some days later," he answered. "The young lady was abed mending her bruises, then the tragedy occurred. Afterward, she took a fever—something to do with female things not happening as they ought—and *that* was what killed her."

It was an interesting but subtle difference. "A fascinating story, Mr. Laudrey," said Kemble. "Who did the postmortem? Osborne?"

"No, no," said Laudrey. "He had not come down from Oxford. It was probably Dr. Frith here in Widding, but he is dead now."

"Was he any good?"

Laudrey nodded appreciatively. "Very good indeed."

Kemble looked at Laudrey a little coyly. "And is Osborne any good?"

Laudrey hesitated. "Osborne is a fine physician too," he said. "But perhaps more beholden to opinion than to science."

Kemble looked at the man with a new appreciation. "You mean Osborne is more apt to find what the family wishes to find, do you not?"

"I didn't say that," Laudrey answered. "But he obviously catered to Warneham's whims and fancies. I never saw such a lot of powders and pills and unguents in my life."

Having seen the bulging box of medications, Kemble did not disagree. "What was she like, the second duchess?"

Laudrey shook his head. "Too far above my social circle," he said. "I never heard any ill spoken of her. She was very young, and doted on a bit by the village ladies."

"Which ones, specifically?" asked Kemble.

Laudrey considered it. "Well, there was the rector's wife."

"Mrs. Hamm?"

Laudrey slowly shook his head. "I believe this was in the time of the previous rector," he said. "The name escapes me. And then there was Mrs. Osborne. And Lady Ingham—her husband had just bought North End Farm, and she is a bit—well, pardon my saying—"

"Yes, a social climber," Kemble added ruefully. "I had noticed."

Laudrey seemed to relax in his chair.

"Tell me, Mr. Laudrey," he said, "since you seem a man of sense. What was the duke's third wife like?"

Laudrey pulled a sad face. "Oh, a quiet girl, and terribly nervous. She simply was not up to the duties of a duchess, I never thought."

"Oh, dear," said Kemble. "It sounds tragic already."

"It was, rather," said Laudrey pensively. "She was the eldest daughter of Lord Orleston, whose seat was just to the south of here. His younger girls had married, but Lady Helen was not a beauty, and it was said she preferred church work and gardening to marriage."

"Why did she marry, then?"

"Well, Warneham offered for her—because she was convenient, I always thought," Laudrey said, shrugging his big shoulders again. "And like the duke, Lord Orleston hadn't a son, so all he possessed was to pass to a nephew. I daresay he wished to be sure the girl had a home of her own when he was gone—which he is now. But then, she is too, isn't she, poor girl?"

"She became overly fond of her laudanum tonic, it sounded," said Kemble.

Laudrey's eyes narrowed. "Doctors nowadays are bit

quick with the laudanum, I'd say," he answered. "And all the other things in those tonics."

"What do you mean?" asked Kemble. "What, precisely, was she taking?"

Laudrey shrugged. "I cannot recall," he admitted. "Just the usual hodgepodge of opiates, herbs, and sedatives which ought just as well be dispensed off the back of a Gypsy's cart, if you ask me. And nearly any apothecary will sell you laudanum. Peddle it like gin, they do."

"Heavens," said Kemble. "Do you think the duchess was addicted?"

Laudrey shook his head. "Who's to say?" he answered. "A hundred babes a month die up in Middlesex parish alone from ingesting too much black drop—no one really admits that, of course. But that's what it is. Soothe your troubles—or someone else's—with a touch of opiate."

Kemble looked at him curiously. "What, precisely, are you saying, Mr. Laudrey? Was Dr. Osborne overprescribing his tonics?"

"No more so than any of his kind," the justice admitted. "We took an account of his medicine chest, of course. A bottle of tincture of opium was found to be missing, but then his mother remembered knocking something off the windowsill and breaking it as she watered her violets. She never bothered to see what it was. Frankly, I find this every time I have call to go through a doctor's chemicals and records. They leave things sitting around their clinic, they keep shoddy notes."

Kemble tried to turn the subject back to the dead duchess. "Could this young lady have suffered from melancholia?"

Laudrey nodded a little sadly. "Everyone later said she was downcast over her childlessness—and they were married a good many years. The duke was terribly disappointed by it. I am sure she knew it, too. Frankly, the lady looked outright sick to me when last I saw her."

"Sick as in how?" asked Kemble.

The justice looked uncomfortable. "I hardly know," he admitted. "I wondered if she was eating, to be honest. But she never struck me as a suicide. She was too devout. But what good would my pressing forward with an inquiry have done?"

"I understand," Kemble murmured. "One would not wish to inconvenience the duke in any way when his barren wife had so conveniently obliged him by dying."

Ire flashed in Laudrey's eyes. "Now you may wait just a moment, sir!" he countered. "I do my job—insomuch as I am able. I thought the death ought to have been looked into, and I told the duke so."

"Did you indeed?"

"Most certainly!" Laudrey narrowed his gaze. "But the duke said he didn't want the gossip, and he threatened my job if I pursued it. I got the impression that since the girl was of no more use to him, he wished her buried, literally and figuratively. I thought it chilling, myself."

Kemble was beginning to agree with him.

"And that is one reason I have not bestirred myself too thoroughly over *his* death, if you must know," Laudrey went on. "Perhaps the duchess did do him in. But I wonder if perhaps he simply got what was coming to him?"

Kemble smiled thinly and rose. "Perhaps he did, Mr. Laudrey," he said pensively. "Perhaps he did at that."

Laudrey, too, got up from his chair. "Well, there you have it, sir. That's the whole of what I know." ·

Kemble bowed stiffly. "Thank you, Mr. Laudrey," he said. "The new duke is most grateful for your kind assistance."

Late that evening, Mr. Statton's weather prediction came true in a flash of light and a low, distant rumble from the sky. Unable to sleep, Gareth lay in bed to the sound of the rain, this time a steady downpour instead of lashing, wind-driven sheets. Good Lord, they scarcely needed more rain, he considered, as the time for harvest neared.

Unaccountably restless, Gareth got out of bed, put on his dressing gown, and lit a lamp by his reading chair. He picked up one of Watson's agricultural magazines and flipped randomly through it. Some of it actually made sense to him now. He was gaining his sea legs, he thought, where this business of growing things was concerned.

While he had not wanted to return to Selsdon—and still had not faced a great many of his demons—Gareth was beginning to appreciate the importance of the place. He had meant his stay here to be but a short one, but now he was not so sure. The estate needed a great deal of oversight, and Gareth was beginning to feel pride in his ability to comprehend and to make good decisions. Pride in Selsdon itself. The work was not as tangible, perhaps, as sending ships and commodities flying around the world, but managing a large estate, he had discovered, was not so very different from managing a large shipping company.

Mr. Watson seemed surprised at Gareth's hands-on

approach and his easy grasp of the accounting. Warneham had done no more than plow in enough cash to keep crops in the ground and the income stream flowing. Long-term improvements such as Knollwood had been let go for decades save for the threshing machine, which Watson had pressed for. Gareth felt a growing eagerness to see just what could be done when the place was treated as the piece of real business capital it was.

Despite all this eagerness, however, Watson's agricultural magazine could not hold Gareth's interest. His mind was elsewhere, really. It was still on the path to Knollwood, in the little folly by the pond. In talking with Antonia today, it had frightened him a little, the rage he still held inside. The seething resentment toward Warneham. A part of his youth had been stripped from him— and his grandmother's life quite likely shortened—by a selfish, vindictive man. A man who had then spinelessly lied to his friends and his family about the truth of what he had done.

Even now, if he closed his eyes, the sound of the rain could take him back to his life aboard ship. He could still smell the filth, the heat and stench of leering, unwashed sailors. He remembered what it had been like to go hungry, and to gratefully eat food so rancid and worm-riddled that it had not been fit for human consumption. He remembered storms so vile they could make a man pray for a painless death. He remembered weeping like the child he had been with longing for his grandmother, and his old life in London. A life among people he had trusted and understood. Had his grandfather lived, Gareth would likely have been a prosperous merchant or a goldsmith by now. Perhaps even a money lender. All, even the latter, were honorable professions so far as Gareth was concerned.

As if driven by Gareth's thoughts, another low rumble passed over the house, this one very near. Unable to stop himself, he went to the window and looked out over the curtain wall. Just to make sure. He did not have to wait long for the next flash of lightning. This time, his eyes were quick. This time, he knew just what—and who— to look for. The rampart was empty, thank God.

But that did not necessarily mean that Antonia was not frightened, did it? He did not know her habits. Perhaps even as he stood here with his hand pressed to the cold glass, she was wandering the house, trapped in that dreamlike state between wakefulness and sleep, grieving for her children. And tonight there would be no Mrs. Waters to depend upon—she was likely lying in her bed upstairs with her throat wrapped in flannel and her cough soothed by some of Osborne's infamous laudanum.

Gareth left the window and paced across the room, one hand on his hip. He had to restrain himself from giving in to the impulse to go to her. It was not his place to do so, was it? They were becoming too close. A friendship—no, much more than that—had sprung up between them, two lost and damaged souls. It might be all too easy for Antonia to come to lean on him, to depend on him, when what she should be doing was moving in the opposite direction. Away from Selsdon, and all the whispers and memories. Sometimes he wondered if even Knollwood would be far enough.

Suddenly thunder sounded again, this time loud enough to rattle the windows. As before, Gareth was out the door and halfway down the corridor before he realized what he intended. But by the time he reached the turn which would take him to the ducal apartments, there was no chance of his forcing himself to turn back. He plunged ahead heedlessly, as he had done from the very first. Antonia was alone, and if she was awake, quite likely terrified. Gareth went in through the sitting room, which was shrouded in darkness. Gingerly he made his way to her bedchamber door, then hesitated. Should he knock so that she might put on a robe? Or simply slip in, in the hope that she slept soundly? It was not as if they hadn't already seen one another in a state of undress.

He pushed open the door to see that in the depths of the room, a lone candle burned. Antonia stood by the window, draperies thrown wide, her arms crossed tight over her chest. Her shoulders were bent, as if she wished to somehow draw inside herself, and her feet were bare. Her long hair hung in heavy waves to her waist, making her look like a wraith in the gloom—an agonizingly beautiful figment of his imagination.

He whispered her name, and she turned at once. Her face was contorted into a mask of grief, but when she saw him, her gaze softened until her eyes were but limpid pools. "Gabriel," she whispered, darting straight into his arms. "Gabriel. My angel."

He pulled her hard against his chest and drew a deep, steadying breath. And suddenly he wondered precisely who was comforting whom. Antonia felt so small and so right against his chest. So reassuring and so . . . innocent. It was as if his worry for her was transcended by his need for her—a need which ran deeper than the sensual and was more insidious than ordinary lust. But perhaps he simply needed her to need him. Perhaps when she no longer did so, when she was well and strong again, she would be able to use him for whatever she needed and move on, as so many others had done.

He should have set her away once the moment had passed; should have murmured something blandly reassuring in her ear. But instead, he buried his face in her hair. "Antonia," he whispered. "Antonia, I was worried. The storm . . ."

She trembled a little in his arms. "Gabriel, I feel so foolish," she answered. "Why must I be this way? It's just rain—and this is England, after all. It is not apt to quit, is it? I just want to be normal again."

"I think perhaps you are normal, Antonia," he whispered. "Besides, what would be the alternative? To feel less? To love less? Would you rather have a life half lived?"

She shook her head, her hair scrubbing against his dressing gown. "No," she said, her voice a little tremulous. "No, I wouldn't. I never thought of it like that."

"I think, Antonia, that when you love someone, you love deeply and immeasurably," he said quietly. "But even the deepest of affections cannot save us from losing what we love. And then we must go on. That is what you are doing. You are going on. You are coping the best way you know how. Don't be harsh with yourself, my dear, for the world is harsh enough as it is."

She looked up at him then with a tremulous smile. "Thank you for that," she said. "You are a man of great common sense, I think. I—I honestly don't know what I would have done without you these past weeks."

Gareth tucked a strand of hair behind her ear and felt his chest go tight with the aching need to protect her. He had just slipped another inch down that black, bottomless well of unrequited love. *Falling in love.* It was an apt description of the awful thing which was happening to him. Antonia needed a friend, not a lover. Not another set of expectations which might crush her just as she was beginning, perhaps, to find herself again.

But he continued drawing his fingers down through her hair. "Have you not slept at all?"

She shook her head. "No, I was unable—well, actually *afraid*—to go to sleep once I heard the thunder. Tonight I cannot depend on poor Nellie to come fish me out of the fountain or drag me down off the roof, can I?"

He led her with one hand to the bed, where the covers were already thrown back and the pillows were in disarray. "Here," he said, laying his dressing gown aside, "I shall lie down with you until the storm has passed."

She looked at him hesitantly. "Please don't do anything for me that you will later regret," she said. "I know how you feel about me, Gareth. You feel a duty—"

"Shh," he said, pulling her nearer. "Don't talk—isn't that what you always say? Don't talk. Don't think."

"But we won't just lie down, will we?" she said softly, as if reading his mind. "I will beg you for more. And you will give in to me."

Gareth knew she was right, and he hadn't the strength to simply walk out of the room—the room which smelled of gardenias and of temptation. Of *her.* "Do you want me to make love to you, Antonia?" he rasped. "Is that what will help you forget?"

Her tongue came out to lightly touch the corner of her mouth. "Yes," she said swiftly. "You have a gift for it, I think."

"God, Antonia," he whispered. "I have a gift for making a muddle of things, too."

But he kissed her, long and deep, cradling her face delicately between his hands as his tongue plumbed the sweet depths of her mouth. In response, Antonia moaned and opened fully, twining her tongue silkily with his and rising onto her tiptoes.

Gareth plunged his fingers into her hair, stroking over her temples. He told himself he had meant only to comfort her, but he knew in his heart it was a lie. He could feel Antonia's breathing ratcheting up and his groin pooling with heat and blood. As if emboldened, Antonia delved into his mouth with her tongue, and to his shock, he shivered like an eager stallion. This was wrong. It was another step in the direction neither of them should take. But Antonia pressed her lithe, warm body fully against his, and Gareth gave in. The mess could be sorted out tomorrow. Or another day. This day—this *night*—was for loving her.

He drew her higher against him and kept kissing her. Antonia's hands slid up his back as her tongue teased at his, sending another wave of lust shuddering through him. He wanted her so desperately. And she wanted him—for the pleasure and the comfort he could give her, of course. It was nothing more.

Deliberately, he set his hands on her waist and lifted her against the straining weight of his erection. He wanted her to know what he felt; what she did to him. Perhaps he hoped to warn her off. It did not work.

Antonia lifted her lips from his. "Take me to bed, Gabriel," she pleaded.

He followed her onto the mattress, then drew her

firmly against him so that she lay with her back against his chest. After wrapping both arms firmly about her, he set his lips to the back of her head. "There," he said. "You see? The storm cannot get you now."

She wiggled back against him, her derriere doing delightful things to his cock. Gareth tried not to think about that, and to merely listen to the sound of her breathing. Tried to remember his purpose in coming here. But it was too late. She had addled his brain with her touch. He was not strong enough to keep his hand from sliding up to cup the warm weight of her breast. He felt Antonia make a sound of pleasure, a little vibration in the back of her throat.

Her hands went to the tie at the neck of her night-gown, loosening it. "Gabriel," she murmured, her voice now seductively lethargic, "I want you."

He cupped her breast almost possessively. "Antonia," he rasped. "I keep telling myself this must stop—for your sake."

"And for yours," she answered. "But . . . but must it stop this very night?"

He knew he should say yes, but the weight of his cock was pressed eagerly against her lush backside. She moved urgently against him again. "You are so good, Gabriel. So good at making me forget."

Outside, the rain was still hammering down. Inside the dimly lit room, Gareth could have believed that they were the only two people on earth. There was a sense of intimacy and warmth surrounding them which was impossible to deny. Indeed, he had probably come here tonight planning precisely this.

But unwilling to too closely consider his own ignoble

motivations, Gareth ran one hand down her leg, then slowly pushed up her nightgown with his thumb as his fingers skimmed up the tender flesh of her thigh. At her hip, he pushed it higher, baring the lovely swells of her derriere. Almost lazily, he reached around and brushed his hand down her belly, feeling her shiver with anticipation. He kissed the side of her neck and kept nuzzling her lightly as his fingers stroked lower, to the soft tangle of curls between her legs. Gently he teased her until she moaned faintly and shifted one leg to open herself to his touch.

"Ahh," she whispered when his fingers stroked deeper. Lightly he kissed her neck from the back of her jaw down to the elegant curve of her shoulder, pushing the nightgown away as he went. He felt her grow silky and wet to his touch, and he yearned to turn her over and simply plunge himself inside, but that would not do. It was not what she needed. He had found the nub of her desire now, and lightly stroked it with the tip of his finger.

"Gabriel?" Her voice was thready.

"Shh," he said again, pressing his lips behind her earlobe. "No talking, remember? Just sweet sounds of pleasure."

He felt her swallow hard. Felt her body roll back against him in a position that was total surrender. He lifted her leg and pulled it back against him. "Imagine," he whispered, "that this is about nothing but you, and this beautiful sweet place between your legs."

"Yes?" she whispered.

"And no talking," he said again. "I want you to think only of your body. Of your satisfaction."

"But I want you inside me," she protested. "Please . . . let me feel . . ."

Unable to resist, Gareth pushed up the hem of his nightshirt and let his erection spring free. The feel of her bare buttocks against his heated flesh was a torment. He lifted her leg and let himself slide into the smooth wetness between her legs. "Hold your leg like that," he whispered, "just for a moment."

He pressed the head of his cock into the silken heat. She was ready; beyond ready. Gently he pushed himself inside, just an inch, to allow her to grow accustomed to the new sensation.

"G-Gabriel?" she whispered again.

Unable to hold back, he pushed deeper. "Good God," he choked. "Are you all right?"

She nodded. "Yes."

"Press back against me," he said. When she did, he thrust more firmly, sliding deep inside her, joining his body to hers. Antonia moaned. Gareth reached around her to touch her again, and she shivered with need. "That's it," he encouraged. "Just let me hold myself deep inside you," he murmured. "Open your legs, and let me stroke you."

In his embrace, her entire body trembled. He struggled not to move but to let the weight of his cock and the intensity of his touch drive her passion higher, until she started to gasp and to shake almost uncontrollably. Her release, when it came, was powerful and bone deep. Satisfied with his careful restraint, he stilled his hand and felt her tremble until the pleasure had drained through her and she lay still in his arms.

Antonia came back to earth, feeling languid and

sated. "Oh, Gareth," she whispered. "That was . . . quite remarkable."

His mouth skimmed along her jaw. "*You* are remarkable," he whispered, lightly kissing her neck.

Tentatively, she rocked her hips back against his. "Gabriel . . . did you?—"

"It does not matter," he whispered, drawing himself from her body. Gently he pulled her over onto her back and came onto his knees, stripping away his nightshirt to reveal his tautly muscled chest and well-sculpted arms. He tossed the shirt into the floor as her eyes fell to his slender waist, and lower still.

"Here, let's take this off." His hands grasped the hem of her nightgown, which was already rucked up to her waist. She lifted a few inches and allowed him to pull it off.

Antonia was not entirely sure what had just happened—but she was sure she had enjoyed it. Only now did she begin to realize that the rain was still peppering down beyond the windows, and that thunder still rumbled in the distance.

In the faint candlelight, Gabriel's hungry eyes swept over her body. Impatiently, she reached for him, pulling his weight down on top of her. "Now you," she whispered.

"Patience, my dear." Braced on his knees, Gareth cradled her head in his arms and kissed her deeply. His heat and his unique scent surrounded her. His big body seemed to shelter her. In response, Antonia delved into his mouth, entwining her tongue with his, and felt great satisfaction when a shudder ran through him.

"Umm, like that," she said when he drew back again.

"Do . . . *that*—not with just your tongue, but with . . . you know."

He smiled a little at her insistence. "We needn't rush, Antonia," he whispered. "The night is long and the storm is still raging." He bent his head and suckled her breast, drawing the pink-brown areola fully into his mouth, then flicking his tongue over her taut, aching nipple.

Antonia shifted restlessly beneath him, and reached down to twine her fingers in Gabriel's luxurious blond locks, but he looked up, his eyes glittering, and brought her hand to his mouth. Almost reverently, he kissed her open palm, and then, surprisingly, the scar across her wrist. Feeling awkward, Antonia tried to draw her hand back to hide the disfigurement, but he held on. "I think you are beautiful," he murmured, holding her gaze as he dotted kisses down her hand. "Every inch, every scar, every freckle."

"I—I don't have freckles," she murmured, almost mesmerized by the intensity in his eyes. She gasped when his tongue lightly flicked across her palm. Then, still watching her, he drew her index finger into his mouth and gently sucked. Something inside her stomach turned a flip-flop, and she felt that warm ribbon of hunger go twisting through her, pulling at her very core.

Impatient, she lifted one leg to pull him down with it, but he moved his hand and pressed it firmly back down into the softness of the bedcovers. He shifted his mouth to the other breast, laving her, teasing her, and drawing out her need as if it were a fine, taut thread of silk. Her breathing ratcheted up just a notch, and Gareth slipped lower until he was planting kisses between her breasts, down her belly, and lower still.

When he was between her legs, he slid his palms up to push her thighs apart. With one knee, he nudged them still wider. "Antonia, I want to love you like this," he rasped, looking up at her. "Will you let me?"

Scarcely comprehending what it was she agreed to, she nodded. Watching her with his heavy, hooded eyes, Gabriel skimmed his warm, elegant hands up her inner thighs until she was fully open. Fully exposed. Antonia let her head fall back into the pillow, unable to hold his gaze. Other than his light teasing that afternoon at Knollwood, Antonia had never known such decadence could exist; that one human being could instill in another such a rush of joy and yearning.

Lightly, Gabriel touched her with his tongue, making her whole body jolt and sending a rush of heat across her cheeks. And then he stroked her in earnest, and she almost came off the bed with a cry of pure pleasure. She cried out, her voice weak and thready. "Gabriel?"

He looked up but did not release her. Instead, he bore her hips down into the bed's softness and held her there. Again his eyes, hot and hungry, swept down her, holding her in thrall.

Her hand fluttered uncertainly. "Please, Gabriel . . . just—"

"What, love?" he murmured. "Shall I . . . shall I stop? Is that your wish?"

Antonia felt her throat work up and down. "No," she rasped. "Don't stop, Gabriel. Don't ever stop."

With a satisfied smile, he lowered his head and drew his tongue deep, making her whimper. And then he touched her with one finger, slipping it inside. She heard herself moan, a soft but desperate sound. Gabriel's clever fingers and teasing tongue delighted her. Tormented her. Left her aching for more.

Another finger slipped inside, and his tongue began to graze her feminine nub in deliberate, delicate little flicks, leaving her trembling on the precipice. Antonia had never experienced such intense pleasure. For long, exquisite moments, Gabriel loved her with his tongue and with his hands. Antonia's hands dug into the blankets as if she were fighting to remain earthbound, and then she was arching off the bed like a wanton and begging him for release. Chanting into the darkness, "*Gabriel. Gabriel. Gabriel.*"

He stroked deeper, more intently, lingering in that sweet, perfect spot. Again and again, his skill pitched her higher until Antonia imploded with ecstasy, her body seizing with spasms of raw pleasure, her throat working soundlessly as she drowned in it.

She came awake to the present to see Gabriel kneeling between her legs. His gaze was fierce in a way she had never seen before. Possessive. Demanding. And Antonia wanted to be his, at least in this wonderful, exquisite moment. She no longer heard the storm. There was only the here and the now, and the perfect intimacy between them. She reached out and murmured Gabriel's name.

His hand was on his erection. He drew back his flesh, and planting one strong arm on the pillow near her head, he leaned over her, again urging her legs wide. "I want to be inside you, Antonia," he said roughly.

Antonia reached out and took his erection into her hands. His eyes squeezed shut, and he made a sound— something between a hiss and a groan. His heated flesh felt as if it were covered in warm velvet. She felt

Gabriel's strength, the power of his virile male body, coursing through him. Gently she guided him to her, lifting her hips, and pleading for him to take her. When it felt as though he hesitated, Antonia stroked him lightly, and a pearl of fluid seeped out onto her hand. He closed his eyes and shuddered, the muscles of his arm and his throat going taut and sinewy.

He was on the edge, she sensed. On the edge of a foolish, noble gesture. "Gabriel," she whispered, drawing her hand down his length again. "Come to me. Come inside me. Don't cheat me of the pleasure of pleasuring you."

Gareth heard her words, and what little hesitation he had managed to dredge up fell away. Antonia stroked his length again, a delicious torment. He shut his eyes and prayed he would not disgrace himself.

"Don't stop," she whispered as their bodies met. "Don't think."

He could not possibly. There was no stopping the inevitable. He pressed himself into her warm, womanly flesh, and it was as if they melded together. As if he was drawn down into her, becoming one with her, driven by some transcendental force which was beyond him. He thrust deep on his first stroke and cried out, the sound raw and carnal.

Antonia opened fully to him as her hands slid around his buttocks, then up to his waist, stroking him. Murmuring to him. This was not just pleasure. This was not just sex. He was lost to it, drowning in it. Drowning in Antonia. He felt touched in a place so deep and so vulnerable that he marveled she could even reach it.

When he opened his eyes, he could see her—almost into her soul, it seemed. Eyes which had once seemed otherworldly were now startlingly clear, and the depth of emotion contained there was both surprising and gratifying. Gareth thrust inside her, reveling in her feminine softness, and in her ardent, urgent desire to pleasure him. Always, always it had seemed the other way round to Gareth.

Something in him spiraled, and drove higher. He tried to hold back; tried to stretch out the moment of earthly joy, but it was not to be. His release came upon him in a powerful and unexpected rush. He tried to withdraw from her body, but he was an instant too late. The last of his seed spilt across the soft ivory flesh of her thigh as his body spasmed and shook.

His breath still heaving roughly, Gareth dropped his head and waited for the onslaught to stop. It had been beautiful. Magnificent and precious—save for one small mistake. Gareth set his forehead to hers. "Oh, Antonia," he whispered, bearing his weight onto his elbows. "I tried, love, to be careful."

"Gabriel, it is all right," she murmured, stroking the hair back from his high, elegant forehead. "It will be all right."

"Let us hope so," he said a little grimly.

He reached across the bed to snare his nightshirt, then made swift work of the evidence. After tossing it to the floor, he rolled to one side and propped himself on his elbow. His eyes drifted over her face, wondering what she was thinking. Probably what he was thinking—that he'd taken another grave risk with her body, and with her precious, hard-won freedom.

If, God forbid, his seed took root, Antonia would be stuck with him. There would be another marriage she would not have chosen. Another brick wall, narrowing down her life and her choices. Good God.

Somehow, he managed to smile down at her and to pick up a strand of her silken hair to nonchalantly toy with. But there was nothing nonchalant about what they had just done. For him, it had been a life-altering moment. A moment of exquisite passion and extreme apprehension. Oh, he wanted Antonia. He was beginning to think he had done so all along. He knew beyond a doubt he was in love. But he would rather not have her at all than to have her under such regrettable circumstances.

"Gabriel?" Her small, warm hands came up to cradle his face. "Please don't worry."

He grinned. "I'm not."

"And don't lie to me," she added. "I am still not entirely sane sometimes, it is true. But I was a fool only once."

He felt his gaze soften and dipped his head to kiss her softly on the cheek. "You are right," he murmured, brushing his lips over her ear. "I am worrying."

She rolled toward him and tucked her head beneath his chin. "You are very large," she said against his chest. "You make me feel . . . *safe,* Gabriel. If an accident happened—if your fear came true—would it be . . . so dreadfully awful?"

He made her feel safe. Was that it? Roughly, he laughed. "Awful for you, love? Or for me?"

"It wouldn't be awful for me," she whispered, her voice a little hollow.

He gripped her fiercely then. "Listen to me, Antonia," he said. "You don't want me. Stick with your own kind—that's the advice my grandfather always gave me. And he was right, too."

"And you . . . you aren't my kind?"

"You know, Antonia, that I am not," he answered. "You were brought up to be something that I never was. You have a birthright that was never mine to claim."

Her gaze moved slowly over his face. "That is not true, Gabriel."

He searched for the words that would make it clear to her. "Antonia," he said quietly. "For three years I lived here amongst these people at Selsdon. But I was never, ever one of them. And if I forgot for one instant that I was not, someone—Warneham, his wife, even the servants—would remind me, quite firmly and clearly. So do you really think—do you truly imagine . . ." He let his words fall away and slowly shook his head.

She laid her hand against his chest. "Do I really think what?"

With a wistful smile, he stroked the turn of her cheek. "Do you really think, Antonia, that your family and your friends would agree with you?" he whispered. "Do you think for one moment they would not find me unsuitable? Beneath you?"

"But . . . but you are a duke now," she answered. "Society will forgive a duke almost anything."

"Outwardly, perhaps, yes," he returned, gentling his voice. "But what is that worth? Do I want society to begrudgingly accept me simply because of some twist of fate? Most of them would not otherwise have acknowledged me had we tripped over one another."

Antonia looked at him sadly—and far too knowingly. "You are so hurt inside, Gabriel," she whispered. "It breaks my heart."

He rolled onto his back and dragged an arm over his

eyes. "But pain, Antonia, can be a useful emotion," he said. "Pain can drive you. Spur you on to make something of yourself."

"Is that what happened to you?" she asked.

"I daresay it was," he answered. "I wanted control of my own life. Of my destiny. I did not want to be at anyone else's mercy ever again."

She curled against him, and he drew her tight to his side, then lifted the other arm from his eyes. "The thunder has ended, I think," he said. "Perhaps the rain will soon stop, too."

"Gabriel, you may go if you wish," she said quietly. "I shall be fine. As you say, the worst is over."

"Yes, perhaps," he murmured.

But he could not find the will to rise from her bed and leave her. Her hand was playing through the hair on his chest, and her small, warm body was wrapped around his. It was bliss. Almost without deciding to, he reached down and pulled up the disheveled bedcovers, all the way to their chins.

Antonia nuzzled nearer. "How did you know, Gabriel, when you fell in love?" she asked. "How did it feel?"

Her questions shook him. "I . . . I beg your pardon?" he asked, crooking his head to look down at her.

Antonia shrugged. "Did she make your heart skip a beat? Did you feel unable to sleep or to eat?"

Xanthia. She meant Xanthia. "It . . . it wasn't like that," he said. "I just came to feel that we should be together. That it was fated in some way."

"That does not sound like love," Antonia murmured.

"I loved her," he said a little defensively. "It was not

the head-over-heels, sick-to-your-stomach kind of falling in love, perhaps. It was a slow recognition of what would be best."

"Best for both of you?" Antonia asked. "You did not feel beneath her? After all, her brother was a nobleman."

Gareth opened his mouth to answer, then closed it again. He considered her question. "Rothewell is not like other noblemen," he finally said. "The three of them grew up with nothing, and in frightful conditions. They were orphans, too, you see, sent out to Barbados by a family that did not want them. I suppose we shared that. In a way, we all grew up together, clinging to the wreckage of our old lives, and trying to come out strong."

"I see," she murmured, her voice vibrating faintly against his chest. "And was there a pivotal moment for you? An instant when you realized you wished to marry her?"

For a long moment, he did not answer. "It was in a storm," he finally confessed. "Not like this, but a sort of hurricane. We were trapped alone in our shipping office near the careenage, and we thought . . . well, we thought we were going to die. I had prepared myself for such a death many times before—life at sea requires it—but Zee was terrified. The storm felled trees and shattered windows. Small skiffs were thrown up from the ocean like so much seaweed. One corner of our roof kept lifting off. And in the end, we hid behind some of the furniture, and I—"

"What?" she encouraged. "Go on."

He gave a rueful shake of his head. "I cannot," he said. "I have spoken too freely."

"I see," said Antonia gently. "The lady's honor, and

all that. Never mind. Knowing you, Gabriel, I can easily guess what happened."

"Let us just say that I did the only thing I knew to do," he admitted. "And frankly, I—I thought it meant something. But when the daylight came and the storm settled, Zee was her strong, competent self again. She did not need me. She never really had."

Antonia drew his hand to her heart and set it flat against her chest. "Gabriel, what we did tonight—it *means* something," she whispered. "I . . . I don't quite know what—but when the rain stops and the morning comes, I shall still need—" Abruptly, she broke off her words and drew a steadying breath. "I will always be grateful to you," she finished.

He held her close and pressed his lips to the top of her head. "I don't want your gratitude, Antonia," he said again. "I want only your happiness."

"I know," she murmured, her voice drowsy now. "I know that, Gabriel."

And with their arms bound tightly about one another, they slipped away into a restless sleep, as the rain rattled through the downspouts and morning edged near, each of them dreaming of what might have been.

Chapter Fourteen

*T*he Portsmouth seafront lay in darkness, the tang of salt and seaweed thick in the night air. The fine carriage swung into a narrow, cobbled lane and rocked to an immediate halt. Gabriel heard the ominous slap-slosh-slap of the rising tide as it pummeled the harbor's stonework, and a chill ran down his spine.

They had stopped before a pub. Its iron lantern was swinging in its bracket, throwing a murky light up the alley. Four disreputable-looking fellows stood in the shadows. The largest of them pushed away from the wall with his booted foot and strolled languidly toward the carriage. "You'd be Warneham?" he asked through the window.

"Yes," the duke hissed. He pulled out his purse and shoved a banknote at the man.

The man tucked the money into his coat. "Where's 'e at, then?"

The duke lifted his gloved hand and pointed across the carriage. "There," he gritted. "Just get him out of my sight.

And make damned sure he never sees England again, do you hear?"

The man laughed, a low, raspy sound, and yanked open the door. Only then did Gabriel realize what was happening. "No!" he shouted. "Wait—sir!—I want my grandmother! Just let me go. Let me go back!"

"Ooh, wants 'is granny, does 'e?" The man moved as if to seize Gabriel by his coat collar.

"No, wait!" Gabriel caught the doorframe as the man jerked him out. "Stop! Your Grace! You—you cannot let them take me!"

"Oh, you think not?" Warneham lifted his boot and rammed his heel hard against the door's edge, crushing Gabriel's knuckles. He yelped with pain, and let go. The man had an arm about Gabriel's waist now. He hefted him backward across his hip, as if he were balancing a sack of potatoes.

Warneham craned his head through the door as they left. "Scared of water, eh?" he called out. "Well, by God, I'm going to give you something to be scared of, you little Hebrew bastard."

By the third day of her illness, Nellie Waters was champing at her bit like an old warhorse and beginning to trundle downstairs to her mistress's room on all manner of pretexts. She had forgotten to lay out my lady's hairpins. She wished to sort out some things for Monday's laundry. All feeble excuses at best, so Antonia paid them no heed, turning Nellie on her heels as soon as she was caught and promptly sending her upstairs to bed again.

On Nellie's last such foray, however, she managed to make away with a sack full of stockings to be mended and her darning needles. But when she returned to her quarters, she found George Kemble waiting in the narrow passageway outside her bedchamber door, one elegant shoulder propped languidly against the doorframe.

"Ah, Mrs. Waters, good morning! I see you are making a splendid recovery."

"Not to hear my lady tell it," said the maid irritably. "What do you want anyways, Mr. Kemble? These are the maids' chambers, I'll have you know."

"Are they?" said Kemble speciously. "How exciting! Perhaps I shall catch just a teasing glimpse of your wellturned ankles, Mrs. Waters—in those attractive brown brogues you seem to favor?"

Mr. Kemble did not see the sack of stockings coming. Mrs. Waters caught him squarely across the ear and was greatly pleased to hear his teeth clack resoundingly.

"Good God, woman!" Mr. Kemble drew warily away. "It was a jest! A jest!"

Mrs. Waters glared at him. "I find my sense of humor sadly wanting nowadays," she returned. "Now good day to you and your pert tongue, sir. I am bedridden, in case you had not heard."

"Damned if I should like you to swing that sack at me when you were feeling hale and hearty, then." Kemble was tugging at his earlobe in an attempt to restore his hearing. "Look, Mrs. Waters, I really did think we were getting along splendidly. Now I need your help—"

"I know your type, Mr. Kemble," she said warningly. "You have come up here to poke about and stir up trouble, so—"

"Precisely!" Kemble interjected. "And I thought by

now you must be quite bored to tears and ready for a little intrigue."

"Intrigue?" Mrs. Waters drew back an inch, squinting.

Kemble slipped just the neck of his silver flask from his pocket. "Intrigue, and some of my special medicinal care for invalids?" he said, waggling it. "But please, my dear woman, not here in the passageway?"

With a somewhat guilty glance up and down the corridor, Mrs. Waters pushed open her door and motioned him in.

There being but one teacup and one chair in the room, Kemble was forced to strain gentility by perching on the edge of Mrs. Waters's bed, and sipping straight from the flask. Though the room was tucked under an eave, it was nicely furnished with a small four-poster bed, chintz curtains, and a worn but beautiful Axminster carpet. The good lady sat across a small mahogany table, in a wing chair which looked old and comfortable. A paroxysm of coughing struck her, and she picked up the teacup for a long, restorative sip.

"Well, what manner of intrigue did you have in mind, sir?" asked Mrs. Waters when her throat was clear and her mood had been improved by the expensive brandy.

Kemble smiled serenely. "Well, first I must ask your opinion on a matter of some delicacy," he said. "It concerns one of the few subjects—possibly the *only* subject—about which I know nothing."

"Oh?" Mrs. Waters looked at him strangely. "And what would that be, pray?"

Kemble swallowed hard. "Well, *female* things," he finally said.

"Female things?" The look was deepening toward suspicion. "What manner of female things? We are not talking about hat ribbons here, are we?"

"I am afraid not," said Mr. Kemble. "I mean female . . . er, *functions*."

Mrs. Waters scowled disapprovingly. "Mr. Kemble, I really do not think—"

Kemble set the flask down with a *thunk*! "Madam, have you any notion how unpleasant a task this is for me?" he said tightly. "I am trying to help your mistress. If I did not need to know these things, would I really be asking?"

Mrs. Waters considered it. "No, I daresay not."

"Fine," he said impatiently. "Now, I want you to tell me what happens when a woman conceives a child? What are the symptoms? What, precisely, would she notice?"

Mrs. Waters flushed faintly. "Well, she would gain weight, of course."

"Always?" he interjected. "From the very first? What if she were sickly?"

"Yes, I see your point," said Mrs. Waters. "Some do take on a queasy stomach. But not usually at the very first."

"But does it ever happen?"

"Oh, bless me, yes!" said the woman. "With her first child, my sister Anne clung to the chamber pot every day for three months, and thereafter was the picture of health. Some poor souls are ill the whole time—'tis rare, though."

"And in those cases, the woman might actually lose weight at first?"

"'Tis possible," said Mrs. Waters.

"What other symptoms might she have?" asked Kemble. "Her . . . her monthly courses would cease, would they not?"

Face flushing pink, the maid nodded. "Yes, 'tis the first sign, actually."

"But could such a cessation be caused by something else?"

"Well, age, of course," acknowledged Mrs. Waters. "Illness. A fright or a shock—especially one that lingers."

"Melancholia?"

Mrs. Waters's eyebrows drew together. "Well, it could be possible, I suppose," she said. "Particularly if she fell off significantly—with her weight, I mean."

"Another good point!" said Kemble. "Some women are obsessed with weight, are they not? I do not mean that they strive to have a good figure—it is something more obsessive than that."

"I have heard tell of women who would starve themselves to death, 'tis true," Mrs. Walters acknowledged. "But I never knew why, nor ever knew of one personally."

Kemble tapped his finger pensively. "In any case," he finally said, "could severe weight loss cause a cessation of a woman's courses?"

"Oh, indeed it could do," said the maid. "'Tis nature's way of seeing they don't conceive when they are too thin or too ill to bear a child. Nature knows what's best, I always say."

Kemble unscrewed the cap on his flask and took a small, pensive sip. "So which came first?" he muttered. "The chicken? Or the egg?"

"I beg your pardon?"

Kemble tipped the flask over Mrs. Waters's teacup again. "If a woman became nauseous and her courses stopped, how would she know if pregnancy was the cause?"

The maid seemed beyond embarrassment now. "If she were married and healthy, 'twould be a safe assumption," said Mrs. Walters. "Otherwise, why, it could be some time. Three months, perhaps—and then only if the doctor could feel it in the womb. A babe won't quicken until much later than that."

Kemble tucked the flask back into his pocket. "Thank you," he said. "Thank you so much. You have been an invaluable help to me."

Mrs. Waters's eyes widened, and she gave another cough into her handkerchief. "Have I indeed?" she finally said. "That was simple enough."

He had already started toward the door when he thought of something else and turned around. "Mrs. Waters, may I ask—have you any notion who might have been the previous lady's maid here at Selsdon?"

She pulled a thoughtful face. "Well, I've heard Musbury mention it on occasion," she said, then shook her head. "I'm sorry. I'm not at my best. I cannot call it to mind."

"Mrs. Musbury," said Kemble pensively. "Do you gather she knew the lady well?"

"Yes, I collect she did," said Mrs. Waters. "She was from these parts, I believe, as was the last duchess."

"Excellent!" Kemble rubbed his hands together. "Thank you, Mrs. Waters. You are, as always, perfectly brilliant."

* * *

Gareth found Antonia in the parlor shortly before noon. He had not seen her since slipping from her bed in the early hours before dawn. She sat at the giltwood escritoire jotting out a letter, her head bent to the sun, which shot her hair with strands of brilliant gold. Her jaw was set somewhat rigidly over her task. She had not even heard him come in.

For a moment, he hesitated. She was beautiful, yes, but it was no longer her beauty which drew him. He thought of how she had felt in his arms last night. How loathe he had been to leave her. The almost ethereal intimacy they had shared. And now, when he had thought the reality of her situation would creep in to buck up his resolve, he found instead that it was flagging.

He was done for, he realized, watching her small, capable hand scratch across the page. He was in love with her, head over heels. There was no point in pretending otherwise. The only thing now was to decide what ought to be done about it. Would he do the right thing? Or the selfish thing?

And what *was* the right thing? Today he was not sure. Her questions last night about Zee had forced him to look inward and to face a certain truth. What Gareth felt now was very different from anything he had felt before, and far more complex. There was no impatience, none of the frustration he had felt with Zee. There was only a deep and abiding certainty that he needed this woman. A seemingly delicate and fragile woman who, Gareth was beginning to think, was actually neither.

He tucked his hat in the crook of his arm and stepped a little closer. "A penny for your thoughts?" he said quietly.

Antonia gave a little gasp. "Oh, heavens!" she said, her

hand going to her heart. "Gabriel. I was lost in thought, was I not?"

With a muted smile, he peered over her shoulder. "Writing to one of your frustrated admirers in London?" he asked.

Antonia looked up and smiled. "It is very odd, but all those scoundrels seem to have vanished," she said. "Could it have anything to do with the new duke who is in residence, I wonder?"

"I can't think why I would put them off," he confessed, taking one of her hands in his.

But perhaps he had done precisely that, he belatedly realized. Perhaps those sort of men feared being too closely examined by someone who might have Antonia's best interests in mind.

She looked down at their entwined fingers. "I am writing to my father, Gabriel," she said quietly. "I am telling him . . . telling him that I shall come. I shall do as he asks, and come to Town to celebrate the birth of the new child. I shall pay a few social calls with him, perhaps, and see how people receive me. There will be whispers behind my back, I know, but perhaps they will fade. Beyond that—well, I make Papa no promises."

Gareth felt his heart sink and the floor seemingly shift beneath his feet. He was suddenly at a loss for words. "You have had a change of heart, then," he finally managed. "When do you leave?"

Antonia glanced up, her eyes softening as she caught his gaze. "I think I should go at once, if Nellie is up to it," she answered. "I—I have become a distraction to you, Gabriel. Please don't say I haven't. Besides, I shall need new clothes. My mourning is all but over."

"Yes, I see," he said quietly.

"I thank you, Gabriel," she said, her voice soft. "You have given me strength and encouragement. You have made me feel as if—well, as if I really do have some say over my destiny. I *can* control my father. And perhaps I can have a life again. Perhaps I need not shut myself away in the country, or in Bath, for God's sake, like some widow on her last legs."

He still held his hat and was fighting not to crush it. "No, you are a widow with a pair of very lithe, very shapely legs," he said, forcing himself to smile. "I think they will stand you in good stead whilst you waltz around London breaking hearts."

She studied him quizzically, then the expression smoothed away, as if she had forced it. "Well, have you come in search for me?" she asked brightly, changing the subject. "Am I needed elsewhere in the house?"

Yes, he wanted to say. *You are needed in my bed. In my heart. In my home, wherever it may be.*

Her leaving so suddenly was a development he had not anticipated. And while it had sounded wise in the abstract, the reality of her going was another thing altogether. He wanted, inexplicably, to beg her to stay. To take back all his wise and cavalier words and simply throw himself on her mercy.

But whose needs did that serve? His, and only his. A return to society was precisely what Antonia deserved. She had every right to reach out for the life she wanted, not simply settle for the life which was at hand. And if, by some miracle, he and Kemble could lay to rest any of the doubt surrounding Warneham's death, her path to her new life would be even smoother.

But she was still looking at him and awaiting his answer to her question. "No, I just wandered in," he lied. "Everything is fine. I was just looking . . . for something."

"Whilst carrying your hat?" She leapt to her feet and lightly kissed his cheek. "Come now, Gabriel. I thought we were to be honest with one another?"

"Yes, we did say that, didn't we?" He gave a muted smile. "Actually, I was going to ask if you would go for a walk with me."

"I should love to," she answered. "May I have a moment to change my shoes?"

"Antonia." He caught her lightly by the arm. "You need not go."

She set her head to one side and studied him. "Perhaps I want to. Where are you going?"

He dropped his gaze. He felt suddenly twelve again. "To the pavilion in the deer park," he said. "But I just . . . didn't really want to go alone."

"I should be pleased to go. I love the pavilion." She gave his hand one last reassuring squeeze and started toward the door. "I will meet you in the great hall."

A few minutes later, Gareth watched her come dashing back down the stairs. She wore a somewhat loose, old-fashioned gown of sprigged muslin in a fetching shade of green with a matching green-and-yellow shawl tossed over her shoulders. "I decided to wear something colorful and comfortable," she said, her eyes sparkling. "And—well, it was the only thing I could quickly get on without Nellie's help. Oh, what do you have in the basket?"

Gareth smiled and lifted his arm. "A cold luncheon,

I'm told," he said. "Mrs. Musbury thinks I am skipping my midday meal too often."

Antonia laughed. "A picnic!" she said. "How lovely."

They went out through the conservatory into the back gardens, her hand resting lightly upon his arm. The air today was touched with a hint of autumn, and if one looked quite closely, a flash of red or gold could sometimes be seen in the lush foliage of the orchard which bordered Selsdon's formal gardens. The orchard gave onto a swath of woodland, and below it lay the deer park.

The road which led down to the deer park was easy to find and, like the road to Knollwood, well kept. "I used to walk this way often as a child," he said. "The pavilion was Cyril's favorite place to play. We would pretend it was our castle and stage mock battles to defend it. Or sometimes we would treat it as a sort of amphitheater and act out one of Shakespeare's plays—not *Romeo and Juliet,* mind. One of the more bloodthirsty ones."

She looked up at him and smiled. "I found this little lane on my own," she said. "Warneham never mentioned it. I suppose it is just as well, for it gave me a place to hide myself away occasionally."

They strolled in silence for some time, her hand lying lightly on his arm. The path narrowed as it descended, and the foliage grew more untamed. It was beautiful, but a little haunting as the wood enfolded them, shutting out the sky. Gareth looked up and thought of little Beatrice. From time to time, Antonia too glanced up into the canopy of green, but she said little.

"Are you thinking of Beatrice?" he finally asked. "I mention it because . . . well, I suppose I am."

She looked at him with a soft smile. "Always," she said quietly. "She is never far from my mind or my heart, Gareth. But I think perhaps—oh, I don't know—I still feel the loss so deeply. I still feel at fault. The grief is ever present, but I have begun to hope that perhaps one day I might understand. I must accept, someday, that nothing I can say or do—no amount of prayer or penance—will ever bring my babies back. What would you call that? Resignation?"

"Wisdom," he answered. "I would call it wisdom, Antonia. And a giving in to the ways of God."

"Yes, perhaps that is it," she murmured, giving his arm a little squeeze. "Perhaps I am surrendering unto God that which was always his."

"Yes, but that part, Antonia, about feeling at fault," he continued. "That part, I hope, you will carefully consider as you go forward with this next part of your life. You cannot hold yourself responsible for . . . for the actions of a capricious, narcissistic ass."

"Oh, my!" she murmured appreciatively. "I never heard Eric described better."

Gareth managed to smile down at her. They walked on in silence for a moment, but finally Antonia spoke. "Tell me more about mourning," she said. "Jewish mourning, I mean."

Gareth was not sure how to explain it. His impressions were those of a child. "Well, after the funeral, the family goes home to meditate on the life of the departed, and to pray for them," he said. "This is done for seven days, and it is supposed to be a period of intense grief."

"*Seven* days?"

"Yes, and in that time, one does not leave one's home,"

he went on. "Visitors may call upon the bereaved to pray and to talk about the departed, but that is all. Mourners may eat only very simple foods. They cannot enjoy any luxury, such as a leisurely bath or even the wearing of shoes. We cover our mirrors, and we take the cushions off the chairs. We may not work, nor even think of work, and we light a special candle of remembrance. It is a time to begin to heal ourselves, and sanctify the memory of the one who is lost to us."

He glanced down to see Antonia looking at him in wonder. He realized that somewhere in his narrative he had gone from "they" to "we." It was characteristic of his life, perhaps. The chronic confusion of never knowing just where one belonged.

"It almost sounds like a luxury to me." Antonia's voice was low and raw with emotion. "To be encouraged in one's grief . . . I cannot imagine it."

"When I was a boy, I thought sitting shiva very dull," Gareth confessed. "But now that I am older, I wonder if it isn't very wise indeed. Yes, it is a sort of luxury. In a shiva house, it is thought wrong to try to cajole the bereaved from their grief, or to distract them from thinking of their loss."

"You are surprisingly knowledgeable, Gabriel, for one who did not worship in the faith."

They had started down the hill which led to the pavilion and the small lake beyond. Gareth found himself growing unaccountably tense. "Everyone I knew, Antonia, was a Jew," he said quietly. "As a small boy, I had seen no other way. And yet I was kept from *being* a Jew. I know my mother meant well, but—"

"Oh, Gabriel, I am quite sure of it." Antonia stopped

abruptly and turned to look at him. "She just never knew she would die so young. She never knew your father would not come home again. How well I understand that a mother cannot foresee and prepare her child for life's every tragedy. You must not think ill of her. You mustn't."

Gareth nodded, and resumed their walking, but at a slower pace. He did not want to reach the foot of the hill. And he did not want, particularly, to carry on this conversation any further. There was a part of him that was still irrationally angry with his mother. He felt as if her choice had left him hanging, suspended between two worlds, and belonging to neither.

He kicked a rotting walnut from the path and felt mild satisfaction when it cracked solidly against a tree. "I know, Antonia, that everything my mother did, she did out of love," he said. "Love for me, and for my father. But to a small boy, there are few things more important than fitting in with the world around you—and few things more reassuring. And frankly, I think my grandparents' faith was a grounding influence. I believe it would have done me a vast deal of good."

"Do you believe what they believed?" There was no hint of judgment in her voice; merely curiosity.

"Some days, Antonia, I don't know what I believe." He paused to lift a wayward briar from Antonia's path. "For me, this isn't even about faith. It is about a nurturing community of good and honest people."

She ducked under the briar, then glanced toward him with a faint smile. "Perhaps I understand better than you might imagine, Gabriel."

Gareth looked up to see the pavilion through the trees

up ahead. Beyond it lay the lake. He picked up their pace a little. He had come this far; it was best to get it over with.

The pavilion was round and entirely open. Eight Ionic columns of white stone supported the pavilion's dome, and three white marble steps encircled its base. Once it had been furnished with chaises and chairs, but now it held nothing but a rough-hewn wooden bench and a swath of dead leaves.

Antonia sensed Gabriel's hesitation well before they reached the end of the path. But when the pavilion came into view, he marched on like a soldier to battle. He did not give the impression of a man who had come to savor the outdoors and admire the greenery.

"It is lovely, isn't it?" she said when he finally stopped to take in the view. "Lovely, but a bit ostentatious, I always thought."

Gabriel did not answer. After a moment had passed, he picked up his pace again, and together they went up the steps. Gabriel put down Mrs. Musbury's basket and drifted toward the opposite side of the circle. Antonia let her hand fall away from his arm, and for a moment, she simply watched him. There was a hesitance to his gait and a rigidity to his posture which was unusual. He had apparently left his hat behind at Selsdon, for his luxurious golden hair now tossed lightly in the breeze coming off the lake.

He went to the very edge of the pavilion and set one hand high against the nearest column. The other hand went to his hip, pushing back the front of his coat to reveal the slender turn of his waist. Gabriel stared out across the water, in the direction of what had once been a boathouse but was now just a pile of rotting timber, which was slowly sliding into the lake and taking its sagging roof along with it.

Gabriel was thinking, she knew, of his cousin Cyril's death. It was here that Warneham's son and heir had died during a family picnic—at least that was the story Nellie had got belowstairs. Antonia's husband had never spoken of it, save to say that Gabriel had done it deliberately, out of jealousy and spite. Knowing him as she did now, however, she knew that was not remotely possible. Despite his cold, formal edges, the man had a heart that was kind, perhaps to a fault.

Since his arrival at Selsdon, Gabriel had been exceptionally good to her, when he had no reason whatever to trouble himself and when many in his shoes might have been bitter. He had accepted almost unquestioningly her protestations of innocence surrounding Warneham's death. He had come to Selsdon with his heart newly broken, his lover newly wed, and thrust into a position she was now convinced he had not wanted, but he had still opened at least a little piece of his heart to her. He could not love her, perhaps, in the way she might wish when she let her silly, girlish fantasies run free, but he cared for her. And yes, he wanted her, too—but it was a desire, she believed, which had arisen from his tenderness and his concern.

The least she could do was repay him in kind. Slowly, she walked through the dead leaves which littered the marble floor. She hardly knew what to say. Gabriel had obviously come here for a reason, and she must trust he would deal with it in his own way, and in his own time.

He apparently heard her approach, for he turned, one hand still on the column, and extended his arm as if to invite her to his side. Antonia smiled and joined him. Gabriel set his arm about her waist, and his warm, heavy hand came to rest lightly on her hip.

"The lake is beautiful, isn't it?" she murmured. "Like glass, almost. One can see the reflection of the clouds, and the low-hanging branches along the edge."

When he said nothing, she went on. "When I first came to Selsdon, I used to walk down here alone," she said. "It was a sort of escape for me, I suppose. I used to imagine just walking into the water—that beautiful, pure, glasslike water—and . . . simply disappearing into it. Becoming one with it, in some elemental way. And leaving my troubles behind."

His hand, which had rested so lightly upon her hip, tightened. "You mustn't say such things." His voice was suddenly taut with emotion. "That is like wishing yourself dead, Antonia. You must not ever think such a thing again."

She shook her head. "No, no, it was not like that, Gabriel," she vowed. "I never . . . thought of it as death. I thought of it as just—I don't know—escaping, I suppose? I apologize. I can't think why I brought it up."

"You were not thinking clearly, Antonia, if you had such fancies," he returned.

"No, I daresay I wasn't."

He turned and pierced her with his gaze. "You must promise me that if you ever do so again, you will tell me at once."

"Tell you?"

"Yes," he said firmly. Then his voice hitched. "Or . . .

someone. Nellie. Your brother. Promise me, Antonia." He sounded unaccountably angry.

"Yes, I promise," she said. "I am sorry, Gabriel. I did not mean to frighten you."

He withdrew into himself again. She could see it in the way his eyes grew distant and a little glassy. Uncertain what to do, she went to the bench and swept it off. But she did not sit down. Instead, acting on instinct, she returned to him and set her hand at the small of his back.

He turned at once to look at her, awareness returning to his gaze.

"Gabriel," she said quietly. "Do you wish to tell me about it? About Cyril's death?"

He shook his head.

For an instant, Antonia hesitated to interfere. She knew what it was like to be poked and prodded by the annoyingly well-intentioned. "Well, I think you should," she finally said, hoping her voice sounded decisive. "After all, you brought me down here for a reason, did you not? It cannot have been simply to admire the scenery."

For a long, heavy moment, Gabriel did not speak. "Are you really going away, Antonia?" he asked, his voice a little hoarse.

She hesitated. "I wish only to do what is best for us both," she answered. "I don't wish to be a burden to you. I have a family. I . . . I have people who care for me, in their own way. What do you want me to say, Gabriel? Tell me, and I shall say it."

He looked up at the sky above the lake and narrowed his eyes against the sun. "That we shall always have a regard for one another, I suppose," he said. "That we will be . . . friends. Always, Antonia. Friends who are able to share things. To—To wish one another well. To remember one another fondly."

She set her hand against his cheek. "Oh, Gabriel," she whispered. "That is such an easy request to grant."

His eyes had returned to the water. They were distant again; a little haunted. "Cyril drowned," he finally said, his voice hollow. "He drowned. There." He lifted his hand, perfectly steady, and pointed to the center of the lake. "I—I hit him. I did not mean to do it, but I did. And then he just . . . died."

"I see," Antonia murmured. "And you were boating? Or swimming?"

Gabriel's gaze still focused on the lake, which seemingly held him in thrall. "I cannot swim," he choked. "I . . . never learnt how."

"You cannot swim?"

"No," he blurted. "The water, it . . . it terrifies me. I—I have learnt to cope. To hide it."

This Antonia could not fathom. *Gabriel afraid of the water?* He had lived over a year at sea and come to manage a vast shipping empire. He had spent a lifetime on the docks and piers and quays of the West Indies. How could such a man *fear* water?

Antonia took him by the arm and led him to the old bench. "I want you to sit down," she said. "I wish to ask you a question."

He dragged his fingers through his curling blond locks, but finally he sat. "I never meant to do it." His voice was still flat. "I told them. It was an accident—a sort of accident, I suppose."

"No, you do not strike me as a person who would

deliberately hit someone in such a way," said Antonia soothingly.

He turned to look at her, his expression stark. "No, I meant to hit *Jeremy,*" he said. "I wanted . . . I think, in that moment, I *wanted* to kill him."

Antonia furrowed her brow. "Jeremy?"

"Lord Litting," he said. "The duchess's nephew."

"Oh," said Antonia. She had met Litting on two or three occasions, the last one being the day before her husband's death, when he had come to Selsdon to spend the evening. "I know him vaguely," she said. "And yes, I can imagine that one might occasionally wish to swing something at him."

"Oh, Antonia, he was just a boy then," said Gabriel almost wearily. "He was full of the devil, yes, and a bit of a bully, as bigger boys are wont to be. But he was not . . . evil. Just cocksure and stupid."

Antonia wondered if that was true. "Very well then," she murmured. "And the three of you were playing?"

"We were rowing," said Gabriel, pointing again toward the distant water. "Way out there."

"Rowing when you could not swim?" said Antonia sharply. "That seems unwise."

He dragged a hand down his face. "I didn't wish to go," he whispered. "I didn't. But everyone else had taken a turn. The duchess's entire family was here. I wasn't even supposed to be invited—but at the last minute, Cyril had begged his mother, and she gave in to him. There were no other children Cyril's age. Jeremy was the closest."

"So you were twelve," Antonia mused. "And Cyril was what? Eleven?"

"Almost twelve," said Gabriel hollowly. "And Jeremy was . . . fourteen, I think? He wanted to go back out in the boat, but the men were all tired. So Jeremy decided Cyril and I should go. I refused, so he began to taunt me and say that I was afraid of the water—which I was."

"Oh, dear," said Antonia quietly. "Children can be so terribly cruel."

Gabriel's jaw clenched until it twitched. "I should have held firm," he gritted. "I was used to standing up to Jeremy, especially if he was after Cyril. I was almost as big. But some of the men—the duchess's brothers, perhaps?—they began to laugh at the notion I might be afraid of the water."

"And adults can be crueler still," she added.

His expression was bleak. "Then one of them said that perhaps they should just take me and chuck me in the lake," he continued. "He said it was the best way to learn to swim. Then another one quietly joked that perhaps Jews were like witches and would simply float. Looking back, I don't think he meant me to hear, but—but I began to fear that they really might do it. And that was a far more frightening prospect than rowing with Jeremy. So . . . I got in the boat."

"What can those men have been thinking!" Antonia whispered.

Vaguely, Gabriel shrugged. "Jeremy wanted to row into the center of the lake." He sounded deathly tired now, his words flat and emotionless. "He and I had taken the ends, because Cyril was the smaller. His mother insisted he sit in the middle. But once we were there, Jeremy stood up and began to rock the rowboat back and forth with his feet spread wide, laughing. He wanted to see me panic—and I did. Water was sloshing up over the sides. I was terrified. Cyril wasn't much better. He began to scream."

"Dear God," said Antonia. "What dangerous behavior."

Gabriel shook his head very slowly. "I just wanted Jeremy to stop," he whispered. "I just wanted him to *stop*. I wanted Cyril to stop crying. So I—I got to my feet and—and I *swung*. I swung my oar at Jeremy. And by God, I meant to hit him, too. But Cyril—I don't know—he must have stood up or something. The oar caught him across the temple. And then the boat—it just went over. I remember going under, but I—I came back up somehow. I grabbed for the boat and clung for dear life. I did not know, you see, that Cyril was underneath."

Antonia winced. "He was unconscious when he hit the water, I daresay."

"They said I'd knocked him cold," Gabriel admitted. "I suppose that I had. I'd swung for my life, meaning to hit Jeremy. He swam for shore. I must have been screaming. Two of the footmen swam out, and the duchess's brothers brought the other rowboat. But it was . . . too late. Cyril was facedown in the water all that time."

"And Jeremy swam for shore," Antonia echoed. "Knowing that you could not swim, and that Cyril had gone under?"

"I don't know," said Gareth. "I don't know what Jeremy thought. Perhaps he was as frightened as we were. He certainly seemed shaken afterward. And he didn't precisely deny what he had done. But all the duchess could see was that I had hit Cyril in the head. She convinced herself I had meant to do it; that I had been just waiting for the chance. I suppose . . . I suppose that was easier than blaming her own nephew."

Antonia threaded her fingers through his and gave his hand a strong squeeze. "Dear Lord," she murmured. "You were just a child."

"Not to her," he whispered. "Not to her, or to Warneham. To them, I was the embodiment of evil. She cried, and said that I was scheming to get what was Cyril's. That I had been jealous, and meant to do it all along—that they should have known 'a Jew would do anything for money.' At the time, I was utterly clueless. I was twelve, for Christ's sake. Now I realize that even then, she was afraid I might inherit. But how could such a thing have crossed my mind, Antonia? I was a nobody. I was here on charity. Until Cavendish turned up in my office a few weeks past, I had no notion such a thing could even happen."

"But they had known it all along," Antonia murmured. "They had to have known."

"To me, it made no difference," he said sadly. "Cyril was dead, and I had loved him. He had taken me as his friend, blind to the prejudices around him. To Cyril, it did not matter if I were Jew or a Red Indian or a Barbary pirate. He just wanted a playmate. He was a kind boy with a good heart—and I killed him. It was an accident, but he died by my hand, and I have had to live with that every day of my life. I did not need Warneham to punish me. I did not want this"—here, he lifted his hands expansively—"my friend's birthright."

Antonia wanted to cry. Not just for Gabriel, who had been wronged, but for Cyril as well. And strangely, for the former duchess, who had lost a child and had perhaps gone a little mad in her grief. Antonia could sympathize.

"I am so sorry," she whispered. "I can only imagine what such a loss would be like when you were twelve. And then to lose everything else. Your grandmother. Your home. And then Warneham took you deliberately down to Portsmouth, did he not? To the *water*."

Gabriel was silent for a moment. "He came at dawn the next morning," he whispered, "and tossed me into his carriage by the coat collar. He said that he was going to give me something, by God, to be scared of. And he did."

Antonia set one hand to her forehead and imagined the terror. What was it Gabriel had said of Portsmouth? *"Just walking along the docks made my stomach churn."* He had been so naïve that he had not been afraid of the people, he had been afraid of the water. But Antonia was sinkingly certain he should have been afraid of the people. He had been a child amongst wolves.

It was as if Gabriel read her mind. He bent forward, legs splayed, and set his elbows on his knees. "Do you know what life is like, Antonia, for boys who go to sea on such ships?" he asked, holding his head in his hands. "Have you any notion of the . . . the degradation to which they are exposed?"

"No." The word came out very small. "But I have a feeling it is a life too ugly for me to imagine."

"It is a life which someone as gently bred as you should know nothing of." Gabriel seemed unable to look at her. "It strips the humanity from you. It reduces you to—to something less than an object. It taints you."

"You were gently bred, too," she answered. "And

you are not tainted. You are a strong and decent man, Gabriel."

"I know more of the world than I should wish to, Antonia," he whispered. His fingers were pressed to his temples now, as if his head hurt. "Luke and Kieran— Lord Rothewell—they understood, I think, without our even discussing it," he went on. "They could guess what life on the *Saint-Nazaire* had been like for me—and frankly, I am not sure they had had a life much better."

"Were you . . . beaten?"

"Oh, God, yes," he said quietly. "But not like the regular sailors. They did not want to mar me in any way, you see. I was worth more to them if I were . . . pleasing to the eye. Antonia, do you understand what I'm saying?"

"I . . . I am not sure." Hoping to comfort him, she reached down and set her hand lightly on his knee. Gabriel flinched as if she had struck him. She jerked her hand away. "Were they going to sell you, perhaps?" she asked, conjuring up the worst horror she could imagine. "Or—or trade you, like an African slave?"

He shook his head. "No. No, not like that."

Antonia felt frustrated with herself, and with her inability to grasp something which Gabriel seemed so deeply affected by. "I want to understand," she whispered. "I want to know what you lived through. It is a part of you, Gabriel, for good or ill."

"Yes, it is a part of me." He lifted his head from his hands, but for a long moment, he looked at the lake, not at her. "Antonia, a ship goes to sea for weeks, often months, at a time," he finally continued. "Generally, there are no women on board. So it is tacitly understood that the officers and crew . . . that they may use the younger, more powerless sailors—cabin boys, and the like—for their . . . their sexual gratification."

Antonia felt vaguely ill. "For sexual gratification?" she echoed. "I don't . . . I cannot . . ."

At last he swiveled his head to look at her. His face was a mask of agony, his beautiful features twisted. "Do you understand, Antonia, what I am telling you? Or have you heard enough to be thoroughly revolted?"

She shook her head. She felt a little light-headed, as if the world about her was floating away.

His features hardened. "It's called *buggery,* Antonia." Gabriel's voice came as if from a distance. "That's what those sorts of sailors like to keep young boys for. They rape them. Sodomize them—and sometimes worse."

Antonia's hands began to shake. "My God," she whispered. "How? How can they just . . . do that?"

Gabriel misunderstood her question. "How?" he asked. "They wear you down with whipping and humiliation until they make you into—into this perverted *thing*. A weak, frightened thing which they can use for their own satisfaction. And after a while, you . . . you just quietly let them do it. You learn to give them pleasure—and you learn to be damned good at it. Because you have no choice. It's how you survive."

"Oh, dear God!" She felt a sudden explosion of nausea—a surge of bile scorching up her throat like scalding vinegar. Clapping a hand over her mouth, Antonia leapt from the bench and bolted for the edge of the pavilion. *The rape of a child.* The pain he must have felt was incomprehensible. Clinging to one of the columns, she bent nearly double and retched. And when at last the nausea subsided, the mortification set in. For an instant, she closed her eyes.

When she moved to straighten up, Gabriel slid a warm, strong hand beneath her elbow. "Christ, I am so sorry," he whispered, his voice laced with agony. "Oh, Antonia. I should never have—"

"No, it—it is all right." She turned her face away and dragged the back of her hand across her mouth. "I believe it is I who ought to apologize. Please forgive me. I just—never imagined—"

At last she turned back to look at him. His face was utterly without emotion. Abruptly, he went down the steps toward the stream which fed the lake. There, he knelt, returning with his fine lawn handkerchief soaked with cool water.

Gratefully, she took it. "I am so sorry," she said again, wiping her face. "I never thought—never dreamt—dear God, Gabriel, you were just a *boy*."

He turned away and cursed again. "I ought to be horsewhipped," he said, walking away from her toward the next column. "There was no need to tell you how—"

"But there *was*," she interjected. She followed him and caught him by the arm. "I asked you, Gabriel, didn't I?"

He spun to face her, his face twisted with sudden rage. "But it is my duty to know what you should and should not hear," he said, his voice trembling with emotion. "You are a gently bred aristocrat, Antonia. And I am *not*. I have seen and done things which—which I have no right to expose you to."

She laid her hand on his arm. "Gabriel, don't treat me like a child."

"But in this respect, Antonia, you *are* a child," he gritted. "You have a childlike view of the world—and that is as it should be. You are a lady, and ladies are to be shielded from evil and filth. But I—I took it upon myself to tell you . . . because—hell, I don't even know why. I guess I wanted to give you a good and proper disgust of me."

Antonia grappled with her temper. This was not about her, and she knew it. "Gabriel, I am not a child," she said again. "Kindly do not patronize me or take it upon yourself to decide what I should or should not know."

"That is what a man does," he gritted, turning his face away. "That is his job."

"Then it is a damned disservice," she snapped, striding around the column until he was forced to look at her. "Perhaps if my father had not shielded me from all the world's filth, I would have known it for what it was when I brushed up against it."

"You are talking nonsense," Gabriel muttered.

"If I had known what iniquity was, perhaps I would have seen my first husband for the liar and cheat that he was," she pressed on. "Perhaps I would not have been so naïve as to think married men didn't keep mistresses. Perhaps I would have known that fathers sometimes barter their daughters away for expediency's sake, and that innocent little girls do in fact die young—and for no good reason."

"Antonia, don't," he said. "Don't do this to yourself. These things are not at all the same."

"They are precisely the same!" she insisted. "They are part and parcel of why women are left ignorant and vulnerable. I was not prepared for life's ugliness, Gabriel. That is what hurt me. That is why I came apart."

"Oh, so now you know the man you've been so cheerfully bedding was a whore," he rasped. "Do you honestly feel better about yourself, Antonia? Do you?"

She felt herself go rigid with anger. "No," she snapped, her whole body trembling. "But at least this time, I know what I am up against. At least it will be a fair and even fight."

He looked at her with unutterable sorrow in his eyes and cursed again beneath his breath. Then he turned on one heel and strode from the pavilion.

Antonia grabbed the basket and followed him. "Gabriel, wait."

But he did not wait. He kept walking, and at a pace which made clear his intentions. He did not want her. She would not disgrace herself by running after him.

Antonia sat down on the white marble steps and let the basket drop. Her hands—no, her entire body, inside and out, was trembling. Never in her whole life had she felt such raw, barely restrained anger. Anger at what had been done to him. A rage against all mankind for allowing such evil to exist. But with the tumbling rush of emotion came a realization. She was alive; alive to the pain and to the anger. To the injustice. Antonia felt as if she had been living in an emotional wilderness—a wasteland with no feelings, save for grief and hopelessness—and now the pain was surging back into her limbs, as she had been frozen numb for all these years.

Gabriel. Poor Gabriel. With a knot in her throat and tears in her eyes, she watched him stride up the hill and into the wood. But Gabriel never looked back.

Chapter Fifteen

*G*abriel walked the deck in the gloom, one hand feeling his way along, the other carrying a pewter tray. Not for the first time, his stomach churned. He swallowed hard, struggling not to be ill. The captain's quarters were just a little further along. He found the door and went in.

Captain Larchmont sat at his map table, thoughtfully stroking one end of his mustache, his booted legs splayed wide. He glanced up at the sound of the door. "That had best be my tea, you little whelp," he growled.

"Y-yes, sir," Gabriel whispered. "W-with biscuits."

"Set it down, then," the captain ordered. "No, not over there. Here, by God."

Gabriel approached the map table with trepidation, set the tray down hastily, and stepped back.

Larchmont looked at him and grinned. "You're a pretty little thing," he murmured. "Come here."

Gabriel stepped forward an inch.

"I said come here, damn you!" Larchmont's huge fist pounded the map table, making his teaspoon jump.

Gabriel did as he was ordered. Larchmont dragged him between his legs, one arm banded about his waist. "Why, you're as pale and pretty as a girl," he said, wrapping one of Gabriel's blond curls around a dirty, callused finger. "Tell me, laddie, has the crew been too rough?"

Gabriel squeezed his eyes shut and felt a tear leak out. Larchmont laughed. "Perhaps I ought to just keep you myself," he murmured, stroking the backs of his fingers along Gabriel's cheek. "What would you say to that? A real bed? A little more food? No more rough, stinking sailors up your arse at every turn? Not too bad, eh?"

"Y-yes, sir."

Larchmont wheezed with laughter. "Well, let's have a little more enthusiasm, laddie!"

"Y-yes, sir," he said, more loudly this time.

Larchmont stood and began to unhitch his breeches. When Gareth backed away, the captain grabbed him by the hair and shoved his face down against the map table. "Drop your trousers, lad," he growled, his mouth pressed to Gabriel's ear, his body bearing him down.

Promptly at twenty past three, the last of the kitchen maids rose from Mrs. Musbury's worktable, taking the dirty cups and saucers along with them. Tea was over, and it was time to begin the preparations for dinner. Mrs. Musbury had taken up the tablecloth—she was appropriately particular, Kemble had noticed, that propriety be always observed—and begun to lay out her account books for the afternoon.

The housekeeper was a small, colorless woman, but her quiet demeanor, Kemble had learned, hid a spine of Sheffield steel. She peered over her wire spectacles at him. "May I help you in some way, Mr. Kemble?"

Kemble smiled. "Yes, ma'am," he said. "I was wondering if you might be so kind—"

"—as to answer another question for you?" She gave a prim frown. "You really are quite full of them, are you not?"

Kemble tried to look shamefaced, but it was a stretch. "It is true I am possessed of a naturally inquisitive nature," he confessed.

"It is more than that, I think," murmured the housekeeper. "But go ahead, Mr. Kemble, and keep your secrets. I am sure the new master knows what he is about. How may I help?"

Kemble pulled out a chair. "Might we have a seat?"

"Dear me," she said, laying aside her spectacles. "By all means."

Kemble crossed one leg over the other and flashed another of his smiles. "I was just wondering, Mrs. Musbury, what became of the lady's maid who was here before Mrs. Waters?"

The housekeeper looked surprised. "Miss Pilson?" she said. "Why, she came here in service to the duchess—the third duchess—and after her tragic passing, Miss Pilson went to one of the duchess's sisters, I believe. She was an old family retainer."

"While she was here, were you on good terms with Miss Pilson?"

"Oh, indeed!" said the housekeeper. "She was a most amiable creature, and very diligent in her duties."

Kemble carefully considered how to pose the next

question. "Might I ask, ma'am, did Miss Pilson ever confide in you anything of a personal nature? About the duchess, I mean."

Mrs. Musbury looked vaguely affronted. "I cannot think what you are trying to suggest."

"Nothing at all, I do assure you." Kemble gave a dismissive toss of his hand. "But I should think, frankly, that her job was very worrying. She must have been constantly concerned about her mistress when—and pardon me for listening to gossip—when her mistress was so decidedly unhappy."

Mrs. Musbury was silent for a long moment. "You are not really here as a valet or a secretary, are you, Mr. Kemble?"

Kemble deepened his smile. "Let us just say that His Grace has some things he would like tidied up," he said. "And who better to tidy things up than a good valet? Or a good secretary, for that matter?"

The housekeeper seemed to consider his argument. "You must understand that I have been at Selsdon a relatively short while," she said quietly. "I manage the household and all the female servants associated with maintaining the house. The lady's maid does not fall under my purview. I joined the household during Miss Pilson's tenure, and we became friends, after a fashion. Yes, she was very worried about her mistress. The duchess was not an especially happy woman."

"Was she ill?"

"She was under a great deal of strain," said Mrs. Musbury. "She was also a shy lady who was not comfortable with people she did not know well."

"How about people she did know?" asked Kemble. "Did she have friends?"

"A few," said the housekeeper. "You must understand that as the duke's wife, there were not many people hereabouts who were her social equal. But she enjoyed the company of the local gentry."

Kemble smiled. "I'll bet Lady Ingham was here quite regularly."

Mrs. Musbury's smile was muted. "Yes, she was," agreed the housekeeper. "Mary Osborne, the doctor's mother, was often with her. They quite doted on the duchess. And about the time I arrived here, the Hamms came to St. Alban's. She and Mrs. Hamm were close in age, but Mrs. Hamm always visited with her husband. The late duke seemed to enjoy their company vastly."

Yes, I'll bet he did, thought Kemble.

"Was he a religious man?" he asked, trying to keep a straight face.

"Not particularly," said Mrs. Musbury. But she would not be further led.

"Is it true the late duchess used a vast deal of tonic? Specifically, a tonic with laudanum in it?"

Again, the housekeeper gave her faint smile. "She came to depend on it, I believe, to sleep," she answered. "I think the doctor in West Widding prescribed it initially, and when Dr. Osborne came down from university to practice, he continued it."

"Was Miss Pilson worried about the amount she consumed?"

"A bit, yes."

"I wonder, Mrs. Musbury—did Miss Pilson ever

confide in you that the duchess was having problems . . . well, problems of a female nature?"

Mrs. Musbury was silent a long while. "What strange questions you do ask, Mr. Kemble," she murmured. "As the duchess's weight slowly dropped away—she never had any sort of appetite—Miss Pilson confided in me that some . . . well, some female troubles arose."

"Could she have been with child?" asked Kemble pointedly.

"It would have been a natural assumption, given her symptoms," said the housekeeper. "But Miss Pilson was reasonably confident that was not the case."

"Would the duchess have discussed these problems with Dr. Osborne?"

The faint, doubtful smile returned. "Oh, I doubt it," said Mrs. Musbury. "Perhaps she would have discussed them with her lady friends."

Kemble tapped his finger upon the worktable. "I see," he murmured. Abruptly, he rose. "Thank you so much, Mrs. Musbury, for your help."

The housekeeper accompanied him to the door. "Might I ask, Mr. Kemble, if you are anywhere near finished with your questions?"

His hand already on the doorknob, Kemble paused to consider it. "Very nearly, I believe," he murmured. "Yes, very nearly finished."

Gareth was in the study, regretting almost every word he had ever spoken to Antonia, while mindlessly signing the huge pile of letters which Mr. Kemble had left out for him when the gentleman himself came into the room. Gareth was almost glad to see him. He was tired of sitting in this dreary room with no company save his own, and guilt enough for an entire cricket team.

"Good afternoon," said Gareth, flicking a quick glance up at him. "It appears that you have been busy today."

"Yes, thanks," said Kemble vaguely. He went to the bank of windows which overlooked the somewhat gloomy north gardens and simply stood there, staring into the afternoon shadows, his hands clasped behind his back. His usual mordant personality seemed to have deserted him, and the man was quite obviously deep in thought.

Feeling inordinately weary, Gareth laid aside his pen and pushed away the letters. He did not ask Kemble why he had come in; he did not care. He was simply glad for a distraction. Still, he kept looking about the somber, sunless room, and thinking of Antonia. She hated Selsdon's northerly rooms, Coggins had said.

Antonia. Good Lord. Gareth pushed himself away from the desk in disgust. What had he been thinking to confess to her such horrors? He doubted he would even sleep tonight for having so freely relived them. One could only imagine what Antonia's night would be like. She was the last sort of person with whom one ought to share such things. She had seen so little of the world, and that which she had seen had too often hurt. He still was not sure why he had told her.

But there was only one reason a person would do such a thing, wasn't there? He had wanted to see how she would react. And now he had seen. She had been disgusted. Physically disgusted. Gareth pushed his chair from the desk with a violent shove. He had never confessed that filth to any living person, and then he had chosen perhaps the one person in his life who was the most fragile. A woman who knew so little about the dark side of human nature, she had not even grasped his meaning.

Well, if he had been looking for an answer, he now had it. Antonia would never get past what he had once been. There could be no future. Every time they made love, she would look at him and remember just how he had honed his skills. He had traded his body for shelter and for safety. For the chance to stay *alive*. For over a year, he had been a whore. The fact that he had not chosen his path did not change what he had done or what had been done to him. He was forever altered by it. And even Antonia, guileless though she might be, had to know that.

Suddenly, Kemble turned from the window. "What is it, Lloyd, that drives a man?" he asked, his brow furrowed.

"I beg your pardon?"

"The essential nature of man," Kemble said, slowly pacing along the bank of velvet-draped windows. "I am pondering it. And I think at base, all men are driven to attain the same two things, are they not? It is either money or sex—or both. Money, of course, equates to power. And power gets you sex."

Gareth was not entirely clear what they were discussing. "There is always revenge," he remarked, the late duke being much on his mind today. "Men will do a great deal to attain revenge."

Kemble paused, his brow furrowed. "It is odd, but I have always thought revenge more a woman's motivation," he said musingly. "Men will do it, yes. But usually to maintain power—whereas a woman will seek revenge out of spite, I think."

Gareth just shook his head. "You are waxing philosophical today, old fellow," he said. "I am not capable of such deep thought and—"

Just then, the door opened again. Coggins stood in the doorway, looking a little confused himself. "I beg your pardon, Your Grace," he said. "But a guest has arrived. It is Lord Litting, a nephew of the late duke."

"Litting?" Gareth rose. "What the devil can he want?"

"Do you know him?" asked the butler.

Gareth propped one hip on his desk. "Yes, but only from childhood," he answered. "There is nothing he could possibly want from me."

Coggins gave a little cough. "Might I show him in, Your Grace?"

Gareth motioned at the door. "By all means," he said. "Bring him in and let him have his say."

Litting! Today of all days, damn it. As the door closed, Kemble leaned near. "It may be that I have inadvertently caused Litting's visit," he said quietly. "May I remain?"

Gareth wanted to roll his eyes. "Say no more," he answered. "I should probably rather not know the details of what you've been up to. And yes, you are staying."

A few moments later, Coggins returned. Litting came in like a whirlwind, still wearing his driving coat, and quite obviously agitated. With his rapidly receding hair and an ample paunch beneath his expensive waistcoat, he looked very little like the boy Gareth had once known.

As soon as the door was closed, Litting tossed a letter onto Gareth's desk and sent it skidding almost into his lap. "I should like to know the meaning of this, Ventnor," he demanded, stripping off his driving gloves. "You have a lot of gall setting your hounds loose upon me."

Gareth picked up the letter and skimmed it. To his shock, it was signed by the Home Secretary. Awkwardly, he cleared his throat. "I can assure you, Jeremy, that I have not even a passing acquaintance with Mr. Robert Peel. In fact, I am so far removed from that lofty sphere, I don't even *know* anyone who *knows* Peel."

"Actually, Your Grace, you do." Kemble leaned gracefully across his desk, and snatched the letter from his grasp. His eyes swept over it, then he glanced at Litting with a simpering smile. "Allow me to introduce myself, my lord. I am Kemble, the duke's personal secretary. I think perhaps I indirectly caused this letter to be sent."

"Sent?" bellowed Litting. "It was not *sent*. It was hand carried to my house by some Grim Reaper of a chap from the Home Office. And he has been back *five times*."

Kemble gave a breezy smile. "Well, he must find you simply fascinating!"

"He has not found me at all," snapped Litting. "I have thus far refused to see him—and I mean to continue refusing."

Suddenly, the door opened again. Gareth was shocked to see Antonia enter. She had changed from her green frock back into a somber but elegant gown of charcoal gray and a black lace shawl which set off her blond hair to great advantage. "Lord Litting!" she said, coming toward him with her hands outstretched and a bright smile upon her face. "How lovely to see you."

Left with little choice, Litting caught her hands and allowed her to kiss his cheek. "Your Grace," he grumbled awkwardly. "A pleasure, as always. I did not realize you were still in residence."

"Yes, I am to remove to the dower house as soon as it is renovated," she said a little breathlessly. "Unless I decide to stay in London. His Grace has kindly given me time in which to ponder my options."

Gareth wondered if Antonia's cheery tone seemed false to anyone save himself. He was a little surprised to see her in this part of the house, which Coggins had professed her to abhor. But here she was, clasping her hands demurely before her and playing the welcoming hostess.

"Do pardon my barging in," she said. "Coggins said Lord Litting had come to call, and I just thought perhaps I should pop in."

Gareth waved toward a chair. "You are most welcome, Antonia, to join us," he said. "But I collect this is not precisely a social call."

"No, by God, it is not," said Litting, who repeated his complaint to Antonia, who had perched herself on the edge of the chair nearest Gareth's desk.

"Oh, dear," said Antonia, her brow furrowing.

"Well, I simply don't see what the problem is, my lord," said Kemble in a solicitous voice. "If the Home Office has questions about your uncle's untimely demise, you should feel free to answer them. We none of us have anything to hide, I hope."

Litting sneered at Kemble, then looked back and forth between Antonia and Gareth. "We none of us have anything to hide, eh?" he said mockingly. "Well, I want you to put a stop to this, Ventnor, do you hear? Whomever these dogs belong to, you call them off—or you may learn something you'd as soon not know."

"I know my cousin is dead," said Gareth quietly. "And I should like to know why."

Litting looked at him incredulously. "*You* should like to know?" he echoed. "Oh, Ventnor, that is rich indeed. No one gained more by my uncle's death than the two of you"—here, he thrust a finger at Antonia—"as sorry as I am to say it."

"I beg your pardon," said Antonia stiffly. "I fail to see what I have gained."

Gareth, who still stood, came from behind his desk and leaned very near Lord Litting. "Actually, *Jeremy,* you don't sound sorry in the least to say it," he answered in a lethally quiet voice. "So let me warn you that if you say it again, or if you impugn that lady's good name by word or deed or even the slightest insinuation, you will be meeting me over a brace of pistols."

Litting drew back, still sneering. "I am not at all sure I should trouble myself," he said. "I am not sure I account you a gentleman, Ventnor."

Kemble interjected himself between them. "Now, now, sirs," he said. "And Lord Litting, in case you had not heard, Ventnor is now Warneham. I am sure he would appreciate the courtesy of your using his title. And if I may, Your Grace, I do not think Litting fancies being called *Jeremy*."

Litting backed away first, looking just a little shaken. Kemble extended his hand. "Why do you not give me your coat, my lord, then take a seat?" he said calmly. "We are all on the same side here, I believe."

Litting divested himself of his driving coat, then

shoved his gloves into the pocket while watching them all warily. "No one is going to pack this murder off on me," he said darkly. "I have already had to endure that presumptuous justice of the peace following me back to Town. I won't have it, do you hear? I had absolutely no wish to see Warneham dead. None whatsoever. The man was not even my blood kin." This last was said with a sniff which held a hint of disdain.

As an act of contrition, Gareth sat down in the chair opposite Antonia, rather than return to the more distant and authoritative position behind his desk. Kemble went to the small sideboard between the windows and drew the stopper from a bottle of sherry. "No one suspects you of anything, Litting," he said, pouring. "Not so far as I know. Now I think we should all have a drink."

When he returned with a tray of four glasses, everyone gratefully took one. Gareth continued to watch Antonia. She seemed reasonably composed, but she kept cutting long, assessing glances at him when she thought no one else was paying attention. Suddenly, it struck him. Antonia was *worried* about him.

"Now," said Kemble brightly. "Why do you not simply tell all of us what you know, Litting?"

"That's the very point, damn it," he grumbled. "I don't know a bloody thing."

"Well, you must have come down here for a reason that day," Kemble pressed. "You were not, I collect, in the habit of calling upon your—well, let's just call him your uncle-in-law."

Litting's narrow shoulders seemed to fall. "Call him what you damned well please," he said. Then he flicked a quick glance at Antonia. "Your pardon, Your Grace. I do not mean to sound unsympathetic, but I am not pleased that Warneham has caused me to be mixed up in this."

Kemble was tapping one finger lightly on his wineglass. "You came down to Selsdon on the afternoon of Warneham's death. Why? Did he send for you?"

Litting twisted uncomfortably in his chair. "Yes, not that it's any of your business," he finally said. "And he sent for Sir Harold Hardell as well. Has anyone questioned him? Has anyone been pounding at *his* door night and day? That's what I should like to know."

"Why?" asked Kemble pointedly. "Did he have cause to wish Warneham ill?"

Litting tossed his hand with weary disdain. "Oh, good God, no," he said. "He came down here because the duke asked him to, just as I did. He said he needed advice, and Sir Harold could scarcely refuse him. *Who* are you, precisely?"

"Advice?" said Kemble sharply. "Legal advice?"

Litting's gaze moved back and forth between Antonia and Gareth again. He licked his lips, a nervous gesture Gareth remembered from childhood. "Yes, legal advice."

Gareth suddenly felt the hair on the back of his neck stand up. "What sort of legal advice?" he demanded. "Damn it, Litting, if it could have had any bearing on his death, you are obligated to say."

Lord Litting seemed to swell with indignation. "So you really wish to know, do you?" he said, the nasty edge returning to his voice. "And you think it will help you, eh? I ought to tell you, by God. Right here and now."

Suddenly, Antonia half rose from her chair. "Well, *do*

tell it, then, Litting," she said, her voice arching. "Get on with it, please. I vow, I grow sick of this."

"Well, you may grow a good deal sicker, madam," said Litting. "Fine, then. The duke told us he was planning to press forward a suit of nullity."

"A what?" said Gareth. "What the devil is nullity?"

Kemble flashed him a dark look. "Oh, dear," he murmured. "It sounds as if the duke wished to annul his marriage to the duchess."

Antonia gasped. "An annulment? Of our marriage? Why? How?"

Litting was looking at them in mild satisfaction. "Well, there you have it," he said. "Are you pleased? He said he was desperate to get rid of her—that he had grounds to do so—and he wished Sir Harold's advice as to how to most smoothly extricate himself. And then Warneham turned up *dead* before he could further pursue it. Now, do either of you really wish me to tell that to Mr. Peel's vulture? For my part, regardless of what happened to Warneham, I should prefer that no more of our family linen be hung in Fleet Street to dry."

"A most intriguing story!" Kemble murmured, holding his chin pensively. "And what about you, Lord Litting?"

"What about me, pray?" The man turned his haughty gaze on Kemble.

"Why were you here? You are not a barrister—are you?"

"I—well—no, of course I am not!" he said. "It is a ridiculous question."

"Then why were you here?" asked Kemble again.

"What did Warneham want of you? The two of you were not especially close, were you?"

"I—well—that's none of your business," Litting finally said. "I was asked. I came. And I did not do a damned thing more—your pardon, ma'am."

But Antonia had taken on a pale, anxious demeanor. Her hands were braced tightly on her chair arms, as if she meant to leap up. "But this—this is horrible!" she said softly. "How can he have done such a thing? I would have been ruined. I do not understand."

Kemble reached out and covered one of her hands with his. "Your Grace, the duke could have been given an annulment under very few circumstances."

She turned and looked at him dully. "Yes," she whispered. "Yes, he would have had to claim we did not consummate the marriage—which, I daresay, he would never have done, for his pride wouldn't let him. Perhaps he meant to claim that I was hopelessly mad, and that he did not know it. But he knew that I . . . that I had suffered a mental collapse. Papa made that clear before the wedding. And I am not mad. I am *not*."

Gareth had risen and gone at once to her chair. This was bad. Very bad. To some, this could conceivably give Antonia grounds for wishing Warneham dead. Gareth now stood behind Antonia, one hand resting protectively on her shoulder. Almost instinctively, her fingers fluttered up to grasp at his. Litting was right, damn his hide. It would be most imprudent to allow this to get out. It would not simply blight Antonia's future; it would obliterate it. Gareth was beginning to fear that before all this was done with, his meddling would have caused Antonia more harm than good.

"Did Warneham say, Lord Litting, why he wished to do this?" asked Kemble. "Was there . . . someone else whom he wished to marry?"

"No, no," said Litting irritably. "It was nothing like that."

Kemble took a long, slow sip of his sherry, then swallowed with equal languor. "Warneham was desperate for an heir," he said musingly. "Did he mean to find another bride? Attend the season, perhaps?"

"What good would that have done him?" Antonia cried, springing from her chair. "He could not—it was not—it was not me who was the problem!"

Gareth caught her by the hand. "Please, Antonia, sit down," he said. "We shall get to the bottom of this. No one will learn of it, I swear."

"You had better hope, Ventnor, for her sake, that they do not." Litting finished off his sherry in one hearty gulp. "The old gossip hasn't yet died down. She does not need more on the heels of it."

Kemble set his glass down with a sharp clatter. "Forgive me, Lord Litting, but Warneham simply *must* have said more than this," he pressed. "I will go to London and speak with Sir Harold if I must, but I really should rather not."

Litting shifted his weight uneasily. "Warneham simply claimed that his marriage to the duchess mightn't be legally valid, and that—"

"If the marriage was not valid, why annul it?" Kemble swiftly interjected. "Must one do such a thing?"

Litting opened his hands questioningly. "All I can tell you is that Warneham said he wished to minimize the damage to the duchess, to the extent he could," he said.

"I think he was concerned about angering her father. He said Lord Swinburne had too many friends in Parliament, and that he would rather quietly sue for nullity and buy Swinburne off."

"Buy him off?" said Kemble sharply.

"In a manner of speaking." Litting made an equivocal gesture with his hand. "He was going to settle fifty thousand pounds on the duchess through her father, and give her his house in Bruton Street in exchange for Swinburne's not contesting the suit."

"Nonetheless, he was going to ruin me forever." Antonia's hands were shaking. Her eyes darted to their faces in turn, wide and anxious. "He was going to say I was mad. Wasn't he? *Wasn't* he?"

Gareth set his hand on her arm. "It is all right, Antonia," he murmured. "No one can hurt you now."

Kemble lifted his elegant shoulders. "We may never know what he meant to say, Your Grace," he said quietly. "I rather doubt he could have got away with a claim of madness were you to appear."

"He would not have let me," she whispered. "He would have shut me away, just as Father did. He—why, he would have called witnesses. To say things. Vile things."

Kemble looked at her pensively. "I am not at all sure that is what he meant to do," he answered. "He may have been prepared to claim non-consummation."

"And then what?" said Gareth sardonically. "Marry again?"

"Yes, to what end?" asked Antonia witheringly. "Did he think that someone else would be able to—oh, never mind! This is mortifying. Simply mortifying."

Litting rose abruptly. "And it is also none of my concern," he said. "I've told all of you what little I know. Now the two of you had best advise your friends in Whitehall to call off the dogs, for if they darken my door again, I'll tell to them what I've just told you. And it will look dashed nasty for the duchess when I do."

With obvious reluctance, Kemble retrieved Litting's coat.

"It is rather late in the day to be driving back to London," said Gareth, hating what he must say next. "May we put you up for the night?"

Lord Litting sneered. "Given the luck I've had, I should rather not spend another evening under this roof," he said. "But thank you. I have a sister near Croydon with whom I shall stay."

Kemble held open the door. "Allow me to show you out," he said smoothly.

In an instant, they were gone.

Gareth was half hoping Antonia would bolt into his arms, but she did not. She was pacing restlessly through the room, her hands fisted in the delicate lace of her shawl. Gareth went to her and deftly extracted the ends. She looked down as his fingers unfurled the fine fabric, watching almost as if the hands were not hers but someone else's.

Gareth flicked an anxious glance up at her. He hoped desperately that Lord Litting's visit did not set Antonia back, for it had seemed lately that she was far more in charge of her emotions.

"Antonia, I won't let this hurt you," he said quietly. "I swear to you I *won't*. I will shut Litting up if it comes to that, but I think he has no reason to talk. I will see that you are protected."

But Antonia's mind had taken a different turn. "Oh, Gabriel," she said, sinking back down into her chair. "I had no idea Warneham was even contemplating such a thing as an annulment! Please say that you believe me."

"Of course I believe you, Antonia," he answered.

She looked up at him at little grimly. "Many people would not," she said. "Some would say it gives me a motive for murder."

Gareth shook his head. "I believe you, Antonia," he said quietly. "And I believe *in* you, too. There is nothing anyone could say that would make me doubt you—certainly not Litting. He was speaking in half-truths, anyway. We do not yet have the whole story—but I will get it. I swear to you."

Antonia set the heel of her hand to her forehead, her expression one of indescribable fatigue and defeat. "I cannot believe this is happening," she said. "I feel like such a gudgeon for coming in here. For imagining, even for a moment, that I might be of . . ." She let her words break off and shook her head.

Gabriel knelt down and held her gaze. "That you might what, Antonia?"

She glanced away as if she was unable to look at him. "I did not know Mr. Kemble was with you," she said. "I did not wish you to have to see Litting alone. I feared he had come to do some sort of mischief. I thought for once I might be of help to you, instead of it being the other way round. It was silly of me."

He took her hands in his and gave them what he hoped was a squeeze. "Thank you, Antonia, for worrying about me."

She still did not look at him. "I am sorry he came here, Gabriel, to cut up your peace."

Gabriel gave a muted smile. "I think we both know my peace had already been sliced pretty well to ribbons," he said quietly. "And that the doing of it was all mine. As to this business with Litting, well, I am sure you know that, too, was my doing. I have asked Kemble to help me uncover the truth, to try to dispel all the uncertainty surrounding Warneham's death. And now it seems I have but deepened it."

At last she looked at him, her gaze locked with his as he stood. "Oh, Gabriel," she whispered.

But Antonia was forestalled from whatever remark she had meant to make. The door latch clicked, and Kemble came back into the room. "Well!" he said speciously. "Wasn't that a pleasant little chat!"

Gareth gave a disgusted grunt. "I think we should all have another glass of sherry to wash it down with," he said, crossing the room to get the decanter.

Antonia turned to Mr. Kemble at once. "None of this makes any sense, does it?" she said. "First the rumor-mongers whisper that I poisoned Warneham because I was unhappy in our marriage. And now Litting suggests I killed him so that he could not end our marriage? Is it too much to ask that they should all settle on one lurid tale or the other?"

Kemble, for once, looked confused, too. "Here is what I cannot comprehend," he said, settling gracefully into a chair as Gareth refilled the wineglasses. "Why didn't Litting simply tell the truth about Warneham's plans when the justice of the peace questioned him? Why would he bother to protect you, Your Grace, from a charge of murder?"

"Indeed, I barely know him," she agreed.

Gareth watched Kemble carefully. One could almost see the cogs of his mind meshing together. "I think that the answer is that he was *not* protecting you," Kemble said pensively. "He was protecting someone—or some-*thing*—else."

"That makes no sense," said Gareth, falling back into his chair. "What was Litting doing here in the first place? And why did Warneham fear Lord Swinburne's wrath?"

"Papa can be very vindictive," said Antonia.

"I do not doubt that, my dear," said Gareth. "But what did Warneham have to lose? He did not go about in society. He was not remotely involved or interested in what went on in London. He had even let out his town house for the last five years. I fully expect he could have lived the remainder of his life without ever laying eyes on Swinburne again."

Antonia looked unconvinced. "Papa wields a great deal of influence in the House."

Gareth shook his head. "What could the Lords do to make his life difficult?"

Kemble sipped at his wine. "The House of Lords is the only institution that can grant a peer a divorce," he said pensively.

"But he was going to annul our marriage," said Antonia. "And all his other wives were dead."

Gareth leaned forward anxiously. "Perhaps he feared his suit of nullity would fail, and he would have to resort to a divorce?"

Kemble seemed to consider it. "No, there is not a chance in hell," he said, almost to himself. "It would have taken years, possibly. He would first have to appeal to the ecclesiastical courts for a separation, then file the bill for divorce with the House. And what grounds could he use? He would need two witnesses to the adultery or the—"

"The adultery?" cried Antonia, almost coming out of her chair.

Kemble waved her back down again. "I am speaking theoretically, Your Grace," he said soothingly. "No, there would have been no possibility of a divorce."

"Perhaps he feared he might need the House's support in some other sort of unpleasantness?" Gareth suggested.

Suddenly, Kemble turned in his chair to face Antonia. "Your Grace, you earlier gave the impression your marriage was never consummated," he said. "I must ask you why."

"I beg your pardon?" Antonia's face flooded with pink.

"Damn it, Kemble," said Gareth.

Kemble looked at him and opened his hands expressively. "Your Grace, I work for you," he said. "Do you wish this cloud of blame lifted from her shoulders or not?"

Gareth merely glared at him.

"I do not mind to answer your question, Mr. Kemble," said Antonia quietly. "I am sure it was whispered about within the house anyway."

Kemble shot a triumphant smirk at Gareth, then turned to Antonia. "Thank you, Your Grace," he said magnanimously. "Was celibacy your idea, or was your husband impotent?"

"He was impotent."

"Ah, I thought as much," said Kemble. "Did he blame you?"

Antonia shook her head. "I blamed me," she said. "He seemed frustrated with himself."

Clinically, Kemble let his eyes run down Antonia's length. "Well, you cannot possibly have disappointed him in any way," he said, as if he discussed the merits of a piece of furniture. "If you could not please him, then the man cannot possibly have expected another bride to bring him back from the dead—so to speak."

"Oh, good Lord!" said Gareth. "Antonia, you may leave the room, since Mr. Kemble seems intent on breaching all bounds of civility."

"No, I think I shall stay, thank you," said Antonia. She was watching Kemble almost raptly now.

For his part, Kemble was lost in thought. "So we must now ask ourselves how he meant to remedy this situation," he muttered to himself. "What, precisely, did Warneham want? And what confluence of events might have given it to him?"

"Oh, he wanted an heir of his blood to dispossess me," said Gareth. "And frankly, I would have been pleased had he found one."

"Yes, there was no other motivator that I can see," Kemble agreed.

"Perhaps he meant to claim our old friend Metcaff?" Gareth sourly suggested.

Kemble looked at him in amazement. "Your Grace, you are perfectly brilliant!"

"Am I? How? Could he have done so?"

"No, the notion is ridiculous, but . . ." Kemble's words

trailed away as he turned to look at Antonia. "Is there any chance, ma'am, however slight, that someone might have murdered Warneham on your behalf?"

Antonia's blue eyes widened. "Lord, no."

Gareth shot her a questioning look. "That maid of yours is a bit of a battle-ax," he said quietly. "And she very nearly killed *me*."

Antonia looked askance at him. "Oh, Gabriel, that's utter nonsense. Nellie wouldn't hurt a flea."

"Oh, I think Nellie would hurt anyone she thought capable of wounding you," Kemble asserted. "But I do not see how she could have learnt of his plans to dissolve the marriage. And even if she had, she might have thought it a good thing."

"I daresay you are right," Gareth reluctantly admitted.

Kemble finished his sherry and pushed his glass away. "Well, I think we can do no more here for today," he said musingly. "Tomorrow it is going to rain—heavily, I think, if my sinuses are any judge—but the day after, Your Grace, perhaps we should go up to London if the roads are dry? I would very much like to hear what this barrister has to say for himself."

"Yes, perhaps we should," said Gareth wearily. "Let me think on it for now." Together, they all rose. Antonia set a hand to her temple.

"Will you be so kind as to excuse me from dinner tonight, Your Grace?" she said a little stiffly. "I feel a bit of a headache coming on. As Mr. Kemble says, it is probably just the rain approaching. Perhaps I shall have a tray brought up."

Gareth bowed. "By all means," he said. "It has been a difficult day for us all."

On that note, Antonia left the room, taking what little warmth and comfort there had been along with her. Gareth felt downcast and thwarted. As if his outburst this afternoon at the pavilion had not been enough of a fiasco, his meddling in Warneham's death might now prove to be Antonia's undoing. And he was not at all sure she could forgive him for any of it.

Chapter Sixteen

*G*abriel lay perfectly motionless, listening to the sway of the Saint-Nazaire and the creaking of the ropes which bound her. The ship was still as death save for the scuttling rats below. The other hammocks hung empty from their pegs, lifeless, shriveled cocoons, their occupants long since flown ashore, in search of drink and sport.

Just then, footfalls sounded on the deck above, some heavy and certain, others light and hesitant. The sound of someone being dragged, perhaps. Raucous, raspy laughter. The beam which held the door above slid free, and Gabriel froze with fear. A tremulous light appeared, followed by a stumbling tangle of legs. More laughter. Gabriel peeked around a timber beam to better see. Creavy and Ruiz. He began to shake with dread. And then he saw. No, they would not be coming for him tonight. They had dragged a woman down between them, her arms bound behind her, her blue dress ripped from sleeve to waist.

Ruiz shifted his hand from her lips, and she screamed. Creavy backhanded her, bloodying her mouth and sending *her hair tumbling down over one shoulder. "Ooh, I likes me a tart wiv a little fight in 'er," Creavy crooned, rubbing a strand of her hair between his filthy, gnarled fingers. Gabriel could see the woman's eyes widen with fear.*

"Dios mío! Get on weeth it!" Ruiz sounded impatient.

Creavy ripped down the rest of her dress until her breasts were exposed; small white orbs heaving in the lantern's light. Ruiz held her tight as Creavy unbuttoned his trousers and threw up her skirts. Gabriel drew the blanket over his head as she screamed. Then the screams became a whimper, and the whimper a slow, mournful sobbing.

He should do something. Anything. Offer up himself, perhaps? But he did not—he was too afraid—and the whimpering went on, long into the night. Gabriel held himself deathly still beneath the blanket, sickened by the sounds of the woman's suffering. Sickened by his own pathetic weakness.

Gareth dined alone that night in the small dining room, feeling lost and more desolate than he wished to admit. This was the shape of things to come, he very much feared. He pushed away his plate and let his eyes drift over the empty room. He had foolishly begun to rely upon Antonia, almost without realizing he'd been doing so.

Antonia was someone with whom he could discuss his questions and ideas about Selsdon. And in spending time with her, he had begun to see pieces of the laughing, vivacious girl she had once been and hints of the gracious, levelheaded woman she should have become. It was not too late for her.

When a footman came in to clear his plate, Gareth waved away the next course. He had no appetite—not for food, at any rate.

After dinner he took his glass and his bottle of port and went not to the study, as had become his habit, but to the cream-and-gold parlor, where he had first laid eyes upon Antonia. Where, just this morning, she had told him of her plans to do precisely what he had recommended—leave Selsdon. In this room, he always imagined that he could smell her; smell the faint scent of gardenias and something else—something clean and a little sweet.

Cradling his port between his legs, Gareth slumped in a wide leather armchair opposite the row of French windows and stared morosely out into the gardens, toward the shadowy row of estate buildings beyond. The days were growing rapidly shorter now, and at this late hour, he could see only their looming dark outlines. The near end of the granary. The stables. The carriage house. Orderly, well-kept buildings of slate and stone and timber, all in a row; all as neat and tidy as he wished his emotions were.

She was going to leave, she had said, as soon as her maid was well enough to travel. That might well be tomorrow, or possibly the next day. She had not said that her going was permanent. But Gareth had the strangest premonition that it would be. Once Antonia arrived in London, if her father's power and influence could indeed restore her to even some modest level of society, what would there be for her to return to? If she had formed any attachment to him—if she had harbored any silly, romantic notions—his revelations this afternoon would have shattered it.

On that thought, Gareth drained the dregs of his wine. Perhaps, deep in the recesses of his mind, that was precisely what he had meant to do. Perhaps there was a part of him that wished to drive Antonia away; a part that feared the sort of intimacy she would require. He poured a second glass of port and slid a little lower into his chair. He was not perfectly sure when the light on the horizon caught his eye—well, *caught* was the wrong word. It was more of a slow awareness that something was not right.

He looked up to see that a warm, rosy light limned the roofline of the carriage house beyond the gardens. Gareth blinked and scooted up in his chair. Not daylight, surely? No. It was too isolated. *Too vivid.*

"Fire!" he bellowed, coming out of his chair. The glass of port tumbled to the floor. "Fire," he called again, going to the bell and yanking vigorously. He rushed down the passageway toward the great hall. A footman usually slept on the cot in Coggins's office. Gareth pounded on the door. "Fire!" he bellowed again. "Get up, for God's sake!"

The door flew open. One of the younger footmen stood in his shirtsleeves, eyes bleary. "Y-yes, Your Grace!"

"How many people sleep above the carriage house?" Gareth roughly demanded.

"Six, I think." The footman was awake now. "What's amiss?"

"There is a fire," he said.

"Christ Jesus!"

"The carriage house, from the looks of it," said Gareth. "Wake all the servants who aren't ill. I want them at the stable well in five minutes—with buckets!"

"Yes, Your Grace." He was throwing on his coat now. His hands were shaking.

Gareth was already halfway down the corridor when

a thought struck. He turned around and shouted at the footman, who was partway up the curved staircase. "And send someone to the village," he added. "I want Osborne up here. *Now*."

Once outside, Gareth dashed onto the pergola and looked about. From this angle, he could see that the glow had heightened beyond the roofline of the carriage house. Behind him, doors were slamming and chaos was erupting. He set off at a run, but feet came pounding after him.

"It's a bad one." Kemble's voice rang out behind him. "I saw it from the library. Are there servants above?"

"The stable staff," Gareth shouted. "Come on! We'll cut through Watson's office."

Watson had not yet locked up for the night, thank God. Gareth bolted inside to see that the back windows were alight with a sickening glow. Dashing around the desks and tables, he pushed through the back door, which gave onto the service courtyard. A set of carriage doors had been flung wide, and flames were rolling out onto the cobblestones and licking their way up the doors.

Kemble drew up beside him. "It's going up the walls—inside and out." He ran to the windows on the other side. "Fire! Get out! Fire!"

Flames were licking up the wooden doors and trim. In seconds, two of the window frames were afire. "We've got to get upstairs," said Gareth, circling along the courtyard in search of the staircase. "Find the stairs. Some of the lads are ill, and likely full of laudanum."

The stairs. The stairs. *Where were the bloody stairs?*

"Fire! Fire!" Kemble cried, pausing to peek inside the next set of doors. "Over here!" he shouted at Gareth.

Quickly, they unbolted the doors, but the fire was licking its way up and over. The heat in the courtyard was becoming fierce.

"Wait! We need water!" Gareth ran to the trough near the well and doused himself. He scooped another bucket and crossed the courtyard to drench Kemble. "Take off your neckcloth," he ordered. "We must wrap them round our mouths."

Together they did so, then dragged open the second set of doors. The right-hand wall was already aflame. Behind them, servants were dashing into the courtyard. Mrs. Musbury was barking orders to line up at the well. Just then, above them, an explosion blew out a window. Glass rained down on the cobbles. Gareth dashed inside, Kemble on his heels.

"Your traveling coach!" Kemble shouted through the roiling smoke. "We can pull it out by the tongue!"

"No, go up! Up!" Gareth words were muffled by his neckcloth. He waved toward the stairs. "There!"

Together, they thundered up the steps. Kemble paused at the first landing. "No," Gareth cried, pointing upward. "That's storage."

At the top, there was just one door. Gareth flung it open. The room was filled with tack and supplies. "Over there!" Kemble gestured through the faint smoke.

Gareth could see flames licking at the top of the window casing. He set his shoulder to the interior door and burst in to find a sort of parlor with a rough-hewn table and two cupboards. The next door, surely? "Fire! Get up! Fire!" he bellowed, shoving through it to find three beds, and Terrence standing at the window in his nightshirt, his expression petrified.

"Terry, get out!" Gareth's shouts were muffled by the cloth. "Good God, man, get out!"

Terrence turned and ran directly into Kemble. The other two men roused quickly. "Who else sleeps up here?" Gareth demanded.

A second groom was shoving on his shoes. "The stable boys," he answered. "Through there."

"Is there a second staircase?" Kemble shouted from the tack room. "Because we are going to need it."

"No stairs that a'way." Talford, the coachman, was yanking on his breeches. "Just windows."

Kemble slammed the door tight. "Mary, Jesus, and Joseph!" prayed Terrence. "We're going to die."

"Don't be ridiculous!" snapped Kemble, returning. "Hurry along now! We're going out a window." He shooed them forward, away from the thickening smoke, like a goose herding her goslings. The roaring heat was oppressive now.

Gareth was rousting the stable boys. "What's happening?" he shouted back at Kemble. "Have the stairs caught?"

"I fear so," said Kemble. "Find a window."

"Which window is lowest?" Gareth shouted at the coachman who was behind Kemble.

"Through there," said Talford. "It's a tad lower on the laundry side."

They were essentially circling around the estate shops' courtyard. People were beginning to cough. Gareth had no clue where the laundry was, but he pushed his way into a room full of old furniture. He went to the left window and threw it open. "We need a ladder!" he shouted down. "A ladder—round to the laundry side! Hurry!"

Coggins looked up. "Right away, Your Grace!"

Gareth closed the window to cut down the draw. "How bad is it?" he asked Kemble.

"It's stone—but with dry timber framing," he said grimly. "The stairs are going and your coach is afire."

"Musbury's got a bucket line going on that side," Gareth said. "Let's get that back window up and see how far down it is."

This window was stuck from disuse. It took the both of them to shove up the casement. Behind them, the stable boys and grooms were filing in.

"The stairs are falling in," Talford shouted through the smoke. "It's out that window or nothing."

The youngest boy began to cry. One of the grooms was wheezing. Kemble had his head out the window, assessing the view. Gareth set a hand on the boy's shoulder. "Look, we can jump out if we must," he said. "The worst you'll get is a broken leg."

This, unfortunately, did not comfort the lad, whose sobs became great, gulping heaves.

Kemble drew his head in. "It's pitch black on that side," he said. "But I'd judge it no more than seventeen feet."

Just then a clatter arose from below. Gareth leaned out to see a tremulous halo of light moving across the grass, and one of the footmen dragging a ladder.

"Put it there!" ordered Coggins, holding the lamp aloft. "Your Grace, we have it! You must come down at once."

Gareth drew his head back in. "You," he said, grabbing the youngest boy. "You go down first."

The boy cast a glance out the window. "I c-cannot, Your Grace," he sobbed. "I—I am afraid."

Gareth grabbed one of the grooms. "You go first," he said, winking. "You must catch the others if they fall."

The groom had one leg out the window as the ladder scraped into place.

"All right!" cried Coggins. "Come on down!"

The groom wasted no time. "Next!" cried Coggins. "Your Grace, you must come down!"

Kemble shoved forward another stable boy. "Youth before beauty!" he trilled. "I daresay I shall have to go last."

This stable boy made his way gingerly out as the men below bellowed orders up at him. "Set your hand on the sill! Shift your foot! To the left, now. Steady."

Just then, fire burst to life through the most distant doorway. "There goes the tack storage!" Kemble shouted. "And likely some solvents, too."

Gareth grabbed Talford, the coachman. "What's in there? Any idea?"

The coachman winced. "Turpentine, certainly, Your Grace. Linseed oil. And some old paint, I daresay."

"Bloody hell!" Gareth grabbed the next groom. "Down you go. Hurry."

This man was more nimble than he looked, and down in a trice. Gareth grabbed the youngest boy again. "Now you must go," he said sternly. "If you fall, someone will catch you."

"B-but it's dark," said the boy. "H-how will they see me?"

"Well, wait another minute, and the frigging roof will

be afire," said Kemble under his breath. "That ought to light it up rather nicely."

"Kemble, hush." Gareth pushed the boy forward. "You must go now, so that the rest of us may follow."

It seemed an eternity before the boy was down. "Kemble, go," Gareth ordered.

"I'm afraid of heights." Kemble waved one arm. "Mr. Talford? Your ladder awaits."

Just then, something in the distant room exploded. Gareth looked back to see a small fireball roll beneath the old parlor table. Glass shattered, and a cry rang out from the courtyard side.

"Another window blew," said Kemble grimly. "Now we've got a cross draft. We don't have long now."

Talford was almost down. Gareth grabbed the next stable boy, a big lad with a red nose and rheumy eyes who had been hanging well back from the others. "Come on," he said. "Down you go."

The lad backed away, almost cringing. "You must go next, Your Grace. I shall go last."

"The hell you will," said Gareth. "Go. *Now*. That's an order."

The boy did as he was bid, but he looked about ready to cast up his accounts. Gareth watched him nimbly descend. It was not the ladder he feared, then. "You're next," he said over his shoulder to Kemble. "And none of your damned theatrics."

"You must go first," said Kemble as Gareth withdrew from the window.

A few feet away, Talford's bed burst into flame, along with the rug beneath it.

"You will go, by God," said Gareth. "Or I shall throw

you bodily, and you'll likely break that perfect nose of yours—perhaps even a leg to go with it."

Kemble's eyes swept down him. "Yes, you might, mightn't you?" he murmured. "Fine, Lloyd, go fricassee yourself for all I care." He swung a leg out, and the rest of him smoothly followed. Kemble descended the rungs so gracefully that one would imagine he did so every night of the week. Hell, perhaps he did, for all Gareth knew.

"Your Grace, please!" Coggins's voice was strident. "You really must come down now!"

Gareth already had a leg out. Just as his second foot found a rung, with his hands still on the windowsill, a clap of thunder sounded that resonated off Selsdon's walls and sent a tangible shudder through the carriage house.

Please, please God, Gareth prayed as he clambered down. *Please let it pour.*

"Your Grace!" Coggins was holding his own hands prayerfully before him as Gareth turned. "Oh, thank the good Lord!"

The footmen pulled down the ladder. Gareth surveyed the crowd. "Is that everyone?" he said. "Has anyone gone unaccounted for?" he asked, unfurling the wet cloth from his mouth.

Talford stepped forward just as a dollop of rain struck Gareth's forehead. "All my men are accounted for, Your Grace," he said. "God bless you both."

"Fine, then," said Gareth. "Those of you who are ill, get the hell out of this rain. Go into the kitchen and put on some tea. The rest of you get round to the courtyard and join the brigade."

Everyone hastened round the buildings, but the rain was now pelting down. The smaller patches of fire were turning to steam and smoke. In the courtyard, Mrs. Musbury was still barking orders like a sergeant major, the hem of her nightgown dragging soddenly over the cobbles. Someone had wisely turned all the horses out to pasture. Watson stood to one side of the courtyard, grimly surveying the damage.

"Gabriel!" To Gareth's shock, Antonia darted from the crowd, looking small and rather terrified. She wore a heavy woolen cloak, but beneath it one could see the flannel of her wrapper and a pair of dainty pink bed slippers. "Oh, thank God!" she cried, flying to him. *"Gabriel!"*

Gareth caught her by the shoulders, an unexpected joy surging through him. "Antonia, what are you doing out here?"

"Oh, Gabriel, I could not find you!" Another clap of thunder sounded and she jumped, but held fast to his arms. "They said you had gone into the carriage house! I imagined the worst."

The rain was steadily picking up. Gareth managed to smile at her. "But as you see, Antonia, I really am safe," he said. "Please, my dear, go back inside. This storm is coming on so fast."

She clung to his arms, her blue eyes wide, her lashes tipped with raindrops. "I don't care about the storm!" she cried. "I care only for you. Oh, Gabriel, I—I know you don't wish me to say it—but I care for you so much."

She was speaking rashly, out of panic, he knew, but his heart felt a stirring of hope. He just prayed for her sake they did not have an audience. "My dear girl," he said quietly. "Don't do this."

"No." Her voice was sharp. "I cannot help it. Don't be angry with me, *please*. I have been so frightened. When I could not find you, I thought . . . I thought my life was over again. I need you, Gabriel. Even if you do not feel quite the same, please just—"

He cut her off, tightening his grip on her shoulders so that he would not drag her into his arms as he so desperately wished. "Antonia, we cannot speak of it here."

"When, Gabriel?" she whispered. "I must see you. *Tonight*."

He glanced worriedly about the crowd. "Very well," he murmured. "But please, go back into the house, my dear. That is what I need you to do just now—keep yourself safe. For me, Antonia?"

Just then, Nellie Waters shoved her way through the crowd. "Lady Antonia, this is madness!" she whispered. "For the love of God, please go back inside the house before you catch your death!"

Gareth turned Antonia gently around. "I suspect if you refuse Mrs. Waters, she will simply stay out here with you and make herself sicker," he said quietly.

With obvious reluctance, Antonia nodded and walked away. For an instant, Gareth hesitated, wishing to go after her, but someone saved him from his folly by clearing his throat sharply behind him. "Mr. Watson needs you, Your Grace," said one of the footmen.

"Yes, of course." Hastily, Gareth crossed the courtyard. The bucket brigade was breaking up. The fire would soon be out. "It's bad, isn't it?" he said, joining Watson.

The estate manager nodded. "But everyone got out alive, thanks to you and Mr. Kemble," he said. "And the rain is coming on fast. I think the worst is over—well, almost."

"Almost?" Gareth looked at him, disconcerted. "What do you mean by that?"

The estate agent flicked a troubled glance at Gareth. "There is something you are going to have to see, I suppose," he said, starting across the courtyard toward the bay in which the fire had begun.

The doors still sat wide open, their interior sides charred. "What was in here?" Gareth asked Watson as they surveyed the damage. "Some sort of wagon?"

Watson pointed into the dark, smoldering depths. "The new threshing machine," he said grimly.

Gareth cursed beneath his breath. "Machine breakers?"

Watson shrugged. "So I first assumed," he said, dragging one of the doors shut. "Until I saw *this*."

The door's interior was blackened, but on the front side, much of the white paint was intact—as were the bloodred letters scrawled across it. Gareth felt as if someone had knocked the wind out of him. As if the boys from Shoreditch had just hammered him to the ground again and left him gasping for air.

Burn in hell, Jew.

For an inestimable moment, Gareth could only stare at it, the rain running down his face. Watson looked pained. "I am sorry, Your Grace," he finally said. "I felt . . . well, I felt you ought to see it."

Behind him, he could feel the servants' eyes as they took in the scene. "Leave it open," said Gareth sharply. "Just . . . leave it open so everyone doesn't have to see it."

"It's filth, Your Grace," said Watson firmly. "Pure, unadulterated filth—and I am sorry. People don't believe that way any longer. They truly do not. England is beginning to change."

"Well, someone hasn't," Gareth murmured.

Watson surprised him then by setting a hand on his shoulder. "I shall tear it down tomorrow, Your Grace," he said quietly, "and finish the job of burning it."

Someone appeared at Gareth's elbow with a black umbrella. "Mother of God," whispered Dr. Osborne, looking at the door. "Someone needs to hang for this."

Gareth turned and dragged a filthy hand through his wet hair. "Thank you for coming, Osborne," he said. "Come on. Let's get inside and—"

Another clap of thunder cut him off, and it was as if the heavens split wide open. The deluge began in earnest. Gareth grabbed the doctor's arm. "Inside Watson's office," he shouted over the din. He grabbed Mrs. Musbury and dragged her along with him.

"Into the kitchens, everyone else!" she shouted. "Go! Go, quickly!"

The servants went around the office toward the lower kitchen door. Osborne and Watson followed Gareth and Mrs. Musbury into the office. Kemble brought up the rear. Coggins had vanished. They burst inside just as a bolt of lightning tore through the sky.

"Oh, I have never been so glad in all my life for a thunderstorm!" said the housekeeper, shaking herself off. "Oh, Your Grace. Mr. Kemble. You were very brave indeed!"

"Who amongst the staff has been injured?" Gareth asked, his gaze shifting from Mrs. Musbury to Watson. "Was anyone burnt?"

"Edwards, the second footman, broke a finger, I

think," Mrs. Musbury offered. "An accident passing the water buckets."

"Fine, Edwards is your first patient," Gareth ordered the doctor. "And then you must see to everyone who is still nursing swollen tonsils. I have a notion every damned one of them was out here in this smoke and rain tonight."

"Yes, I fear so," Osborne agreed, checking the contents of his satchel.

"Then kindly see to Mrs. Musbury," Gareth continued. "She has a weak chest, and the duchess has already chided me about keeping her standing in the rain."

The housekeeper looked affronted until Gareth winked at her. She allowed Osborne to escort her away.

Watson sat down at his desk. Gareth flopped down into a nearby chair, feeling filthy and weary. A heavy silence fell across the room. Gareth saw Kemble had a streak of soot across his high, usually immaculate collar, and a tuft of his hair had been scorched. Poor devil. He had not signed on for this.

"Machine breakers, eh?" said Kemble skeptically. "But in this case, *anti-Semitic* machine breakers? I wonder how many of those are wandering about the south of England with red paint and a tinder box?"

"You have a theory?" asked Gareth quietly.

"A theory, yes." Propped casually against Watson's drawer-stack, Kemble was looking grim. "But no more than that."

Watson sat wearily back in his desk chair, his hands shoved deep into his coat pockets. "It is almost as if whoever did this could not resist one last malicious stab," he said. "And it *could* be machine breakers, I daresay. And yet I do not think so. We haven't even used the bloody thing yet. And we've put no one out of work—nor planned to. The entire staff knows that."

"I know what I should like," said Kemble, coming away from the file cabinet to brace his arms wide on Watson's desk. "I should like ten minutes alone with that last stable hand you shoved out the carriage house window."

Gareth looked at him in surprise. "What, the lad with the runny nose? Whatever for?"

Kemble frowned pensively. "The boy looked . . . guilty," he answered. "He was sick, yes. But it was more than that. Had you not ordered him out the window, I'm not at all sure he meant to go. And then, when you ordered the sick into the kitchens, he didn't leave. He joined Musbury's bucket line."

"Damn," said Gareth. "Did he indeed?"

Watson pushed his chair away from the desk. "You are speaking of Howell, I think?" he remarked. "A big lad of about fifteen? He's been abed and feverish the last two days. I can't think what he could have done to feel guilty for."

Kemble slowly shook his head. "It may not be what the boy has *done*," he answered. "It may be more a case of what he has heard or seen."

This time Gareth dragged both of his filthy hands through his hair. "Christ, another mystery!" he said. "Kemble, speak with the lad tomorrow. Find out what he knows."

"By all means, Your Grace," said Kemble, his gravity

giving way to waggishness. "After all, my hair has been singed and my favorite coat ruined. Someone *really* must pay."

Gareth crossed his arms over his chest and regarded him assessingly. "So, do you care to share with us your theory?" he asked. "Who is to do this paying?"

Kemble set his head to one side. "I am not perfectly sure," he admitted. "But if I were a wagering man, I should guess it will be our old friend Mr. Metcaff."

Chapter Seventeen

Gabriel pressed his back to the damp stone wall of the galley, his heart pounding. He heard nothing; nothing but the clatter and clamor of a busy port. The rumble of barrels rolling across wood. The creak of the cranes. The familiar hue and cry of the dockyard—much of it in foreign tongues. But they had lost him. He was free. Gabriel drew in a deep, shuddering breath and turned the corner toward freedom.

The shouts rang out at once. "Oy, there's the lit'le bastard! After 'im, Ruiz!"

Gabriel was off in a flash. Feet pounded down the cobbles behind him as he dashed through the twisting, turning streets of Bridgetown. His lungs were about to burst. He saw a shadowy alley up ahead, but as he made for it, a tavern door flew open. A thin, dark-haired man stepped out, and snatched him up as if he weighed nothing.

"Ho, what have we here?" he chortled. "A little pickpocket, perhaps?"

"P-please, sir." Gabriel had begun to shake. "Don't let them take me. Please."

The three sailors drew up near the door, panting. "Thank you, sir," *said Creavy.* "The lad gave us the slip on the dock."

The man did not relinquish his grip. "And what would be the name of your ship?"

Creavy hesitated. "The Saint-Nazaire. Why?"

"Not all captains are reputable," *said the dark-haired man.* "What is your interest in this boy?"

"Why, he's indentured, sir," *said Creavy almost defensively.* "We have a right to seize him."

The dark man sneered. "Indentured? He doesn't look old enough to shave!" *He glanced again at Gabriel.* "In fact, the lad looks awfully like my long-lost cousin from Shropshire. I believe I shall just take him home with me."

Creavy's eyes narrowed wickedly. He took a step nearer.

In a flash, the dark man drew a knife—a long, lethal-looking thing which had been strapped to his thigh. "Don't even think of it." *His voice was soft and calm.* "There are a dozen men inside that tavern. Half are my friends—and the other half my employees."

"But—but the boy's ours by rights," *rasped Creavy.*

"Fine," *said the dark man.* "You go get the lad's papers of indenture from Larchmont—yes, I know all about the Saint-Nazaire—then bring them to Neville Shipping down by the careenage. I shall have a look at them—and then, if I'm satisfied, why, I'll give you the lad. What could be more fair?"

As the men walked away, Gabriel drew in his breath on a shuddering sob. "Will they be back, sir?"

The dark man patted his shoulder. "Not a chance in hell. Come on, boy. Let's get you to safety."

* * *

As the fire hissed and steamed its last, Gareth returned to the house through the kitchens to make sure everyone was accounted for. Mrs. Musbury had put on one of her gray serge gowns and was pouring coffee for the exhausted crowd which was gathered in her sitting room. Nellie Waters was bustling about with a mop, sopping up puddles of water and tidying the piles of wet coats and boots. Gareth found Dr. Osborne in the stillroom splinting the broken finger.

He flicked a glance up at Gareth. "I believe we have escaped without serious injury," he said. "Have you any idea who might have done this?"

Gareth shook his head. "No, not yet," he said grimly. "But I will—and may God help him."

Seated at the narrow worktable, the footman was looking a tad pale. Gareth set a hand on the servant's shoulder. "All right there, Edwards?"

"Yes, Your Grace," he said. "It is a clean break. It does not hurt—well, not much."

Gareth smiled wearily. "Thank you for your efforts tonight," he said. "Go back to your bed, Osborne, if this is the worst of it. I thank you for coming so quickly."

With that, he hastened upstairs, stripped to the waist, and sluiced off the worst of the smoke and the grime at the washstand. He forced himself to forget about the fire, but he could not forget the stark, almost hopeless, expression in Antonia's eyes tonight. She really had been terrified for him; so terrified she had put aside her own fear of storms to come looking for him. Patting his face dry with a towel, Gareth caught his own gaze in the mirror. The man who looked back seemed . . . different, somehow. His face, shadowed with a day's worth of beard, seemed leaner, his eyes harder. These few weeks at Selsdon had changed him, and not in the way he had anticipated.

Gareth wondered what his father had looked like at this age. Much the same, he supposed. Major Charles Ventnor had been thirty-six years of age upon leaving for the Peninsula, already battle-hard and battle-weary. Gareth remembered that his father had been tall, broad-shouldered, and golden-haired. That his laugh had been rich and deep. That his eyes had lit with happiness when he'd looked at his wife. And that was about it. Gareth's was a child's memory, all he would have to sustain him throughout the rest of his life.

He was surprised to find himself missing his father so much. But perhaps now, of all times, it was understandable. Had he lived, Gareth could have asked him what it was like when a staid and serious-minded man fell head over heels in love at such an age. Would it go away? Get worse? Or would it grow and become something beautiful and all-encompassing, as his parents' devotion had done? Even time and distance had not lessened their love. Religion and class-consciousness had not altered it one whit.

And suddenly, Gareth knew what his father's advice would have been. To chance it. To risk it all—regret, hope, happiness—with Antonia. But Antonia's situation was not quite the same, was it? She had never been allowed to make her own decisions. She had never been given choices. And so long as her husband's death hung like a shadow over her head, she would have few.

But Warneham and his father were in the past. Antonia, perhaps, was his future, though in what form, he was not entirely sure. Her words tonight had given him hope when they should not have. And now he burned with the need to see her. To hold her. Gareth threw down the towel and went to the dressing room for clean clothes.

When he reached her sitting room door, Antonia answered on his first soft knock, wearing nothing but her nightgown. "Gabriel!" she cried, diving into his arms. "Oh, I am so glad to see you. Are you unhurt? Is everyone safe?"

He set his lips to the warm turn of her neck. "Everyone is fine, love," he said. "We were fortunate."

"No, we were not fortunate, *you* were brave," she answered. "You and Mr. Kemble. Everyone was speaking of it. Why, if the two of you had not risked . . . had not risked your lives to—oh, God!"

"What, love?"

"Gabriel, you could have been *killed!*" she whispered, her voice choking. "And now I don't know whether to kiss you or to slap you senseless."

He speared his fingers into the thick, loose hair at the back of her head. "I vote for *kiss,*" he murmured. "Being slapped senseless isn't nearly as exciting."

Antonia leaned fully against him, turning her face to his. He molded his lips over hers, gently at first. And then it was as if a spark burst to flame between them. As with that night on the rampart, it was a sudden, fierce longing which could not be contained. An elated relief to find that they were alive and together despite whatever tragedy the world had thrown at them. Gareth deepened the kiss and was lost to her.

Antonia felt Gabriel's arms come about her, warm and strong. She gave herself up to it; the allure of his touch, the hunger of his body. She felt that sweet, familiar ache go twisting through her, drawing at her very core. His mouth moved over her face, kissing her temple, her eyebrow. But it was not what she wanted. Sensing it, Gabriel returned his lips to hers, surging inside on a kiss that left her knees trembling.

His touch was insistent. Commanding. What she burned for. She pressed her body fully against his, offering herself out of love and desperation. His hands flowed over her, firing her skin. One hand slid beneath the curve of her buttock, and Gabriel pulled her firmly against the hardening ridge of his arousal.

Antonia knew she should urge him toward the bedroom, but there was a delicious wickedness to making love in the middle of one's sitting room. "Take me," she murmured against his mouth. "Now, Gabriel, please."

"Antonia," he whispered. "Oh, God."

She felt Gabriel urge her backward. The edge of her rosewood secretary struck the backs of her legs. His mouth never leaving hers, he lifted her up. Her pens skidded off the desktop, landing somewhere on the carpet. They ignored them. His hands found her breasts, weighing them and rubbing them until her nipples ached and she was arching almost off the table, aching for more.

Antonia's fingers went to the tie at the throat of her gown. Gabriel pushed the soft flannel off her shoulder and bit gently at the bare flesh. Inexplicably, a tremor ran through her. She sought out his lips, and he took her with a renewed desperation, exploring the recesses of her mouth with deep, hungry strokes. Antonia felt reality swirl away as he pushed up the hem of her gown.

Parting her legs, she let herself swim in the sensation of his touch, and as he plunged into her mouth again, she let her hand slide round his waist. She drew out his shirt-tails and skimmed her palms up the warm, hard muscles of his back. "Gabriel," she murmured. "So beautiful." She felt his body shiver with pleasure as his heat and tantalizing scent surrounded her. Soap and citrus. Wood smoke and a hint of musky male. His breath was sawing in and out now, his hands heavy and demanding.

Antonia slid a little nearer to the edge of the table and let her fingers go to the buttons of his trousers. In a heated rush, she unfastened them. The satiny head of his erection sprang away from the taut muscles of his belly. "God, Antonia," he rasped. "I have to have you."

"Then have me," she whispered, frantically pushing away the fabric of his drawers. "Here and now. Don't think. Don't talk."

"Why do I always find those words so persuasive?" he muttered, rucking up her nightgown. He stepped nearer and kissed her neck, his teeth nipping none too gently down her throat. Swiftly, his hand eased fully between her legs, touching her flesh, which was already wet with need.

He moaned and slipped one finger inside. "More," she choked, sliding her hand up his warm, velvety erection. "Now. *Please?*"

In response, he pulled her to the very edge of the table. Antonia listened to her breath roughen. He pressed himself into her and entered her hard on one stroke. "Oh!" she said. "*Yes.*"

He thrust again, making the table thump hard against the wall. Antonia did not care. She let her head roll backward, almost emboldened by the fear of discovery; by the almost desperate need they felt for one another. Again and again, Gabriel plunged into her, holding her on the very edge of the desk, on the very edge of implosion. Unable to restrain herself, Antonia strained instinctively against him, an urgent, physical need building and building.

"Antonia," he choked, one hand going to her breast. "Antonia, I can't resist . . ."

She could think of nothing but the driving force inside her, of the desperate need to ease her torment as she urged herself against the heat and weight of him inside her. Gabriel's hands and mouth were desperate, too. The urgency ratcheted up. She felt him thrust and thrust again. She cried out, and Gabriel's head went back, his spine drawn taut as a bow. The rhythm drove them, dragging her to that fine, sweet precipice until her climax seized her. Her body shattered with sensation. Gabriel withdrew almost completely, then thrust deep on one last stroke. His head went back, the tendons of his neck straining, his cry of pleasure soundless as his warmth flooded inside her.

For long moments, they simply held one another, his head resting on her shoulder, his brow damp with perspiration. Then Gabriel's conscience seemed to prick him. "Good Lord, Antonia," he whispered. "I cannot believe I did this to you. Here. On a desk, for God's sake."

She lightly kissed the curve of his ear. She didn't care. She couldn't even fathom the risk they had just run. Every logical thought had been obliterated by her need for him. The desire which kept springing up between them seemed eternal and white-hot. "Gabriel," she said quietly. "I love you. I know . . . I know you don't wish me to say it. Perhaps not even to think it. But there, it is said."

Gabriel lifted his head, and their gazes met. He cupped the side of her face in his hand, his eyes a little sad. "Perhaps, Antonia, you simply love how I make you feel?"

"Stop it, Gabriel." She laid her hand over his alongside her face. "I am not like . . . like anyone else you have had sex with. This is not about physical pleasure."

"No?" He lifted one eyebrow.

She felt her face flame. "Well, it *is*," she admitted. "But it is so much more than that."

His smile was muted. Wordlessly, he pulled his body from hers, then lifted her off the desk, and restored her nightgown to order. He shoved his shirttails back in with a few quick stabs. "Antonia, I care for you," he finally said, without looking at her. "A great deal. You deserve to know that."

"Do you?" Her voice was amazingly steady.

He turned his back and walked to the window. The very window at which she had stood on that awful morning when she had denied making love to him. But her need for him could not be denied; she knew that now.

"I care for you, yes," he said again, staring out into the rain. "Do I love you? Yes, Antonia. Desperately. I think you know that."

He loved her? Yes, he must. Gabriel was not the sort of man who said things he did not mean. Hope stirring in her heart, Antonia followed him and set both her hands on his upper arm. "I cannot know, Gabriel, unless you tell me," she answered. "I cannot guess. I am afraid, even, to hope."

He shook his head, his eyes focused somewhere in the distance. "Antonia, let us not rush into anything," he cautioned. "You have been through so much. You have had so little opportunity to choose what you want."

"I *want* you, Gabriel," she said quietly. "I *choose* you."

He hesitated, but Antonia could feel his resolve giving way. She waited and said nothing. It was not as though she did not understand his concerns. With her history, she was a grave responsibility to take on. Gabriel was also convinced his ancestry would be objectionable to her father—and he was probably right. But Antonia no longer cared what her father thought. And somehow, she must convince Gabriel of that.

Just then, a door opened and thumped shut again. Someone was rummaging about in the adjoining bedchamber. "It must be Nellie," Antonia whispered. "She has come back."

Gabriel kissed her lightly on the nose. "To check on you, God bless her," he said. "Go, quickly. Go to sleep, my dear, and know that yes, I do love you. To distraction."

And then he was gone. Antonia was left standing by the little rosewood desk. From the bedchamber, Nellie called out her name. With a vague sense of disappointment, Antonia turned and went in to prepare for bed.

Gareth was up at dawn the following morning to survey the damage with Mr. Watson. The estate agent had had the good sense to call over the carpenters and stonemasons who had been at Knollwood, and he set them straight to work on the carriage house. Three bays, their contents, and all the rooms above them were beyond hope, and demolition was begun. By nine o'clock, the damaged doors were taken down and, just as Watson had promised, tossed to a refuse heap for burning.

Fortunately, at that moment, Mr. Kemble turned up and reminded them that the doors were evidence and must not be burnt until the perpetrator was found. Then he sent Talford off in the gig, which was amongst the equipment which had survived the fire, to fetch the justice of the peace from West Widding. Everything, Gareth realized, was in good hands. He returned to the house with Antonia much on his mind.

In the long, narrow office by the great hall, he found Coggins going about his usual schedule of sorting out the mail and assigning the day's duties to the footmen. Gareth lingered in the corridor beyond as the last of the servants were dealt with.

It had become a part of his routine, this dropping by Coggins's narrow office each morning to enquire about Antonia and to review the work which was planned for the day. He remembered the first occasion on which he had done so, just a few weeks past.

After leaving her last night, Gareth had realized that they had never discussed their quarrel by the lake. Perhaps they never would. Perhaps it had not even been a quarrel. He had wanted, he supposed, absolution of his sins. But absolution was not always the same as understanding. Could Antonia ever understand? Could anyone?

Her words last night had made his heart soar. But as

he had said to her, he did not want her to throw away her choices, for life thus far had given her so very few. He meant it—and yet he was beginning to believe that Antonia knew her own mind. She had begun to break out of the shadows of the past. She was becoming the beautiful, gracious woman she had always been destined to be.

It was time they had a long and earnest talk. He knew that. He wished only that the truth would come out about Warneham's death. If Antonia came to him, he wanted it to be because she truly could not live without him. He could not live in peace if he was left harboring even a shred of fear that he was only the best Antonia could do under the circumstances. And he needed her to understand and to accept not just what he was but what he had once been. It seemed like a lot to hope for.

Coggins was ticking down the last of the day's schedule with the footmen. When they were finished, Gareth went in. Coggins snapped to attention, though he looked worn and a little on edge. His gray hair seemed a little thinner, and his long, solemn face seemed rather more so.

"Good morning," said Gareth. "Has the duchess come down yet?"

"No, Your Grace," he said, laying aside his ledger. "I have not seen her."

"Very well." Gareth tried to relax. "When you have a moment, Coggins, there are some things I should like you to take care of."

"Of course, Your Grace," he said. "How may I help?"

Gareth set one shoulder to the door frame. "Talford and the stable staff are going to need their things replaced," he said. "Clothing, boots, razors, Bibles, you name it. They have nothing left. Do what you can. Go up to London for a day if need be."

"Certainly, sir," said Coggins. "I think Plymouth will have what they need. What more may I do?"

Gareth crossed his arms over his chest and considered his next words. "Mr. Kemble has a theory about the fire," he finally said. "He thinks Mr. Metcaff may have returned to the neighborhood. Have you any knowledge of that?"

Coggins looked alarmed. "Heavens no, Your Grace," he answered. "That is disturbing indeed. I shall make inquiries amongst the staff."

Slowly, Gareth nodded. "Yes, do that," he responded, letting his arms fall. "If anyone has seen or heard anything of Metcaff, I want you to inform Kemble at once."

Coggins nodded. Gareth thanked him and turned to go, but at the last instant, the butler spoke again. "Your Grace, if I might have a word? A . . . a rather frank word?"

Gareth turned back around. "By all means, Coggins," he answered. "I hope we are beyond walking on eggshells around here."

Coggins clasped his hands behind him. "It—well, it is about the fire, Your Grace," he began. The butler was not a man much given to emotion, but today he looked oddly pained. "Not about the fire, per se, but the . . . the writing which was found?"

Slowly, Gareth nodded. "Yes, what of it?"

Coggins looked at him plaintively. "I know, sir, that I speak for all the staff in saying—well, in saying that no one really cares, sir, if you are a . . . a Jewish person."

Gareth managed to smile. "Thank you, Coggins. That is good to know."

"And no one here would have written those words, Your Grace," Coggins solemnly continued. "The staff is very happy to work for you, and pleased to see the many improvements which are being made to the estate. Indeed, Mr. Watson says you are quite a genius. Truly, sir, Metcaff was the only real rabble-rouser, and we believed, of course, that he was gone. So . . . that's it, sir. That is what the staff wished me to say. We are all so deeply sorry for what happened."

Gareth set a hand on the man's shoulder. "I thought as much, Coggins, when everyone turned up in their nightclothes to haul water last night," he said. "But thank you for saying so."

Again, he turned to go, then thought better of it. "And Coggins?"

"Yes, Your Grace?"

"Just for the record, I was confirmed in the same place as most everyone else here at Selsdon," he said. "At St. Alban's, to be specific. I recall it vividly. I was eleven."

Coggins looked surprised.

Gareth hesitated for a moment. "My mother was a Jew," he said. "Her parents were forced from their homes in Bohemia when they were young and fled to England in hope of a better life. I was deeply fond of them and proud of their piety. But for good or ill, I am just like everyone else around here. And if things ever settle down, I might actually shock them all speechless and turn up one Sunday for services."

Coggins looked a little embarrassed. "Then we should be pleased indeed to see you there, Your Grace."

Suddenly, a racket sounded in the carriage drive. Coggins went to his narrow window, which overlooked the front steps. "Why, I believe it is your friend Baron Rothewell, Your Grace. Were you expecting him?"

"Lord, no." Gareth followed him to the window and looked out over Coggins's shoulder. It was indeed Rothewell leaping down from his glossy black high-perch phaeton. "Poor devil," Gareth muttered. "He really is quite desperate."

Coggins looked up. "Desperate, sir?"

Gareth smiled faintly. "His sister recently married," he said. "Now Lord Rothewell does not know what to do with himself. He has no one to quarrel with over dinner. Why else would he come back?"

A few minutes later, Rothewell was being shown into Gareth's study. Kemble was already there, seated at the small writing desk and scratching out some sort of document. He did not look especially surprised to see Rothewell.

Gareth rang for coffee, then took one of the wide armchairs which flanked the hearth.

"Well, it looks as though there's been some excitement here." Rothewell stretched his long, booted legs out before him and made himself look entirely at ease. "The back of your carriage house has soot-blackened holes where some of its windows should be. What the hell happened?"

Kemble laid down his pen with a snap. "I was just making some notes on that little fiasco for our justice of the peace," he said tartly. "We had a rogue footman exacting a little revenge, it would now appear."

Gareth turned in his chair. "Are we certain of that?"

"It is as good as proven," said Kemble with a sniff. "That rheumy stable boy of yours? He heard some racket in the tack room two days ago. He crawled out of his sickbed long enough to peek through the door. Metcaff was rifling the cupboards—looking for red paint and turpentine, I don't doubt."

"Good God!" said Gareth. "And the boy did nothing?"

Kemble reclined gracefully in his chair. "And the boy did nothing," he echoed, opening his hands. "Now, in his defense—a slender reed though it may be—he was sick, and he had a snootful of Osborne's infamous cough remedy. Care to guess what's in it?"

Gareth could only groan.

"Perhaps we ought to go looking for the bastard?" Rothewell offered, rather too cheerfully. "The footman, I mean."

"Oh, you really *must* be bored." Kemble gave one of his dismissive hand tosses. "Don't bother looking. Metcaff has already been spotted over in West Widding. Mr. Laudrey will have him under arrest"—Kemble pulled out what looked like a solid gold pocket-watch—"oh, right about luncheon, I daresay."

"And then what will happen?" asked Gareth.

"A swift trial and a quick hanging—unless you wish to intervene," said Kemble a little mordantly. "Perhaps you'd like to press for transportation to Australia? The man is, after all, your own blood kin."

Rothewell was looking confused. "Yes, Metcaff's the by-blow, is he not? How did he come to be involved in all this murder and whatnot?"

"In Warneham's death, do you mean?" Kemble's dramatic black eyebrows went up a notch. "That, I begin to believe, is a lot more *not* than *what*—though it's the *why*, frankly, that I cannot quite make out."

"I beg your pardon?" said Rothewell.

"Metcaff didn't kill anyone, I am quite sure," said Kemble impatiently. "He is completely innocent of that, if nothing else."

Just then, one of the footmen came in with the coffee. Gareth gladly began to pour. "So, Rothewell," he said, casually passing a cup, "what brings you back? Surely our little contretemps cannot compare to the excitement of London?"

"Actually," said Rothewell, "I have come at the behest of the Vicomte de Vendenheim and his friends at the Home Office."

"Have you indeed?" Kemble was up from the desk in a flash and swishing his way around the furniture. "Well, why didn't you say so? This must be delicious!"

Rothewell looked at Kemble a little charily. "It is just that de Vendenheim wished me to convey some information he was not comfortable putting in writing," he said. "Though it makes dashed little sense to me."

Kemble's eyes were alight. "What has happened to Max? Why didn't he come himself?"

Rothewell looked vaguely uncomfortable. "I collect his twins had the chicken pox," the baron reported. "Besides, I drive faster."

"It sounds as if something exciting must have happened," said Gareth.

"Well, in part, it is more about what *didn't* happen," said Rothewell. "He said I was to tell you that Lord Litting was avoiding him, and that he'd had no success running him to ground. He said you would understand what he meant."

Gareth felt the excitement wane. "Oh, that," he said.

"Yes, Litting already came down here in a fit of pique. Accused us of setting our hounds on him. We didn't get much more out of him, I'm afraid."

"It doesn't matter," said the baron. "De Vendenheim went to see the barrister, Sir Harold Somebody-or-other."

"Indeed?" Kemble sat down, his eyes widening. "And did he talk?"

"Jabbered like a magpie, as I understand it." Rothewell paused to sip his coffee. "Apparently, de Vendenheim invoked Peel's name, and that did the trick."

"So?" said Kemble breathlessly. "Out with it. What did he say?"

Rothewell's gaze turned inward. "I'll tell it to you as best I can," he said. "It is quite an amazing story—but de Vendenheim wouldn't let me write anything down."

"Well, get it straight," snapped Kemble. "Leave nothing out."

The baron's eyes flashed with ire, but his temper held. "This Sir Harold fellow said the Duke of Warneham asked him down here to discuss a touchy legal situation," said Rothewell. "The whole story was couched, I gather, in mights and maybes, but the gist of it was that Warneham hinted that he had made a Gretna Green marriage in his youth—this was prior to his inheriting the dukedom—and he wanted this barrister to explain the ramifications of the marriage."

"What do you mean, *hinted*?" asked Gareth. "And why was he confessing such a thing now?"

Rothewell's broad shoulders rose. "He said he was in his cups, and may have done it on a lark," said the baron. "The barrister thought he was lying about that part, for what it's worth. Anyway, Warneham wanted to know what the punishment would be if he confessed publicly."

"Punishment for what?" asked Gareth. "Eloping to Gretna Green was thought scandalous, but it was hardly illegal."

"No, not punishment for eloping." Kemble had slid to the edge of his chair. "Punishment for bigamy—*that* is what he meant, wasn't it, Rothewell? The man married four other women *that we knew of*. That could mean four bigamous marriages, depending on how long his Gretna Green bride lived. And he was going to own up to *that*?"

The baron nodded. "Apparently, he was considering it," said Rothewell. "According to this barrister, Warneham claimed he first wished to annul his marriage to the present duchess so as to limit her father's anger."

Kemble had leapt to his feet and was pacing the room. "So Warneham was essentially claiming that his marriage to the *first* duchess was bigamous," he said, rubbing his chin with one hand. "Not to mention the other three."

"And he was willing to literally bastardize poor Cyril by making the story public," Gareth said angrily. "That was why he wanted Litting's blessing. And it is why Litting would not tell us the whole truth—he was outraged, no doubt."

"But why would Warneham care what this Litting chap thought?" asked Rothewell. "The story is scandalous and outlandish on its face."

Kemble stood before the cold hearth, his hands clasped tightly behind his back, his eyes afire with some inscrutable emotion. "He would care about Lord Litting

for the same reason he would care about Lord Swinburne," he said. "Because if Warneham managed to get
himself charged with four counts of bigamy, the whole
bloody mess was apt to land in the House of Lords like
the fetid, steaming pile of horse manure that it is."

"And *that* would have been a grave embarrassment to
Litting's family." Gareth rolled his shoulders uncomfortably. It felt as if his coat was suddenly too tight. By God,
there was something else—something in the back of his
mind, nagging at him.

Suddenly Kemble stopped his pacing and clutched
madly at his throat. "Oh, dear!" he cried.

"What now?" asked Rothewell sourly.

"I believe I have just been seized with the quinsy!" he
wheezed. "Someone must fetch Dr. Osborne!"

Fifteen minutes later, Kemble had swooned himself
onto Gareth's red leather divan, declaring himself too
overtaken with illness to even go upstairs. A eucalyptus
salve was sent for, and in this way, Nellie Waters caught
wind of the situation and came in herself to deal with
it, saying that since she had already had it, there was no
possibility of her contracting it again. She sat down by
the divan, stripped off Kemble's cravat, and began to
apply the salve up and down his neck with a vigor which
suggested she was rubbing down a sweating horse, and
producing all manner of moaning and groaning from
her patient.

Gareth was watching it all through a veil of suspicion
when Antonia came in with a blanket. He was beginning
to grasp just what Kemble was about.

"Oh, Mr. Kemble!" she cried, going at once to the

divan. "What perfectly dreadful news. I thought we'd got beyond this."

Nellie took the blanket and shooed her mistress across the room. "Get back, all of you," she said authoritatively. "This is a nasty business we're dealing with here."

Gareth believed it might indeed be nasty, but he was not at all sure it was of the contagious sort. Nonetheless, mere moments later, Coggins brought the doctor in. Osborne greeted everyone cheerfully. Nellie Waters relinquished her seat, and if the doctor thought it odd to perform before a crowd, he said nothing of it.

"I thought we were done with this quinsy," said Osborne sympathetically as he poked about inside Kemble's mouth with a little wooden stick. "There, yes, just turn to the light a bit."

"Unggghh," said Kemble.

Osborne turned to Gareth. "A sudden onset, did you say?"

Lord Rothewell opened his hands. "Well, one moment he was quite fine, and the next—"

"Unggkk," Kemble interjected.

Osborne withdrew the stick.

"Actually, I felt a little ill in the rain last night, now that I think on it," said Kemble.

Osborne looked doubtful. "Well, there is no abscess of the peritonsillar tissue, as one would expect," he said. "And your mucous membranes look fine. Perhaps you simply inhaled too much smoke last night?"

Kemble seemed to seize upon the notion. "Yes, yes, I daresay you are right," he said. "Well! I am much reassured." He sat up and laid a hand on Osborne's coat sleeve. "You must excuse me, Doctor. I do worry inordinately about my health—much as poor Warneham did, you know. Almost obsessively, one might say?"

Osborne cleared his throat a little pompously. "It is true that the late duke was not entirely well," he said. "He was plagued by a great many health problems."

"And you are, in point of fact, an amazing diagnostician, are you not, Dr. Osborne?" said Kemble. "I am fortunate you could rush up here and see me, and give me such reassurance. After all, you were able to diagnose Warneham's severe asthma after only"—he looked at Mrs. Waters—"three short days of coughing?"

Mrs. Waters nodded.

Osborne was beginning to look uncomfortable. "Asthma can be dangerous if left untreated."

Kemble smiled. "Indeed, in an acute attack, one wheezes and gasps for breath, do they not?" he said almost solicitously. "But you were able to diagnose the duke's problem well before any of those symptoms set in, thank God—and just days before His Grace's wedding, too. Yet poor Mrs. Musbury coughs for nearly three months out of every year, but you have never once prescribed potassium nitrate for her. Why is that, Dr. Osborne?"

Osborne drew himself up quite rigidly. "Why, I resent what you are implying, Mr. Kemble." The doctor snapped his bag shut and stood. "I care for each and every one of my patients, regardless of circumstance or birth."

"Oh, I never thought otherwise!" Kemble tried to wave him back down again. "I am sure potassium nitrate would not be appropriate for Mrs. Musbury. It can be a very dangerous and debilitating drug. In fact, a mere layman such as myself might refer to it by an altogether different name, mightn't he? It is commonly called saltpeter, I believe."

"Kemble," said Gareth warningly, "be sure you know where you are going with this."

But the two men were focused on one another. "That is a misnomer," said Osborne hotly. "It is a legitimate drug when used appropriately."

"Yes, and you were using it appropriate to your purpose, were you not?" said Kemble sweetly. "As an anaphrodisiac—in hope of making certain that Warneham never begat an heir, an heir who might displace you in his affections?"

From the back of the room, Antonia and Mrs. Waters gasped. Rothewell cursed appreciatively beneath his breath. Intrigued, Gareth stepped nearer. "But saltpeter doesn't really work, does it?"

Kemble shrugged. "Osborne obviously thought it worth a shot."

Osborne looked truly stricken now. "I don't know what the two of you mean to imply!" he said tightly. "I never, ever wished Warneham ill. Good God, we—we were friends! We dined together! We played chess together! I would never do anything—*anything*—to hurt him."

"Oh, I think you were more than friends," said Kemble quietly. "I think you were *his son*."

At this, Osborne froze. Suddenly, everything clicked into place for Gareth. The nagging thoughts. The snippets of familiarity. The afternoon sun was slanting through the window now, turning Osborne's dark hair to a shade of warm brown. For the first time, Gareth truly looked at the man—at his elegant profile and his expensive coat. At the set of his jaw and the way he held his head. It was as if time hurled him back almost twenty years. Yes, it was there—if one looked for it.

Then suddenly, Osborne drew in his breath on a wretched sob. He sat back down in his chair, and covered his face with his hands. "Oh, God!" he cried. "Oh, dear God!"

Antonia set her fingertips to her mouth and sank slowly into a chair. Mrs. Waters edged closer and set a protective hand upon her mistress's shoulder.

Gareth moved to Osborne's side. "Do you want to know what I think, Doctor?" he asked quietly. "I think that you *wanted* Warneham to be dependent on you. I think you encouraged his delusions about his health and fed into his fear of dying without a legitimate heir."

"Quite so." Kemble exchanged a knowing glance with Gareth. "In fact, we think you came to the village from London with every intention of either blackmailing Warneham or ingratiating yourself with him—I am still pondering that one."

Finally, Osborne looked up. *"No!—"* The word came out on a ragged sob. "That is a vile lie! I was just a lad! I wanted only to see my father. To—to know who he was. What he looked like. Is that so terrible? *Is* it?"

"No," said Kemble, casting his gaze around the room at his audience, who all stood rapt, as if frozen to the floor. "I daresay any of us here might have done the same. And yes, you were just a lad. But your mother— when I knew her, by the way, she called herself Mrs. de la Croix—she was a woman of great . . . er, *experience,* was she not?"

"She was a woman who had suffered a difficult life,"

snapped Osborne. "You people cannot know what that does to a person. At times, we were nearly destitute. And yes, de la Croix *was* her name. We . . . we changed it when we came here."

Gareth crossed his arms over his chest. "Yes, but Warneham recognized the two of you at once, didn't he?" he suggested. "Certainly he recognized Mrs. de la Croix—his first love. His first bride. Your mother was a very beautiful woman, Osborne. I can well imagine he might be persuaded to elope with her."

At last, Antonia spoke. "I do not understand," she rasped. "Gabriel? Mr. Kemble? Are you two claiming that my husband was already *married*? Married to Mary Osborne?"

Gareth looked at her in sympathy. "Well, the duke had married her, yes," he answered. "In his youth. At Greta Green. Without his father's permission."

"And I am sure Mrs. Osborne still had the papers to prove it," Kemble chimed. "She was a sly one. You had to be, to survive in her sort of world—the world of the demimondaine. Trust me, I know."

The doctor was still quiet.

"What happened, Dr. Osborne?" Kemble gently urged. "You came to see Warneham on the morning of his death, did you not? You brought him some things, his medication amongst them. But you made a mistake, did you not?"

"Yes," rasped the doctor. "Yes, damn you. I made a mistake."

"Tell us what happened," said Kemble. "I know that it has been a burden to you. If it was an accident—why, I am sure no one here will wish to prosecute you. And you no longer have any secrets to keep. We know them all, Osborne. I am quite sure of it now."

A long, pregnant silence fell over the room. Then the doctor drew a great, heaving breath. "I brought the wrong medication," he whispered. "I realized it as soon as I was called to his room that morning. But no one else knew, you see."

"No, the medication I saw was potassium nitrate, all right," said Kemble. "It was not simply the *wrong* medication."

Osborne shook his head. He looked weary beyond words. "I always bought the medication from my regular chemist's in Wapping," he admitted. "But . . . but then I cut it, you see, with sodium chloride."

"With *salt*?" said Gareth. "Common . . . table salt?"

"Yes," the doctor whispered. "It lasted longer that way, and Warneham was able to take a larger dose. That was important to him."

"Why?" Gareth demanded.

Osborne gave a halfhearted shrug. "I often did such things," he admitted. "Warneham took a great many medications, most of them harmless. It comforted him, and the more the better. He was persuaded, you see, that he was going to die of something soon, and he wished me to treat his illnesses aggressively."

"That was aggressive, all right," muttered Kemble.

"I never let him take it full strength," said Osborne. "I only wished him to have . . . to have—"

"Just enough to render him impotent?" Kemble suggested. "It probably didn't take much. Indeed, given his age and his fanciful notions, he probably *was* impotent."

Osborne looked down and slowly shook his head. "I

just didn't want . . . I just didn't want there to be another child," he said pleadingly. "As long as Cyril lived, Mother knew Warneham would never look twice at me. But the instant he was gone, Mother packed our bags. She knew that if Warneham could just meet me—could just *see* me—how bright I was, how handsome I was—that he would at least befriend me, if no more. After all, he had no one else."

It was beginning to come clear. Gareth marveled at Kemble's perspicacity. But if Osborne was Warneham's son, why wasn't he standing here, in the shoes Gareth had so reluctantly filled?

Kemble, however, was still speaking. "Oh, I think Warneham did a great deal more than befriend you," he suggested. "He educated you—and in a grand style, at the very best school. He brought you and your mother into his social circle—probably to placate her."

"And he likely paid for that house your mother lived in—through some discreet third party, of course," Gareth added. Suddenly, he remembered something the old groom Statton had said. "And that nonsensical story she made up about your saving his favorite mare was precisely that, was it not? Nonsense devised to explain away his generosity. Warneham never kept mares—for breeding or for riding."

"It was so stupid of Mother!" said Osborne, sounding suddenly more angry than grief-stricken. "I begged her never to tell it again, and she didn't—but Lady Ingham just *won't hush up*."

"Yes, and Warneham wished his involvement in your life kept a secret, I daresay," said Gareth. "He wanted no one to know of his youthful folly."

"Why?" Antonia suddenly blurted. "If—why, if Mrs. Osborne was his wife—why should he?"

"Ah, therein lies the coil!" said Kemble. "She married him—but she was not *his* wife, was she, Doctor?"

Osborne shook his head. "No," he whispered. "No, Mother was already married. To a man named Jean de la Croix."

"Who the hell was he?" said Gareth.

Osborne shrugged. "A disreputable Frenchman whom she married in Paris," he said. "He would leave her for months at a time to go drifting about the Continent, playing at cards and dice. Petticoat-chasing. Once he was gone for over a year, so Mother returned to London to live her own life. And after a few months, she just decided—"

"She decided her husband must be dead," Kemble supplied. "It was a gamble, of course. But a handsome young English nobleman had fallen desperately in love with her, and she was carrying his child. As it happened, however, de la Croix was not so obliging as to actually *be* dead, was he?"

"No." Osborne hung his head. "He got wind of the wedding before they had even returned from Scotland. He left whatever woman's bed he'd been warming to come to London to laugh, and to demand money for his silence. Warneham did not take that too well—and since he had kept the marriage a secret from his father, he simply left her."

"When did de la Croix die?" Gareth demanded.

Osborne lifted his shoulders beneath the expensive fabric of his coat. "I . . . don't recall," he said. "I was six or seven. He was stabbed to death over a pack of marked cards in some hell near the *Quartier Latin*."

Kemble still looked pensive. He was playing with Osborne as a cat might a mouse, but the doctor was too distraught to realize it—or perhaps too guilty to care. "So, returning to that morning before Warneham's death," he went on, "you brought him his usual medication. But you were in a rush. You were excited over something, I think? And you made a terrible mistake, didn't you?"

"Yes." The word was just a whimper. "Father sent a note asking me to come up to Selsdon, and to bring Mother's papers and her Bible."

"The documents she had kept which proved their marriage at Gretna Green?"

Osborne nodded. "He said someone was coming from London who might look at them. A barrister he knew. My heart leapt into my throat when I read his note. I thought—I thought he meant to acknowledge me."

"Oh, I suspect you thought a lot more than that," said Gareth. "And if he had truly wanted to acknowledge you, Osborne, he could have done so at any time—certainly after the first duchess's death."

"He *loved* me." The doctor looked up, his eyes bleary, and shook his head. "He hated you, and he *loved* me. He knew I never wanted the title. I just wanted people to know I was his son. Mother—yes, she wanted the dukedom. After a time, it came to obsess her."

"Yes," said Kemble dryly. "I daresay it did. So, you got the papers together. Then what did you do?"

"I realized I needed to take up his asthma medication," said Osborne. "So I rushed into my clinic and dropped the brown bottle into my pocket. But I did not realize I had got the *wrong* bottle. The bottle with the uncut potassium nitrate—without the salt."

"Oh, God!" Antonia's voice was just a whisper.

"Where are your mother's papers now?" Gareth pressed. "We should like to see them."

Osborne shook his head and looked up at them plaintively. "I don't know. I never saw Warneham again." He cast a wary glance up at Gareth. "I was quite sure you had found them that day you turned up at my office. I was sick with worry. And to be honest, I'm glad it is over with."

"Oh, it is far from over with," said Gareth, looking at Rothewell. "Could Sir Harold Hartsell have the papers?"

Rothewell shook his head. "I got the impression he never actually *saw* them."

"Well, they will turn up," said Kemble. "Warneham would never have thrown them away, and just now, that is hardly our most pressing concern."

"If they are here, I shall find them." Gareth dragged a hand through his hair. "To think that all this time . . . Well, what must we do now?"

"*We* must do nothing," said Kemble. "*Dr. Osborne* must go to that writing desk and pen his confession so that any shadow of doubt can be lifted from the duchess's name—and we should like *two* copies, if you please!"

Osborne looked horrified. "You cannot be serious. Tell . . . *everything*?"

Kemble shrugged. "You may tell what you please," he returned. "Save for the part about mixing up Warneham's medicine. That you must confess. And in exchange for your cooperation, the duke shall do his best to see that you are not unfairly implicated in the other murders."

"Other murders?" Antonia had risen a little unsteadily. "Dear God, *what* other murders?"

Gareth went to her and slid an arm beneath her elbow. "I fear Mr. Kemble is about to tell us, my dear," he said quietly.

"Lord Gawd," whispered Mrs. Waters. "What else has he turned up?"

Kemble flashed her a knowing smile. "As I think Mrs. Waters is aware, I have for some time been convinced that the last two duchesses were murdered," he explained. "And that the only likely perpetrators were Mrs. Osborne and Lady Ingham—who, so far as I could tell, is an incurable rattle, which sometimes makes one wish for an early death, 'tis true. But it is not quite the same thing as outright murder."

Osborne would not look at Kemble. "What about this, Doctor?" Gareth demanded, circling around until he could see his face. "Have you any knowledge your mother may have done such a thing?"

Osborne looked up, his eyes a little glassy now. Nervously, he licked his lips. "Mother . . . was not well," he finally said. "She became obsessed, as I said, over the possibility of the dukedom."

"Yes?" said Gareth a little harshly. "And precisely what did she do about it?"

"Nothing, so far as I know," he whispered. "Once or twice she tried to convince Warneham to fall back on their old marriage lines. She wanted to pay someone to destroy the record of her first marriage—it was made in France, after all, and de la Croix was dead. This, she said, could give Warneham his heir—the heir he so desperately wanted to displace *you*. But I discouraged such insanity. It would never have worked." Here, he glanced bitterly between Gareth and Kemble. "Someone always turns up the truth."

Kemble ignored the look. "But with Warneham unwilling to endure the scandal, it hardly mattered," he said musingly. "Until he realized he was impotent, and that there was absolutely no chance of his begetting an heir—my apologies to you, Your Grace. I can only imagine how this discussion must make you feel."

"No," said Antonia. "You cannot know. It makes me feel . . . free, somehow."

Osborne looked at Antonia with hurt in his eyes. Suddenly Gareth remembered the look in the doctor's eyes the first night they had all dined together. The many times he had admonished her to take her medication. There had been other things, too—small but telling things. In the only way he'd known how, Osborne had perhaps tried to make Antonia dependent upon him. But in that, she had held fast, thank God.

Gareth turned to Kemble. "I don't understand," he said. "How did Mrs. Osborne commit these murders?"

"Well, the second duchess was silly and rather spirited," said Kemble quietly. "Like most young people, she had no sense of her own mortality. I think Mrs. Osborne enticed her to take a jump she was not skilled enough to handle, and when that did not induce a miscarriage, I suspect Mrs. Osborne somehow dosed her with an abortifactant—something so strong it killed her. Ladies of the demimonde often have more than a passing acquaintance with such things."

"Yes, they would, wouldn't they?" Gareth scrubbed his hand across the stubble of his beard. "And she pulled a similar trick with the third duchess, too, I daresay."

Kemble nodded. "Yes, I think the poor girl confessed to her dear friend Mrs. Osborne that she had some hope of being with child," he said musingly. "It was unlikely, of course. The girl was ill, I think, not *enceinte*. But it was a chance Mrs. Osborne dared not take. And once again, it was easy to substitute a pure opiate for the duchess's regular sleeping draught."

"Good Lord," said Antonia.

Gareth looked at her in sympathy. "The poor girl just went to sleep and never woke," he said quietly. "And you did not dare look too closely, did you, Dr. Osborne, for fear of what you might find?"

"It's not true!" Osborne swore. "It is not. If Mother did *anything,* I know nothing of it."

"Your mother frequently delivered medications for you, did she not, Dr. Osborne?" Gareth challenged. "Especially to the ladies? You told me that yourself."

Osborne made a sound, somewhere between a sob and a laugh.

Kemble opened his hands expressively. "It would be a simple matter indeed to deliver a bottle of pure opiate when only a weak tincture was prescribed. I wonder, Doctor—did you ever have a bottle go missing?"

"I don't recall," he rasped. "Sometimes things get broken, you know. It is very hard to keep account."

"Yes, I'll just bet it is," said Kemble softly.

"When did your mother die, Dr. Osborne?" Gareth demanded.

"Over two years ago," Osborne snapped.

"Yes, less than two months after Antonia's marriage to the duke, I believe?" said Kemble. "Would you care to tell us how she died?"

Osborne was glaring at Kemble now. "She fell down the stairs," he retorted. "She broke her neck. For God's sake, do you mean to make me relive it?"

"Why?" asked Kemble softly. "Were you there?"

This time, the doctor went for Kemble's throat. "You bastard!" Osborne roared. "You goddamned meddling bastard!"

Gareth grabbed him almost as he leapt, wrapping one arm around his neck and dragging him backward across the carpet.

To his shock, Kemble followed them, his gaze never leaving Osborne's. His eyes were afire with an almost unholy light. "Did you fall in love with the duchess, Dr. Osborne?" Kemble demanded. "Did you? Did you push your mother down the stairs because you knew what she was capable of? Did you fear who her next victim might be? *Did* you?"

"To hell with you!" said Osborne, wrestling backward against Gareth's relentless grip. "Let me go, damn you! Let it be a fair fight."

From the back of the room, Rothewell softly chuckled. "Osborne, the duke is protecting your worthless arse, had you but sense enough to know it."

Suddenly, all of the anger and pugnacity seemed to drain out of Kemble. "No, the acorn never falls far from the tree, does it?" he murmured to no one in particular. "Let him go, Your Grace. He is as impotent as his father—and as manipulative, perhaps, as his mother."

Gareth did as Kemble asked. Osborne shrugged his

coat back into place, his hot glare sweeping over them. "You people know nothing!" he said. "You cannot know what I have been through! I said there had been an overdose from the very first, didn't I? I said they had been smoking cigars and that Warneham must have overreacted. I tried to protect Antonia! I *tried!*"

Kemble waved his hand. "Too little, too late, Osborne," he said wearily. "If you'd loved her more than you loved yourself, you would have explained it fully, then and there. Now all we want from you is that signed statement that you accidentally mixed up the drugs. I think you're probably hedging a bit about the rest of it, but I cannot prove it, and if the duke agrees, I am content to let God sort it out."

"I want what I have always wanted," said Gareth darkly. "I want Antonia's name cleared. You may do it willingly, Osborne. Or I can beat it out of you. The choice is yours."

Osborne grabbed his leather satchel. "I am going home, damn you," he said. "I shall write the statement and send it at my leisure."

Kemble made a little *tsk-tsk* sound in the back of his throat and stepped in front of the door. "You are not leaving my sight to so much as piss, Osborne, until the ink is dry on your statement. I won't have you go home and stick a pistol in your mouth, thereby leaving a cloud over the duchess's good name."

Apparently, the doctor did not properly estimate his adversary. This time he leapt, and when Gareth did not catch him, he got his hands round Kemble's throat. Gareth moved to tear him off, but suddenly the tables were turned. In a flash, one of Osborne's arms was twisted up behind him and he was facedown on the Axminster carpet with Kemble's knee between his shoulder blades and blood spewing from his nose.

"Christ, my finger!" cried Osborne. "You son of a bitch! You deliberately broke my finger!"

His left index finger, Gareth noted, was indeed lying crookedly to one side.

Rothewell peered over the tea table. "Now that's a nasty piece of work," he said admiringly.

Kemble pressed his knee in harder. "You've got nine more to go, Osborne," he growled against the doctor's ear. "What will it be? A thumb? Or the statement?"

Antonia was looking a little faint, Gareth realized. He cut a glance at Mrs. Waters. "I think the ladies should leave the room," he gently suggested. "Actually, they should never have been here."

Mrs. Waters was looking at the scene in obvious satisfaction. She clearly would not have missed it for the world. But Antonia's gaze was fixed upon the man bleeding on the carpet.

Mrs. Waters laid a hand on her arm. "My lady?"

Antonia jerked into motion. "No, we should have been here," she said, casting one last disdainful glance at Osborne. "I am *glad* I was here. But now I have seen—and heard—quite enough."

Chapter Eighteen

*T*he place called Neville Shipping was stuffed near to bursting with desks, tables, and stacking drawers. The clamor of the port rang through the open windows, most of which had wide white shutters, and people dashed in and out so fast, the front door never shut. But the place was tidy, and it smelled familiar; of ink and of fresh paper, as his grandfather's office once had—it was the smell, Zayde always said, of money being made.

At a copy stand by the windows, a young girl sat on a tall stool with her head bent to her work, her tongue poking out one corner of her mouth and a tatty quill pen clutched in her hand. Her long dark hair hung to her waist, and her eyes were serious.

Gabriel took a step nearer. The girl laid down her pen. "Hullo," she said shyly. "Are you the boy Luke found?"

Gabriel nodded and flicked a glance at her desk. "What are you doing?"

"Copying contracts." The girl smiled. "It's frightfully te-

dious, but Luke says it improves my script. Anyway, I'm Zee. What's your name?"

"An excellent question!" The man named Luke Neville *had stepped back out of his office. "What is your name, lad? We must know what to call you around here."*

Did they mean to let him stay? "It—It's Gabriel, sir." He felt himself almost sag with relief. "But I don't think I like that name any longer."

Luke Neville grinned hugely. "Feeling the hot breath of pursuit on the back of your neck, eh?" he remarked. "Have you another name you like better?"

"Gareth," he said. "Just Gareth Lloyd, sir—if that's all right?"

The man laughed. "People often come to the islands to lose themselves," he said. "All right, Gareth Lloyd—tell me, how's your arithmetic? Have you any sort of head for numbers?"

Gabriel nodded with alacrity. "I like numbers sir," he said. "I do them in my head."

Luke Neville bent over and set his hands on his knees. He looked Gabriel straight in the eyes. "So, if my hold is filled with fifty crates of bananas at one pound twelve shillings profit per, but I lose forty percent to black rot en route to port, what is my profit? And what have I lost?"

Gabriel didn't hesitate. "You would lose thirty-two pounds even on the twenty crates' spoilage, sir. And turn forty-eight pounds profit on the thirty good crates."

"Well, damn!" Luke Neville's eyebrows went up. "I think we can find something for you to do, boy."

Late that afternoon, Gareth was in the great hall saying good-bye to George Kemble when Antonia came in through the conservatory carrying a basket of roses on her arm. She had once again put on her green-and-yellow walking dress, and her hair was falling down on one side. On the whole, it was a charming combination.

"Mr. Kemble, surely you are not leaving?" she said, hastening toward them. "Please do stay—at least for dinner?"

Kemble sketched a graceful bow. "I fear pressing business calls me to London, Your Grace," he said. "But I remain, of course, your humble servant."

Antonia's eyes danced with laughter. "You may be a great many things, Mr. Kemble," she said, handing him one of the roses. "But I think humble is not one of them."

Kemble smiled and snapped off the stem. "This must be the last of the season's blooms," he mused, neatly tucking the rose into his hatband. "Well, there! Now, kindly make my good-byes to Mrs. Waters. I did not get the chance."

"Yes, I left Nellie upstairs pouring all my tonics into the chamber pot," Antonia confessed. "She was rather enjoying it."

"The things Osborne prescribed?" Gareth slid a hand beneath her elbow and drew her protectively nearer. "I confess, I was going to ask you not to take them. God only knows what they might contain."

"Well, I rarely ever really took them," Antonia confessed. "But most were harmless, I daresay."

"Most likely," Kemble agreed. "Perhaps his intentions were not initially so benign, but Warneham's cough before the wedding gave him a better idea than to simply let his mother commit outright murder. I still am not certain, however, that the saltpeter caused impotence."

"Perhaps it was just guilt?" Gareth suggested darkly.

"It is all quite tragic, is it not?" said Antonia almost wistfully. "I do think Dr. Osborne wished people to become dependent upon him. But I intend to do without any medications. From now on, if I cannot sleep"—she paused to look at Gareth almost coquettishly—"well, I am persuaded I must simply find something else to do."

"*Ahem!*" Mr. Kemble slapped his very elegant beaver hat onto his head. "I'd best be off, then."

Antonia laid a hand on his coat sleeve. "Mr. Kemble, could I just ask one more thing?"

Swiftly, he removed the hat. "By all means, Your Grace."

Antonia seemed to carefully consider her words. "Do you think Dr. Osborne is truly sorry?" she asked. "Especially about the two duchesses who died? I mean, he confessed what he knew rather readily. Couldn't he have insisted that he was legitimate and forced us to look for his mother's papers? Perhaps even forced the issue of the dukedom?"

Kemble smiled. "An excellent question!" he answered. "Alas, we found the Bible, Your Grace."

"Yes, I hadn't had an opportunity to tell you, my dear," said Gareth. "It was in plain sight on my bookshelf—and inside it we found *all* of Mrs. Osborne's papers, including the record of her marriage to Jean de la Croix. Osborne believed he was only confessing what we already knew—or would soon discover."

Antonia gave a muted smile. "And you were very clever to make him think that, Mr. Kemble," she said.

"Do the two of you believe Dr. Osborne is a murderer?"

Kemble drew a deep, pensive breath. "I think him venal and manipulative like his mother," he said. "But has he gone so far as to kill deliberately? No, I think not."

Gareth shook his head. "He hasn't the stomach for it—I hope."

Antonia frowned faintly. "What will happen to him now?"

"I cannot say," Kemble answered. "I doubt he has done anything for which he can be successfully tried, save for perhaps diagnosing Warneham with asthma when he didn't have it—but what can be done to prove that now? We can't very well dig the poor devil up. And perhaps Osborne had some degree of complicity in his mother's shenanigans. But her actions will be hard to prove after so many years, therefore his will be nearly impossible."

"It is just as well, I suppose," said Antonia quietly. "I am a little surprised my husband never suspected. I think, you know, that had he loved his wives, he would have. Don't you?"

Kemble shook his head. "I cannot suppose to understand such a man, my dear."

"Nor can I," Gareth added. "But it is over now, Antonia. At last it is well and truly over."

Together the three of them walked out into the brilliant afternoon. To the left, the sun was slanting from the clouds to form a perfect pool of light over the village, and from beyond the carriage house and stable block, the sounds of hammers and saws rang out sharp and clear in the warm air. Gareth looked down to see that Rothewell's high-perch phaeton waited in the carriage drive, his fine matched blacks tossing their heads and literally chomping at their bits.

"Good Lord," he said appreciatively. "How did you manage this?"

"Well, it was this or your gig," said Kemble. "And I am *not* returning in glory and triumph to London driving anything so ordinary as *that*. Besides, Rothewell is a danger to the general populace in this thing."

"But how is he to get home?"

Kemble smiled. "Oh, I'm sending my barouche for him in a day or two."

Gareth turned serious as Kemble climbed up into the high seat and took the reins from the groom. "I really don't know how to thank you," he said, looking up. "Antonia and I owe you so much."

Beneath his fine beaver hat, Kemble's sharp black eyebrows went up a notch. "Dear me, did Rothewell not tell you?" he said, shaking out his whip. "I shall be sending you a bill—quite a large one, I daresay—unless, that is, I get an invitation."

"An invitation?" asked Gareth, confused. "To what?"

"Why, to the wedding, of course." With that, Kemble touched his whip smartly to his hat brim, then snapped it above Rothewell's horses' heads. The phaeton set off at a fine clip.

Suddenly the door opened behind them. The baron himself came out, looking rather the worse for wear, with one hand lifted to his eyes as if to shield the sun. "Gone, then, is he?" said Rothewell. "Wait! Good God!—is that—is that my phaeton he's driving?"

"Well . . . yes," said Gareth.

Rothewell looked at him incredulously. "Damn it,

Gareth! You—you just *let* him take my phaeton? It's brand-new! And I am on my way to the village. How the hell am I to get there?"

"You may walk, I daresay," Gareth suggested, "and spare my gateposts."

Antonia looped her arm through Gareth's. "I am so sorry, but if you mean to quarrel with Lord Rothewell, you must wait," she said sweetly. "I was here first, and I have something I wish to quarrel about."

With a grunt, Rothewell stepped back and made a sweeping motion toward the door. "Have at it, ma'am."

With her stomach in a bit of a knot, Antonia led Gabriel back into the conservatory and closed the door on Lord Rothewell's blazing visage. She drew her quarry into the center of the greenery, to a little fountain surrounded by ornamental palms. She felt as if her head were still swimming from all the day's incredible events—but her mind was perfectly clear now. It always had been, really, where Gabriel was concerned. From the very first, something deep inside her had been drawn to him; to his strength, and to his essential goodness.

She took one of Gabriel's hands in hers. His thick, golden hair had grown too long, and it had fallen a little forward to shadow his eyes—eyes which looked tired and more than a little anxious.

"It is quite ironic, is it not?" she said. "Just as the golden egg was almost within his grasp, Osborne killed his goose?"

Gabriel smiled softly. "I like to think that in the end, we all get what we deserve, Antonia."

Antonia lifted her chin. "But you do not think that you deserve all this," she said quietly.

"All what, my dear?"

She tilted her head toward Selsdon's great hall. "The house. The land. The dukedom. Indeed, I was a little bit afraid you were going to tell Osborne to take it all and go hang this morning," she said, only half in jest.

"Oh, for one fleeting moment, my dear, I thought about it," he confessed. "But then I realized . . ."

Antonia laid her hand lightly against his lapel. "What, Gabriel?" she asked, leaning into him. "What did you realize?"

He smiled a little ruefully. "I realized, Antonia, that a man who toiled the livelong day in a shipping office in Wapping would never be thought good enough for . . . well, for someone like you."

She set her head a little to one side and studied him through her soft blue eyes. "Thought by whom?" she finally asked. "Does anyone's opinion of you matter, save mine? You must understand, Gabriel, that I have stopped living my life by other people's standards."

Gabriel looked down at their clasped hands. "You may regret that choice, Antonia," he said quietly. "I want only your happiness, you know."

"And I have decided, Gabriel, that I want my happiness, too," she whispered. "I want it quite desperately. I have spent a very long time being miserably unhappy. I shan't do it any longer, no more than I can help, at any rate. I told you when we argued at the pavilion—this time I mean to fight for what I want."

He lowered his sweeping, dark brown lashes for an instant. "Is that what you meant?"

"What did you think I meant?" she asked. "I mean to grab what happiness I can, however little it may be."

"You deserve more than just a little happiness, Antonia," he said. "Now that we have Osborne's confession, your life will be different, in that respect, at least. I cannot restore to you your fairy-tale dreams or your lost children, but at least your name has been cleared completely."

"I do not want fairy tales any longer, Gabriel," she answered. "I want only what is real, and what is true."

He bowed his head, and took both her hands in his. "Antonia, I know that I have done things in my past which make me feel . . . ashamed, and I just—"

Antonia cut him off. "Oh, Gabriel, you have it all wrong," she whispered, her eyes going soft with pain. "You have had things done *to* you. That is not at all the same! I am not speaking of just the—the physical horrors you have been forced to endure, but of the way you were treated here, by your cousin, by other people. Your abandonment. The shame you have been made to feel. It . . . it breaks my heart."

He looked at her with an old pain in his eyes. "We all make choices, Antonia," he said. "And I have made some which I regret. Things which are repulsive to you, and—"

"Gabriel, thirteen-year-old boys do *not* make choices like that," she said stridently. "They choose between whether to conjugate their Latin or go skipping stones. Whether to run barefoot in tall grass or dance about in the rain without a hat, or do the thousand other foolhardy little things boys are told not to do. But they *do not* choose to be beaten and to let—*oh, God*!" She squeezed her eyes shut.

"You cannot even say it," he whispered. "It disgusts you."

Antonia gathered her strength and forced her eyes open. She looked at him very directly. "I cannot even say it," she repeated hollowly. "It disgusts me. But it is not what *you* chose. I am not so emotionally fragile, Gabriel, that I cannot tell the difference."

"You are not fragile," he said hotly. "You are *strong*, Antonia. You had an emotional collapse—and for a very good reason. You will fully recover someday, if you have not already."

Antonia was beginning to believe he was right. "There was a time, Gabriel, when I was considered a great catch," she said. "When I was very young and very naïve and knew nothing of the world's cruelty. Now my strength and my resolve are returning. And yet, some days, I worry I mightn't be capable of being a good wife. The doctors have said I am 'not well,' but that sounds as if I am . . . sick. I am not sick. I am broken into pieces. And on those very darkest days, Gabriel, I sometimes still fear I will never be whole again."

Gabriel's smile warmed with tenderness. "Perhaps, Antonia, to the right man, a few broken pieces of you would be better than a whole and perfect someone else?" he suggested.

Antonia's expression grew more poignant, if such a thing were possible. "Oh, Gabriel," she whispered. "Oh, my dear, that is so beautiful. And I know, sadly, that you once had that perfect someone in your life. Someone long before me. I wish I could say I am sorry things did not work out for you. But I . . . well, I am not sorry. I am greedy. I would not give you back to her. No, not even were it within my power. I love you too much to be unselfish."

He pulled her back to him and set his cheek to hers. "It was not like that, Antonia," he said. "It certainly was not like *this*. What I felt for her—for Zee—was more about security. We'd come up hard, both of us, in sometimes squalid circumstances. I felt she would not judge me harshly. And I feared losing the only family I had. But what I feel for you, Antonia—it defies all explanation. It is a love which takes my breath. It leaves me in awe."

Antonia leaned forward and put her hands around his neck. "Then ask me to marry you, Gabriel," she whispered. "Ask me, and I shall be the very best wife I can be. Ask me, and together we will make one another stronger. I know that we will. Just please . . . *ask me*."

Gareth looked down into her bottomless blue eyes. "You once said, my dear, that you wanted an independent life," he reminded her. "Will you give all that up, just to marry me?"

"Oh, Gabriel, don't you see?" she whispered. "You have *given* me my independence. You have helped me break those awful chains which bound me to the past. I know that life isn't perfect—that even you, my love, are not perfect. But you are so close. So very, very close. Yes, whatever it is I would be giving up, I give it up willingly."

"You do not wish to return to London, not even to clear your head, or—or give society another try?" he asked, his voice choking. "You know what you want? You will stay with me, and bear your father's disapproval if it comes?"

Wordlessly, she nodded.

Gareth drew a deep breath. "Well, then, Antonia," he

whispered. "Will you marry me? Will you bind yourself to me for all eternity? Will you be my duchess? For there is nothing—*nothing*—that would make me happier."

She stood on her tiptoes and lightly kissed him. "For all eternity, Gabriel," she answered. "And into the great hereafter."

Baron Rothewell pulled his hat down over his eyes to shield the sun and set off in the direction of the village proper. He did not like the sun. Indeed, since leaving Barbados, he had rarely ever seen it. Men of his ilk were almost never awake at such a godforsaken time of day as—well, as daylight.

The trek down the hill was not a long one, but Rothewell allowed himself to steep in misery all the way. He was going to knock George Kemble's perfect, pearl-white teeth down his throat as soon as he got back to London. Well, he might have to sober up first and get a little sleep. But he could do it. At present, however, a higher and more noble duty called. Rothewell rarely did anything which was either high or noble, but he tried to get into the spirit of the thing.

Martin Osborne lived in a lovely old half-timbered house that had certainly cost someone a tidy sum, and he had plenty of servants to staff it with, too. One let the baron in, another came carrying the doctor's apologies—not once, but twice—and yet a third brought tea. And eventually, Osborne must have decided Rothewell simply wasn't going to leave, and he, too, came in. He appeared to have splinted his finger, and his nose had turned a swollen and nasty shade of red which, Rothewell knew from personal experience, was destined to turn blue,

en purple, and finally, an appallingly jaundiced shade
f yellow.

"What did you tell the staff?" Rothewell asked with-
ut preamble. "That you walked into a door?"

Osborne quivered with indignation, then relented.
That I tripped, if you must know," he said. "On a chair
the duke's study."

"Oh, I must know," said Rothewell, "since it would be
est we all get our stories straight."

"Then do sit down, Lord Rothewell," said the doctor
ghtly. "And by all means tell me what I can do for you."

Rothewell rubbed a finger along the side of his nose.
See, here's the thing, Osborne," he began. "I have been
inking about what happened today, and I am not at all
re the justice of the peace over in West Widding isn't
oing to cut up a little rusty when this confession you've
gned gets out."

"It was an accident," hissed the doctor.

"Nonetheless, Osborne, you are a physician," said the
aron. "As unfair as it may seem, you do not get to have
ccidents. And let's face it, there have been so many *acci-
ents* in this little village, there are bound to be questions
ver this one. Hard, awful questions. Do you really wish
answer them?"

"What do you care?" Osborne demanded. "It's my
ide, not yours. Besides, there's no avoiding it now that
ve written your bloody statement."

"I care because the new duke has already been
rough hell—twice," said the baron. "And I'll be
amned if I'll have him put through it again. They do
ot need any more gossip or innuendo up there; they've
ad enough to choke on already, thanks to you and your

father. As to avoiding it, yes, you can avoid it. You mu
leave town. No, you must leave England—and prefe
ably Europe. You must go someplace with a vast deal
water between here and there."

"You must be insane," said the doctor.

"I think it quite likely," said Rothewell. "But that
neither here nor there, no pun intended. You are ruin
in Lower Addington, Osborne. You were never destin
to become wealthy working in this village backw
ter—and you damned sure won't do it now. But in, s
Barbados—why, the white ruling class is filthy rich, a
physicians are both rare and welcome. That, I am p
suaded, is where you shall go."

The doctor's eyes widened. "There is no way in he
am going to the godforsaken West Indies!" There wa
hint of umbrage in Osborne's tone. "It's hot. They ha
insects. Large ones. And horrific, infectious diseases. N
I demand to see the duke."

"That's why they need doctors," said Lord Rothew
with a logical shrug. "And the duke cannot be involv
in something which might later be construed as obstru
tion of justice."

"And what of yourself, Rothewell?" asked the doct
with a soft sneer. "Above the law, are you? You certair
behave it."

Rothewell smiled faintly. "Let us just say that I belie
I can more zealously safeguard the Ventnor family's i
terests than your incompetent justice of the peace cou
ever do," he murmured, withdrawing a fold of pape
from his coat pocket. "And English law, I long a
learnt, is often apt to protect the criminal far more th
the victim." He handed the papers to the doctor.

"What is this?"

"My signature granting you passage on Neville's frigate, the *Belle Weather,*" he answered. "She embarks with the evening tide from the West India Docks a se'nnight hence. You will sail with her, Dr. Osborne, or you will be accountable to me—and I have far less to lose than my friend the duke."

"But—but this is ridiculous!" the doctor gritted.

"Do remember, by the way," Rothewell continued, "that we have retained the second copy of your confession, if you should be tempted to commit any malpractice whilst in Barbados. I am not without influence there, and I will not hesitate to see that you are prosecuted to the furthest extent of the law—and then some."

"You think me guilty of murder." Osborne looked outraged.

"I think you guilty as sin, Osborne—of negligence, at the very least," Rothewell replied. "But the duke and duchess have already been touched by enough scandal. The man is like a brother to me, so this, you might say, is my wedding gift to him. I am getting rid of his problem."

"Your wedding gift?" Osborne sneered. "So he has convinced her, has he?"

"By now, yes, I expect so." Rothewell looked at him pathetically as he rose from his chair. "Or she, perhaps, has convinced him. In any case, Osborne, she was never going to have you."

Osborne's face went white with anger. "You think I don't know that? Do you? Well, let him have her. She's as fragile as a piece of Sevres, so I wish him very happy. I never wanted her anyway. I should never have felt sorry for her. Never."

"Wishing you'd let Mamma do your dirty work again, are you?" Rothewell laughed nastily. "It takes a mighty small pair of ballocks to hide behind a woman's skirts 'til you're damned near forty."

Osborne started to come out of his chair, but Rothewell lifted his boot and planted it squarely in the doctor's chest. "Not another word, Doctor, for you're about to convince me you aren't nearly as stupid as you've been pretending. Now I want your assurance, sir, that you will sail with the *Belle Weather* and that thereafter you will never draw another breath in England again."

"Or what?" said the doctor snidely. "You shall turn the justice of the peace on me?"

Rothewell leaned very near. He wanted Osborne to see the pupils of his eyes and smell the anger on his skin. "Now mark me, sir, and mark me well," he whispered. "For what *I* shall do to *you,* the justice of the peace will be the very *last* tool I shall need."

He removed his boot to see that Osborne was now shaking. His work here was done. Rothewell threw open the door and started the long hike back through the village and up the hill.

Epilogue

The gossip rags read that Duke and Duchess of Warneham were wed on a beautiful autumn day during a weeklong house party at the country estate of the notorious Marquis of Nash. Much was made of the duchess's good fortune in reclaiming her old position, and the fact that her groom was the grandson of Malachi Gottfried, a Jewish money-lender.

What they did *not* say was that the bride wore cerulean blue to match her eyes or that the groom danced with her beneath the stars until midnight, or that they did not give a damn what the gossip rags said. Over a buffet of roasted sturgeon, fresh prawns, and very expensive champagne, old Malachi was toasted—not once, but at least half a dozen times—and mostly by the Neville family, who had been amongst the chief beneficiaries of his extraordinary wisdom.

After the sun had vanished, Lord Nash had ordered a bonfire built and a table laden with sumptuous sweets laid out. His bride Xanthia tried to ignore the trifles and cakes. Instead, she floated amongst the guests, attempting to keep her burgeoning belly obscured by her shawl, and her brother from flirting with the bride's stepmother, a deceptively fresh-faced girl of perhaps twenty, who quite obviously had a penchant for dangerous-looking men. Lord Swinburne seemed destined to wear the cuckold's horns in his May-December marriage.

"I have tried to distract Kieran, Gareth, but he is quite unmanageable," Xanthia whispered to the groom as the evening drew to a close. "I shall ask him to give me his arm and escort me inside." She turned then to Antonia and lightly kissed her cheek. "My dear, I am so glad you have given Nash and me the honor of hosting your wedding. I hope from this day forward, you will think of me as a sister, as Kieran and I think of Gareth as our brother."

Antonia smiled and returned the kiss. She had not thought to like Lady Nash, but it was a challenge.

"Gabriel, does everyone save me call you Gareth?" she asked her husband as they strolled through the dark toward the house. "It sounds so strange to my ears."

He was silent for a long moment, but he wrapped his arm a little tighter about her waist. "I changed my name when I arrived in Barbados," he said. "In the West Indies, it is easy to—to reinvent oneself. To become someone else—someone stronger than you were."

Antonia curled her arm beneath the warmth of his coat and hugged him to her. "I understand."

As if by mutual agreement, they stopped beneath a canopy of trees and let the others proceed on in the gloom. Antonia set her head on his shoulder. "Shall I call you Gareth, then?" she asked. "Would that be better?"

He pondered it for a time. "No, I think perhaps that I am ready to be Gabriel again," he eventually answered. "I think, Antonia, that I have found the part of me that was . . . lost. Or perhaps shut away is the better term? I begin to believe that with you, I can bring together the good parts of both my lives. I have begun to believe that perhaps—just *perhaps*—I can be whole again."

Antonia did not know what to say. Gabriel had given her an inestimable gift— the gift of his strength and his wisdom. That she might have given him something in return had never occurred to her.

Gabriel looked down at her and pulled her fully against him. "Kiss me, Antonia," he whispered. "Kiss me, and make me—for about the hundredth time today—the happiest man on earth."

Gladly, she did so, rising onto her toes and cradling his beautiful face in her hands. "Gabriel," she whispered. "Gabriel, my angel."

Pocket Books
proudly presents

Never Romance a Rake

Available in paperback June 2008
from Pocket Books

Turn the page for a preview of
Never Romance a Rake. . . .

Après elle, le déluge

Her shoulders set stiffly back, the Comte de Valigny's daughter pushed through the sitting-room door with a quick, capable swish of her hips, turned up the lamp, and motioned Lord Rothewell toward a chair, all without pause. Despite her brisk demeanor, Rothewell still found the woman strangely seductive.

He ignored the chair, since she did not deign to sit. Inside the small chamber, a low fire glowed in the hearth, and a second lamp burned by a worn but elegant chair which sat adjacent. Rothewell let his gaze sweep over the room, as if by taking it in, he might divine something of the woman's character.

Unlike the gilt and gaudy splendor of de Valigny's parlor, this tidy sitting room was appointed with French furniture which looked tasteful but far from new. Leather-bound books lined the whole of one wall, and the air smelled vaguely of lilies instead of smoke, soured wine, and too much male perspiration. Clearly, this was not de Valigny's territory, but his daughter's—and unless Rothewell missed his guess, the twain rarely met.

He turned to face her. "Have you a name, *mademoiselle*?" he enquired with a stiff bow. "I gather *mon chou* is not your preferred form of address?"

Her smile was bitter. "What's in a name?" she quoted pithily. "You may call me Mademoiselle Marchand."

"Your Christian name," he pressed. "Under the circumstances, *mademoiselle,* I think it necessary."

There was another flicker of annoyance in her eyes. "Camille," she finally answered.

"And I am Kieran," he said quietly.

His name seemed of no consequence to the woman. She paced to the window and stared out into the gaslit street beyond. A carriage went spinning past, the driver's shadowy form barely visible in the gloom. Unasked, he started across the room to join her, but she cut an immediate and forbidding glance over her shoulder.

He hesitated. Why press forward with this travesty? Indeed, what had possessed him to pursue it at all? Pity? Lust? One last effort to redeem his hopelessly blackened soul? Or was it simply a gnawing hunger for something which he had not already tasted to nauseating excess?

What had brought such a beautiful creature to such a desperate point—and she must indeed be desperate, though she hid it like a master.

Rothewell dropped his gaze. A glass of what looked like strong claret sat on a dainty pie-crust table by her chair, and a book lay open beside it. He glanced at the spine. It was not a novel, as one might expect, but a work of French philosophy by Rousseau. Good Lord, was the woman a bluestocking? He glanced again at her face, now in profile as she stared into the night.

No. With lips as lush as those, it simply was not possible. Moreover, she was too cool. Too continental and sophisticated.

"Mademoiselle Marchand," he said quietly, "why are you cooperating with your father in this unholy scheme?"

At last she turned from the window, her hands held serenely at her waist, one laid neatly over the other. "I do it, *monsieur,* for the same reason as you," she replied in her faintly accented French. "Because there is something in it for me."

"What, a title?" Rothewell sneered. "I assure you, my dear, mine is scarcely known. It will do you little good."

"I don't give a damn for your title, sir," she calmly returned. "I need an English husband—one who can do his duty."

"I beg your pardon?"

"A husband who can get me with child—and quickly." She crooked one dark eyebrow and let her gaze run down him as if he were a piece of horseflesh on the block. "Surely you can accomplish that much, *monsieur,* despite your haggard appearance?"

Strangely, it was not the insult but her apathy which stirred his ire. "There are many eligible bachelors in London, *mademoiselle,*" he said darkly. "Why haven't you found one?"

"Alas, I am told they have all gone to the country for shooting season." She laughed lightly. "Oh, come, *monsieur!* With de Valigny's reputation? And my mother's? I am thought scandalous, my lord. But you—ah, *you* do not look as if scandal much disturbs you."

"You have a tart tongue, madam," he returned. "Perhaps that is your problem?"

"*Oui,* but you'll not be long burdened with it," she

answered evenly. "Just wed me, Rothewell, and do you duty. As soon as the child is born healthy, I will split my in heritance with you—less de Valigny's cut, *naturellement*— and then you may go on your merry way."

"Good God," he said. "I begin to believe you are a coldhearted as de Valigny."

A bitter smile curved her full, sensuous lips. "And begin to believe it is your precious title which concern you after all," she answered. "You are a hardened game ster, are you not? *Prendre un risqué!* You have a fifty-fift chance the child will be female."

"Yes?" he growled. "And what then?"

She gave a Gallic shrug. "*Alors, monsieur,* you ca divorce me," she replied. "I will gladly give you cause, i need be."

Like the snap of a whip, his hand seized her arm "You will not dare, *mademoiselle,*" he gritted. "For if yo do, it won't be a divorce you'll get."

The woman had the audacity to laugh in his fac "Ah, suddenly principled, are you?"

He released her arm, but she did not back away. " don't give a damn for my title, either, Mademoisel Marchand," he snapped. "But I care a great deal abou being made a cuckold."

"Oh, everyone has a price." Was there an unexpecte note of melancholy in her voice? "You. Lord Enders. D Valigny. *Oui, monsieur,* even me. I have just proven i have I not?"

"A price?" he returned. "There may be little abou me that is honorable, *mademoiselle,* but I have no nee to marry a woman for her money. Indeed, I have n need—or desire—to marry at all."

"What nonsense!" She cut another of her cool glance

at him. "That is precisely why you remained at the card table, *n'est-ce pas?*"

"No, damn you, it is not," he snarled.

Mademoiselle Marchand blinked her eyes, as if attempting to clear her vision. *"Non?"* she murmured, drifting back to the window. "Then why did you play de Valigny's little game, Rothewell? What other reason could you possibly have?"

It was on the tip of his tongue to tell her it was because he could not bear the thought of Lord Enders heaving himself atop so lovely and so innocent a young woman—but no. That would not do. It probably wasn't even true. Why should he give a damn what happened to de Valigny's insolent by-blow? Oh, she was beautiful, yes. And infinitely beddable. But she had a tongue like a serpent, and eyes which seemed determined to pierce his darkest recesses.

How the devil had he got himself into this mess? There was nothing of the gentleman in him, and there never had been. He was no better than that scoundrel de Valigny, or the sick, twisted Lord Enders.

Her piercing eyes were on him now, watchful. Insistent. "Why, Rothewell?" she said. "I demand the truth."

"The truth!" he said bitterly. "Would either of us recognize it, I wonder?"

She stepped toward him, her eyes glinting. "Why did you gamble with de Valigny?" she demanded. "If not the money, why?"

His frustration finally exploded. He caught her by the elbow and dragged her against him. "Because I wanted to have you, damn it," he snarled down at her. "Why else? I think I should like you under my thumb, *mademoiselle*. In my bed. Beneath me. I should dearly love to make you eat a few of your prideful words and do my every bidding. That is *why*."

Satisfaction glinted in her eyes. *"Très bien,"* she murmured, stepping back as he released her. "At least I know what I am dealing with."

Rothewell forced down his anger. He was a liar—and he felt suddenly weary and ashamed. "Oh, you have no idea, Mademoiselle Marchand," he said quietly. "For all your avant-garde upbringing, you cannot possibly know what you are *dealing with*. I release you, my dear, from this foolish, Faustian bargain of your father's. You are not his to barter—no matter what he might imagine when he is in his cups."

Mademoiselle Marchand had resumed her lonely vigil by the window, and no longer faced him. Her delicate narrow shoulders had rolled inward with fatigue now, and much of the hauteur had left her frame. Slowly, she turned and let her gaze take him in again, but this time it was his face which she studied.

"No," she said quietly. "No, Lord Rothewell, I think I shall stand by my father's bargain."

Rothewell gave a sharp laugh. "I don't think you understand, *mademoiselle*," he answered. "I have no need of a wife."

For a long, expectant moment, she hesitated, her mind toying with the knife's edge of something he could not fathom. She was weighing him. Judging him again with her all-seeing eyes. And it made him acutely uncomfortable.

"Très bien," she finally answered. "Is Lord Enders still in my father's parlor?"

Rothewell shrugged. "I daresay. Why?"

She set off briskly toward the door. "Then I shall marry him after all," she replied over her shoulder. "It will be worth a vast deal of money to him—and to my ather."

Rothewell beat her to the door, slamming his open palm against it. "Good God, woman, don't be a fool!" His voice was a low growl. "Enders is a lecher—and that term is a generous one."

"*Oui?* And what business is it of yours?" She turned and set her back to the door, bravado flaring in her eyes. But like the hardened gambler he was, Rothewell smelled fear.

Suddenly, a moment of clarity struck. He let his arm drop. "Tell me, my dear, how much longer do you have?" he murmured, his gaze taking in her wide brown eyes and fine cheekbones. "I think I hear the fatal sound of a ticking clock—and I don't mean the one on your mantelpiece."

"Three weeks." Her voice was calm. "Until the middle of next month."

"Three weeks?" he echoed. "And then what happens?"

She lifted her chin a fraction. "My . . . *vingt-huitième,*" she said. "My twenty-eighth—how do you say it?—my anniversary of birth?"

"Your birthday?" said Rothewell incredulously. "You must be married by your twenty-eighth birthday?"

"To obtain my inheritance, *oui,* I must first marry."

"And your father knows this?" Rothewell growled. "He knows it, and he used you? To stake a card game?"

"De Valigny, I fear, is without scruple," she said motionlessly. Her eyes were still upon him, dark and glowing. "So what is it to be, my Lord Rothewell?" she

quietly continued. "Am I to marry you? Or must I t:
the licentious Lord Enders to my bed?"

Good Lord, she really meant to marry one of the
And the choice was to be his?

He looked again into her bottomless brown eyes. S
was serious. Deadly serious.

Rothewell felt as if someone had just crushed the
from his lungs.

The past is heating up...
Don't miss these bestselling historical
romances from Pocket Books!

A Malory Novel!

Captive of My Desires ❖ Johanna Lindsey
On the high seas, love takes no prisoners...

A Wicked Gentleman ❖ Jane Feather
Someone wicked this way comes...

How to Abduct a Highland Lord ❖ Karen Hawkins
She took his freedom...He'll steal her heart...
How can two wrongs feel so *right*?

Indiscretion ❖ Jillian Hunter
A steamy reunion on the Scottish Highlands results in
desire, in delight, and indiscretion.

Caroline and the Raider ❖ Linda Lael Miller
She plotted a daring rescue—but never planned on a
dangerous passion.

The Perils of Pursuing a Prince ❖ Julia London
Some passions are worth the risk.

If You Desire ❖ Kresley Cole
How much desire can a Highlander resist?

Lose yourself in the passion...
Lose yourself in the past...
Lose yourself in a Pocket Book.

The School for Heiresses ❧ Sabrina Jeffries

Experience unforgettable lessons in love for
daring young ladies in this anthology featuring
sizzling stories by Sabrina Jeffries, Liz Carlyle, Julia
London, and Renee Bernard.

Emma and the Outlaw ❧ Linda Lael Miller

Loving a man with a mysterious past can force you
to risk your heart...and your future.

His Boots Under Her Bed ❧ Ana Leigh

Will he be hers forever...or just for one night?

Available wherever books are sold
or at **www.simonsayslove.com**.

156